THE
KING OF LIES

THE
KING OF LIES

John Hart

THOMAS DUNNE BOOKS
St. Martin's Minotaur
New York

This is a work of fiction. All of the characters portrayed in this novel are products of the author's imagination.

THOMAS DUNNE BOOKS.
An imprint of St. Martin's Press.

www.minotaurbooks.com

Design by Kathryn Parise

LIBRARY OF CONGRESS CATALOGING-IN-PUBLICATION DATA

Hart, John.
    The king of lies / John Hart.—1st ed.
        p. cm.
    ISBN-13: 978-0-312-34161-9
    ISBN-10: 0-312-34161-X
        1. Murder victims' families—Fiction. 2. Fathers—Death—Fiction. 3. Fathers and sons—Fiction. 4. North Carolina—Fiction. 5. Mystery fiction—Fiction. 6. Legal stories—Fiction. I. Title.
    PS3608.A78575 E37 2006
    813'.6—dc22

                                                        2005049774

10 9 8 7 6 5 4 3

For Katie

ACKNOWLEDGMENTS

Nothing happens in a vacuum, and bringing a novel to publication is no exception. It takes time and faith, and the road can be long. To those who walked it with me, I would like to express my sincerest gratitude.

First and foremost, I would like to thank my wife, Katie, a source of constant support and invaluable advice—and the finest eye for fiction that a writer could ask to have looking over his shoulder. I love you, baby. To my agent and good friend, Mickey Choate, who wasn't scared to take a chance on a new guy—thanks for the faith and for the lessons. And along those lines, many thanks to my editor, Pete Wolverton, the most irreverent man I've ever met and the most capable. Let it never be said that you don't step to the plate. To Katie Gilligan, who is as sharp as a tack—thanks for putting up with me; you're the best. And a comprehensive and sincere thank-you to everyone at St. Martin's Press, St. Martin's Minotaur, and Thomas Dunne Books who worked so diligently to make this book possible.

To everyone who read the manuscript at its worst and still calls me a friend, my most profound gratitude. And to the following people, whose goodwill was so evident: Nancy and Bill Stanback, Kay and Norde Wilson, John and Annie Hart, Mary Hart, Charlotte and Doug Scudder, Sterling Hart, Ken Peck, Annie P. Hart, John and Megan Stanback, Anne Stanback, Charlotte Kinlock,

ACKNOWLEDGMENTS

Mark Stanback, Nancy Popkin, Joy Hart, John Betts, Boyd Miller, Stan and Ashley Dunham, Sanders Cockman, Sean Scapelatto, George Guise, Linda Parker, Darby Henley, Debbie Bernhardt Gray and Allison Wilson, and David and Jennifer Wilson. Special thanks to Clint and Jody Robins, who were always there, and to Mark Witte, a friend of the written word, who had a very fine idea. Thanks as well to James Randolph, attorney and friend, who took the time to make sure I'd not forgotten too much about the law, and to Erick Ellsweig, who knows why. If I have failed to mention anyone, the fault is purely mine. Rest assured that I know who you are and that you have my thanks as well.

There are others whom I have encountered along the way—people whose paths I never imagined I would cross—who have helped to make the whole experience more than I ever hoped it could be. My warmest gratitude to Mark Bozek and Russell Nuce, who bought the movie rights, and to the wonderful authors who have been kind enough to read this book and share their thoughts on it: Pat Conroy, Martin Clark, Steve Hamilton, Thomas Perry, Mark Childress, and Sheri Reynolds. What a privilege this has been for me.

Finally, an extra-special thanks to Saylor and Sophie, my daughters, for hanging the moon.

THE
KING OF LIES

CHAPTER

1

I've heard it said that jail stinks of despair. What a load. If jail stinks of any emotion, it's fear: fear of the guards, fear of being beaten or gang-raped, fear of being forgotten by those who once loved you and may or may not anymore. But mostly, I think, it's fear of time and of those dark things that dwell in the unexplored corners of the mind. Doing time, they call it—what a joke. I've been around long enough to know the reality: It's the time that does you.

For some time, I'd been bathed in that jailhouse perfume, sitting knee-to-knee with a client who'd just gotten life without parole. The trial had damned him, as I'd told him it would. The state's evidence was overwhelming, and the jury had zero sympathy for a three-time loser who had shot his brother during an argument about who'd get control of the remote. Twelve of his supposed peers, and not one cared that he'd been drinking, that he was cracked to the gills, or that he didn't mean to do it. No one cared that his brother was an ass and a felon in his own right, not the jury and least of all me. All I wanted was to explain his appeal rights, answer any legal questions, and get the hell out. My fee application to the state of North Carolina would wait until the morning.

On most days I was ambivalent, at best, about my chosen profession, but on days like this I hated being a lawyer; that hatred ran so deep that I feared something must be wrong with me. I hid it as others would a perversion. And this day was worse than most. Maybe it was the case or the client or the emotional aftermath of one more needless tragedy. I'd been in that room a hundred times, but for some reason it felt different this time. The walls seemed to shift and I felt a momentary disorientation. I tried to shake it off, cleared my throat, and stood. We'd had bad facts, but the decision to go to trial had not been mine to make. When he'd stumbled from the trailer, bloody and weeping, he'd had the gun in one hand, the remote control in the other. It was broad daylight and he was out-of-his-head drunk. The neighbor looked out the window when my client started screaming. He saw the blood, the gun, and called the cops. No lawyer could have won the trial—I'd told him as much. I could have had him out in ten, but he refused to take the plea arrangement I'd negotiated. He wouldn't even talk about it.

The guilt may have been too much, or perhaps some part of him needed the punishment. Whatever the case, it was over now.

He finally tore his gaze from the jail-issue flip-flops that had known a thousand feet before his and forced his eyes to mine. Wet nostrils shone in the hard light, and his red eyes jittered, terrified of whatever they saw in that jigsaw mind of his. He'd pulled the trigger, and that brutal truth had finally taken root. The trail had wound its way across his face as we'd talked for the past few hours. His denials had sputtered to a halt, and I'd watched, untouchable, as hope shriveled and died. I'd seen it all before.

A sopping wet cough, his right forearm smearing mucus across his cheek. "So that's it, then?" he asked.

I didn't bother to answer. He was already nodding to himself, and I could see his thoughts as if written in the dank air that hung between us: life without parole and him not yet twenty-three. It generally took days for this brutal truth to bore through the bullshit tough-guy act that every dumb-ass killer carried into this place like some kind of sick birthright. Maybe this joker was smarter than I'd given him credit for. In the brief time since the judge handed down his sentence, he'd grown the lifer stare. Fifty, maybe sixty years behind the same redbrick walls. No chance of parole. Not twenty years, not thirty or even forty, but life, in caps. It would kill me, and that is God's own truth.

A glance at my watch told me I'd been in there for almost two hours, which was my limit. I knew from experience that the smell had by now permeated my clothes, and I could see the dampness where his hands had pawed at my jacket. He saw the watch come up and he lowered his eyes. His words evaporated in the still air, leaving a vacuum that my body settled into as I stood. I didn't reach to shake his hand and he didn't reach for mine, but I noticed a new palsy in his fingers.

He was old before his time, all but broken at twenty-three, and what might have been sympathy wormed into a heart I'd thought forever beyond such things. He started to cry, and his tears fell to the filthy floor. He was a killer, no question, but he was going to hell on earth first thing the next morning. Almost against my will, I reached out and put a hand on his shoulder. He didn't look up, but he said that he was sorry, and I knew that this time he truly was. I was his last touch with the real world, the one with trees. All else had been pared away by the razor-sharp reality of his sentence. His shoulders began to heave beneath my hand, and I felt a nothingness so great, it almost had physical weight. That's where I was when they came to tell me that my father's body had finally been found. The irony was not lost on me.

The bailiff who escorted me out of the Rowan County Jail and to the office of the district attorney was a tall, wide-boned man with gray bristles where most of us have hair. He didn't bother to make small talk as we wound through the halls packed with courthouse penitents, and I didn't push it. I'd never been much of a talker.

The district attorney was a short, disarmingly round man who could turn off his eye's natural twinkle at will; it was an amazing thing to watch. To some, he was a politician, open and warm. To others, he was the cold, lifeless instrument of his office. For a few of us behind the curtain, he was a regular guy; we knew him and liked him. He'd taken two bullets for his country, yet he never looked down on people like myself, what my father had often called "the soft underbelly of a warless generation." He respected my father, but he liked me as a person, and I'd never been sure why. Maybe because I didn't shout the innocence of my guilty clients the way most defense lawyers did. Or maybe because of my sister, but that was a whole different story.

"Work," he said as I entered the room, not bothering to get up. "I'm damn sorry about this. Ezra was a great lawyer."

The only son of Ezra Pickens, I was known to a few as Jackson Workman Pickens. Everybody else liked to call me "Work," which was humorous I guess.

"Douglas." I nodded, turning at the sound of the office door closing behind me as the bailiff left. "Where'd you find him?" I asked.

Douglas tucked a pen into his shirt pocket and took the twinkle from his eye. "This is unusual, Work, so don't look for any special treatment. You're here because I thought you should hear it from me before the story breaks." He paused, looked out the window. "I thought maybe you could tell Jean."

"What does my sister have to do with this?" I asked, aware that my voice sounded loud in the cramped, cluttered space. His eyes swiveled onto me and for a moment we were strangers.

"I don't want her to read about it in the papers. Do you?" His voice had chilled; the moment had not played well. "This is a courtesy call, Work. I can't go beyond the fact that we've found his body."

"It's been eighteen months since he disappeared, Douglas, a long damn time with nothing but questions, whispers, and the looks that people give when they think you can't tell. Do you have any idea how hard this has been?"

"I'm not unsympathetic, Work, but it doesn't change anything. We haven't even finished working the crime scene. I can't discuss the case with a member of the defense bar. You know how bad that would look."

"Come on, Douglas. This is my father, not some nameless drug dealer." He was clearly unmoved. "For God's sake, you've known me my whole life."

It was true—he had known me since I was a kid—but if there was any cause for sentiment, it failed to reach the surface of his lightless eyes. I sat down and rubbed a palm across my face, smelling the jailhouse stink that lingered there and wondering if he smelled it, too.

"We can do the rounds," I continued in a softer tone, "but you know that telling me is the right thing."

"We're calling it murder, Work, and it's going to be the biggest story to hit this county in a decade. That puts me in a tough spot. It'll be a media frenzy."

"I need to know, Douglas. This has hit Jean the hardest. She's not been the same since that night—you've seen it. If I'm going to tell her about our father's death, I'll need to give her some details; she'll want them. Hell, she'll need them. But most of all, I need to know how bad it is. I'll need to prepare her. Like you said, she shouldn't read it in the paper." I paused, took in a breath, and focused. I needed to visit the crime scene, and for that I needed his agreement. "Jean needs to be handled just right."

He steepled his fingers under his chin, as I'd seen him do a thousand times, but Jean was my trump, and he knew it. My sister had shared a special friendship with the DA's daughter. They'd grown up together, best friends, and Jean was in the same car when a drunk driver crossed the centerline and hit them

4

head-on. Jean suffered a mild concussion; his daughter was nearly decapitated. It was one of those things, they said, and it could just as easily have been the other way around. Jean sang at her funeral, and the sight of her could pull tears from Douglas's eyes even now. She'd grown up under his roof and, apart from myself, I doubted that any one person felt her pain the way Douglas did.

The silence stretched out, and I knew that my arrow had slipped through this one small chink in his armor. I pressed on before he could think too much.

"It's been a long time. Are you sure it's him?"

"It's Ezra. The coroner is on-scene now and he'll make the official call, but I've spoken with Detective Mills and she assures me that it's him."

"I want to see where it happened."

That stopped him, caught him with his mouth open. I watched as he closed it.

"Once the scene is cleared—"

"Now, Douglas. Please."

Maybe it was something in my face, or maybe it was a lifetime of knowing me and ten years of liking me. Maybe it was Jean after all. Whatever the reason, I beat the odds.

"Five minutes," he said. "And you don't leave Detective Mills's side."

Mills met me in the parking lot of the abandoned mall where the body had been found, and she was not pleased. She radiated pissed-off from the bottom of her expensive shoes to the top of her mannish haircut. She had a pointed face, which emphasized her look of natural suspicion; because of this, it was impossible for anyone to find her beautiful, but she had a good figure. She was in her midthirties—about my age—yet lived alone and always had. Contrary to speculation around the lawyer's lounge, she wasn't gay. She just hated lawyers, which made her okay in my book.

"You must have kissed the DA's ass to get this, Work. I can't even believe I've agreed to it." Mills stood only five five or so but seemed taller. What she lacked in physical strength, she made up for in smarts. I'd seen her shred more than one of my colleagues who had presumed to challenge her on cross.

"I told him I won't leave your side, and I won't. I just need to see. That's all."

She studied me in the gray afternoon light and her animosity seemed to drain away. The sight of a softening expression in a face rigorously trained against such things was vaguely repellant, yet I appreciated it nonetheless.

"Stay behind me and touch nothing. I mean it, Work. Not one damn thing."

She began a purposeful stride across the cracked, weed-filled parking lot, and for a moment I was unable to follow. My eyes moved over the mall, the parking lot, and then found the creek. It was a dirty creek, choked with litter and red clay; it flowed into a concrete tunnel that ran underneath the parking lot. I could still remember the stink of it, the chemical reek of gasoline and mud. For an instant, I forgot why I'd come.

It could have happened yesterday, I thought.

I heard Mills call my name and I tore my eyes away from that dark place and the childhood it had come to represent. I was thirty-five now and here for a very different reason. I walked away from it, walked to Mills, and together we approached what had once been the Towne Mall. Even in its prime, it had been ugly, a prefab strip mall sandwiched between the interstate and a power-transfer station that chewed at the sky with towers and high-tension lines. Built in the late sixties, it had struggled for years with imminent closure. Only a third of the stores had had tenants as of a year ago, and the last one had fled with winter. Now the place crawled with bulldozers, wrecking balls, and itinerant workers, one of whom, according to Mills, had located the body in a storage closet at the back of one of the stores.

I wanted the details and she gave them to me in short, bitten sentences that the warm spring breeze could not soften.

"At first all he saw were ribs, and he thought they were dog bones." She threw me a glance. "Not bones that a dog would eat, but a dog skeleton."

I nodded foolishly, as if we weren't talking about my father. To my right, a hydraulic jackhammer gnawed concrete. To my left, the land rose to the heart of downtown Salisbury; the buildings there seemed to gleam, as if made of gold, and in a sense they were. Salisbury was a rich town, with a lot of old money and a fair amount of new. But in places, the beauty was thin as paint and could barely hide the cracks; for there was poverty here, too, although many pretended there was not.

Mills lifted the yellow crime-scene tape and ushered me underneath. We entered the mall through what used to be a double door, now a ragged mouth with crushed cinder-block teeth. We moved past boarded-up storefronts to the last in the row. The door was open beneath a sign that read NATURE'S OWN: PETS AND EXOTICA. Nothing more exotic than rats had been behind those plywood sheets for years—rats and the decaying corpse of Ezra Pickens, my father.

The power was off, but the crime-scene unit had set up portable spotlights. I recognized the coroner, whose pinched face I would forever remember from the night my mother died. He refused to meet my eyes, which was unsurprising. There had been many difficult questions that night. From the rest, I got a few polite nods, but most of the cops, I could tell, weren't happy to see me. Nevertheless, they moved aside as Mills guided me through the dusty store to the closet at the back. My gut told me that they moved out of respect for Mills and my father more than they did for any grief they might imagine me to feel.

And just like that, there he was, ribs gleaming palely through a long rip in a shirt that I had forgotten but now remembered quite well. He looked something like a broken crucifix, with one arm outflung and his legs folded together. Most of his face lay hidden beneath what looked to be a candy striper's shirt still on its hanger, but I saw a porcelain stretch of jawbone and remembered whiskers there, pale and wet under a streetlamp on the last night I saw him alive.

I felt eyes upon me, and they pulled me away. I looked at the gathering of eager cops; some were merely curious, while others, I knew, sought their own secret satisfaction. They all wanted to see it, my face, a defense attorney's face, here in this musty place where murder was more than a case file, where the victim was flesh and blood, the smell that of family gone to dust.

I felt their eyes. I knew what they wanted, and so I turned to look again upon the almost empty clothes, the flash of bone so pale and curving. But I would give them nothing, and my body did not betray me, for which I was grateful. For what I felt was the return of a long-quiescent rage, and the certain conviction that this was the most human my father had ever appeared to me.

CHAPTER

2

I stared at my father's corpse, doubting that I could forget the sight and wondering if I should even try. I bent, as if to touch him, and felt Mills shift behind me. She dropped a hand onto my shoulder, pulled me back. "Enough," she said, and her eyes were hard as she herded me away from the scene and back into my expensive but aging car. I watched her walk back to the gaping door, and twice she turned back to look at me. I gave her a nod as she turned for the last time and disappeared inside. Then I tried to call Jean from my cell phone. Her housemate, a rough-edged woman named Alex, picked up on the first ring. She was tight-lipped and physical. We didn't get along, and my list of questions was longer than her supply of answers. Her relationship with my sister had long ago poisoned the family well, and she made no bones of how she felt about me. I was a threat.

"May I speak to Jean?" I asked.

"No."

"Why not?"

"She's not here."

"Where can I find her?" There was silence on the other end, then the sound of a cigarette lighter. "It's important," I insisted.

I heard her inhale, as if she was thinking about it, but I knew better. Alex never gave willingly, not to me.

"At work," she finally said, making me wonder when was the last time my voice had been welcome in that home.

"Thanks," I said, but she had already hung up.

Confronting Jean was the last thing I wanted to do, especially at her work, where the stink of decline must have ground deepest into her skin. Yet it was the smell of pepperoni and mushroom that struck me first as I stepped into the old Pizza Hut on West Innes Street. It was a stale smell, one that churned up memories of junior high dates and fumbled kisses. We used to laugh at people like my sister, and the memory of that pulled my shoulders even lower as I walked to the counter.

I knew the manager by sight only, and was again informed that Jean was not available. "On a delivery," he told me. "Welcome to wait."

I took a seat in a red vinyl booth and ordered a beer to keep me company. It was cold and tasteless, which on this day was exactly what I needed. I sipped it as I watched the door. Eventually, my eyes wandered, exploring the people who clustered around their tables. There was an attractive black couple being served by a skinny white girl with studs in her tongue and a silver crucifix jammed through her eyebrow. They smiled at her as if they had something in common. Nearest to the buffet, two women challenged chair legs that looked spindly yet weren't, and I watched them urge their children to eat yet more, since it was all-you-can-eat Thursday.

Three young men sat at the table next to mine, probably from the local college and in for an early-afternoon beer buzz. They were loud and coarse, but having fun. I felt the rhythms of their chatter and tried to remember what that age had been like. I envied their illusions.

The door opened to a spill of weak sunlight and I turned to see my sister move into the restaurant. My melancholy ripened as I watched. She carried her decline as I carried a briefcase, businesslike, and the red pizza box seemed at home under her arm. But her pale skin and haunted eyes would never fit my memories of her—no more so than the grubby running shoes or tattered jeans. I studied her face in profile as she stopped by the counter. It used to be soft but had grown angular, with a new tightness at the eyes and mouth. And her expression was hard to pin down. I couldn't read her anymore.

She was a year over thirty, still attractive, at least physically. But she'd not been right for some time, not the same. There was something off about her. It was clear to me, who knew her best, but others picked up on it. It was as if she'd ceased trying.

She stopped at the counter, put down the hot box, and stared at the dirty pizza ovens as if waiting for someone to cross her field of vision. She did not move once. Not even a twitch. I could feel the misery coming off of her in waves.

A sudden silence at the table of young men pulled my eyes away, and I saw them staring at my sister, who stood, oblivious, there in the gloom of the front counter.

"Hey," one of them said to her. Then again, a little louder: "Hey."

His friends watched him with open grins. He leaned half out of his seat, toward my sister. "How about I take some of that *ass* home in a box?"

One of his friends whistled lowly. They were all staring at her now.

I almost rose—it was a reflex—but when she turned to the table of young drunks and stared them down, I froze. Something twisted behind her face. She could have been anybody.

Or nobody.

She raised both hands and flipped them off, holding it for a few good long seconds.

Then the manager materialized from the back of the kitchen. He hitched at his belt, put the belly that covered it against the counter, and said something to Jean that I could not hear. She nodded as he spoke, and her back rounded as she seemed to sink under his words. He gestured minutely at the table, said a few more words, and then pointed in my direction. She turned and her eyes focused on me. At first, I thought she didn't recognize me; her mouth seemed to tighten with distaste, but then she came over, passing the table of drunks and giving them the finger one more time, her hand tucked against her chest, where the manager could not see it.

The boys laughed and went back to their drinking. She slipped into the booth opposite me.

"What are you doing here?" she asked without preamble or smile. Her eyes were empty above skin smudged purple.

I studied her more closely, trying to find the reason that she seemed so disjointed to me. She had the same clear skin, so pale that it was almost translucent; large, tilted eyes; a delicate chin; and dark hair that spilled across her forehead and down to her shoulders in an unkempt wave. Up close, she was steady. Study her one piece at a time and she looked fine; nevertheless, it was wrong.

Something in the eyes, maybe.

"What did he say to you?" I asked, nodding toward the manager. She didn't bother to follow the gesture. Her gaze remained fixed on me; there was no warmth in it.

"Does it matter?" she asked.

"I guess not."

She lifted her eyebrows, turned her palms up. "So?"

I didn't know how to get to the place I needed to go. I spread my fingers on the slick red-checked material that covered the table.

"You never come here," she said. "Not even to eat."

I had barely seen my sister in the past year, so I didn't blame her. Wrong as it was, avoiding her had become something of a religion for me. Most times, I could never admit that, but those bruised eyes pained me. There was too much of our mother in them, and they'd not worked for her, either.

Indecision twisted my lips.

"They found Ezra's body," she stated. It wasn't a question, and for an instant I felt pressure behind my eyes. "I'm guessing that's why you're here." There was no forgiveness in her face, just a sudden intensity, and in the place of surprise or remorse, it unsettled me.

"Yes," I said.

"Where?"

I told her.

"How?"

"They're calling it murder." I studied her face. Not a flicker. "But nobody knows much more than that."

"Did Douglas tell you?" she asked.

"He did."

She leaned closer. "Do they know who did it?" she asked.

"No," I responded. Unexpectedly, her hands settled around my own and I felt the warm sweat on her palms, which surprised me. It was as if I'd come to believe that no blood flowed in her—that's how cold she'd appeared to me. She squeezed my hands as her eyes moved over my face and picked me apart. Then she pushed back against the cracked and yielding vinyl.

"So," she said. "How are you taking all this?"

"I saw the body," I replied, appalled by my own words. In spite of what I'd said to Douglas, I'd not planned to tell her this.

"And . . ."

"He was dead," I said, ushering in a silence that lasted over a minute.

"The king is dead," she finally said, her eyes immobile on mine. "I hope he's rotting in hell."

"That's pretty harsh," I told her.

"Yes," she replied flatly, and I waited for something more.

"You don't seem surprised," I finally said.

Jean shrugged. "I knew he was dead," she said, and I stared at her.

"Why?" I asked, feeling something hard and sharp coalesce in my stomach.

"Ezra would never detach himself from his money or his prestige for so long. Nothing else would keep him away."

"But he was murdered," I said.

She looked away, down at the decomposing carpet. "Our father made a lot of enemies."

I sipped my beer to buy a few seconds. I tried to make sense of her attitude.

"Are you okay?" I finally asked.

She laughed, a lost sound that had no connection to her eyes. "No," she said. "I'm not. But it's got nothing to do with his death. He died for me on the same night as Mom, if not before. If you don't get that, then we've got nothing to say to each other."

"I don't know what you're talking about."

"You do," she said, an edge in her voice that I'd never heard before. "As far as I'm concerned, he died that night, the second Mom went down those stairs. If you don't see it that way, it's your problem, not mine."

I'd expected tears and found anger, but it was directed at me as much as at Ezra, and that troubled me. How far down separate paths had we traveled in so short a time?

"Look, Jean. Mom fell down those stairs and died. I feel that pain as much as you do."

She barked another laugh, but this one was ugly. " 'Fell,' " she echoed. "That's rich, Work. Just fucking rich." She swiped a hand across her face and sniffed loudly. "Mom . . ." she began, then faltered. Sudden honeysuckle tears appeared at the corners of her eyes, and it occurred to me that until now I had seen no emotion in her, not since we'd buried our mother. She pulled herself together, raised unapologetic eyes.

"He's dead, Work, and you're still his monkey boy." Her voice strength-ened. "His truth is dead, too." She blew her nose, crumpled the napkin, and dropped it on the table. I stared at it. "The sooner you come to terms with the only truth that matters, the better off you'll be."

"I'm sorry, Jean, if I've upset you."

She turned her gaze away and directed it out the window, where two starlings squabbled in the parking lot. The momentary tears had gone; with-out the sudden color in her face, you would never have known she'd been upset.

I smelled garlic and suddenly two pizza boxes appeared on the table. I looked up to see the manager, who ignored me and spoke to Jean.

"It's your favorite," he said. "Sorry." Then he turned and walked back to the kitchen, taking most of the garlic smell with him.

"I've got to go," Jean said flatly. "Delivery." She pulled herself out of the booth, jiggling the table and sloshing my beer. Her eyes didn't meet mine, and I knew that my silence would send her away without another word. But before I could think of something to say, she had scooped up the boxes and turned away.

I fumbled for my wallet, threw a couple of singles on the table, and caught her at the door. When she ignored me, I followed her into the sun and to her time-ravaged car. I still didn't know what I wanted to say, however. How dare you judge me? . . . Where have you found such strength? . . . You're all I have and I love you. Something like that.

"What did he mean?" I asked, my hand upon her arm, her body wedged into the open car door.

"Who?" she responded.

"Your manager. When he said 'It's your favorite,' what did he mean?"

"Nothing," she said, her face looking as if she'd swallowed something bitter. "It's just work."

For whatever reason, I didn't want her to go, but my imagination failed me.

"Well," I finally managed. "Can we do dinner sometime? Alex, too, of course."

"Sure," she said in the same voice I'd heard so many times. "I'll talk to Alex and call you."

And that, I knew, was that. Alex would make damn sure the dinner never happened.

"Give her my best," I said as she rocked into the tiny car and started the tired engine. I thumped the roof as she pulled off, thinking that the sight of her face in the window of that shitty car with the Pizza Hut sign strapped on top was the most pitiful thing I would ever see.

I almost got in my car then, and I wish now that I had. Instead, I went to the manager and asked what he'd meant and where Jean had gone. His answer revealed the cruel pull-the-wings-off-flies kind of torment I'd not seen since high school, and it was part of my sister's daily life. I was in my car and out of the lot before the restaurant door had closed behind me.

I used to look at homeless people and try to imagine what they had once looked like. It's not easy. Beneath the grime and degradation is a face once adored by someone. It's a truth that tricks the eye; our glances slide away. But something happened to ruin that life, to strip it bare; and it wasn't something big like war or famine or plague. It was something small, something that but for the grace of God could take us, too. It was an ugly truth, one my sister knew too well. She wasn't homeless, but fate and the callousness of others had conspired to take from her a life I knew her to love very much. It was a good life—many would say great—and were I to close my eyes, I could see it even now. She had been trusting then, aglow with the promise of years that stretched out like silver rails.

But fate can be a wayward bitch.

So can people.

My hands steered the car along a route I knew by heart, and I looked around as I drove. I passed the massive house we'd known since childhood, empty but for my father's dusty belongings and the tracks I'd left on those rare occasions when I stopped by to check on things. Two blocks more and my own house swam into view. It crowned a small hill and looked down its nose at passing traffic and the park that lay beyond. It was a beautiful old home, with good bones, as my wife often said; but still it needed paint, and the roof was green with moss.

Beyond my house was the country club, with its Donald Ross golf course, clay tennis courts, clubhouse, and swimming pool lined with idle tanned bodies. My wife was up there somewhere, pretending we were rich, happy, or both.

On the other side of the golf course, if you knew how, you could find a beautiful development full of Salisbury's finest new homes. It was chock-full of doctors and lawyers and other assorted rich people, including Dr. Bert Werster and his wife, Glena, the queen bitch herself. Glena and Jean used to run together, back when Jean, too, was married to a surgeon and had tanned tennis-player legs and a diamond charm bracelet. There had been a group of them, in fact, six or seven women who alternated bridge and tennis with margaritas and long husbandless weekends to Figure Eight Island.

Jean's nameless manager had told me the women still played bridge every Thursday, and they liked to order pizza.

This was my sister's life.

I pulled to the curb a block down from Dr. Werster's house, a tower of stone and ivy. I watched as Jean heaved herself up steps that to anyone else might have seemed welcoming, and imagined that pizza had never weighed quite so much.

I wanted to carry her burden. I wanted to take Glena Werster out with a long rifle shot.

Instead, I backed slowly away, worried that sight of me would only compound the load on her troubled and fragile shoulders.

I drove home, past the club, and did not see the bright clothes that flashed in the sun. At the top of my driveway, I killed the engine and sat under tall walls whose peeling paint mocked me. I checked to see that I was unobserved, rolled up my windows, and wept for my sister.

CHAPTER

3

It took twenty minutes to pull myself together; then I went in for a beer. Mail littered the kitchen counter and the answering machine blinked five new messages at me. I couldn't have cared less. I went straight for the fridge and wrapped my fingers around two bottle necks. They clanked, and I sipped from the first as I dropped my coat on the kitchen chair and moved through the empty, childless house to the front door, which opened to the world below. I sat on the top step, closed my eyes to the warm sun, and pulled hard on the bottle.

I'd bought the house several years ago, when Ezra's presence imbued the law practice with a patina of respectability and desperate souls paid dearly to touch the hem of his robe. He'd been the best lawyer in the county, which had made my job easy. We'd shared an office and a name. That meant I could cherry-pick my cases, and six weeks after a local grocery truck backed over an eight-year-old kid in the parking lot, I plunked down a $100,000 down payment.

I took another sip and sudden panic struck me as I realized that I couldn't remember the name of that poor kid. For a long minute, I agonized over just how soulless this made me, and then, like a breath, his name flooded my mind.

Leon William McRae. I pictured his mother's face on the day of the funeral, the way tears had channeled down dark grief-cut furrows to drip on the white lace collar of her best dress. I remembered her strangled words, her shame over her little boy's pine casket and his plot in the poor man's cemetery that lay in the shadow of the water tower; how she worried that he'd never feel the afternoon sun there.

I wondered now what she'd done with the money his death had brought, and hoped she'd made better use of it than I. Truth be told, I disliked the house; it was too big, too visible. I rattled in it like a quarter in a tin can. But I always liked to sit there at the end of the day. It was warm in the sun. I could see the park, and the oak trees made music of the wind. I would try not to think about choices or the past. It was a place for emptiness, for absolution, and rarely was it mine alone. Usually, Barbara fucked it up.

I finished my second beer and decided on a third. I dusted myself off and went inside. As I passed through the kitchen, I saw that the answering machine now had seven messages on it, and I wondered vaguely if one might be from my wife. Back outside, I reclaimed my seat in time to see one of my favorite park-walking regulars round the corner.

There was a certain magnificence to his ugliness. He wore a fur-lined hunting cap regardless of the weather and liked the earflaps down. Threadbare khaki pants flapped around legs walked scrawny, and his arms were as skinny as those of a starved child. Heavy glasses pulled at his nose, and his mouth, always whiskered, turned up as if in pain. He kept no schedule whatsoever, and walked compulsively: midnight in the pouring rain, stalking the tracks on the east side of town, or steaming in the morning sun as he marched through the historic district.

No one knew much about him, although he'd been around for years. I'd picked up his name once at a party—Maxwell Creason. There'd been talk about him that night. He was a regular fixture in town, and everyone saw him out walking, but, apparently, no one had ever spoken to him. No one knew how he supported himself and everyone assumed that he was homeless, one of the regulars at the town's few shelters, maybe a patient at the local VA hospital; but the speculation was never very profound. Mostly, there was laughter— about how he looked, why he walked so obsessively. None of the comments were pleasant.

I never saw him like that. For me, he was a question mark, and in some ways the most fascinating person in Rowan County. I would daydream of falling into stride so that I might ask him, What do you see, in these places that you go?

I did not hear the door open, but suddenly Barbara was behind me, and her voice made me jump.

"Honestly, Work," she began. "How often do I have to ask you to drink your beer on the back patio? You look like white trash squatting out here for the world to see."

"Evening, Barbara," I said, not turning around, eyes still on my mysterious walker.

As if realizing how harsh her words had been, she softened her tone.

"Of course, honey. I'm sorry. Good evening." I could feel her as she stepped closer, a mixture of perfume and disdain that fell around me like ashes. "What are you doing?" she asked.

I couldn't bring myself to answer. What could I say? "Isn't he magnificent?" I said instead, gesturing.

"Who? Him?" she asked, pointing as if with a gun.

"Yes."

"Oh for heaven's sake, Work. Sometimes I don't understand you. Really, I don't."

I turned finally, looked up at her, and found her beautiful. "Come sit with me," I said. "Like we used to."

She laughed in a way that made her suddenly ugly, and I knew that hope would change nothing.

"I used to wear blue jeans, too. But now I need to make dinner."

"Please, Barbara. Just for a minute or two." There must have been something in my voice, for she stopped in midturn and came to my side. Her lips flirted with a smile, and although the flirtation was brief, it made me think of smiles that were neither so bland nor so insincere, of times not so far back when her smile could blind me. I'd loved her then, or believed I did, and never doubted the choices that I had made. Back then, she was so confident in the rightness of us, and spoke of our future with a passion that felt prophetic. She said that we would be the perfect couple, that we would have the perfect life; and I believed her. She made me her disciple, showed me the future through her eyes, and it was dazzling and bright.

That was a long time ago, but even now I could close my eyes and see a yellowed shadow of that vision. It had seemed so easy.

I brushed the resin of a southern spring from the step and patted the broken tile. She bent slowly, and when she sat, forearms on her knees, I thought I saw the old love flutter in her eyes.

"Are you okay?" she asked, and looking at her, I thought she meant it.

For an instant, my throat closed, and I felt that if I let the words out, the tears might follow. Instead, I gestured once more at the dwindling figure of my park walker and said again, "Isn't he magnificent?"

"Oh Jesus, Work," she said, getting back to her feet. "He's a horrible old man, and I wish he'd stop walking past our house." She stared at me as if at a stranger, and I had no words for her. "Damn it. Why do you have to make it so hard? Just take your beer and sit out back. Will you do that for me, please?"

As she stalked into the house, I rubbed at my face. Until then, it had never occurred to me that the man was old, and I wondered why my wife had picked up on the fact while I had not. I watched as he moved down a grassy bank to the shore of the small city lake that was the heart of the park, then faded into the playground, which seemed to grow smaller each passing year.

Inside, the house was cold. I called to Barbara, got no answer, and so moved into the kitchen for a beer that I knew better than to drink yet planned to anyway. I saw Barbara through the door to the living room, hunched over the paper, a glass of white wine untouched beside her. Rarely had I seen her so still.

"Anything in the paper?" I asked, my voice sounding small even to my own ears.

I carried my beer into the well of her silence and sat in my favorite chair. Her head was bowed; her skin shone pale as Ezra's bones and a still darkness filled the hollows of her cheeks. When she looked up, her eyes were red and getting redder. Her lips seemed to have thinned, and for a moment she looked scared, but then her eyes softened.

"Oh, Work," she said, tears leaking out to slide like oil down the high planes of her face. "I am so sorry."

I saw the headline then, and felt it odd that she could cry while I could not.

That night, as I lay in bed waiting for Barbara to finish in the bathroom, I thought of the newspaper article and the things it had said and left unsaid. It portrayed my father as some kind of saint, a defender of the people and pillar of the community. This brought my mind again to truth as a concept, and the naked subjectivity of something that should be pure essence. My father would have found the article a fitting epitaph; it made me want to vomit.

I stared through the window at a night made beautiful by a waxing moon, turning away only at the sound of Barbara's self-conscious cough. She stood transfixed, pinned between the moon and a soft spill of light from the bathroom closet. She wore something filmy that I had never seen, and her body was a ghost beneath it. She shifted under my scrutiny and her breasts moved in unison. Her legs were as long as always, yet they seemed more so tonight, and the darkness of their joining pulled my eyes down.

We'd not had sex for weeks, and I knew that she offered herself thus from a sense of duty. Strangely, that moved me, and I responded with a hard, almost painful need. I didn't want a wife just then. No communication. No feeling. I wanted to wall myself in soft flesh and pound the reality of this day from my bones.

She took my proffered hand and slid beneath the sheets, saying nothing, as if for her, too, this remained impersonal. I kissed her hard, tasting the salt of barely dried tears. My hands moved on her and in her, and somewhere along the way, her nightclothes vanished. She trailed her hair across my chest and offered her breasts to my mouth. I bit down, heard her stifled cry, and then was lost in the rush of blood and the *slap slap* of wet, happy flesh.

CHAPTER

4

I'd discovered in recent years that there was often a special silence in my wife's absence. It was as if the house itself had finally exhaled. And when I woke the next morning, I knew before opening swollen eyes that I was alone. As I lay there, five seconds into the first day of the rest of my life, I came to know that my wife no longer loved me. I didn't know why the realization struck, but I couldn't dispute it. It was fact, like my bones are fact.

I glanced at the bedside table, seeing nothing but the lamp and a water glass with smeared lipstick on its silvered edge. She used to leave little notes: "At the bookstore"; "Coffee with the girls"; "Love you." But that was before the money got tight. I wondered where she'd gone, and guessed the gym, there to sweat out what remained of me from the night before. She'd study her figure in the mirror, carve a smile onto careworn cheeks, and pretend she hadn't prostituted her life for a lukewarm marriage and a handful of shiny nickels.

I swung my feet from beneath the covers and stood. A glance at the clock showed it was almost seven. I felt the day loom and knew it would be a big one. By now, word of Ezra's death would have spread across the county and I expected to leave a wake in the day wherever I went. I carried this thought to the bathroom, where I showered, shaved, and brushed teeth in desperate need of

it. A single clean suit remained in the closet and I pulled it on without pleasure, thinking of blue jeans and flip-flops. In the kitchen, I found a half-filled
pot of coffee, poured a cup, and added milk. I took my coffee outside, under a
diffuse and lowering sky.

It was early for the office and court didn't open until nine, so I went for a
drive. I told myself it would be aimless, but I knew better. Roads lead somewhere; it's just a question of choice. This road carried me out of town and
across Grant's Creek. I passed the Johnson place and saw a hand-lettered sign
offering free puppies to a good home. My foot came off the gas and I slowed.
For an instant, I considered it, but then I pictured Barbara's reaction and knew
that I would never stop. Yet my speed trailed away, and I kept one eye on the
rearview mirror until the sign dwindled to a whitish speck and then was gone.
Around the bend, the speed limit climbed to fifty-five and I goosed it, rolling
down the windows and missing my own dog, now two years in the ground. I
tried to put him out of my mind, but it was hard; he'd been a damn good dog.
So I concentrated on driving. I followed the yellow line past small brick houses
and developments with trendy names like Plantation Ridge and Saint John's
Wood.

"Country come to town," my wife would say, forgetting that my father was
raised white trash.

Ten miles out, I came to the faded, shot-up road sign for Stolen Farm Road.
I slowed and turned, liking the feel of tires on gravel, the steering wheel that
hummed under my hand. The road passed through a wall of trees and entered
a place untouched.

Stolen Farm was old, like the county was old, generations in the same family, with cedars grown tall along fence lines established before the Civil War.
The farm had once been huge, but things change. Time had whittled it down
to ninety acres, and I knew it teetered at the brink of bankruptcy and had for
years. Only Vanessa Stolen remained of the family, and she'd been considered
white trash since childhood.

What right did I have to bring my troubles to this place? I knew the answer,
as I always did. None whatsoever. But I was tempted. Dew was on the grass, and
she'd be up with coffee on the back porch. There'd be worry on her face as she
stared out over fields that could make anyone else feel young again, but she'd
be naked under that old cotton shirt she wore. I wanted to go to her, because I
knew that she would take me as she always had; knew that she would put my
hands on her warm belly, kiss my eyes, and tell me everything would be all

right. And I'd want to believe her as I so often had, but this time she'd be wrong, so very fucking wrong.

I stopped at a bend in the drive and nosed forward until I could see the house. It sagged in on itself, and I ached to see more boards on the windows of the top floor, where in the past I'd stood at night to watch the distant river. A year and half had passed since I'd last been to Stolen Farm, but I remembered her arms and how they wrapped around my naked chest.

"What are you thinking?" she'd asked, her face above my shoulder, a ghost in the window.

"About how we met," I'd told her.

"Don't think about such nasty things," she'd replied. "Come to bed."

That was the last time I'd seen her; but a light still burned on the front porch, and I knew that it did so for me.

I put the car in reverse, yet remained for a moment longer. I'd always felt Vanessa's connection to the place. She'd never leave, I knew, and would one day be buried in the small cemetery tucked away in her woods. I thought then that it must be nice to know where you will spend eternity, and wondered if such knowledge brought peace. I thought that it might.

I turned and left, leaving, as I always did, some small piece of me behind.

Back on black pavement, the world lost its soft edge, and the drive to the office seemed harsh and full of noise. For nine years, I'd worked from a narrow shotgun office on what the locals called "lawyers' row." It was around the corner from the courthouse and across the street from the old Episcopal church. Other than a couple of secretaries next door, the church was the only attractive thing on the block; I knew every piece of stained glass by heart.

I parked the car and locked it. The sky above was growing darker, and I guessed the weatherman out of Charlotte might be right about a late-morning rain; it felt somehow appropriate. At the threshold of my office, I stopped and looked back at the red clay that rimmed my tires like lipstick, then went inside.

My secretary, the only one left, met me at the door with coffee and a hug that devolved into helpless sobs. For whatever reasons, she'd loved my father, and liked to imagine him on a beach somewhere, recharging just a little before storming back into her life. She told me that there had been numerous phone calls, mostly from other attorneys, sending their respects, but some from the local newspapers and even one reporter calling all the way from Raleigh. Murdered lawyers, it would appear, still had some print value. She gave me the stack of files I needed for court, mostly traffic matters and one juvenile offender, and promised that she would guard the fort.

I left the office a few minutes before nine, planning to enter court after it started and thus avoid any unnecessary encounters with well-wishers or the idle curious. So I entered the building through the magistrate's office. The tiny waiting room, even at this time of day, was crowded with the usual reprobates and deadbeats. Two men were cuffed to the bench, their arresting officers sharing a paper and looking bored. There was a couple swearing out an assault complaint against their teenage son, as well as two men in their sixties who were bloody and torn but too tired or sober to be mad at each other anymore. I recognized at least half of them from district criminal court. They were what we in the trade called "clients for life"—in and out of the system every couple months on one minor charge or another: trespass, assault, simple possession, whatever. One of them recognized me and asked for a card. I patted empty pockets and moved on.

Out of the mag's office, I headed into the new part of the building, where district court would be held. I passed the concession stand run by a half-blind woman named Alice, then slipped into an unobtrusive door with a small plaque that read LAWYERS ONLY. Beyond that door was another, this one with a security keypad.

I entered court from the rear and got my first nod from one of the bailiffs. It was like a signal, and suddenly every lawyer in the room was looking at me. I saw so many genuinely concerned faces that I froze momentarily. When your life is shit, it's easy to forget just how many good people are in the world. Even the judge, an attractive older woman, stopped calendar call and invited me to the bench, where she expressed her sorrow in a quiet and remarkably tender tone. I saw for the first time that her eyes were very blue. She pressed my hand lightly with her own and I looked down in momentary embarrassment, noticing the childish doodle she'd made on her judge's pad. She offered to continue my cases, but I declined. She patted my hand again, told me Ezra had been a great lawyer, and then asked me to take my seat.

Over the next two hours, I acted sad and negotiated pleas for clients I might never meet; then I went next door to juvenile court. My client was ten years old, charged with felony arson for burning down an abandoned trailer where older kids went to smoke pot and screw. The kid had done it, of course, but swore it was an accident. I didn't believe him.

The assistant district attorney running court was a cocky little twerp, two years out of law school. He swaggered, and was disliked by prosecutors and the defense bar alike—an idiot who'd never figured out that juvenile court is about helping kids more than it is about conviction rates. We tried the case before an ex-prosecutor turned judge, who found the child delinquent; but, like the rest of us with half a brain, the judge believed that the kid had probably done a public service and so let him off with juvie probation, a punishment designed to straighten out the parents as much as the kid. For me, it was standard fare. The kid needed help.

The assistant DA smirked. He walked to the defense table, pulled his lips back from too-large teeth, and told me he'd heard about my father. He flicked at those teeth with a purple-bottomed tongue and observed that Ezra's death raised as many questions as my mother's had.

I almost decked him, but I realized just in time that he would love it. Instead, I gave him the finger. Then I saw Detective Mills; she stood in the shadows near the exit, and I realized, once I saw her, that she'd been there for some time. If I hadn't been numb, that might have freaked me out; she was the kind of person you liked to keep track of. When I packed up my briefcase and walked to meet her, she gestured curtly.

"Outside," she said, and I followed her.

The hall was packed with warm bodies, and the lawyers stopped and stared. Detective Mills was lead investigator. I was the son of a murdered colleague. I didn't blame them.

"What's up?" I asked her.

"Not here," she said, seizing my arm and turning me against the flow of people, toward the stairs. We walked in silence until we turned down the corridor leading to the DA's office.

"Douglas wants you," she said, as if I'd asked another question.

"I guessed as much," I responded. "Do you have any leads?"

Her face was all sharp angles, making me guess that the previous day still bothered her; but I knew the drill. If anything went wrong, Mills would catch the heat, and I guessed word was already out about my visit to the scene. It broke all the taboos. Cops did not allow defense lawyers to walk through the crime scene and possibly contaminate evidence. Mills, bright as she was and no stranger to cover-your-ass politics, had probably papered the file with testimonials from other cops as to exactly what I had and had not touched. Douglas, too, would be prominently mentioned.

Her silence was thus not surprising.

Douglas looked like he had not slept at all.

"I don't know how the damn papers got hold of this so fast," he said as soon as I stepped through his door, coming half out of his seat. "But you damn well better not be involved, Work."

I just stared at him.

"Well come in," he continued, dropping back into his chair. "Mills, close that door."

Detective Mills closed the door and moved to stand behind Douglas's right shoulder. She jammed her hands into the pockets of her jeans, pulling back her jacket to show the butt of her pistol in its shoulder holster. She leaned against the wall and stared at me as if I were a suspect.

It was an old trick, probably done out of habit, but standing there she looked every inch the bulldog she was. I watched Douglas settle back in his chair, deflating as if shot with a dart. He was good people and knew that I was, too.

"Do you have any leads?" I asked.

"Nothing solid."

"How about suspects?" I pressed.

"Every fucking body," he replied. "Your father had a lot of enemies. Unhappy clients, businessmen on the wrong end of the stick, who knows what else. Ezra did many things, but walking lightly was not one of them."

An understatement.

"Anybody in particular?" I asked.

"No," he said, tugging at an eyebrow.

Mills cleared her throat and Douglas let go of his eyebrow. It was obvious that she was unhappy, and I guessed that she and the DA had exchanged words on how much to tell me.

"What else?" I asked.

"We believe that he died on the same night he disappeared."

Mills rolled her eyes and began to pace the office like a man ten years in the same cell.

"How do you know that?" I asked. No way could the medical examiner have been that specific. Not after a year and a half.

"Your father's watch," Douglas said, too long in this business to gloat over his own cleverness. "It was self-winding. The jeweler tells me it will run for thirty-six hours after the person wearing it stops moving. We counted backward."

I thought back to my father's watch, trying to remember if it had a date function.

"Was he shot?" I asked.

"In the head," the DA told me. "Twice."

I remembered the candy striper shirt over my father's head, the pale curve of exposed jawbone. Someone had covered his face after killing him, an unusual act for a murderer.

Mills stopped in front of the wide windows that looked across Main Street at the local bank. A light rain fell and thin gray clouds covered the sky like lint, but the sun still shone through, and I remembered my mother and how she always told me that rain and sun together meant that the devil was beating his wife.

Mills planted herself on the windowsill, arms crossed, the sky behind her darkening as the clouds thickened. The last sunlight disappeared, and I guessed that the devil's wife was down and bleeding.

"We'll need to examine Ezra's house," Douglas continued, and I nodded, suddenly tired. Douglas paused, then went on. "We'll also need to check his office. Go through his files and find out who might have reason to hold a grudge."

This brought my head up, and suddenly it all made sense. Ezra was dead. The practice was mine, which meant that Douglas and the cops needed me. Letting law enforcement paw through a defense attorney's client files was . . . well, it was like letting a defense attorney enter the crime scene. If I refused, they'd need a warrant. There would be a hearing and I would probably win. Judges were loath to undermine the attorney-client privilege.

I realized then that the DA had figured this out before calling me to his office the day before, and that made me ineffably sad. Quid pro quo is an ugly thing between friends.

"Let me think on that for awhile," I said, and Douglas nodded, tossing an enigmatic look at Detective Mills.

"We found the slugs," he said. "Both of them in the closet. One in the wall, one in the floor."

I knew what that meant, and doubted that Ezra had entered the closet voluntarily. He'd been ordered there at gunpoint. The first shot had caught him standing, passed through his skull, and embedded itself in the wall. The second shot had taken him lying down. The killer had wanted to make sure.

"And?" I said.

Douglas looked again at Mills and started tugging on his right eyebrow.

"We don't have full forensics yet, but they came from a three-fifty-seven," Douglas said, leaning forward in his chair, looking as if the movement hurt his ass. "We checked the records. Your father had a three-fifty-seven revolver, a stainless Smith & Wesson." I said nothing. "We need that gun, Work. Do you know where it is?"

His right hand came up again, working at the eyebrow. I thought very carefully before I spoke.

"I have no idea where that gun is."

He leaned back and put his hands in his lap.

"Look for it, will you? Let us know if you find it."

"I will," I said. "Is that it?"

"Yeah," Douglas said. "That's it. Just get back to me on those files. We'll need to get access, and I'd rather not bother the judge."

"I understand," I said, and did. I stood up.

"Just a second," Mills said. "I need to talk to you about the night your father disappeared. There are a lot of unanswered questions. There may be something of value."

The night Ezra disappeared was the same night my mother died. It was not an easy subject for me. "Later," I said. "Okay?"

She looked at the district attorney, who said nothing.

"Later today," she responded.

"Fine." I nodded. "Today."

Douglas kept his seat as Mills opened the door.

"Stay in touch," Douglas said, and lifted his hand as Detective Mills closed the door in my face. In the hall outside, with eyes like fingers upon me, I felt very alone.

I slipped down the back stairs and passed again through the magistrate's office. It was all but empty and I nodded at the woman behind the wire-mesh window. She popped gum at me and looked silently away. Outside, the sun still hid itself, but the rain had dwindled to mist, when what I wanted most was pounding rain. I wanted the grayness, the steady hiss and crackle of water straight from the void; I wanted purity on my face and the heaviness of a three-season suit ruined beyond repair. Without decision or action, I wanted to fade away, to be taken from view and put, for a whisper of time, in a place where no one knew me. Instead, I got the passing stare of two young boys; instead, I got damp.

It was not yet noon when I entered the office, and my secretary looked unsettled when I told her to go home. She packed her bag with uneaten lunch, a stack of legal pads, and a thesaurus, then left with a wounded step. I wanted to go upstairs and search Ezra's personal office, but his ghost stopped me on the stairs. I'd not been up there for six months and was too depressed to face the dusty splendor of a straw empire improvidently made mine. I decided instead to find an innocuous lunch and the courage to face again my childhood home and the memories of broken bones that lay like stained carpet on the formal staircase.

For twenty minutes, I drove, searching for a lunch spot that offered a chance of anonymity. Eventually, I just gave up and hit the drive-through at Burger King. I ate two cheeseburgers as I drove twice past my father's house. It challenged me with its thick columns, blank dull-eyed windows, and perfect alabaster paint. More castle than house, it hunkered behind hedgerows and box bushes that reminded me of pillboxes I'd once seen when Ezra took the family to the beaches of Normandy. My father, I knew, had willed the beast to me so that I could carry on his war against the old-money snobbery of this town that for years had dulled the lacquer of his magnificent achievement. But I knew now, as I always had, that that would never happen. Waging war took conviction, and while I understood the forces that drove my father, I could not relate to them. There are many kinds of poison, and I was not a fucking idiot.

I turned into the driveway, passed beneath the crossed arms of sentinel trees, and so stepped back in time, my childhood around me like broken glass. Keys jingled and I sat in the silence that followed. I saw many things that no longer were: my first bike and toys, long gone to ruin; a father flushed with early triumph; and my mother, alive, still happy, gazing at Jean's questioning smile. I saw it all, unyellowed by time; then I blinked and it was gone, ashes in a sudden wind.

The police were not there yet and the door was heavy with disuse as I stepped inside. I disengaged the alarm system and flipped on lights as I moved through the house. Dust lay thick on the floor and on the sheets that draped my father's furniture. Old tracks were visible as I walked slowly through the downstairs, passing the two dining rooms, the den, the billiards room, and the door to my father's wine cellar. Stainless steel gleamed dully in the kitchen, making me think of knives with ebony handles and my mother's pale, narrow hands.

I checked his study first, thinking to find the pistol in the top drawer with his silver letter opener and the leather journal that Jean had given him in place of a grandson. It was not there. I sat in his chair for a few seconds and stared at the only framed photograph, a faded black-and-white shot of a tumbledown shack and the unsmiling family that lived in it. Ezra was the youngest, a thick, dirty-legged boy in denim shorts, his feet bare. I peered into the black spots of his eyes and wondered at his thoughts on that day. I picked up the journal and riffed the pages, knowing that my father would never have trusted his secret self to paper, yet feeling some hope in spite of myself. It was empty, so I replaced it as I'd found it. My eyes wandered as I tried to find some sense of this man I had once presumed to know, but the room meant nothing to me. It was resplendent in old maps, leather furniture, and the mementos of a lifetime, and yet it rang so empty. The room itself was a trophy, I realized, and I could see him sitting there, and knew that he could smile at this room while his wife lay weeping in the big bed upstairs.

Sitting in his chair felt vaguely incestuous and I didn't stay long. As I left his study, I noticed that my tracks on the dusty floor were not alone. There were other tracks, smaller ones, and I knew that Jean had been here. The tracks led from the study back to the hall and then to the wide staircase. The prints disappeared into the carpet runner that climbed the stairs, then reappeared on the hardwood of the hall that led to my parents' room. I'd not been upstairs in over a year and the prints were obvious. They vanished on the Persian carpet that covered the bedroom floor, but by the bed, and the table where I'd hoped to find the gun, I found a half print in the dust. I looked at the bed and saw a circular indentation in the covers, as if some animal had curled there to nest.

I checked for the gun, found nothing, then sat on the bed and rubbed the impression away. After a thoughtful moment, I got up, and as I left the house, I shuffled my feet to make mute the dusty floor where once two children had played.

Outside, I leaned against the locked door, half-expecting Detective Mills to roll up the drive with a dozen squad cars in her wake. I tried to slow breathing that sounded very loud in a world of unusual quiet. From somewhere came a smell of new-mown grass.

I remembered my father's gun from the night I saw it shoved into my mother's face. When he saw me, there in the bedroom door, he tried to play it off as a joke, but my mother's terror was real. I saw it in her tear-stained eyes, in her posture, and in the way her hands pulled at the belt of her robe when she told me to go back to bed. I went because she asked me to, but I now remembered the still house and the creak of bedsprings as she made peace the only way she knew how. I came to hate my father that night, but it took a long time for me to realize the magnitude of that emotion.

I never learned what they'd been fighting about, but the image never scabbed over; and as I turned away from that place, I thought of my own wife's tears and her limp submission the night before—the bleak satisfaction I took from her smallness as I used her shamelessly. She'd cried out, and remembering the taste of salted tears, I thought, for that instant, that I knew how the devil felt. Sex and tears, like sun and rain, were never meant to share a moment; but for a fallen soul, an act of wrong could, at times, feel very right, and that scared the hell out of me.

I descended into my car and started the engine, and as I passed again beneath the trees that guarded this place and turned toward the park and home, my thoughts were dark with the dust of places the mind should never go.

CHAPTER

5

All I wanted was to peel off my suit, fall into bed, and find something better across the black, sandy gulf; but the moment I turned onto my block, I saw that it wasn't going to happen. The curving slope of driveway that should welcome a man at times like this glittered instead with shiny black and silver cars. The sharks had gathered. The friends of my wife had come, bearing their honeyed hams, their casseroles, and their eager questions. How did he die? How's Work holding up? Then, sotto voce, when Barbara couldn't hear: What was he mixed up in? Two bullets in the head, so I heard. Then lower still: *Probably deserved it.* Sooner or later, one of them would say what so many thought. White trash, they'd say, and eyes would glint above lips chapped by one too many tight smiles. Poor Barbara. She really should have known better.

On principle, I declined to be chased from my own home, but my car refused to make the turn into the driveway. Instead, I bought beer and cigarettes at the convenience store next to the high school. I wanted to carry the bag into the football stadium, mount the bleachers, and get slowly drunk above that rectangle of brown grass. But the gate was locked, and the chain was loud when I yanked on it. So I drove back to my father's house and drank in his driveway. I killed most of the six-pack before I managed to go home.

As I turned onto my block, I saw that the number of cars had grown, giving my house an unfortunate festive air. I parked on the street two houses down and walked. Inside, I found the crowd I suspected: our neighbors, several acquaintances from out of town, doctors and their wives, business owners, and half of the local bar, including Clarence Hambly, who, in many ways, had been my father's greatest rival. He immediately drew my gaze, for he stood tall and disdainful even in this monied gathering. He had his back to the wall, one elbow on the mantel, and a drink in his hand. He was the first to notice me, but looked away when our eyes met. I dismissed him, a minor irritation, and scanned the crowd for my wife, finding her across the room. Looking at her, I could say, without pause or reflection, that she was a beautiful woman. She had flawless skin, high cheekbones, and eyes that flashed. That night, she had salon-perfect hair and looked stunning in last season's most expensive dress. She was cloistered with her most regular companions, women whose hands were cold with jewels and thin blood. When she saw me, she stopped talking, and her friends turned as one. Their eyes dissected me, settling on the beer bottle I'd carried in; and when Barbara left their circle, they said nothing, yet I imagined sharp tongues poised to flay my naked back. I lit another cigarette and thought of the funeral yet to plan. Then Barbara materialized, and for a moment we were alone together.

"Nice party," I said, and then smiled so that my words would not sound so cruel.

She pressed hard lips against my cheek.

"You're drunk," she said. "Don't embarrass me."

That would have been the low point, had Glena Werster not chosen that moment to sweep through the front door. She flashed a smile that made her teeth look oiled, and her black dress was short and tight. The sight of her in my home made me ill. I thought of Jean and the weight of her tread as she'd mounted the steps to Glena Werster's pillared mansion.

"What's she doing here?" I asked.

Barbara watched over her wineglass as Glena nestled into the bosom of her little clique in the corner, and I saw worry in my wife's eyes. When she turned to me, her whisper was fierce.

"You be nice, Work. She's very important in this town."

By "important," I knew my wife meant that Glena Werster sat on the board of the country club, was filthy rich, and mean enough to ruin reputations for the joy of it.

"I don't want her here," I said, and gestured vaguely at the group of women huddled under the portrait of Barbara's father. "I don't want any of them here." I leaned closer and she pulled back so quickly that it stank of pure instinct. I spoke anyway. "We need to talk, Barbara."

"You've sweated through your shirt," she said, flicking three fingers across the buttons beneath my collar. "Why don't you go change." She started to turn away, but then she turned back. She reached for my face and I leaned forward. "Shave, too, would you?" Then she was gone, back to her circle of tight-lipped friends.

So I stood alone, lost in my own home as people uttered kind words, and I nodded as if I agreed with everything they said; yet I existed in an eerie kind of silence, and the warm words broke over me like surf on a half-deaf man. A few were sincere, but none understood the first thing about my father—what made him so inexplicable, so extraordinary, and so evil.

In a pilgrimage of fumbled words, I made it to the kitchen, where I'd hoped to find a cold beer. Instead, I saw that a full bar had been arranged, and I marveled darkly at my wife, who, in the cold wake of death, could make of the impromptu an occasion. I ordered bourbon on the rocks, then felt a hand on my shoulder and a voice like crushed ice asking the bartender to make it two. I turned to see Dr. Stokes, my neighbor, whose boot-leather features and white beard made him look very much like Mark Twain.

"Thank you," he said to the bartender. Then he steered me away from the bar with his firm doctor's hand and said, "Let's take a little walk." He led me through the kitchen and out into the garage, where graying sunlight stretched dusty rectangles on the floor. He released me into the emptiness, then sat on the steps with a grunt and a flourish. He sipped his drink, then smacked his lips. "Now that's a good friend."

"Yes," I said. "It can be."

I watched him watch me as he put down his drink and lit a cigar.

"I've been watching you," he finally said. "You don't look good."

"It's been a bad day."

"I'm not talking about today. I've been worried about you for years. Just not my place to say, if you follow."

"What makes today different?" I asked.

He looked at me and puffed blue smoke. "I've been married fifty-four years," he said. "You think I've never had that look, like your best friend just kicked you in the balls. It doesn't take a genius; my wife saw it, too." He flicked imaginary lint from his pant leg and studied his cigar as he continued. "Now, I can't do anything about your wife—a marriage is a man's own business—but there are some things you ought to hear, and I know damn well that no one else in there will tell you."

Unsure what to say, I balanced my drink on an overturned wheelbarrow and lit a cigarette. The silence stretched out as I fumbled the pack back into my shirt pocket. When I looked up, I saw that shadows filled the doctor's eyes, which made me strangely sad. He had warm eyes; always had.

"Your father was the biggest asshole I ever met," he said, then pulled on his cigar as if he'd commented on the weather. I said nothing, and after a few seconds the old man continued. "He was a self-centered bastard who wanted to own the whole damn world, but you know that."

"Yes," I said, and cleared my throat. "I know that."

"An easy man to hate, your father, but he would look you in the eyes as he slipped the knife in, if you know what I mean."

"No."

"He was honest about his avarice. Other honest men could see that."

"So?" I asked.

"Am I finished yet?" he asked, and I said nothing. "Then let me talk. There was also Jean. I never liked the way he raised your sister. Seemed like a waste of a perfectly good mind. But we can't choose our parents, and that's her bad luck. I've watched her, too, and now that Ezra's dead, I think she'll be all right."

A harsh laugh escaped me. "How closely have you watched her?" I asked, thinking that Jean was so far from being all right.

He leaned forward, a sharp glint in his eyes. "Closer than you, I bet," he said, and the truth of it stung. "I'm not worried about her. It's you that troubles me."

"Me?"

"Yes, now shut up. This is what I came out here to tell you. So pay attention. Your father was a big man, with big visions and big dreams. But you, Work, are a better man."

I felt tears sting my eyes and wished fervently that this man had been my father. There was blunt honesty in his face and in the way he moved his thickened hands, and for a moment I believed him.

"You're better because you don't want big things for small reasons. You're better because you care—about your friends and family, things that are right; you favor your mother that way." He paused for an instant and nodded. "Don't choke on Ezra's burdens, Work. I'm eighty-three years old, old enough to know a thing or two, and the most important is this. Life is goddamn short. Figure out what *you* want. Be your own man and you'll be better for it."

He stood slowly and I heard his joints pop. Ice rattled on glass as he drained his drink.

"Bury your old man, Work, and when you're ready, we'd love to have you over for dinner. I knew your mother well, God rest her soul, and I'd love to tell you about her happy times. And one last thing—don't lose any sleep over Barbara. She's a bitch by nature, not by choice. So don't be hard on yourself."

He winked at me and smiled around his cigar. I thanked him for coming, because I didn't know what else to say; then I closed the door behind him and sat where he had, on wood still warm from his narrow haunches. I sipped ice-watered bourbon, thought about my life, and wished the old man were right about all the things he'd said.

Eventually, my glass ran dry, but this I could fix. My watch showed it was almost five, and as I stood, I thought briefly of Detective Mills. I'd not called her and at the moment didn't care; all I wanted was that drink. I was in and out of the kitchen without a word, and if that offended people, then too bad. I'd had enough. So I returned to my dank cell to watch the shadows crawl and to drink my bourbon warm.

I stayed in that awful place long enough for the light to dim and the walls to tilt. I was not an angry drunk; I didn't get weepy and I didn't figure out a damn thing. My jacket went into a box filled with lawn clippings I'd never emptied and my tie ended up twisted around a nail in the wall, but I kept the rest of my clothes on, which was hard. I wanted to shake things up, break the complacency bowl, and for one crazy moment I pictured myself running naked through the house. I'd chat with my wife's friends and dare them to pretend, at the next inane social gathering, that it had never happened. And they would—that's what kept my clothes on. Every last one of them could look me in the eye over drinks or dinner the next week, ask in all earnestness how the practice was doing, and then tell me what a fine funeral it had been.

I wanted to laugh and I wanted to kill somebody.

But I did neither. I went back inside; I mingled and I talked. I kept my clothes on, and if I made an ass of myself, no one said a word to me about it. Eventually, I left, and as I sat in my car, windows down and purple light on me like a second skin, I thanked God for one thing: that, drunk as hell and drowning in faces and words without meaning, I had not uttered the one irretrievable thought that had haunted me. And searching my ruined eyes in the mirror, I acknowledged, to myself at least, that I thought I knew who had killed my father.

Motive. Means. Opportunity.

It was all there if you knew where to look.

But I did not want to look. I never had. So I twisted the mirror up and away. Then I closed my eyes and thought of my sister, and of times that were no less hard for their simplicity.

"Are you okay?" I asked Jean.

She nodded, tears dripping off her tiny pointed chin to soak into her white jeans like rain into sand. Her shoulders hunched lower with each sob, until she looked bent and broken, her hair hanging just low enough to cover the top of her face. I pulled my eyes off the little gray teardrop circles, trying not to look at the blood that spread from between her legs. Red and wet, it soaked the new pants she was so proud of, the ones our mother had given her on that morning of her twelfth birthday.

"I called Dad and he said he'd come get us. Soon. I promise. He said so."

She didn't say anything and I watched the red stain darken. Without a word, I took off my jacket and spread it across her lap. She looked at me then in a way that made me proud to be her big brother, like I made a difference. I slipped an arm around her shoulders and pretended that I was not half-scared to death.

"I'm sorry," she said tearfully.

"Everything's okay," I told her. "Don't worry about it."

We were downtown, at the ice cream parlor. Mom had dropped us off on her way to Charlotte for the afternoon. We had four dollars for ice cream and plans to walk home afterward. I barely knew what a girl's period was. When I first saw the blood, I thought she might be hurt, and only then did I realize that her eyes had been filling with slow tears for awhile. "Don't look," she'd said, and bowed her head to the tears.

Dad never came, and after an hour we walked home, my jacket around her waist. It was almost three miles.

At home, Jean locked herself in the bathroom until Mom got back. I sat on the front porch, looking for the courage to tell my father what a bastard he was—for not caring about Jean, for making a liar of me—but in the end I said nothing.

How I hated myself.

*   *   *

I woke in near darkness. There was a face in my window and I blinked at the thick glasses and heavy whiskers. I pulled back instinctively, not just because the man was so ugly.

"Good," he grunted. "I thought maybe you were dead."

His voice was guttural, with a heavy southern accent.

"What . . ." I said.

"Shouldn't sleep in your car. It's dangerous." He looked me up and down, glanced in the backseat. "Smart boy like you should know better."

The face withdrew and, like that, he was gone, leaving me half-asleep and still drunk. *What the hell was that?* I opened the door and clambered out, stiff and sore. I peered down the street and saw him pass from light to dark, long coat flapping around his ankles, earflaps loose on his ears. It was my park walker, and after years of silent passings, we'd finally spoken. This was my chance. I could put feet to pavement, catch him in the dark, and ask my question; yet I didn't move.

I let him go, the opportunity lost to the paralysis of indecision. I got back into my car, mouth like glue, and I looked for gum or a mint but found neither. I lit a cigarette instead, but it tasted horrible, so I tossed it. My watch showed it was ten o'clock; I'd slept for two, maybe three hours. I peered down the street at my house. The cars were gone, but lights still burned, and I guessed Barbara was up. My head was pounding and I knew that she was more than I could bear right then. What I really wanted was another beer and an empty bed. But what I needed was something entirely different, and as I sat there, I realized that I'd been putting off the inevitable. I needed to go up to Ezra's office, to make peace with his ghost and to look for his gun.

I turned the ignition, thought of all the stupid drunks I'd defended on DWI charges, then drove to the office. It was that kind of day.

I parked in back, where I always did, and let myself into the narrow hallway that ran past the tiny break room, the copy room, and the supply closet. When I got to the main office area, I flipped on a lamp and tossed my keys onto the table.

I heard something upstairs, a scrape followed by a low thump, and I froze. Silence.

I stood and listened, but the sound didn't come again. I thought of Ezra's ghost, found the thought not funny, and wondered if I'd imagined it. Moving slowly, I walked to the front of the office and turned on every light. The stairwell to Ezra's upstairs domain gaped at me, all darkness and slick, shiny walls. My heart was up and running and I felt that unhealthy bourbon sweat. I smelled myself in the stillness and wondered if I was a coward after all. I reached for some kind of calm and told myself that old buildings settle and drunken men imagine things all the time. I reminded myself that Ezra was dead.

I flashed a glance around the place, but everything looked as it always had: desks, chairs, and filing cabinets—all in order. I looked back up the narrow stairwell and started to climb. I moved slowly, one hand on the rail. Five steps up, I stopped, thinking that I saw movement. I took one more hesitant step, heard something, and stopped. Then something huge, dark, and very fast descended upon me. It crashed into my chest and I was falling. I felt a moment of blinding pain; then all was blackness.

CHAPTER

6

I saw light. It flickered and died, then flickered again. It hurt. I didn't want it.

"He's coming around," a voice said.

"Well, that's something at least." I recognized the voice. Detective Mills.

I opened my eyes to bright, fuzzy light. I blinked, but the pain in my head didn't go away.

"Where am I?"

"Hospital," Mills said, and leaned over me. She didn't smile, but I smelled her perfume; it was ripe, like a peach too long in the bag.

"What happened?"

Mills leaned closer. "You tell me," she said.

"I don't remember."

"Your secretary found you this morning at the foot of the stairs. You're lucky you didn't break your neck."

I sat up against the pillows and looked around. Green curtains surrounded my bed. A large nurse stood at my feet, a bucolic smile on her face. I heard hospital voices and smelled hospital smells. I looked for Barbara. She wasn't there.

"Somebody threw a chair at me," I said.

"I beg your pardon," Mills said.

"Ezra's chair, I think. I was walking up the stairs and somebody pushed the chair down on top of me."

Mills said nothing for a long moment. She tapped a pen against her teeth and looked at me.

"I talked to your wife," she said. "According to her, you were drunk last night."

"So?"

"Very drunk."

I stared in dumb amazement at the detective. "Are you suggesting that I fell down the stairs?" Mills said nothing and I felt the first stir of anger. "My wife wouldn't know very drunk if it bit her on the ass."

"I corroborated her story with several people who were at your house last night," Mills said.

"Who?"

"That's hardly relevant."

"Relevant! Christ. You sound like a lawyer." Now I was mad. Mainly because I was being treated as if I were stupid. "Have you been to my office, Detective Mills?"

"No," she replied.

"Then go," I said. "See if the chair is there or not."

She studied me, and I could all but see the debate. Was this guy for real or just being an ass? If she'd ever considered me a friend, I saw right then that she did no longer. Her eyes were intolerant, and I guessed that the pressure was getting to her. There had been many stories in the paper—retrospectives on Ezra's life, thinly worded speculation about the manner of his death, vague details about the investigation—and Mills had been mentioned many times. I understood that this case would make or break her, but for some reason I'd imagined that our personal relationship would remain apart.

"What's your secretary's name?" she asked. I told her and she turned to the nurse, who looked uncomfortable. "Where's your phone?" The nurse told her to use the one in the triage nurse's office. Down the hall. Second door. Mills looked back to me. "Don't go anywhere," she said, and I almost smiled before I realized she wasn't making a funny.

She flapped her way through the curtains and disappeared. I heard her heels on the tile and then I was alone with the nurse. She fluffed my pillow.

"Is this the emergency room?" I asked.

"Yes, but Saturday morning is slow. Shootin' and stabbin' is done until to-night." She smiled and suddenly became a real person.

"What's wrong with me?"

"Oh, nothing but some bruises and such. Your headache might last longer than it would have otherwise." Another smile and I knew I wasn't the first Saturday-morning hangover she'd seen. "You'll be discharged shortly."

I laid my fingers on the warm dough of her forearm. "Has my wife been to see me? Five five. Short black hair. Pretty." She looked blank. "Hard eyes," I added, only half-joking. "Attitude."

"I'm sorry. No."

I looked away from the pity in her face. "Are you married?" I asked.

"Twenty-two years," she said.

"Would you leave your husband alone in the emergency room?" She didn't answer, and I thought, No, of course not; differences end at the hospital door.

"That would depend," she finally said. She smoothed my blankets, her hands moving sure and quick, and I thought she didn't want to finish the sentence.

"On?" I asked.

She looked at me and her hands grew suddenly still. "On whether or not he deserved it."

And there it is, I thought, the difference between her and me. Because I would be there regardless. No matter what. Suddenly, this nurse was not an un-expected friend, and with that bleak realization the warmth in the tiny cur-tained place evaporated. And even though she remained and tried to make further conversation, I found myself alone with my headache and the dis-jointed images of the previous night.

I *had* heard a sound. Wheels on wood flooring. Ezra's big leather chair be-ing rolled to the top of the stairs. I knew I was right about that. I'd felt the weight, damn it.

I hadn't been that drunk.

When Mills appeared, she looked pissed. "I spoke to your secretary," she said. "There's no chair at the bottom of the stairs. There was no chair when she found you this morning. Furthermore, nothing is out of place. No win-dows are broken. No sign of a forced entry."

"But Ezra's chair . . ."

"Is at his desk upstairs," Mills said. "Where it has always been."

I thought back to the day before. I'd sent my secretary home early.

"Maybe I forgot to lock the door," I ventured. "Look, I'm not making this up. I know what happened." Both Mills and the nurse stared at me, wordlessly. "Goddamn it, somebody threw a chair down those stairs!"

"Listen, Pickens. You're not high on my list of favorites right now. I wasted an hour yesterday trying to track you down, and I'm not going to waste more time because you decided to tie one on. Do I make myself clear?"

I didn't know what infuriated me more, that Mills refused to accept what I'd told her or that my wife lacked the decency to come to the hospital. My head was about to split, my body felt like the loser at a Tyson fight, and I thought I might puke hospital green.

"Fine. Whatever."

Mills looked at me as if she'd expected more fight and was disappointed. The nurse said she had some papers for me to sign, then disappeared to fetch them. Mills stared at me and I stared at the ceiling, determined to keep my mouth shut. This day could go two ways. It could get better or it could get worse. After what felt like a long time pretending to be interested in white acoustic tile, Mills finally spoke.

"We still need to discuss the night Ezra disappeared." Her tone was softer, as if it had occurred to her that this information might be *relevant* and that I controlled it. I said nothing, and her temper finally exploded. "Damn it Work, he was your father!"

I looked at her then. "You don't know the first thing about it," I said, and immediately regretted the words. There had been venom in my voice, and I saw the surprise in the detective's eyes. "Listen. I need a shower. I need to talk to my wife. Can we do it this afternoon?" She started to speak and I cut her off. "Your office. Three o'clock. I'll be there."

"Don't make me regret this," she said.

"I'll be there. Three o'clock."

The ripe-peach smell lingered after Mills left. Would I make the meeting? Maybe. The night in question had been a bad one and I'd not talked about it. Ever. Some secrets you keep, and I'd shared this one with my sister alone. It was Ezra's last gift, a lie wrapped in guilt and mortified to pure shame. I'd lost sleep to that lie, and maybe my soul, too. What did Jean call it? *Ezra's truth.* Well, Ezra's truth was my truth; it had to be, and if Jean thought differently, she was kidding herself.

I lifted the sheet. Somebody had put me in a tie-up dress. Perfect.

The nurse let me dangle for almost an hour. When she finally appeared with my paperwork, I still had no clothes, and she left me for another twenty minutes while she collected them for me. The day was getting worse and the feel of dirty clothes against my skin only made it more so.

I limped out of the emergency room and into a day made dull by low scudding clouds. Sweat came instantly in the prickly damp heat. I felt for my keys, couldn't find them, and remembered I had no car, either. So I walked home, and if anyone saw me, they didn't offer a ride. At home, I closed the door as if against a pursuing wind. "I'm home," I called.

The house was empty, as I knew it would be. Barbara's car was gone. The message light blinked its red eye at me, and on the kitchen island I saw a note— a beige rectangle of expensive stationery, with Barbara's tight writing beneath a pen laid across it in a perfect diagonal. I walked over without real interest.

"Dear Work," it began, which surprised me. I expected something different. "I've gone shopping in Charlotte. Figured you could use the space. I'm sorry that last night was so hard for you. Maybe I could have been more supportive. And I agree . . . we do need to talk. How about dinner tonight? Just the two of us. Barbara."

I left the note where it lay and went for a shower. The bed was made, which reminded me that I had no clean suit for Monday. I looked at the clock; the cleaners closed in twenty minutes. I tossed the filthy remnant of my suit into the closet and took a shower.

When I got out, I dressed and went to the office. Inside, I pocketed my keys and looked around. Mills was right about some things. Everything looked normal. But somebody had almost killed me, and I wanted to know why. If there was an answer here, I expected to find it upstairs.

Ezra's office ran the length of the building. The walls were raw brick and looked warm above the twenty-thousand-dollar Persian rug. There were exposed beams, leather furniture, and Tiffany lamps. Ezra had had no taste of his own and had to pay for it. I tried to remember the decorator's name and failed. She'd liked oil paintings and low-cut tops. I saw her breasts once when she bent over to spread some fabric samples. Ezra had caught me looking and winked. It had made my skin crawl, but in sharing the pleasure of those full pale breasts, he'd treated me like an equal for the first and last time. How fucked-up was that?

Ezra's paintings spoke of money—the old kind. Looking at them, you heard the bugle and smelled the dogs. The people in these paintings had gamekeepers, gun bearers, and beaters. They hunted in fine clothes and returned to a silver table service and servants. They hunted hart and stag instead of deer, pheasant rather than quail. Their homes had names.

This was the beast that had ridden my father's back. Old money had humbled him, but more than that it had angered him. Because no matter how good he was, how successful, or how rich, he had always lacked that casual arrogance. Poverty had been his goad; it had driven him, but he'd never understood how strong it made him. Standing on his expensive rug, I wished now that I'd told him. I thought of the photograph of his family that he'd kept on his desk at home. He'd often stared into those tired faces and nodded as if in conversation. He'd fought to escape their world more than to provide for us, and that hurt in ways I'd never explored. Those people were long dead, too cold and rotten to be impressed, but those had been his priorities.

"Shadowboxing the past," Jean had once called it, stunning me with her perception.

I walked to his massive desk and examined the chair. There were scuff marks on the leather, but they could have been old. I rolled it off the carpet and listened to its wheels on the wood floor. It was the same noise I'd heard the night before. I replaced the chair and checked the walls of the stairwell. They were scuffed, too, but that could have been from anything. Back at the desk, I ran my hands over the leather and nodded, satisfied that I'd not imagined anything.

The previous night, I'd caught this chair in the chest. Mills could kiss my ass.

I looked around the office. Someone had come here for a reason.

I sat in Ezra's chair, now mine, and tossed my feet up on the desk. I looked for a sign. What was so important?

After Ezra disappeared, most of our clients followed suit. Ezra had courted them. Ezra had held their hands. He'd gotten the press, and they'd had no idea that most of the underlying work was mine. "Just business," they'd said, before taking their files to the first big city firm they could find. Ezra's death had made plenty of Charlotte lawyers rich, a fact that would kill him if somebody hadn't already done the job. He hated Charlotte lawyers.

And I was left on the court-appointed list, bottom-feeding.

So I doubted anybody was up here for his files. Truth be told, I didn't care if Mills got the files. There was nothing there. I'd combed through them months earlier, looking for crumbs. I just didn't want to make it easy.

Then I remembered why I'd come the night before. I searched Ezra's desk, his filing cabinets, and even the end tables adjacent to the long leather couch that sat against the wall. Nothing. No pistol. I opened the chest under the window and got down on my knees to peer underneath his desk. I went back downstairs and searched every conceivable place where a gun might be hidden. After half an hour, I had no doubt that my office was gun-free.

I climbed the stairs again, turned at the top, and walked out onto Ezra's expensive Persian rug. Immediately, I saw that something was different. It was a small thing, but it leaped out at me. I stopped. I stared at it.

Across the room, near the foot of Ezra's long couch, the corner of the rug was folded under. It lay directly in my line of sight: the corner, along with a foot or more of fringe, tucked under. I quickly scanned the rest of the office, but saw nothing else that seemed out of place. I walked across the room toward the folded corner. Seven long strides, then I felt something yield beneath my foot. I heard the low groan of flexing wood. I stepped back, saw a slight rise beneath the carpet. I stepped on it again. Another creak.

I flipped back the rug and found a section of loose flooring—two wide boards that rose minutely at one end, warped, as if by time or water damage. They were only a quarter inch higher than the rest of the floorboards, but the cut lines did not line up with the rest of the boards. It appeared that the ends had been sawed at some point; they were rough and still pale. The other boards were almost black with age, the cracks between them packed solid.

I dug my nails into the white, rough meat of the cut ends and lifted. The boards rose easily. Beneath them, I found a safe. I should not have been surprised—my father was a secretive man—and yet I stared at it for a long time.

It was long and narrow, set between the floor joists. Its front was brushed metal, with a numeric keypad on the right side. I settled onto my knees, considering this new problem. Should I tell Mills? Not yet, I decided. Not without knowing its secrets.

So I tried to open it. I guessed at the combination. I tried every birthday in the family and every Social Security number, too. I tried the date Ezra passed the bar and the date he married my mother. I tried phone numbers, then I ran everything backward. I wasted half an hour staring at the safe and punching buttons; then I beat on it with my fists. I hit hard. I tore skin. It was that much like my father—hidden, silent, and unbreakable.

Eventually, I rocked away from the hard metal. I wedged the boards back into place and straightened the rug. I studied the scene critically. The lump under the rug remained, small but visible. I stepped on it. The creak was audible.

I went downstairs to the supply closet. On the top shelf I found the claw hammer and nails we used to hang pictures and diplomas. The nails were too small to be of use, but on the back of the shelf I found a half box of ten-penny nails—big, heavy brutes, like you'd use to nail a coffin shut. I grabbed a handful. Upstairs, I drove four of them into the loose boards, two in each one. The hammer was loud, and I swung it a few times too many, scarring the boards when I missed. Two of the nails went in straight and two bent as I drove them; I pounded them flat. When I replaced the rug there was no discernible lump. I stepped on the boards. Silence.

I put the hammer and extra nails on top of Ezra's bookshelf and dropped wearily to the couch. It was deep. "Sleeps one, screws two," Ezra once said, and I'd found that joke funny. Now it was just hard and cold, so I climbed wearily to my feet. Back in my car, I swiped at my face with a shirtsleeve. I was spent and shaky, and blamed it on the hangover; but deep down I wondered if I was coming apart. I turned on the air conditioner and laid my forehead against the hardness of the steering wheel. I breathed in and I breathed out, and after awhile I straightened. I needed to do something, needed to move; so I put the car in drive and pulled into thin traffic.

It was time to see Jean.

You could always hear the trains coming at her house. She lived in the poor part of town, next to the tracks, in a house that time had not spared. It was small, white, and dirty, with a covered front porch and green metal rockers like the blacks used to have when we were kids. A rusty oil tank leaned against the clapboards, and once-bright curtains stirred in the fitful breeze that passed by her open windows. I used to be welcome there. We'd drink beer in the shade of the porch and imagine what it must be like to grow up poor. It wasn't hard; kudzu grew over the fence and there was a crack house a block away.

The trains came by about five times a day, so close that you felt the vibrations in your chest, deep and out of tune with your heart; and the whistle, when it blew, was so loud, you couldn't hear a scream if it came from your own throat. The train gave the air a physical presence, so that if you spread your arms wide enough, it might push you down.

I got out of the car and looked back up the street. Tiny houses settled in silence, and a dog on a chain walked small circles in the dirt of the nearest yard. It's a mean street, I thought, and crossed to my sister's house. The steps sagged under me and there was dirt on the porch. A musty smell wafted from the open window, and I saw shadowed humps beyond. I knocked at the screen door, sensed movement, and heard a woman's voice. "Yeah, yeah. Coming."

The door opened and Alex Shiften blew smoke at me. She leaned against the jamb and looked beyond me. "It's you," she said.

Alex was the most purely physical person I'd ever met. She wore cutoffs and a tank top with no bra. She was long and lean, with wide shoulders and well-defined arms. She was intense, focused, and I thought she could probably kick my ass. I knew she'd like to try.

"Hello, Alex," I said.

"What do you want?" she responded, finally meeting my eyes, cigarette dangling from her lips. Her hair was blond and cropped above broad cheek-bones and narrow, tired-looking eyes. She had five rings in her right ear and wore thick black frames with no glass in them. Beyond naked antagonism, her eyes held nothing for me.

"I'm looking for Jean."

"Yeah, no shit. But Jean's gone." She started to edge back inside, her hand eager on the door.

"Wait a minute," I said. "Where is she?"

"I don't know," Alex answered. "Sometimes she just drives."

"Where?"

She moved back onto the porch, crowding me backward. "I'm not her keeper. She comes and goes. When we want to be together, we are; otherwise, I don't hassle her. That's free advice."

"Her car's here," I stated.

"She took mine."

Looking at her, I wanted a cigarette, so I asked for one. "I'm all out," she said, and my eyes fell to the pack wedged into her front pocket. Her eyes challenged me.

"You don't much care for me, do you?" I asked.

Her voice didn't change. "Nothing personal."

"What, then?" Alex had been around for almost two years; I'd seen her maybe five times. Jean would not talk about her, not where she came from, not what she'd done with her twenty-odd years. All I knew was where they'd met, and that raised some serious questions.

She studied me and flicked her cigarette into the bare dirt yard. "You're bad for Jean," she said. "I won't have it."

Her words stunned me. "I'm bad for Jean?"

"That's right." She inched closer. "You remind Jean of bad times. With you around, she can't let go. You drag her down."

"That's not true," I said, and gestured around me, taking in everything, including Alex. "I remind her of happy times. Before all this. Jean needs me. I'm her past. Her family, damn it."

"Jean doesn't look at you and see happiness. She sees weakness. That's what you bring to the table. She sees you and remembers all the crap that went down in the pile of bricks you grew up in. The years she spent choking on your father's bullshit." Alex stepped closer. She smelled of sweat and cigarettes. I backed away again, hating myself for it. She lowered her voice. "Women are worthless. Women are weak."

I knew what she was doing and felt my throat tighten. It was Ezra's voice. His words.

"Fucking and sucking," she continued. "Isn't that what he would say? Huh? Beyond housekeeping, women are good for two things. How do you think that made Jean feel? She was ten the first time she heard him say that. Ten years old, Work. A child."

I couldn't respond. He'd said that only once, to my knowledge, but once was enough. They are not words a child easily forgets.

"Do you agree with him, Work? Are you your daddy's boy?" She paused and leaned into me. "Your father was a misogynistic bastard. You remind Jean of that, and of your mother; of how she took it and acted like Jean should, too."

"Jean loved our mother," I shot back, holding my ground. "Don't try and twist that around." It was a weak statement and I knew it. I could not defend my father and did not understand why I felt compelled to do so.

Alex continued, firing words at me like spit. "You're a stone around her neck, Work. Plain and simple."

"That's you talking," I said.

"Nope." Her speech was as flat as her gaze, devoid of doubt or question. I looked around the squalid porch but found no help, just dead plants and a porch swing, where, I imagined, Alex filled my sister with lies and hate.

"What have you been telling her?" I demanded.

"You see. There's the problem. I don't need to tell her. She's smart enough to figure it out."

"I know she's smart," I said.

"You don't act like it. You pity her. You condescend."

"I do not."

"I won't have it," she spat out, as if I'd interrupted her. "I've taken her beyond all that. I've made her strong, given her something, and I won't have you fucking it up."

"I do not condescend to my sister," I almost shouted. "I care for her. She needs me."

"Denial won't change fact, and she needs you like a hole in the head. You're arrogant, like your father; she sees that. You presume to know what she needs, as if you could ever understand, but here's the truth of it: You don't know the first thing about who and what your sister is."

"And you do, is that it? You know who my sister is? What she needs?" My voice was up. Anger moved in me and it felt good. Here was the enemy. Something I could see and touch.

"Yeah. That's right," she said. "I absolutely do.

"What?" I asked.

"Not what you want. Not empty dreams and illusions. Not a husband, a station wagon, and a weekly bridge club. Not the goddamn American dream. That package already sucked her dry."

I stared at her glittering eyes and wanted to jam my fingers in them; they saw too clearly how much I was like my father. I'd never trusted Jean to find her own way, a brutal truth, and the fact of that, thrown so bluntly in my face by this woman I barely knew, drained me.

"Are you sleeping with my sister?" I asked.

"You know something, Work, fuck you. I don't need to explain myself. Jean and I are together now. We know what we want, and you're not part of the equation."

"Who are you?" I demanded. "Why are you here?"

"Q and A is over, asshole. I want you out of here."

"What do you want with my sister?" I shot back. She clenched her fists at her sides and I saw the bunch and play of muscles under her skin. Blood suffused her neck. She twisted her lower jaw.

"You need to leave," she said.

"Jean owns this house."

"And I live in it! Now get the hell off my porch."

"Not until I talk to Jean," I said, and crossed my arms. "I'll wait." Alex stiffened, but I refused to back down. I'd been pushed around too much in the past twenty-four hours. I wanted my sister, needed to know that she was all right. I needed her to understand that I was there for her, that I always would be. Indecision fluttered on Alex's face. Then there was movement behind her, and the screen door swung open. Jean stepped onto the porch. I stared dumbly.

Her face was pale and puffy under tousled hair. Red rimmed her eyes and I saw that they were swollen.

"Just leave, Work," she said. "Just go home."

Then she turned and was gone, swallowed by the musty house. Alex grinned in bright triumph, then slammed the door in my face. I put my hands to the wood, then let them fall to my sides, where they twitched. I saw Jean's face; it hung in the air like smoke. There was grief there, and pity, a dread finality.

In numb disbelief, I returned to my car, where I swayed, an emotional cripple. I stared at the house and its dirt yard and heard the whistle of an approaching train. I held my breath to keep from screaming; then all was wind and thunder.

CHAPTER

7

I'd always heard about the last laugh, mostly from Ezra. I never knew that the last laugh could be something real, a thing you could remember and miss.

I could still hear my sister's laugh. It had always been a good one, even when she didn't quite get the joke. Usually soft, it had a peculiar hiccup in the middle. Her lips signaled it with a twitch; then her small white teeth appeared briefly, as if she were nervous; but sometimes it boomed and she snorted through her nose. Those laughs were rare. I loved them, mainly because she could never stop once she started, and tears would track silver down her face. Once, when we were kids, she laughed so hard, she blew a snot bubble with her nose, and we both laughed until we thought we might die for lack of air. It was the single best laugh of my life. That was twenty-five years ago.

I was there when Jean laughed her last laugh. I'd told a really bad joke, something about three lawyers and a dead body. She gave me her small laugh, the one with the hiccup. Then her husband came in and said that he was going to run the baby-sitter home. None of us knew they were sleeping together. So she kissed him on the cheek and told him to drive safely. He honked on his way down the driveway, and she smiled when she told me he always did that.

The accident happened at the rest stop two miles up the interstate. The car was parked. They were naked in the backseat, and he must have been on top, because the impact sent him through the windshield but left her in the car. He suffered a broken jaw, a concussion, and lacerations to his face, chest, and genitals, which seemed about right. The girl never regained consciousness, which was an absolute tragedy.

The state trooper told me that a drunk driver took the exit too fast, lost control, and slammed into their parked car. Just one of those things, he'd said. One of those crazy things.

Jean stood by her man for two months, until the paper announced that the comatose seventeen-year-old girl was pregnant; then she crumbled. I found her the first time she tried to kill herself. There was bloody water running under the bathroom door, and I dislocated my shoulder breaking it down. She'd kept her clothes on, and I later learned that she did that because she knew I'd find her and didn't want to embarrass me. The thought of that broke my heart beyond repair.

Ezra refused to commit her. I begged, I argued, and I yelled, but he was resolute; it would look bad for the family. So Jean stayed with him and with Mother, the three of them alone in that big house.

When her husband left, he took their only child. Too depressed to care, she let him. He presented her with custody papers and she signed them. Had it been a son instead of a daughter, I suspect that Ezra would have fought him over it. But it was a girl, and so he didn't.

That night, she tried again; this time it was pills. She wore her wedding dress and stretched out to die on our parents' bed. After that, she was institutionalized for eight months—Alex Shiften was her roommate. When Jean went home, Alex went, too. We never learned a thing about her. The two shared a conspiracy of silence. Our questions, which began politely, were politely ignored. The questions grew more pointed, as did their reactions to them. When Alex told Ezra to fuck off, I thought the bottom would drop out. We stopped asking. None of us knew how to handle them, and in our discomfort we pretended everything was all right. What a ship of fools.

As I drove away from that ragged dead-end street, I thought about laughter and how it was like breath; you never knew which would be your last. And it saddened me that Jean's last laugh had been such a small one. I wished I'd told a better joke.

I tried to remember my last laugh, but all I could think of was Jean and that snot bubble. That had been grand. But memory can be like a floodgate, once opened hard to close, and as I drove, images and feelings marched upon me like waves. I saw my mother, broken on the floor, then Ezra's safe, his cold smirk, and Alex Shiften's triumphant smile. I saw Jean as a child, and then grown, floating in a bathtub, her diluted blood a translucent shroud that shimmered across the floor and spilled down the stairwell. My wife's hands, cold upon me, and, inevitably, images of Vanessa Stolen—the sweat on her face and on her thighs, her high breasts, which barely moved as she arched her back off the damp flannel sheets. I felt her eyes, heard the stutter in her throat as she gasped my name, and thought of the secret that for so many years had kept me from giving myself to her. And of how profoundly I failed her in that deep dark place where both our lives changed forever.

But some things are stronger than doubt or self-recrimination. Need, for instance. To be accepted. Loved without judgment. Even when I couldn't reciprocate. Time and again, I had returned to the one place, the one person who had never failed me. I'd done this knowing the pain that lingered in my wake. I'd taken all and given nothing. As for something in return, she'd neither asked nor demanded, though hers would have been the right. And I'd tried to stay away; I'd tried and failed. I knew also that I would fail again now. My need was too great, an animal inside me.

So I turned off the road, turned off the world, and drove slowly down the cratered track that was Stolen Farm Road. It felt like a switch had been flicked in my head. Pressures fell away, concerns, too. I could breathe, and so I did, like I'd been long underwater. I passed through the shade of tall oaks and narrow, feathered cedars, and gravel crunched beneath my tires. I saw a shrike with a fence lizard in its claws and felt elemental, as if I, too, belonged here. It was a good feeling, though false, and there were no whispers beyond the wind.

I rounded the last bend and saw Vanessa's house. She stood on the front porch, shading her eyes, and for a moment I believed that she'd felt my approach. My chest tightened and I felt a stirring of body and soul. Even more than this place, this woman did things for me. She was farmwork-lean, with flaxen hair and eyes that shone like sun on water. Her hands were rough, but I loved them for the things they could do. I liked to watch her plant things, those hands in dark earth. It reminded me of what I knew as a child, that dirt is good and the earth forgives. Her breasts were small above a flat stomach, and her eyes were soft where tragedy would have made others hard or indifferent. Small lines cut the corners of her eyes and mouth but were inconsequential.

Looking at her, I felt my weakness. I knew this was wrong, knew that I could never give her what she so richly deserved. I knew it and for an instant

I cared, but only for that instant. Then I was out of the car and in her arms, my mouth on hers, my hands no longer mine to control. I didn't know if I was on the porch or still in the drive. I didn't remember moving, yet all was motion. She rose into me and I was lost. No fear or confusion, just this woman and the world that spun around us like colored mist.

I heard distant sound and recognized my name; it burned in my ear. Then I felt her tongue cool it. Her lips moved over me—my eyes, my neck, my face. Her hands found the back of my head and they pulled my lips back to hers. I tasted plums, kissed her harder, and she weakened against me. I picked her up, felt legs around me. Then more motion and we were inside, up the stairs and onto the bed that knew so well the force of our passion. Clothes evaporated, as if burned away by flesh too hot to bear them. My mouth found her breasts, the hard, ready nipples, and the soft plane of her stomach. I tasted all of her. The dew of her sweat, the deep cleft of her, her legs like velvet bands across my ears. Her fingers clawed at my hair, tangled, and she pulled me up, said words I couldn't possibly understand. She took me in her roughened palm and led me into her. My head rocked back. She was heat, fire; she cried my name again, but I was beyond response, lost and desperate never to be found.

CHAPTER

8

I drifted for what felt like hours. Neither of us spoke; we knew better. Peace like this came rarely and was as fragile as a child's smile. She nestled against me, on her side, one leg thrown across my own. Her hand trailed lazily across my chest, down my stomach. Occasionally, her lips brushed my neck, and they felt like feathers.

I had my arm around her, my hand pressed against the smooth curve of her lower back. I watched the ceiling fan spin, brown blades against her creamy white ceiling. A breeze passed through the window, stroked us like a penitent breath. But I knew it couldn't last, as did she; it never had. We would talk, and as the words came, so, too, would the steady push of reality. I knew the pattern. It always started small, a vague itch in the mind, as if I'd left something undone. Then the face of my wife would make its silent, swift invasion and the guilt would follow on tiny feet. But it was not the guilt of the adulterer; that had passed years ago, soon after Barbara's smile.

This was a different guilt, born of darkness and fear in that stinking creek so many years ago—the day we met, the day I fell in love and the day I failed her. That guilt was a cancer, and under its assault the cocoon would crumble and I would leave, hating myself for again using the only person in this world who loved me, wishing that I could undo the past and make myself worthy. But it was the one thing that I could never do, for if this guilt was a cancer, then the truth was a bullet in the head. She would hate me if she knew. So in time I would leave, as I always did, and already I was dreading the hurt in her eyes when I told her I'd call, and how she'd nod and smile as if she believed me.

I closed my eyes, let myself sink beneath the blanket of this momentary joy, but inside I was hollow, and cold was a fist around my heart.

"Penny for your thoughts," she said.

It had begun, but that was okay. I'd missed the sound of her voice.

"You wouldn't like them," I said. She rose up on an elbow and smiled down at me. I smiled back. "They're dark, horrible thoughts." I kept my voice light.

"Give them to me anyway. A present."

"Kiss me," I told her, and she did. I would give her my thoughts, those that she could bear. "I missed you," I said. "I always miss you."

"Liar." She cupped my chin in one hand. "Filthy rotten liar." She kissed me again. "Do you know how long it's been?"

I did—seventeen months and just under two weeks, each day an agony and an exercise in longing. "No," I told her. "How long?"

"Never mind," she said. "Let's not dwell on it." I saw the pain in her eyes. The last time I'd been with her was the night my mother died. I could still see the reflection of her face suspended in the windowpane as I stared into the night. I was searching then, looking for the strength to give her the truth. But her words had stopped me. "Don't think about such nasty things," she'd said. So I had not.

"Ezra's dead," I told her. "They found his body two days ago."

"I know. I'm sorry. I truly am."

She would never have raised the subject. Just one more way that she was unlike every other. But she'd always been like that. She didn't push or pry, didn't care for details. Vanessa lived in the moment; I'd always envied that about her. It was strength.

"How's Jean taking it?"

She was the first person to ask me that. Not what happened. Not how I was handling it. Her thoughts were of Jean because she knew that would be my biggest concern. I shuddered at the depth of her understanding.

"I'm scared for Jean," I said. "She's gone far away, and I don't know if I can get her back." I told her about my run-in with Alex. About Jean on the porch. "She's left me, Vanessa. I don't know her anymore. I think she's in trouble, but she won't let me help her."

"It's never too late. For anything. All you have to do is reach out."

"I have," I told her.

"Maybe you just think you have."

"I told you, I have."

I felt the force of my words as they passed my lips, and I didn't know where the anger came from. Were we talking about Jean or Vanessa? She sat up in the bed, cross-legged, and stared at me.

"Take it easy, Jackson," she said. "We're just talking."

Vanessa had never called me Work. She used my given name and always had. I'd asked her once why that was, and she'd told me I would never be work for her. I'd told her it was clever, and about the nicest thing I'd ever heard. I could still remember the way she'd looked. Sunlight flooded the open window and I'd noticed for the first time that she was not the young girl I'd once known; time and hard work had left their marks. But I didn't care.

"You're right, just talking. So how have you been?" I asked.

Her face softened. "I'm growing organics now," she told me. "Moving more and more of my production in that direction. Strawberries, blueberries, whatever. People are into that these days. It pays."

"So you're doing okay, then?" I asked.

She laughed. "Hell no. The bank's still after me every month, but I'm ahead of the curve on this organics thing. It will make a difference. This farm will never leave my hands. That, I promise you." She talked more about organic farming, about her aging tractor and the truck that needed a new transmission. She talked about her plans and I listened. At one point, she got up and brought two beers from the kitchen.

To me, Vanessa was a breath of fresh air. She moved to the seasons, touched the living earth every single day. I knew when it was raining, but not until I got wet.

"You know, time's a crazy damn thing," she said, handing me a beer. She slipped back onto the bed and put a pillow in her lap. A strand of hair hung over her left eye. I asked her what she meant. "I was thinking of our families," she told me. "The rise and fall of family fortunes."

I sipped at my beer. "What about them?"

"It's just crazy is all. I mean, think about it. Where was your family at the end of the Civil War?"

She knew exactly where my family had been; we'd talked about it many times. Five generations ago, my ancestor was a foot soldier from Pennsylvania who had the misfortune to get most of his foot shot off. He was captured and delivered to the Confederate prison in Salisbury, where he lingered several weeks before dying of dysentery and infection. He was buried in one of the four trench graves that eventually came to hold over eleven thousand Union soldiers. That was at the end of the war. His wife learned of his death and, pregnant with his unborn child, traveled to Salisbury. But he had no marker; his bones were lost among the thousands of other nameless souls. Word is, it broke her heart. She gave her last dollar to the physician who delivered my great-great-grandfather and died two weeks later. I've often thought of that ancestor, and wondered if her death drained the last true passion from my family.

She died of a broken heart. My God. What a thing.

Her son was passed around the county and spent most of his life shoveling manure on another man's plantation. My great-grandfather delivered ice in the summer and stoked rich men's furnaces in the winter. His son was a worthless drunk who beat my father for the fun of it. The Pickens were poor as dirt and treated like shit in this county until Ezra came along. He changed everything.

The Stolen family was just the opposite. Two hundred years back, this farm had been over a thousand acres, and the Stolens ran things in Rowan County.

"Lot of history in this bed," I said.

"Yep." She nodded. "Lot of love, too." I said nothing, and the silence spoke volumes, an old tale. She loved me and on good days understood that I loved her, too. Why I could not admit that was the problem. She didn't understand and I was too ashamed to explain it to her. So we existed in this horrible undefined state, with nothing to cling to when the nights were cold and endlessly successive. "Why are you here, Jackson?" she asked me.

"Do I need a reason?" I replied, feeling cheap.

"No," she said with feeling. "Never."

I took her grasping hand. "I'm here to see you, Vanessa."

"But not to stay."

I remained silent.

"Never to stay," she continued, and I saw tears in her eyes.

"Vanessa . . ."

"Don't say it, Jackson. Don't. We've been here before. I know you're married. I don't know what came over me. Just ignore me."

"It's not that," I said.

"Then what?" she asked, and I saw such anguish in her face that I lost my voice. I was wrong to have come. So very, very wrong.

She tried to laugh, but it died halfway. "Come on, Jackson. What?" But I couldn't tell her. She stared into my eyes for a long second and I watched as the fire burned out of her face and the resignation settled in. She kissed me, but it was a dead kiss.

"I'm jumping in the shower," she told me. "Don't you dare leave."

I watched her as she padded barefoot and naked from the room. Normally, we'd be in the shower together, her body alive under my soapy hands.

I drained my beer and lay weakly, listening to the birds outside. I heard the shower run in the bathroom and pictured Vanessa's face upturned to water straight from the well. It would taste fresh on her skin. I wanted to wash her hair, but instead I got up and went downstairs. There was more beer in the refrigerator and I carried one to the front porch. The sun felt good on my naked skin and it dried my sweat. Farmland stretched to the distant tree line and I guessed I was looking at strawberries. I leaned against the post and closed my eyes to the breeze. I didn't hear Vanessa come downstairs.

"Oh, my God. What happened to your back?" She moved quickly onto the porch. "It looks like somebody beat you with a bat." She put light hands on me, tracing lines of my bruises.

"I fell down some stairs," I told her.

"Were you drunk?"

I laughed. "A little, I guess."

"Jackson, you need to be careful. You could have killed yourself."

I wasn't sure why I lied to her. I just didn't want to tell her the whole truth. She had enough problems. "I'll be all right."

She took the beer from my hand and sipped. She was in a towel, her hair still wet. I wanted to wrap her into me and promise that I'd never let go. I wanted to tell her that I loved her, that I would spend the rest of my life just like this. Instead, I put one inadequate arm around her shoulder, and even that felt like a stranger's arm. "I love this place," I told her, and she accepted my words without comment. It was the closest I could come to sharing the truth of my feelings for her, and in some small way she knew this. Reality, however, had never been so simple.

"Are you hungry?" she asked, and I nodded. "Let's go to the kitchen." We went into the kitchen and she pulled a robe from the laundry room on the way. "Go put your pants on," she told me. "You can do anything you want naked except sit at my table." She popped me on the rear as I passed by.

She had a trestle table that dated back to the 1800s. It was dented and scarred. Sitting at it, we ate ham and cheese and spoke of little things. I drank another beer. I told her about Ezra's safe and the missing gun. She hesitated for a minute and then asked me how he died. Two bullets to the head, I told her, and she looked out the window.

"Do you feel any different?" she finally asked.

"I don't understand."

She looked at me then. "Does your life feel any different now that Ezra is dead and gone?" I didn't know what she meant and told her so. She didn't speak for awhile, and I realized she was debating whether or not to continue. "Are you happy?" she finally asked.

I shrugged. "Maybe. I don't know. I haven't thought about it in awhile." There was something in her eyes. "What are you getting at, Vanessa?"

She sighed. "I don't think you're living your life, Jackson, not for a long time now."

I grew still and tense. "Whose, then?"

"You know whose." Her voice was soft and she shied away as if afraid I might hit her.

"No, Vanessa, I don't." I was getting angry and didn't know why—didn't want to know why. Denial was a weapon; it killed truth, numbed the mind, and I was a junkie. Part of me recognized this, the same part that knew where she was going, but I ignored that part. That part hurt.

"Damn it, Jackson. I'm trying to help."

"Are you?" I demanded. "Who are you trying to help? Me or you?"

"That is not fair," she said. I knew she was right, but I didn't care. She was taking me places I didn't want to go. "It's you I'm worried about. It's always you!"

"Goddamn it, Vanessa. That's too much pressure. I've never asked for things to be the way they are. They just are."

"*That* is your problem."

I stared at her.

"Things never just are. We make choices, actively or not. You can affect the world, Jackson. Ezra's dead. Don't you feel that?"

"So we're back to Ezra," I said.

"We never left him. And that's the problem. You've never left him. You've been living his life for more than twenty years, and you've never seen it."

I didn't know what she was talking about, and in that instant her face seemed to transform. She was like the rest after all. "No," I said. "Not true."

"Yes." She tried to take my hand, but I pulled it back just in time.

"That is not fucking true!" I yelled.

"Why did you marry Barbara?" she demanded, and there was a stoic calm in her voice.

"What?"

"Why Barbara? Why not me?"

"You don't know what you're talking about."

"I do know. And always have."

"You're not making sense." I watched as she came out of her seat, hands on the table that had fed her family for generations. She leaned closer, and I noticed that her nostrils were flared.

"You listen to me, Jackson, and you listen well, because I swear to God that I will never say this again. But I need it to be said. Ten years ago, you told me you loved me. You damn well meant it, too. Then you married Barbara. Now I want you to tell me why."

I rocked back in my chair, felt my defensiveness, but couldn't do anything about it. My arms crossed over my chest as if to protect my heart. My head rang, and I rubbed at my temples, but the sudden pain refused to die.

"You married Barbara because Ezra told you to." She slapped her palm down on the table and I thought it sounded like a bone breaking. "Admit it. One time, Jackson, and I'll never mention it again. You live Ezra's life, his choices. Barbara's family has a name; she went to the right schools, had the right friends. It's true. Admit it. Damn it, Jackson, be a man."

"No!" I shouted, suddenly on my feet. "I won't admit it because it's not true." I spun from the table and pounded upstairs to get the rest of my clothes and my keys. She was wrong and I refused to take any more. Her voice followed me.

"What about children?" she shouted. "You always wanted children!"

"Shut up, Vanessa!" My voice broke as I said it. I knew that she did not deserve it, but I could not yell loudly enough.

"Whose idea was that? Huh? Whose idea, Jackson? You used to talk about it all the time. Lots of kids! That's what you always planned—a houseful of them, a family to raise right, so you could be the father you wanted Ezra to be. Damn it, Jackson. Don't run away from this. It's too important!"

I ignored her. My shirt was on the floor and I found my keys under the bed. I pulled my shoes on without socks. The house was hot, stifling; I had to get out. I shouldn't have come at all.

She was waiting for me at the bottom of the stairs.

"Don't leave," she said. "Not like this."

Her voice and eyes were both soft, but it wasn't going to work. "Let me by," I told her. She stepped onto the first step, crowding me. Looking down, I saw the part in her hair, the light freckles on the bridge of her nose, eyes that looked too wide to be innocent.

"Please," she said. "Please, Jackson. I'm sorry. I take it back. Please don't go."

"Step aside, Vanessa." The pain in her face cut me, but I couldn't stop. This was her fight, not mine.

"Jackson, please. It's been so long. I can't lose you again. Stay. Have another beer." She reached for my hand.

The stairs were tilting; I couldn't catch my breath, and I didn't know what was wrong with me. I needed air, needed to get out. I shook my hand free and pushed past her.

"I shouldn't have come," I said, hitting the screen door so hard, it slammed against the house.

I felt her behind me, heard her steps on the porch and then on the gravel. Her breath was loud, and I knew that if I turned, I would see tears. So I didn't turn; I marched on, and she caught me at the car.

"Don't go," she said.

I didn't turn around. She put one hand on my shoulder, the other on the side of my neck, where heat still burned. She laid her face upon my back, and I hesitated. I wanted no one thing in my life more than to stay, but she wanted too much. Truth was not my friend.

"Please don't make me beg," she said, and I knew how much the words cost her. But I didn't turn around; I couldn't—one look at her and I would stay. And I wanted to; that's what killed me. If possible, I would never leave, but I needed my anger. I couldn't give it up.

"I'm sorry, Vanessa. I shouldn't have come at all."

She didn't try to stop me as I got into the car. I backed away without looking at her. I drove too fast, wheels loose in the gravel. I kept my eyes down and didn't look up until I was almost to the bend in the road. Then I saw her in the mirror, on her knees in the dust, face buried in her rough farm-girl hands. She looked small. She looked crushed.

My anger drained away and left me shaken to the core. She was the only woman I'd ever loved, and this was all she had of me, a palmful of dusty tears.

Sweet Lord, I thought. *What have I done?*

CHAPTER

9

Istopped at the paved road, as sick as if I'd just stepped on a baby bird. I couldn't bear to think about what had just happened, but it was in me now, inescapable. I felt her tears, her fingers, so light on my neck, and the plane of her cheek against my back. I reached for something solid: the wheel, the dash, the clock that read just after four. I took a deep breath and put the car back into gear. Then I remembered Detective Mills and our three o'clock meeting. Somewhere between cheating on my wife and destroying the woman I loved, I'd forgotten about it.

I stepped on the gas. The road ran black beneath me. I recognized a song on the radio and wondered when I'd turned it on. I punched at the button as hills rolled past on greased tracks and farmland fell away. Trailer parks and strip malls sprang up to follow me as I drove back into town, the smell of sex on me like a scarlet letter. I called the house to see if Barbara was there and hung up when she answered. Her voice was like syrup, and I considered speaking, just to see if it would sour; but if so, it would sour with questions I was not prepared to answer. I needed to calm down, get a grip. Chill the fuck out.

At the office, I used Ezra's shower to rinse sin from my flesh and wondered how many times he'd used it for the same purpose. Never, I thought. Ezra knew women but never knew guilt. Did I envy that in him? No. I nourished my guilt for the soul that it implied, and as I left, I gave Ezra's safe the finger. Fuck everybody. I needed some Work time. Maybe I'd get a dog after all.

Outside, I made it to my car before I saw movement from the corner of my eye. I spun around.

"I saw your car." It was Douglas, the district attorney. He looked tired, his eyes puffy above a nose the color of old wine. He looked at me strangely and I wondered if he'd been drinking. "You didn't answer my knock, so I waited."

I said nothing. For some reason, my heart refused to slow down. He walked across the ten feet that separated us, stopping just before he got too close. His eyes moved over me, taking in my wet hair and disheveled clothes. I felt heat in my cheeks but couldn't stop the flush. Douglas was a hard man to lie to. "Everything okay?" he asked, shoving a piece of gum into his mouth.

"Yes," I said, finding my voice. "Yes." I knew I was repeating myself.

"I ask because I just got off the phone with Detective Mills. She says you'd better be dead already. It's the only excuse that she'll accept." His eyes glittered more than twinkled and I realized they were his black eyes, his courtroom eyes. "Are you dead?" he asked.

"Close," I said, and tried a smile that died on the vine. "Look, I'm sorry about not meeting Mills. I had my reasons."

"Care to share them?" Douglas asked, crowding me without taking a step.

"I do not." He was unimpressed by the anger in my voice. He shoved his hands into his pockets and studied me. I tried to give him my poker face, my lawyer face, but there in the shadow of my dead father's building, it was hard. I had no idea what he saw, but I knew it wasn't the calm, collected face I'd once practiced in the mirror.

"I'm going to tell you something, Work, and I want you to listen well." I didn't even blink. "This is the last thing I can tell you as a friend. It's good advice, so you should take it." He paused, as if waiting for me to thank him, and sighed when I didn't. "Don't fuck around with Mills," he told me. "I mean it. She's pissed-off and frustrated. That makes her the most dangerous person in your world."

I felt a horrible chill move over me. "What are you saying, Douglas?"

"I'm not *saying* anything. This conversation isn't happening."

"Am I a suspect?" I asked.

"I told you the other day that everybody is a suspect."

"That's no answer," I replied.

Douglas rolled his shoulders and looked around the empty lot, up at the roofline, then put his eyes back on mine. He pursed his lips. "Ezra was a rich man," he said, as if that explained it all.

"So?" I didn't get it.

"Jesus, Work." Exasperation was in his voice, and he sucked in a deep breath as if to cool his temper. "Mills is looking for a motive and going through the usual suspects. I assume Ezra had a will."

"Oh shit," I said. "Are you kidding me?"

"Barbara has expensive tastes, and the practice . . ." He paused and shrugged.

"Come on, Douglas."

"I'm just stating the obvious, okay? You're a brilliant tactician, Work. You have one of the sharpest legal minds I've ever known. Hell, you're even decent in the courtroom. But you're no rainmaker. You won't take personal injury cases anymore and you won't kiss ass to get big clients. That's what built the practice and made Ezra rich. But a law practice is a business. Even Mills knows that, and she's been around enough to know that yours is barely solvent.

"Look. I know you didn't kill your father. Just don't give Mills a reason to look your way. Cooperate, for Christ's sake. Don't be a goddamn idiot. Give her what she wants and get on with your life. It's not complicated math."

"It's bullshit math!"

"One plus one is two. Add six or seven zeros and the math gets even more compelling."

I was stunned by his words, and his face had a sharp edge, as if he could cut me open and tell the future in my guts.

"Ezra had a lot of zeros," he concluded.

My insides twisted as if already between his thick, meaty fingers. "Has Mills discussed this with you?" I asked, needing to know.

"Not in so many words," the DA admitted. "But it doesn't take a genius, Work. I know where her mind is going with this. So do yourself a favor. Bend over, take it like a man, and move on with your life."

"Did Mills tell you that someone tried to kill me last night?" I asked.

He frowned at the interruption. "She may have mentioned something about it."

"And?"

Douglas shrugged, his eyes far from mine. "She doesn't believe you."

"And you don't, either." I finished his unspoken thought.

"She's the detective," he said flatly.

"You think I made it up?"

"I don't know what to believe." A simple statement.

"Somebody pushed that chair down the stairs, Douglas. If they didn't mean to kill me, they sure as hell meant to do bodily harm."

"And you're saying it's connected to your father's death?"

I thought about the safe and the missing gun. "Maybe. It's possible."

"You should know that Mills doesn't buy it. She thinks you're generating confusion, clouding the issues. If I thought you did it, and I'm just saying *if*, playing devil's advocate, then I'd be inclined to agree with Mills. It's Occam's Razor, Work. The simplest explanation is usually right."

"That's crap, Douglas. Somebody tried to kill me."

"Just give Mills your alibi, Work, and whatever else she wants. Let her check it out and be done with it."

I thought about what Douglas was asking me to talk about. I could hear the sound of a neck breaking under terrible force. "You know what happened that night, Douglas." It was a statement, a novel writ large.

"I know your mother died in a tragic fall, but that's all I know." His voice was unapologetic.

"It's enough," I said.

"No, Work, it's not. Because it's also the night your father disappeared and for all Mills knows, you and Jean were the last ones to see him alive. It's important, and no one's going to dance around your tender sensibilities. Your father was murdered. This is a murder investigation. Talk to her."

I thought that if he said *murder* one more time, I'd murder him. I didn't need a reminder. I saw my father's fleshless jawbone every time I closed my eyes, and even now I fought the image of his remains under the knives and saws of the medical examiner in Chapel Hill.

Douglas loomed. The silence behind his last words demanded a response, but I didn't look up. He wanted me to cough up the memory of that night like a bloody tumor so that Mills could paw through it, spread it out like finger paint, and discuss it with other cops over coffee and cigarettes. Cops I fought every day in court. I knew how it worked, the twisted voyeurism of people who had seen it all yet never got enough. I knew how they speculated about rape victims in the halls behind the courtrooms, pawed through photographs, and dissected a person's humanity in the quest to be the funniest cop of the day. I'd heard them joke about how people had been killed: Did it hurt? Do you think she begged? Was she alive when they fucked her? Conscious when the knife first touched her pale skin? Did he see it coming? I heard he wet himself.

It was a dark farce, a tragedy played out in the pain of victims in every town in the country. But this time it was my pain. My family. My secrets.

I saw Mother at the bottom of the stairs, her open eyes and blood-flecked mouth, her neck bent like a cruel joke. I saw it all: the red dress she wore, the position of her hands, the Cinderella slipper that lay upon the stairs where it had fallen. The memory was cruel and it cut, but if I looked up, I might see Ezra, and that would be worse. I wasn't ready for that. I couldn't do it. Not again. For if I looked beyond Ezra, I would see Jean. I would see what that night did to her, all of it, frozen on her face in that horrible tableau that still chased through my dreams. There was horror in her face, and rage, an animal force that transformed her. In that face I saw a stranger, someone who could kill, and that terrified me now more than ever. What had that night made of my sister? And was she now forever lost?

If I talked to Mills, it would all come back. She would poke and pry, try with her cop mind to ferret it out. She might see things, and I couldn't have that.

"No problem," I told the district attorney. "I'll talk to her."

"Be sure that you do," he replied.

"Don't worry." I unlocked my car, desperate to escape. "Thanks for worrying about me," I said, but my sarcasm was wasted effort. I climbed into my car, but he stopped me with a hand on my door.

"By the way," he said. "What *were* you doing the night Ezra disappeared?"

I tried to meet his eyes. "Are you asking for my alibi?" I asked, as if he was joking. He said nothing, and I laughed, but it sounded hollow. "As a friend or as the district attorney?"

"Maybe a little of both," he said.

"You're a funny man," I told him.

"Humor me," he said.

I wanted to get out of there, away from his questions and his flat eyes. So I did what any man would have done under the circumstances: I lied.

"I was home," I told him. "In bed. With Barbara."

He smiled a thin smile. "That wasn't so hard, was it?" he asked me.

"No," I told him, surprised. "That wasn't hard at all."

He smiled a wider smile and I saw that food was stuck in his teeth, something brown. "Good boy," he said, trying to be friendly but sounding condescending.

I tried to return his smile but couldn't. A nod was the best I could do, and even that hurt. He wasn't sure about me. I saw it in his eyes. Could I have killed Ezra? It was a question for him, and he would check my alibi. I also knew that he'd discussed this with Detective Mills. This was his county and a media case; he'd never sit on the sidelines. So he'd lied to me as I'd lied to him, and that meant one thing. Our friendship was dead, whether Douglas wanted it that way or not. He could hang someone for my father's death tomorrow, but I could never go back. That bridge was smoking ash.

He left then, and I watched his wide back as he shuffled across the lot to his tired Chevrolet sedan. He got in and drove away. He never looked back, and I realized that he knew it, too. Ezra's death was like a match dropped into damp tinder; it was a slow burn now, but only a matter of time until it flashed. I wondered what else would end a smoking ruin.

I started my own car and left the windows down. I drove my hair dry and smoked a couple of cigarettes to take away the smell of fresh soap. I thought of Vanessa's face in the afternoon light. That's what I would hold on to. How it started, not how it ended. Not what I would say to her the next time I caved to my weakness and sought redemption in her tender mercies.

I said her name once, then tucked it away.

It was almost six o'clock by the time I got home. I knew that something was off the minute I walked in. Candles perfumed the air and soft music played on the stereo. Barbara called from the kitchen and I answered her, dropping my jacket onto a chair back and moving slowly her way. She met me at the kitchen door with a glass of chilled white wine, a chardonnay that probably cost a fortune. She was wearing a smile and a very small black dress.

"Welcome home, baby," she said, and kissed me. Her lips parted and I felt the tip of her tongue. I couldn't remember the last time she'd called me baby, and the last time she kissed me that way, she'd been dead drunk. She pressed against me and, looking down, I saw her breasts swell from the top of her dress with the pressure. She wrapped her arms around my waist.

"Are you drunk?" I asked without thinking.

She didn't flinch. "Not yet," she said. "But two more glasses and you might get lucky." She ground against me, making me vaguely uncomfortable. I felt out of my depth. I looked over the top of her head, saw the pot and pans simmering on the stove.

"Are you cooking?" I asked, surprised. Barbara rarely cooked.

"Beef Wellington," she replied.

"What's the occasion?"

She stepped back, put her wine on the counter. "An apology," she said. "For the way I treated you last night. It was a bad time for you, a horrible time, and I could have been more supportive." She cast her eyes down, but I didn't believe her. "I should have been, Work. I should have been there for you."

Barbara had not apologized to me in years, not for anything. I was struck dumb.

She took my hands and peered at me with what had to be mock concern. "Are you okay?" she asked, referring to my fall, I guessed. "I should have come to the hospital, I know, but I was still mad at you." She made a pout of her lips and I knew that in her mind, that made everything okay. She turned away before I could respond and snatched up her wineglass. Her calm seemed less natural when half of the glass disappeared in one swallow. She turned again to face me and leaned against the sink, her eyes shiny. "So," she began again, her voice too loud. "How was your day?"

I almost laughed. I almost slapped her, just to see what expression would appear on her perfectly prepared face. Somebody tried to kill me last night and you didn't come to the hospital. I made love to a fragile and lonely woman, then ground her spirit into the dirt for reasons I'm too chickenshit to explore. My father is dead with a couple of bullets in his head, and the district attorney wants to know where I was on the night in question. I'd really like to choke the fake smile off your face, which, I think, means my marriage is in trouble. And my sister, whom I have failed in every possible way, hates me. And worst of all, this sister, whom I love—I'm pretty sure that she murdered our father.

"Fine," I told her. "My day was fine. How was yours?"

"The same," she said. "Go sit. The paper is on the table. Dinner will be ready in half an hour."

"I'll go change," I said, and walked from the room on wooden feet. I felt things as I moved: the wall, the banister. What was real? What mattered? If I walked back into the kitchen with shit in my mouth, would she kiss me and tell me I tasted like chocolate?

I splashed water on my face and put on khakis and a cotton roll-neck sweater that Barbara had given me for Christmas several years back. I studied my face in the mirror, amazed at how complete it appeared, how calm and intact. Then I smiled and the illusion collapsed. I thought of the things Vanessa had said.

Barbara still stood at the stove when I walked back into the kitchen. Her glass was full again. She smiled as I poured more for myself. Wordlessly, we clinked glasses and drank. "Ten more minutes," she said. "I'll call you when it's ready."

"Do you want me to set the table?" I asked.

"I've got it. Go and relax."

I turned for the living room and the deep, soft couch. Ten minutes sounded good.

"Douglas stopped by," my wife announced. I stopped and turned.

"What?"

"Yeah, a routine visit, he said. Just to talk about the night Ezra disappeared."

"Routine," I repeated.

"To fill in the blanks, he said. For his forms."

"His forms."

She looked quizzically at me. "Why are you repeating what I say?" she asked.

"Am I?"

"Yes. Almost every word."

"I'm sorry. I didn't know I was."

"Honestly, Work." She laughed. "Sometimes." She turned back to the stove, her hand on a wooden spoon. I stood rooted, dimly aware that numbness was becoming my normal state of existence.

"What did you tell him?" I finally asked.

"The truth," she said. "What else?"

"Of course the truth, Barbara, but what specifically?"

"Don't snap at me, Work," she said. "I'm trying . . ." She trailed off, gesturing with the spoon at the cluttered kitchen. Drops of something yellow landed on the counter and I stared at them because I couldn't meet her eyes. When I did look up, I saw that she had her hand over her mouth and tears shimmered in eyes turned to the floor. Another man would have gone to her and put his arms around her, but my soul was already black with lies.

I gave her an awkward minute and she pulled herself together. "What did you tell him?" I asked again, more gently this time.

"Just what little I know. You've never told me much." Her voice was small. "I told him that after going to the hospital with"—she paused, barely able to finish the sentence; she'd almost said my mother's corpse—"with your mother, you went to your father's house. Then you came here. I told him how upset you were, you and Jean." She looked down again. "About how you two argued."

I stopped her. "I told you about that?"

"Not what you argued about. Not the words. Just that you fought about something. You were very upset."

"What else?"

"Jesus, Work. What is all this?"

"Just tell me, please."

"Nothing else to tell. He wanted to know where you were that night and I told him you were here. He thanked me and left. That's it."

Thank God. But I had to test her. I had to be sure.

I made my voice casual. "Could you swear that I was here all night? Could you testify to that?"

"You're scaring me, Work."

"No reason to be scared," I assured her. "It's just the lawyer in me. I know how some people might think, and it's best if we're clear on this."

She stepped closer, stopping in the kitchen door. She still held the spoon. Her eyes were very steady, and she lowered her voice, as if to give her words a special emphasis. "I would know if you'd left," she stated simply, and something in her face made me wonder if she knew the truth. That I *had* left. That I'd spent long hours weeping on Vanessa's shoulder before creeping back into our bed an hour before dawn, scared weak that she would wake up.

"You were here," she said. "With me. There can be no question about that."

I smiled, praying this time that my face would remain intact. "Good. Then we're settled. Thank you, Barbara." I rubbed my hands together. "Dinner smells great," I added lamely, turning away as quickly as might seem reasonable. I almost made it to the couch, when a thought stopped me. "What time did Douglas come by?"

"Four o'clock," she told me, and I sat down on the couch. Four o'clock. An hour before I spoke to him in the parking lot. I was wrong, then. Our friendship didn't die when he questioned me; the corpse was already cold and starting to stink. The fat bastard was testing me.

Dinner would have been great if I could have tasted it. We had caramelized Brie with slivered almonds, Caesar salad, beef Wellington, and fresh bread. The chardonnay turned out to be Australian. My wife was beautiful in the candlelight and at times I thought that maybe I'd misjudged her. She made clever remarks at the expense of no one, spoke of current events and a book we'd both read. Occasionally, her hand touched mine. I grew mellow with wine and hope. By half past nine, I thought maybe we had a chance after all. It didn't last long.

The plates had been cleared away, stacked in the sink for the people we'd be the next day. The remnants of dessert littered the table and we were halfway through a coffee and Baileys. A quiet contentment filled me, and I looked forward to loving her for the first time in forever. Her hand was on my leg.

"So tell me," she said, leaning closer, seeming to offer herself. "When do you think we'll move?" The question caught me by surprise. I didn't understand, but her eyes had a new glitter and I felt myself sobering, almost against my will. She sipped her wine, her eyes dark above the pale half-moon of the glass's edge. She waited in silence, as if only for me to pluck a date from the air.

"Move where?" I asked, because I had no choice. I dreaded her answer, mainly because I knew what it would be.

She laughed, but there was no humor in it. "Don't joke," she said.

The last of my pleasure vanished, devoured by the cruel hunger in her voice. "I'm not," I said. "Are you?"

I watched as her face softened but saw that it was forced. The muscles still clenched in her once-lovely jawline.

"Into Ezra's house. Into our new house."

"What in the world makes you think that we're moving into that house?"

"I just thought . . . I mean . . ."

"Damn it, Barbara, we can barely afford this house, and it's not even half the size of my father's."

"It's such a lovely home," she said. "I just assumed . . ."

"You assumed we'd move into an eight-thousand-square-foot house we can't afford to heat?"

"But the will—"

"I don't even know what's in the will!" I exclaimed. "I don't have a clue!"

"But Glena said—"

I exploded. "Glena! I should have known. Is that what you two were talking about last night?" I thought of the miserable hours I'd spent in the garage while my wife and her detestable friend planned Barbara's rise to eminence. "You had it all planned out."

A change came over Barbara as I watched. Suddenly, she was cool dispassion.

"It makes sense if we're going to start a family," she said, then sipped her wine and watched me with a hunter's patience. It was not fair. Barbara knew how much I wanted children. I sighed deeply and poured straight Baileys into my cup.

"Are you blackmailing me?" I asked. "Children for Ezra's house?"

"Of course not," she said. "I'm merely suggesting that children would be a logical next step for us, and we could use the extra space."

I tried to calm myself. Exhaustion descended upon me like wet cement, but I decided nonetheless that it might be time to face some ugly truths. Vanessa's tear-streaked face came unbidden to my mind. I thought of the things she'd said, the truths she'd thrust under my nose, truths so abhorrent to me that I'd crushed her rather than face them.

"How come we never had children, Barbara?" I asked.

"You said you needed to concentrate on your career." Her response was immediate and unrehearsed, and I realized that she believed it. An appalling silence filled my head, an arctic calm.

"I never said that," I assured her. The very thought of it was absurd. I had sacrificed more than enough to the hollow idol of my law career. I would never give up the idea of children.

"You most certainly did," Barbara said. "I remember it clearly. You wanted to concentrate on the practice."

"Every time I brought up children, Barbara, you told me that you weren't ready yet. You changed the subject. If it had been up to me, we'd have five by now."

Strange awareness moved across her face, a shadow of understanding. "Maybe it was Ezra," she said, then jerked, as if stunned that she had actually said the words.

" 'Maybe it was Ezra'?" I repeated.

"That's not what I meant," she said, but it was too late. I knew what she meant, and suddenly my ears roared, a cacophony that threatened to knock me from my chair.

Maybe it was Ezra.

Maybe . . . it . . . was . . . Ezra.

I gaped at my wife as if from a distance and I understood. Ezra wanted me to carry on his tradition of greatness. She wanted me to make more money. *Children would distract me.* Her features rippled into something that terrified me. Wife and father had conspired to rob me of my children and I'd let them do it, as plodding and dumb as any farm animal. The clarity overwhelmed me. I stumbled from my chair, her voice a distant buzz. Somehow, I found the bottle of scotch and poured a full tumbler. Barbara was looking at me. Her lips moved, and then she walked to the kitchen on a stranger's legs. Time stood still as she rinsed plates, loaded the dishwasher, and wiped down the counter. She looked at me as she worked, as if worried that I might disappear. But I could not move; there was no one to lead me. I think I laughed at that.

When she finally came for me, I was drunk beyond words, lost in depths I never believed could exist. Stolen! The children I'd always wanted, the family I'd looked forward to since college. By those I should trust the most, my life had been stolen from me. And I'd let it happen. Call it blind trust. Call it cowardice. Call it the complicity of inaction. I shared the guilt, and the enormity of that fact overwhelmed me.

As if through fog, my wife's hand reached for me. She led me to the bedroom, put me down, and stood before me. Her lips moved and the words followed sometime later. "Don't worry, darling. We'll figure it all out. I'm sure Ezra provided." Her words made little sense.

She undressed, hanging her top carefully before turning back to present her breasts to me like manna from some other man's heaven. She slipped off her skirt, revealing legs of carved bronze. She was a statue brought to life, a trophy for good behavior. Her fingers found the fasteners of the clothes that should have armored me but didn't; she took my pants with a victor's smile, told me to relax, and knelt before me. I knew this was wrong but hid behind closed eyes as she spoke in tongues and wove spells of terrible power; so I surrendered myself, and in surrender knew the damnation of the utterly corrupt.

CHAPTER

10

Sunday morning, early, I cracked my eyes to cold gray light. It stole under the blinds to touch the bed but left most of the room dark. Barbara slept beside me, her leg sweaty against my own. I edged to the far side of the bed and held myself still. I felt fragile. Glue bound my eyelids, and the tongue that filled my mouth tasted like something long dead. I thought of the brutal truths so often borne on predawn light. I'd had a few in my time, and they'd all led to this. I was a stranger to myself. I'd gone to law school for my father, married for my father; and for that same man, and for the vile woman who shared my bed, I'd surrendered my dreams of family—my very soul. Now he was dead and all I had was this truth: My life was not my own. It belonged to an empty shell that wore my face. Yet I refused to pity myself.

I lifted my head to peer at Barbara: sleep-matted hair, creased skin, open mouth that glistened on the inside. My face twisted at the sight, but still, even on this dawn of revelation, I had to acknowledge her beauty. But I hadn't married her for her looks; I could tell myself that and believe it. I'd married her for her intensity, her energy. The tail wind of her convictions had swept me into her wake: She would make the perfect wife and only a fool would let her go. Somehow I'd come to believe that, and I thought that now I knew the ugly reasons why. Vanessa had said it: I married her for Ezra. Jesus.

My feet found the floor and I groped my way out of the room. In the laundry room, I found a pair of dirty jeans and some flip-flops. I collected the telephone and a pack of cigarettes and sat on the front porch. Mist was over the park and it was cold. I shivered as I lit up and blew smoke at the world. Nothing moved, and in the stillness I felt very much alive. I dialed Vanessa's number. Her machine answered and I knew that she was already out of bed, barefoot in the wet grass. As I waited for the beep, I decided to tell her the truth: that she was right and that I was sorry. Not that I loved her. Not yet. That had to be face-to-face, and I wasn't ready. There were other issues there, stuff that had nothing to do with truth or with the fact that my life was a mess. But I did want her to know that I understood. That she was right and I was wrong. So I let it all out. The words were just words, a pale start all in all, but they had to count for something. As I turned the phone off, I felt good. I had no idea what the future held, but I didn't care.

So I sat and I smoked, and something moved inside me that I recognized from a long, long time ago. The sun rose and put its warm red fingers upon me, and for a moment I was at peace. Then I felt Barbara's presence and she stepped through the door.

"What are you doing out here?"

"Smoking," I said, and didn't bother to turn around.

"It's six-forty-five in the morning."

"Is it?"

"Look at me, Work."

I turned around. She stood in the open door, wrapped in a fleece robe. Her hair was a mess, eyes puffy above a miserly mouth. I knew that her thoughts, like mine, were on last night. "What are you thinking?" she asked.

I gave Barbara my eyes as a warning, but I knew that she could not decipher even that pale message. She'd have to know me to get it, and we were strangers. So I gave her my thoughts, spelled them out in flat black letters that any moron could read. "I'm thinking that my life has been hijacked, held for ransom that I could never pay. I'm looking at a world that I've never seen before and wondering how the hell I got here."

"Now you're being silly," she said, and smiled like she could play this off.

"I don't know you, Barbara, and I wonder if I ever did."

"Come back to bed," she commanded.

"I don't think so."

"It's freezing out here."

"It's colder inside."

Her frown deepened. "That hurts, Work."

"I've figured out that truth often does," I said, and turned my back to her. In the distance, a man was walking toward us along the street. He wore a long trench coat and a hunting cap.

"Are you coming or not?" she insisted.

"I think I'll go for a walk," I told her.

"You're half-naked," she said.

I turned and smiled at her. "Yes," I said. "Isn't that a hoot?"

"You're frightening me," she said.

I turned back to watch my park walker and felt her step out onto the porch. For a long minute, she stared down at me, and I could only imagine what she might be thinking. Suddenly, her hands were on my shoulders, her fingers kneading me. "Come to bed," she said in her voice of oiled silk and bedroom pleasures.

"I'm awake now," I told her, meaning it in so many ways. "You go." I felt her hands withdraw, and she stood silently — angry, puzzled, or both. She'd spread her angel's wings, offered to lift me up, and I'd shot her down. Where would she go now? What lever could she trust to move me when the last resort of ready flesh had failed her in the end? I knew only that quiet retreat was not an option for her.

"Who've you been talking to?" she asked, a new edge in her voice. I glanced at the phone at my side, thought of Vanessa Stolen, and marveled coldly at my perspicacity.

"Nobody."

"May I have the phone?"

I took another drag.

"The phone," she insisted.

When I looked at her, I saw what I expected to see, thin lips in a face gone pale. "Do you really want to do this?" I asked.

In one movement, she stooped and snatched up the phone. I didn't try to stop her. She pushed the redial button and I turned away, to the strange man in his long coat. He drew nearer, his eyes downcast, his face all but hidden. I wondered if Vanessa would answer and hoped not; beyond that, I felt nothing, not anger or fear, not even regret. I heard Barbara disconnect, and her voice, when she spoke, was tight with anger. "I thought you were done with her."

"I thought so, too."

"How long?" she demanded.

"I don't want to talk about this, Barbara. Not now." I climbed slowly to my feet, hoping as I turned that I would see tears in my wife's eyes, anything to show that she felt more than wounded pride. "I'm tired. I'm hungover."

"Whose fault is that?" she snapped.

I pushed out a deep breath. "I'm going for that walk," I told her. "We can talk later if you still want to."

"Don't walk away from me!"

"Walking won't put any more distance between us."

"Oh. So now your adultery is my fault."

"I'm not talking about this now," I told her.

"I may not be here when you get back," she threatened. I stopped halfway down the steps.

"Do what you have to do, Barbara. Nobody can blame you for that, me least of all." I turned away from her heavy breathing and started down the sidewalk, heading toward the street and the park, which shimmered with cold dew.

"She's a dirty little whore. I've never understood your obsession with her," Barbara said to my back, her voice climbing. "Never!" The last word was a shout.

"Careful, Barbara," I said without turning to face her. "The neighbors will hear." I heard the door slam and imagined that she'd locked it, too. I didn't care. My life dropped away as I stepped off the property and onto the sidewalk. I was a man, like any other. I had taken action, stood my ground. I felt real and it felt good.

At the bottom of the yard, I waited for this man I'd seen a thousand times yet never really met. I got a better look at him as he approached. He was magnificently unattractive, with melted features and a grimace that pulled his lip over brown teeth, which showed only on the right side of his face. He wore grimy glasses with thick black frames and his hair hung limply from beneath the hunting cap.

"Mind if I walk with you?" I asked as he came level with me. He stopped and tilted his head at me. Green irises swam in a yellow sea and his voice, when he spoke, was a smoker's voice. I heard the same heavy accent.

"Why?"

There was distrust there.

"Just because," I said. "Just to talk."

"Still a free country." He resumed his walking and I fell into step with him.

"Thanks."

I felt his eyes on my naked chest. "I'm not gay," he said.

"Me neither."

He grunted, said nothing.

"You're not my type anyway."

He barked a laugh that ended with a snort of approval. "A smart-ass, huh? Who'd have thought?"

We walked down the sidewalk, past the big houses and the length of the park. A few cars were on the streets and some kids were feeding the ducks. The morning mist was slowly burning off the lake.

"I've seen you," he finally said to me. "Seen you for years—sittin' up there on your porch. Must be one heck of a view."

I didn't know what to say to that. "It's a good place to watch the world pass by, I guess."

"Hmph. Better you should pass through the world."

I stopped walking.

"What?" he asked.

"A blinding flash of the obvious," I told him.

"Meaning what?"

"Meaning I think you are a very smart man."

"Yes," he said. "I think you are right." He laughed at my expression. "Come on. We'll walk and you can compliment me. It's a good plan."

"I know your name," I said as we left the park behind and moved toward Main Street and the poor neighborhoods that lined the tracks beyond.

"That right?"

"I just heard it around. Maxwell Creason, right?"

"Just Max."

I held out my hand and he stopped, forcing me to stop alongside him. He held my eyes for an instant, then lifted up his hands to hold in front of my face. The fingers were broken and bent, twisted into claws, and I saw with horror that most of the nails had been ripped off.

"Jesus," I said.

"You know my name," he said. "And I don't mean any offense when I say this, but let's just leave it at that."

"What happened?" I asked.

"Look, I'm glad to talk to you—God knows, it's been long enough—but I don't reckon I know you well enough to talk about that."

I stared down at his hands. They hung like deadwood at the ends of his arms.

"But . . ." I started.

"Why do you care?" he asked sharply.

"You interest me."

"Why?"

"I don't know," I told him. "Because you're different." I shrugged again, feeling the inadequacy of my words. "Because I believe you've never asked a person what he does for a living."

"And that's important to you?"

I thought about it. "I guess so."

He began to shake his head.

"I want to know because you're real."

"What's that supposed to mean?"

I looked away from his face because there was a sudden nakedness there. "I've seen you, too, you know, here and there, walking. But I've never seen you with anybody else. I think there must be honesty in being that alone."

"And you value that?"

I looked back at him. "I envy it."

"Why are you telling me all this?"

"Because you don't know me, I guess. Because for once I'd like to be honest, too—tell somebody that I'd just as soon shoot my wife as look at her again, and that I'd gladly run over her friends on the street just to hear the thump." I shrugged again. "Because I don't think you'd judge me."

Max Creason was not looking at me; he had turned away. "Ain't no priest," he told me.

"Sometimes things just need to be said."

He shrugged. "So do something different."

"That's it? That's your advice? Do something different?"

"Yes," the park walker said. "Stop being a pussy."

The word hung there between us, and on the other side was his face, his very serious face; and in the echo of that blunt honesty, I laughed. I laughed so hard, I almost split myself open; and long before I finished, Max Creason joined me.

Three hours later, I walked up my driveway wearing a blue T-shirt with black letters that read DIG MY ROOT and holding the leash of a nine-week-old yellow Lab I'd decided to call Bone. The Johnsons told me he was the pick of the litter, and I believed them. He was very much like my old dog.

I walked Bone to the backyard and saw my wife through the bathroom window. She wore Sunday church clothes and was practicing smiles in the mirror. I watched for a minute, then gave Bone some water and went inside. It was 9:45.

I found Barbara in the bedroom, clipping on her earrings as she bustled about, looking at the ground as if to find her shoes or the patience to deal with me. She didn't look up, but her voice was chipper.

"I'm going to church. Are you coming?"

This was an old trick. Barbara rarely went to church, and when she did, it was because she knew I'd never go. It was a guilt trip.

"Nope. I've got plans."

"What plans?" She finally looked at me. No other questions. No reference to our fight or to my infidelity.

"Guy stuff," I told her.

"That's nice, Work." She started from the room, then stopped. "That's just perfect." She stormed out.

I followed her through the house and watched her grab her pocketbook and her keys and slam the door behind her. I poured a cup of coffee and waited. It took about five seconds.

The door flew open and Barbara scrambled inside, locking the door behind her and turning, horrified, to me. I leaned against the sink and sipped my coffee.

"There's a bum in our garage!" she said.

"No," I replied in exaggerated disbelief.

She peered through the window blind. "He's just sitting there now, but I think he made a grab for me."

I straightened to my full height. "I'll take care of it. Don't worry." I strode across the kitchen and pulled Barbara away from the door. I stepped outside, my wife crowding behind me with the telephone in her hand. "Hey!" I said. The bum looked up from the old newspaper he'd pulled from our recycling bin. His squint pulled his lips over the dark, rotten teeth. "Come on in," I told him. Max stood. "The bathroom's down the hall."

"Okay," he said, and came inside. It took us five minutes to stop laughing after Barbara burned rubber out of the driveway.

CHAPTER

11

An hour later, I was showered, changed, and clear in my head for the first time in what felt like years. It may have been years. What I knew was this: All you have in life is family. If you are lucky, that includes the kind you married. I was not so fortunate, but I had Jean. I'd take the fall for her if I had to.

I made two phone calls, the first to Clarence Hambly; after my father, he was considered the finest attorney in the county. He drew up Ezra's will. He'd just returned from church but reluctantly agreed to meet me later in the day. Next, I called Hank Robins, a private investigator in Charlotte whom I'd used on most of my murder cases. His machine picked up: "I can't take your call right now, probably because I'm out spying on somebody. Leave your number so I don't have to trace it." Hank was an irreverent bastard. He was thirty now, looked forty on a rough day, and was the most fearless man I'd ever met. Plus, I liked him. I told him to call me on my cell phone.

I left Barbara a note saying I might not be home that night and put Bone in the car. We went shopping. I bought him a new collar, leash, and dog bowls. I also picked up a thirty-pound bag of puppy food and a box of jerky treats. By the time I got back to the car, he'd chewed the leather off one of the headrests, which gave me an idea. I drove a BMW that Barbara had insisted would draw clients, which, in retrospect, was hilarious. I still owed a few grand on it and resented every payment. I took it to a shade-tree lot off Highway 150 and traded it for a five-year-old pickup. It smelled bad, but Bone seemed to like the taste of it.

We were having lunch in the park when Hank finally called. "Work, my man! Been reading about you in the papers. How's my favorite suit holding up?"

"I have to admit that I've been better."

"Yeah. Figured as much."

"How's your schedule these days, Hank?"

"Always busy. I even work sometimes. What've you got for me? Another Rowan County tragedy of love and deception? Rival dope dealers? Not another remote-control killer, I hope."

"It's complicated."

"The best ones always are."

"Are you alone?" I asked.

"I'm still in bed, if that answers your question."

"We need to talk in person."

"Salisbury, Charlotte, or in between. Just tell me when and where."

That was a no-brainer. I'd take any excuse to get out of town and get some breathing room. "How about six tonight at the Dunhill?" The Dunhill Hotel was on Tryon Street in downtown Charlotte. It had a great bar, full of deep and shadowed booths, and would be almost empty on a Sunday night.

"Should I bring you a date?" Hank asked, and I heard a giggle from his end of the phone, a woman.

"Six o'clock, Hank. And that crack will cost you the first round." I hung up, feeling better. Hank was a good man to have on your side.

Ezra's attorney had made it plain that I should not arrive before two. I had half an hour. I put the dog bowls and trash into the truck and whistled for Bone. He was wet from the lake, but I let him ride up front. Halfway there and he was in my lap, head out the window. So, stinking of wet dog and used truck, I walked up the wide steps of the Hambly mansion on its sprawling acres just outside of town. The house was huge, with marble fountains, twelve-foot doors, and a four-room guest house. A plaque beside the door announced that Hambly House had been built circa 1788. I thought maybe I should genuflect.

Judging from Clarence Hambly's face, I did not measure up to the learned colleague he'd expected to appear on this day of holy worship. Hambly was old, lined, and straitlaced, but he stood tall in a dark suit and paisley tie. He had thick white hair and matching eyebrows, which probably added an extra fifty dollars to his hourly rate.

He was genteel, whereas my father had been aggressive, as mannered as Ezra had been bullish, but he was still full of it; I'd seen him in court enough times to know that his Holy Roller attitude never interfered with his shameless quest for high-dollar jury awards. His witnesses were well prepped and slick. The Ten Commandments did not hang on his office wall.

He was old Salisbury money, and I know that my father had hated that about him, but he was good, and my father had insisted on the best, especially where money was concerned.

"I would prefer to do this tomorrow," he said without preamble, his eyes moving up from my scuffed hiking boots to my grass-stained blue jeans and the frayed collar of the shirt I refused to let die.

"It's important, Clarence. I need to do this now. I'm sorry."

He nodded. "Consider it a professional courtesy, then," he said, and ushered me inside. I stepped into his marble foyer, hoping that there was no dog shit on my shoes. "Let's go into my study."

I followed him down a long hall, catching a glimpse through large French doors of the pool outside and the manicured gardens beyond. The place smelled of cigars, oiled leather, and old people; I was willing to bet that his maids wore uniforms.

His study was narrow but deep, with tall windows, more French doors, and floor-to-ceiling bookcases. Apparently, he was into antique guns, fresh-cut flowers, and the color blue. An eight-foot gold-filigree mirror hung behind his desk; in it I looked rumpled and small, which was probably intentional.

"I'm putting your father's estate into probate tomorrow," he told me as he closed double doors and pointed to a leather chair. I sat. He moved behind his desk but remained standing. He looked down at me from this position of assumed authority, reminding me of how much I hated lawyer bullshit. "So there's no reason we can't discuss the details now. For the record, however, I was going to call you this week to schedule a meeting."

"Thank you for that," I said, because I was expected to. Never mind the enormous fee he would collect as executor of Ezra's estate. I steepled my fingers and concentrated on looking deferential, when what I wanted to do was put my feet on his desk.

"Also for the record, accept my condolences on your loss. I know that Barbara must be a great comfort. She comes from a fine family. A beautiful woman."

For the record, I wished there was shit on my shoes. "Thank you," I said.

"Although your father and I were often on opposite sides of the table, I had tremendous respect for his accomplishments. He was a fine attorney." He eyed me from his great height. "Something to aspire to," he concluded meaningfully.

"I don't want to take any more of your time than necessary," I reminded him.

"Yes, of course. To business, then. Your father's estate was sizable."

"How sizable?" I interrupted. Ezra had been secretive about his finances. I knew very little about it.

"Sizable," Hambly reiterated. I looked blank and waited. Once wills are put into probate, they become public record. There was no reason for reticence.

Hambly grudgingly conceded. "Roughly forty million dollars," he said.

I almost fell out of my chair—literally. I would have guessed six or seven million at the most.

"In addition to his skills as a lawyer," Hambly continued, "he was an adept investor. Other than the house and the building on lawyers' row, it's all in liquid securities."

"Forty million dollars," I said.

"A little over, actually." Hambly met my eyes and, to his credit, kept his face neutral. He'd been born rich, yet would never see forty million dollars. It had to gall him, and I suddenly realized that this was another reason my father had gone to Clarence Hambly. I almost smiled, but then I thought of Jean and the miserable house she lived in. I smelled stale pizza and pictured her face in the window of her beaten-down car, the way she'd heaved herself up the steps of Glena Werster's stone monument to greed and ego. At least that will change, I thought.

"And?" I asked.

"The house and the building go to you outright. Ten million dollars will fund the Ezra Pickens Charitable Foundation. You will have a seat on the board. Fifteen million dollars goes into trust for you. Taxes take the rest."

I was stunned. "What about Jean?" I asked.

"Jean gets nothing," Hambly stated, then sniffed loudly.

I came out of my chair. "Nothing?" I repeated.

"Sit down, please."

I complied because I lacked the strength to stand.

"You know how your father felt. Women have no business dealing with money or finances. It might be imprudent to tell you this, but your father changed the will after Alex Shiften came on the scene. Originally, he planned for two million to go into trust for Jean, to be managed by this firm or by her husband, should she marry. But with Alex in the picture . . . You know how your father felt."

"Did he know that they were sleeping together?" I asked.

"He suspected."

"And so he cut her out of the will."

"Basically."

"Was Jean aware of this?"

Hambly shrugged but didn't answer the question. "People do funny things with their money, Work. They use it for their own reasons."

I felt an electric tingle as I realized Hambly wasn't talking about Jean anymore. "There's more, isn't there?"

"The trust for you," Hambly began, finally taking his seat.

"What about it?"

"You will have full, unfettered use of the income it generates until age sixty. Conservatively invested, it should provide at least a million dollars a year. At sixty, you get it all."

"But?" I sensed a catch.

"There are certain requirements."

"Such as?"

"You are required to be actively engaged in the practice of law until such time."

"What?"

'This point is exquisitely clear, Work. Your father felt it important that you carry on the practice, that you maintain your place in society and in the profession. He was concerned that if he just left you the money, you might do something imprudent."

"Like be happy?"

Hambly ignored my sarcasm and the raw, naked emotion that must have been in my voice. Even from the grave, my father was trying to dictate the terms of my life, to manipulate me. "He was not specific in that regard," Hambly said. "But he was very specific in others. This firm will act as trustee. It will be up to us"—he gave me a thin smile—"up to me, actually, to determine whether or not you are actively engaged in the practice of law. One of the criteria, for instance, is that you bill at least twenty thousand dollars a month, adjusted for inflation, of course."

"I don't bill half that now and you know it."

"Yes." Another smile. "Your father thought this might prove to motivate you."

"Unfucking believable," I said, anger finally finding a voice.

Hambly rose to his full height and leaned forward, hands splayed on his desk. "Let me make one thing clear, Mr. Pickens. I will not tolerate profanity in this house. Is that understood?"

"Yes," I said through clenched teeth. "I understand. What else?"

"Any year that you do not satisfy the requirements of the trust document, the income from the trust will go to the Ezra Pickens Foundation. If in two of any five years you fail to meet the requirements of the trust document, the trust will terminate and the full corpus of the trust will transfer irrevocably to the foundation. However, when you reach age sixty, should you comply fully, the entire balance becomes yours to do with as you please. I will provide you with copies of all documents, of course."

"Is that it?" I asked, my sarcasm so thick, no one could miss it. I should have known better.

"In essence," he said. "But there is one last, small thing. Should it ever be shown that you have given any money whatsoever to your sister, Jean Pickens, either directly or indirectly, the trust will terminate and all funds will transfer to the foundation."

"This is too much," I said, on my feet and pacing.

"It's your father's last will and testament," Hambly said, correcting me. "His dying wish. Few would complain after hearing that fifteen million would be theirs to play with. Try to look at it from that perspective."

"There's only one perspective here, Clarence, my father's, and it's twisted as hell." The older lawyer started to speak, but I cut him off, watching his face redden as my voice rose and my respect for the rules of his house vanished. "Ezra Pickens was a twisted, manipulating bastard who never gave two shits for his own daughter and cared just a shade more than a rat's ass for me. Right now, he's laughing in his fucking grave." I leaned over Hambly's desk. I felt spit fly off my lips and didn't care. "He was a first-class asshole and you can keep his money. You hear me. Keep it!"

I subsided backward as the last words left me. I'd never felt such rage, and it left me spent. For an instant, there was silence, broken only by the slight tremble in the old lawyer's clenched fists. His voice, when he spoke, was tightly caged.

"I understand that you are under severe stress, so I'll try to forget your blasphemy, but don't ever come to this house again." His eyes hinted at the strength that made him such a good lawyer. "Ever," he reiterated. "Now, as your father's attorney and the executor of his estate, I'll tell you this: The will is valid. It goes into probate tomorrow. You may find that your position on this matter changes as your temper cools. If so, call me—at the office. As a final matter, I'll tell you something else. I hadn't planned to, but your behavior has changed my mind. Detective Mills has been to see me. She wanted to see your father's will."

If Hambly was watching for a reaction, he wasn't disappointed. My anger fled, replaced by something less honorable, something cold and slick that coiled in my stomach like a snake. It was fear, and with it in me, I felt naked.

"At first, I denied her, but she returned with a court order." Hambly leaned closer and spread his hands; he didn't smile, although I could feel it in him. "I was forced to comply," he said. "She was intrigued. You might wish to explain to *her* how fifteen million dollars does not interest you." He straightened and his fingers snapped shut. "Now, my courtesy has come to an end, as has my patience. Anytime you wish to offer your apology for desecrating my Sunday rest, I will consider it." He gestured at the door. "Now, good day to you."

My mind was awash, but one question had to be asked. "Does Mills know that Ezra cut Jean out of the will?" I asked.

"That question," he replied, seeming to relax into himself, "is best presented to Detective Mills. Now go away."

"I need to know, Clarence." I held my hands out, palm up. "Please."

"I'll not interfere with her investigation. Take it up with her or leave it alone."

"When did he cut her out? What date?"

"My obligation to you does not extend beyond that of executor and primary beneficiary to this will and the trust it establishes. Given the circumstances surrounding your father's death and the police interest in the matter, it would be unwise, for either of us, to take this matter further. I intended no other impression. Once the will is in probate, you may contact me at any time during business hours to discuss any relevant matters. Beyond that, we have nothing to talk about."

"What date was this will executed?" I demanded. A reasonable question, one within my rights.

"November fifteenth," Hambly said. "Year before last."

One week before my father disappeared.

I left, too angry to be scared. But I knew how it would play to the cops. If Jean knew that Ezra was going to cut her out of two million because of her relationship with Alex, it would be one more reason to kill him. That's how Detective Mills would see it. Did Jean know? When did she know? When did Ezra cut her out? I could hear Mills asking those exact questions. But had she?

Damn Clarence Hambly and his petty vindictiveness!

Back in the truck, Bone scrambled into my lap and licked my face. I rubbed his back, glad for the company. I realized that for the past days, while addled by alcohol, grief, and anger, the world had moved on. Mills had not been idle; she'd targeted me. I was a suspect. The concept was too much. I couldn't get my head around it. In the past day, I'd come to understand so many things, none of them pleasant. Now this. I had fifteen million dollars, but only if I surrendered what little remained of myself.

I sat in that driveway, under windows that looked like mirrored eyes, and dark thoughts twisted my mouth into a bitter smile as I thought of Ezra's will and his last effort to manipulate me. My life was still a mess, but in this regard I knew something that Ezra didn't, something that he could never imagine. Black humor moved where the fear snake had been; it bubbled like hot oil and it released me. I pictured Ezra's face, the horror if he only knew, the utter disbelief. I didn't want his money. The price was too high. The thought made me laugh, so that's what I did as I drove away from Hambly House, circa 1788. I laughed like an idiot. I fucking howled.

Yet by the time I got home, the hysteria was gone and I was empty. I felt lacerated inside, as if I were full of glass; but I thought of Max Creason, who'd had his fingers broken and his nails ripped out, yet who still has the strength and humor to tell a total stranger to stop being a pussy. It helped.

I put Bone in the backyard with food, water, and a belly rub, and then I went inside. My note to Barbara was where I'd left it. I picked up the pen and added this: "Don't be surprised to find a dog in the backyard—he's mine. He can come inside if you want." But I knew it wouldn't happen; Barbara didn't like dogs. The one I'd brought to the marriage, another yellow Lab, had never gotten to come inside. We'd been together for three years when I married Barbara; then he went from constant companion to barely tolerated nuisance, another casualty to poor choices. I vowed that would never happen again. As I watched Bone from the kitchen window, I felt the great hollowness of the house around me, its emptiness, and I thought of my mother.

Like my father, she was raised dirt-poor, but, unlike Ezra, she'd been content in her own skin. She'd never wanted the big house, the cars, and the prestige, none of it. Ezra, however, had been ravenous, and as he *bettered* himself, he came to resent her for the constant reminder she was. Ezra had hated his past, been ashamed of it, and history had shared his bed.

This was my theory, for how else could two people rise from abject poverty, bear two children, yet end up worse than strangers?

Years of this resentment had made my mother as hollow as this house, the well into which Ezra had dumped his anger, his frustration, and his hatred. She'd taken it all, borne it, until she was a shadow, and all she had for her children was her fierce embrace and the admonition to be silent. She'd never stood up for us, not until the night she died. It was that brief strength, that incandescent flash of will that had killed her, and I'd let it happen.

The argument had been about Alex.

When I closed my eyes, I could see the ruby red carpet.

We were at the top of the stairs, on the broad landing. I looked at my watch because I had to look away from Jean and from my father. She was defying him, and the explosion was building. It was four minutes after nine, dark out, and I barely recognized my sister. She was not the broken-down wreck that the psychiatric hospital had sent back to us. Not even close.

Mother stood, stunned, hand to her mouth. Ezra was shouting, Jean shouting back, jabbing a finger into his chest. It could not end well, and I stared as if at a train wreck; and I watched my mother reach out, as if she could stop the train with her ten small fingers.

And I did nothing.

"That is enough!" my father yelled, "That is how it's going to be."

"No," Jean said. "Not this time. It's my life!"

Father stepped closer, towered over her. I expected Jean to melt away, but she did not.

"It stopped being your life when you tried to kill yourself," he said. "Then it became mine again. You're barely out of the hospital. You can't possibly think right about anything. We've been patient, we've been nice, but now it's time for her to go."

"Alex is none of your business. You have no right to ask that."

"Let's get one thing clear right now, young lady. I'm not asking. That woman is trouble and I'll not have her messing up your head. She's just using you."

"For what? I'm not rich. I'm not famous."

"You know what."

"You can't even say it, can you? For sex, Dad. Yeah. For sex. We're fucking all the time. What're you going to do about it?"

Father went suddenly still. "You're an embarrassment to this family. It's disgraceful the way you two carry on."

"So there it is," Jean said. "It's got nothing to do with me. It's all about you! It's always been about you! Well, I've had it."

Jean turned to walk away. She didn't look at me, didn't look at Mother; she just turned and took a single step. Then Ezra grabbed her. He jerked her so hard that she fell to her knees.

"Don't you walk away from me! Not ever!"

Jean pulled herself to her feet and twisted her arm free. "That's the last time you'll ever put your hands on me," she told him.

The moment seemed to freeze, Jean's words hanging between them. I saw my mother's face, pure despair, and again her eyes beseeched me. Yet the shadow of my father held me, and Mother must have sensed this.

"Ezra," she said.

"You stay out of this," he commanded, eyes on Jean like a promise of violence.

"Ezra," she repeated, taking a monumental step toward him. "Just let her be. She's grown now, and she's right."

"And I told you to shut it!" His eyes never left Jean, and when she tried again to turn away, he snatched her up and shook her, an angry boy with a boneless doll; but Jean had bones, and I feared they might break. "I said don't you ever walk away from me!" Then he was grunting, incoherent, and Jean's head was loose on her neck. I watched as my mother took hell into her hands.

"Leave her alone, Ezra." She pulled at his massive arm. Jean had gone completely limp, but he continued to shake her. "Damn it, Ezra," she shouted. "Leave my daughter alone!" She began to beat on his shoulders with her narrow fists, and tears shone in the seams of her face. I tried to move, to speak, but I was paralyzed. Then he struck out, a backhand that traveled forever; and then she was falling. Time seemed to stand still but didn't; then she was crumpled at the foot of the stairs, another boneless doll in the house my father made.

Jean collapsed when my father released her. He stared at his hand and then at me.

"It was an accident, boy. You see that, don't you, son?"

I looked into his eyes, saw for the first time that he needed me, and felt myself nod; it was an irrevocable step.

"Good boy," he said. Then the ground fell away and I tumbled into the deep well of self-loathing.

I have yet to find its bottom.

If they'd found Ezra with only one bullet in his head, I'd have called it suicide. How else to deal with the truth of his actions? And yet the greatest sin can be one of omission; such was my burden, the cost of which was my mother's life and my immortal soul. Protecting Jean was my responsibility. I knew my mother's weakness as I knew my father's rage. Without words, she'd begged me to intervene, pleaded as only the weak can plead. I don't know why I didn't act, but I fear that my soul is flawed by some tragic weakness born under my father. For it was not love for him that stayed my hand, never love. Then what? I've never known, and that question haunts me still. So I've lived with my failure, and slept with the memory of a cartwheel dance down ruby-covered stairs.

Jean was barely conscious when it happened; she never knew for certain, but she guessed, and in my eyes she saw the lie that had become Ezra's truth. When asked, I said that Mother had slipped. She had tried to intervene in an argument and she'd slipped. It was just one of those things.

Why did I cover for my father? Because he asked me to, I guess. Because, for the first time, he needed me. Because her death *was* an accident, and because I believed him when he said that nothing good could come of the truth. Because he was my father and because I was his son. Maybe because I blamed myself. Who the hell knows?

So the police asked their questions and I spoke the horrible words; thus Ezra's truth became my own. But the rift between Jean and me was irreparable; it grew into a chasm and she retreated into her life on the other side. I saw her at the funeral, where the last shovel of dirt went onto our relationship as much as it did onto mother's casket. She had Alex, and for her that was enough.

By midnight on the night of my mother's death, the police had gone. We followed the darkened ambulance because we didn't know what else to do. At the back door of the hospital, she left us, carried by strangers into that pale, still building, taken to some cold room where the dead wait in silence. We stood in a light November rain, we three, speechless under a streetlamp and the weight of our own private thoughts. The truth of her death lay upon us, and our eyes refused to meet. But I studied my father when I could, caught the play of water down his face, the clench of muscles under whiskers that gleamed white under the light. And when the words finally came, they came from Ezra, as I knew they must. "Let's go home," he said, and we understood. There was nothing else to say.

At the house, the lights were on, and we sat in the living room while Ezra poured drinks. Jean refused to touch hers, but mine disappeared like magic and Ezra poured another. Jean's hands clenched and unclenched, wrestled on her lap, and I saw bright half-moons where nails bit into her palms. She rocked minutely, wound tight, and at times I heard her keen. I reached for her, but she jerked away. I wanted to tell her that I was not Ezra, not that it would have mattered. I see that now.

No one spoke and the minutes drew out, the only sound that of ice on glass and the heavy tread of Ezra's pacing.

We all jumped when the phone rang. Ezra answered it; he listened, hung up, and looked at us, his children. Then he left the house without a word. We were stunned, floored, and Jean left right behind him, a look on her face that I've never forgotten. At the door, she turned, her words like razors in my soul. "I know he killed her. And damn you for protecting him."

It was the last time I saw Ezra alive. For ten long minutes, I stayed in that house of horrors, that house of broken dolls; then I, too, left. I drove to Jean's, but her car was gone and no one answered when I knocked. The door was locked. I waited for an hour, but she didn't return. I went home and, in the best voice I could manage, informed my wife of the night's events. Then I had another drink. Eventually, I put her to bed, then sneaked out. I spent the rest of the night at Stolen Farm, weeping on Vanessa's shoulder like a goddamn child. At dawn, I crept into bed, where I put my back to my wife and watched gray light swell from beneath the blinds. I kept myself utterly still and held on to Ezra's truth as if for my very life. At the time, I thought it was worth something, but time can be a murderous bitch.

I felt pain and looked down at my hands, clenched so tightly on the kitchen sink that they were bloodless. I released them and they burned, but the pain was relative. I forced the images of that night back into the past, where I'd tried so hard to keep them. I was home. Bone was in the backyard. Ezra was dead.

I heard an engine outside and walked to the laundry-room window. A car was moving slowly up the driveway, and recognizing it, I thought of fate and of inevitability.

My life had become a Greek tragedy, but I'd done what I thought I had to do—to keep the family whole, to save what was left. I could not have known that Ezra would be killed, that Jean would despise me; but there is an undeniable sharpness to fact. Mother was dead. So was Ezra. Nothing would change that, not my own guilt, not a lifetime of pain. Done is done, end of fucking story. So I asked myself, as I had so many times, What price redemption, and where to find it?

I had no answer to that, and I feared that when the time came, I would lack the strength to pay the price. So standing there in that hollow house, I promised myself one thing, that when all this was past and I stood looking back, I would not face the same regret.

I prayed for strength.

Then I walked outside, where I found Detective Mills waiting in the driveway.

CHAPTER

12

Y ou'd better not have car keys in your hands," Mills said as I stepped onto hard concrete and squinted at the light reflected off her windshield. I held my hands out, palms up, to show they were empty.

"Relax," I told her. "I'm not going anywhere." She was wearing loose brown pants, low-heeled boots, and sunglasses. As always, the butt of her pistol showed from beneath her jacket. It was an automatic. The grip was checkered wood; I'd never noticed that before. I tried to remember if Mills had ever shot anyone. Regardless, I had no doubt that she could pull the trigger.

"As God is my witness, I don't know what to do with you, Work. If it weren't for Douglas, we'd be doing this at the station house. I have zero patience for your wounded-bird act. It's bullshit. You're going to tell me what you know and you're going to do it now. Do I make myself clear?"

Strain and fatigue were painted on her face thicker than the makeup she tried to conceal it with. I shook out a cigarette and leaned against her car. I didn't know what she was making of all this, but I had an idea. "You know why defense lawyers lose cases?" I asked her.

"Because they're on the wrong side."

"Because they have stupid clients. I see it all the time. They say things to the police that they can't take back, things that might be misconstrued, especially when there's pressure to break the case." I lit the cigarette, looked down the hill at a passing ambulance, its lights off. "It has always amazed me. It's as if they think that their cooperation will convince the cops to look at somebody else. It's naïve."

"But it keeps people like you in business."

"There is that."

"Are you going to talk to me or not?" Mills demanded.

"I'm talking to you now."

"Don't be a smart-ass. Not today. I don't have the patience for it."

"I've read the papers and I've been in this business a long time. I know the pressure you're under." Mills looked away, as if to deny what I was saying. "If I were smart, I would keep my mouth shut."

"You don't want to be on my bad side, Work. I can promise you that."

"That's what Douglas told me."

Emotion tugged at the corner of Mills's mouth. "Douglas was out of line."

"He just told me to cooperate." Mills crossed her arms. "Are we going to be straight with each other?" I asked. "No crap?"

"No problem," she said.

"I'll be as honest with you as you are with me. Fair?" She nodded. "Am I a suspect?" I asked her.

"No." She didn't hesitate, and I knew she was lying. I almost laughed, she was so transparent, but it would have been an ugly laugh, an "I can't believe this shit is happening" laugh.

"Do you have any suspects?"

"Yes."

"Anybody I know?"

"Everybody," she said, parroting the district attorney. I thought of Jean and prayed that she had not gotten that far in her interview with Clarence Hambly.

"Have you looked into his business dealings? Ex-clients?"

"I can't talk about the investigation."

"I know you talked to Hambly," I told her, watching closely for a reaction, getting none, just the same unbending mouth and eyes I couldn't see. "I know that you know about the will. Seems to me there are fifteen million reasons why you should be looking at me for the murder."

"That Hambly. He's a pompous windbag. He should learn to keep his mouth shut." Watching her, I finally understood why she hated lawyers so much. She couldn't intimidate them, and it killed her.

"So," I prodded. "I'm not a suspect?"

"Douglas says to lay off you. He says there's no way you killed your father, not for money. I can't find any other motive."

"But you've looked."

"I've looked."

"And you're going along with that?"

"As long as you're straight with me, I'll give Douglas his say. For now. But in the end, it's my investigation. Jerk me off and I'll come down on you so hard, your friends will bleed. Is that clear?"

"Crystal," I told her. "What else did you learn from Hambly?" I tried not to show how desperate I was for this information.

Mills shrugged again. "That your father was stinking rich and that if you didn't kill him, you're one lucky bastard."

"It's just money," I said.

"That's good," she told me. "Just money."

"Are we going to do this?" I asked.

"Yeah. Fine. About time."

'Then let's drive," I said. "Barbara will probably be home soon and I don't need her involved in this."

"Oh, I'll talk to Barbara," Mills said pointedly, making it clear that she was still the cop.

"But later, okay? Come on. You drive."

She took off her jacket and tossed it in the backseat. Her car smelled of the same overripe peach perfume I remembered from the hospital. She had the usual cop radios and a shotgun locked to the dash. Voices chattered on the radio and she turned it down as she backed down my driveway. I studied her from the corner of my eye, took in the cuffs, mace, and spare clip on her belt, the way her shirt gapped open, showing a pale lace bra that didn't go with the rest of her. Muscles stood out in her jaw, and I suspected that she would much rather have me in custody than squiring me around town on the city's nickel. I thought about what a good cop she was, reminded myself to be careful of what I said. She was looking for an excuse.

Once on the street, she turned right, past the park. We drove to Main Street in silence; then she pointed the car out of town, toward the long, impossibly narrow roads so typical of the county. "So talk," she said. "And don't leave anything out. I want to know everything that happened on the night your father disappeared. Don't edit. Don't choose. Give me everything."

So we drove, and I tried to speak with great care.

"Why were you there, at his house?"

"My mother's idea. Dinner. Trying to make peace, I guess."

Mills turned fractionally, cut her eyes away from the road. "Peace between . . . ?"

"Jean and my father."

"What were they fighting about?" she asked.

"*Fighting* is too strong a word. There was just a distance there. One of those father-daughter things."

"Specifically what?"

I wanted to lie, to protect Jean completely, but I feared that Mills would find the truth elsewhere. A lie now would only make it seem more important. That was the problem with talking to cops. You never knew what they knew. In the end, that's how they nailed you.

"I think it was about Alex."

"Your sister's girlfriend?"

"Yes."

"Your father didn't approve?"

"No, but it was an old argument. We'd been there before."

"Your sister was not mentioned in your father's will."

"She was never in the will," I said, lying. "My father had old-fashioned views about women."

"And why did your mother intervene?"

"She just got worried. It was a loud argument."

Mills kept her eyes on the road. "Did your father beat Jean?" she asked.

"No."

She looked at me. "Did he beat your mother?"

"No."

"Who was it again that called?"

"I don't know."

"But you were there when the call came in."

"I didn't answer it."

"Tell me exactly what your father said."

I thought back. "'I'll be there in ten minutes.' That's what he said. He answered the phone. He listened. Then he said he'd be there in ten minutes."

"He didn't say where?"

"No."

"He didn't tell you where he was going?"

"No."

"Who had called?"

"No. Nothing. He just left."

"How long was he on the phone?"

I thought about it. "Thirty seconds."

"Thirty seconds is a long time."

"It can be," I said.

"So someone had a lot to say."

"What about phone records?" I asked. "Lugs, pin numbers, anything like that?"

"No luck," Mills said before she caught herself discussing the case and quickly changed the subject. "There had to be something else. Did he take anything with him? Say anything? How did his face look? Was he angry, sad, thoughtful? What direction did he drive?"

I thought about it, really thought about it. That was something I'd never done. How *had* he looked? What was in his face? Something. Resolution, perhaps. Determination. Yes. And anger. But something else, too. Smugness, I thought. The bastard looked smug.

"He looked sad," I told Mills. "His wife had just died and he looked sad."

"What else?" Mills pushed. "Did he take anything? Did he stop between the phone and the door going out? Think."

"He stopped for his keys," I said. "Just for his keys." And then I thought, *My God—his keys.* Ezra kept his keys on a hook board by the kitchen door. One set for his car, one set for his office. I saw it happen like it had been this morning. He moved past me, into the kitchen, his hand reached out—and he took both sets of keys. I saw it. He was planning to go to the office! But why? And had he made it before he was killed?

"There were no keys on his body," Mills said.

"Any sign of his car yet?" I asked, eager to distract her. I didn't want to talk about the keys. Not until I knew what it all meant. Why would Ezra go to the office? I thought about his missing gun, and I thought about his safe. It had to be opened.

"I can't talk about that. Did you ever hear from him again?"

"No."

"Phone calls? Letters?"

"Nothing."

"Why didn't you report him missing?" she asked.

"I did."

"Six weeks later," Mills reminded me. "A long time. That troubles me."

"We assumed he was in mourning somewhere, getting away from it all. He's a grown man."

"*Was* a grown man."

"What's your point?"

"My point is that he didn't even show up for the funeral, and still you didn't report him missing. That's just suspicious. No other word for it."

How to explain that? My father was not at the funeral because he killed her. He knocked her down the stairs and broke her neck! I'd figured that the guilt was destroying him. That he knew better than to face Jean and me with empty words and crocodile tears. Because not even Ezra could eulogize about what a fine person he'd killed. I'd guessed he was dead drunk or at the bottom of a high bridge. To me, that made sense. A lot of sense.

"Grief makes people do funny things," I said.

Mills gave me a very pointed look. "That's what I keep telling myself," she said. "If you know what I mean."

I didn't know what she meant, but her expression helped me guess. She still liked me for the crime. That was good for Jean, which made it good for me. But I couldn't do prison. I'd die before I did life in a box. But it wouldn't come to that; that's what I told myself. There had to be a way.

"I guess that brings us to the big question," Mills said. We were at the park. She turned onto the side street that ran past the lake and stopped the car. I could see my house and I got her message. You're not home yet. That's what she was telling me. Not by a long shot.

The engine ticked as it cooled. I felt her eyes on me. She wanted to look at me now, to focus. The car began to warm in the sun; the air grew stale, and I wanted a cigarette. I met her eyes as steadily as I could. "Where was I on the night in question?" I said.

"Convince me," she replied.

Decision time. I had an alibi. Vanessa would back me up, no matter what. The truth of that coursed through me like cool water. Measured against trial, conviction, and prison, it was the most valuable thing in the world. It's what every cornered criminal would kill to have. But did I want it? The answer was yes. I wanted it so badly, I could taste it. I wanted to turn Mills's withering stare away from me. I wanted to sleep in my own bed and know that I would never be some convict's bitch. I wanted to give her my alibi like a gift. Wrap it in pretty paper with a big bow.

But I couldn't. Not until Jean was in the clear. Should I be absolved, they would look to her. Dig deeply enough and they'd find a reason to like her for the crime, be it our mother's death, Ezra's will, or a lifetime of overpowering abuse. For all I knew, she'd kill for Alex. And thinking back to that night, as I had so many times, I knew that she could have done it. It was all in her face, the rage at her mother's death and the dismay of such utter betrayal. Ezra had left and she'd left right behind him. She could have followed him easily enough. And, like all of us, she'd known where he kept the gun. Motive, means, and opportunity—the holy trinity of criminal prosecution. Douglas would eat her alive if he knew. So I had to know she was safe before playing the alibi card. Yet I felt the weakness in me, fluttering deep and low. Strangely, the knowledge of it made me strong. I looked at Mills, whose face was all hard edges and sharp lines. In her glasses I saw my own features, distorted and unreal. It was too close to what I felt on the inside, so I grasped at that strength, and told one more lie.

"It's like I told Douglas. Dad left. I went home. I was in bed with Barbara all night."

Something moved on her face, a predatory glint, and she nodded as if she'd heard what she expected to hear. Or what she hoped to hear. She gave me a smile that made me nervous without knowing why.

"That's it, then?" she asked. "Think hard."

"That's it."

"Okay." She started the car and drove me the rest of the way home. "Don't leave town," she told me as I stepped out of her car.

"Ha-ha." I said. "That's funny."

"Who's joking?" she asked, flashing that same troubling smile. Then she backed down the driveway and was gone. I lit a cigarette and watched the empty spot in the road where her car had been. Then it occurred to me—why her smile troubled me. I'd seen it before, in court, right before she pulled the rug out from under whichever defense lawyer had the misfortune of underestimating her.

CHAPTER

13

I had a client early on, my first murder case. I was young, still idealistic, and even though he was guilty, I felt for him. He'd killed his neighbor in a drunken fight over a shared driveway. He didn't think the gun was loaded. He just wanted to scare the guy, a common enough story, until a bloody hole appeared in the man's chest.

The trial took eight days. I beat the murder charge, but the jury came back with manslaughter. My client bought seven and a half years, not bad in the big picture. Two hours after the verdict, I got a call to come to the infirmary at the county jail. My client had chugged half a gallon of cleaning fluid in an unsuccessful suicide attempt. The guards were laughing about it at central processing. The jail, they explained between smiles, used nontoxic supplies. My client would shit green for a week, then be okay. Happens all the time. Wink, wink, ha-ha.

I found my client in the infirmary. He was fetal and weeping, oblivious to me and to the guard stuck with suicide watch. It took him five minutes to meet my eyes and another five to respond.

"Don't you get it?" he pleaded.

I was speechless, clueless, I didn't get it.

"Look at me."

I shook my head to show I needed something more.

Then he screamed, veins like cords in his neck. "Look at me!"

I turned to my eyes to the impassive guard, who shrugged. "He's a bitch," the guard said. "Just look at him." My client was small and well formed, with fair skin and straight white teeth. He was attractive, maybe even beautiful.

Suddenly, in a sickening, visceral way, I got it.

"I can't go back to prison," he finally told me. "I'll die first. I'll fucking kill myself." He swore it to me. "One way or another."

Eventually, the story came out. He'd done time before, which I knew. Here's what I didn't know. There was a group of them. Sometimes only three or four. Sometimes seven. They'd tape a centerfold to his naked back and take turns—a screwdriver in his ear to keep him docile. He showed me the scar from the one time he'd fought back. He was still deaf in that ear.

He described it between choking, gut-wrenching sobs. That's what he was going back to. Sometimes for hours at a time.

"I can't do it, man. I just can't."

The next day, he was transported to Central Prison in Raleigh. Two weeks later, he finally managed to kill himself. He was twenty-seven years old, same as I was at the time. I've never forgotten him, for his was the most horrible display of utter despair that I've ever witnessed. Since then, I've skirted the prison system with something like morbid fascination, safe behind my briefcase, yet close enough never to forget what I saw in that young man's eyes.

So, yes. Mills scared me. Terrified me, in fact. I was playing a dangerous game, the stakes brutally real. But Ezra was dead, his shadow as tattered as his flesh, and I was finally learning a few things about myself.

I gave Mills two minutes to disappear, then threw myself into the truck. I had to talk to Jean, to warn her about Mills. Tell her to keep her mouth shut. And if she wouldn't listen, I'd make her. *One way or another.*

Powerful words.

I raced up Main Street but was stopped by an approaching train. So I cut right to Ellis Street and shot across the bridge, the train beneath me a black snake of chattering coal. I didn't know if Mills had talked to Jean or not. She could be en route, even stopped by this very train. So I drove with one eye on the road and dialed Jean's house on the cell phone. I got a busy signal, waited, and hit redial. Twice more I got a busy signal and then it was ringing. I was halfway there, doing fifty in a thirty-five, and the phone kept ringing. I counted fifteen rings, but no one answered. I slammed the phone down, tried to calm myself, but failed. I was near panic. Suddenly, the tension and fear were upon me, hot on my face, like sweat. I pictured Jean in prison and knew that she couldn't make it; it would kill her, sure as the bullets in Ezra's head.

Traffic began to fall away as I moved off the heavily traveled streets and onto the narrow ones where the houses dwindled onto small lots. Children played on the pavement, and I had to slow down for fear of killing one. I passed more and more dirt driveways as the tracks again drew near. Cars littered yards like derelicts and rust streaked the tin roofs of mill houses in their second century. The curbs fell into crumbled ruin and then I was on Jean's street. A tiny boy dangled from the tire-swing in the yard opposite her house, and he watched blank-eyed, his feet trailing in the dust. A face appeared at the window behind him, two eyes and a hint of mouth, then vanished behind mustard yellow curtains that flicked closed as I turned my head away.

I parked in front of Jean's house and turned off the truck. Alex Shiften sat on the front porch, tipped back in a rocking chair, feet on the rail. A cigarette hung from her mouth and she watched me from behind her glassless frames. The corners of her mouth dipped as I got out. I heard the train in the distance, and wind moved the treetops, but I couldn't feel it. The kudzu was still on the banks of the track.

I pulled myself taller and walked into the yard, twigs snapping under my feet. Alex never took her eyes off me. When I got closer, I saw that she had a knife in her hand, calmly shaving down a piece of wood. Her hair was uncombed, sticking up in spiky tufts, and the hard muscles of her arms moved as she whittled. She stood before I got to the steps, barefoot and wearing tight faded jeans.

"What do you want?" she demanded.

"Why didn't you answer your phone?" I shot back.

"Caller ID," she said, and smiled coldly.

I put one foot on the stairs and stopped. Her smile grew into a smirk as she folded the blade away and put the knife into her pocket, as if to say that she didn't need it to deal with me. She leaned against the pillar, and I felt an overwhelming sense of déjà vu. "I need to talk to Jean," I said.

"You always need to talk to Jean."

"Is she here? It's important."

"Gone," Alex replied.

"To work?"

Alex shrugged and looked away, smoke exploring the air around her head.

"Damn it, Alex! Is she at work?"

She stared down at me and slowly gave me the finger. An unrecognizable sound escaped my throat and I pushed past her, into the house. She didn't follow, which surprised me. I'd expected a fight.

The screen slammed behind me and I was in shadow, breathing musty air that smelled of cabbage. Alex's voice followed me. "Look all you want. It won't change anything. Jean's not here and she's got no use for you. So take one last look and then get the hell out."

The rooms were small, with low ceilings, the furniture old and shabby. I moved across the sagging floor in light that fingered through dusty windows to play upon my feet and the thin green rug. I passed the television, saw a framed photo of my mother there, and continued into the kitchen, knowing better than to look for one of me or of Ezra. Pots were stacked in the rack to dry, two places set at the narrow table under the window facing the backyard and the tracks that ran straight into the distance. An African violet was on the windowsill, its purple blossom a bright splash of lonely color.

I called Jean's name but knew already that Alex was right; I knew too well the feel of an empty house. I looked into the bedroom with no real hope and saw the single neatly made bed. I noticed the neat stack of catalogs on the table next to it, the facedown novel, and the water glass on its coaster. I remembered how I used to sit by Jean's bed at night and talk of childish things. Even then she used a coaster. She'd said that wood, like people, needed protection. I understood now that she'd been talking more about herself than about the table. I didn't get it—not then.

Suddenly, I missed her. Not the idea of her, but the intimacy we'd once shared, back when the world was smaller and sharing secrets was an easier thing to do. I put my fingers on the table, looked around the room, and wondered if they shared laughter here, if there was joy in their lives. I hoped so, but I doubted it. Alex was all about control. And Jean, she wanted direction, needed it desperately, and she'd take her cue from anybody.

I searched for some sign of our shared past, anything to indicate that she thought of those days or missed them at all, but there was nothing. My eyes traveled over the bare walls, the bookshelves, and then back to the bed. I turned to leave as the train passed so close, it shook the house; it screamed its mournful scream and was past, fading like memories of childhood.

I was almost to the door when it registered. I stopped and turned, walked back to the tall, narrow bookshelf in the corner, and stooped, my knees popping

like an old man's. Wedged into the corner of the bottom shelf, almost as if hidden, was a tattered copy of *The Hobbit*, my gift to Jean on her ninth birthday.
The cover was creased, the spine broken and fragile under my fingers. I'd put an
inscription on the second page. I still remembered it: "For Jean—because little
people can have adventures, too." I opened the book, but the second page was
gone. Torn out or fallen out, I didn't know.

I put the book carefully back on the shelf.

Outside, I found Alex in her chair. "Satisfied?" she asked.

I fought to keep my temper down. Angering Alex wouldn't get me what I
wanted.

"Do you know when to expect her?" I asked.

"No."

I removed a business card from my wallet and extended it to Alex. She
looked at it but didn't take it. I placed it on the porch rail. "Will you ask Jean to
call me when you see her? My cell-phone number is on the bottom."

"She won't call you, but I'll tell her."

"It's important, Alex."

"You already said that."

"Please. Just tell her." Alex hitched her hands behind her head. "If she calls
me, I won't need to come back and bother you," I said. "Think about it."

"What's it about?" she asked.

"That's for me and Jean," I told her.

"I'll find out anyway."

"That's fine, but not from me." I stepped off the porch, turned, and gestured at my card on the rail. "It's the number on the bottom."

"Yeah, yeah."

I moved into the yard, anxious to be away from Alex and her quiet smugness; then I heard the knife blade click open and the sound of a small laugh. "I
know what it's about anyway," Alex said. I kept walking, tired of her bullshit. I
was almost to the truck. "'You have the right to remain silent. . . .'" she said,
and I froze.

"What did you say?" I asked, stepping away from the truck, keys dangling in
my hand. Her smile spread like a cancer.

"'Anything you say may be used against you in a court of law.'" She was on
her feet, hands on the rail, hips thrust against the wood, leaning out, taunting.
I walked toward her and she leaned farther out over the rail, her mouth open
beneath shiny eyes; she was enjoying herself.

"'If you cannot afford a lawyer, one will be appointed for you.'" Then she laughed, either at my expression or at her own cleverness. Both perhaps.

"What the hell are you talking about?" I asked.

She looked down at me and I up at her. The moment drew out. "We met a very pretty lady," she finally said. "Me and Jean."

"What?"

"A very pretty lady. A very curious lady." She waited, as if for me to speak, but I couldn't. "A very well-armed lady."

"Mills." The name tunneled past my lips.

"She had lots of fun questions," Alex said.

I knew that Alex was toying with me, twisting this in my guts for her own amusement. I shrank beneath a terrible sense of failure, of impending doom. I should have spoken to Jean immediately after I learned of Ezra's body. I should have warned her, used my law degree for something good for a change. But at first, I'd been scared, that day at Pizza Hut, scared that she would walk away, leave me forever. Scared that I would see the truth in her eyes, that she *had* killed him. Scared that my suspicions would be made irrevocable fact. Scared of how I'd handle that. Then, for days, I'd been drunk and full of self-pity. I'd said nothing, and opened the door to ruin. What had Jean told her? How far down the road had she traveled while I wallowed in the trough of my fetid marriage and wasted life? I tasted despair like bile. Mills was no fool. Of course she would investigate Jean.

"Questions about you," Alex continued.

I felt the return of a certain calm. "Why do you hate me so much?" I asked.

"I don't hate you at all," she said. "You're just in my way."

"You're not going to tell me what I want to know, are you? About Mills?"

"Like you said . . . that's for you and Jean."

I saw in her face that she was done. She'd had the last word and was content. She settled back into her chair and picked up the piece of whittled wood, gestured to my truck with it. "Go on," she told me. "I'll tell Jean you stopped by."

I walked away and didn't look back until I was in the truck with the engine on. She didn't know it, but she'd given me something. More than what she'd intended. I was in her way, she'd said. That meant that Jean still cared for me, one way or another, and that was better than nothing.

I called Pizza Hut as I drove away and was told that Jean was not working today. For the next hour, I drove around town, looking for her car. I checked the mall, the movie theaters, and doughnut shops. She was nowhere. Finally, in quiet desperation, I called her house again. No one answered.

At five o'clock, I left for Charlotte to meet Hank Robins. Traffic was unusually light on I-85, so I made good time. By six, I was ensconced in a deep leather booth at the back of the bar. The place was dimly lighted, and there was soft music that sounded vaguely Celtic. I found a half-empty pack of Gitanes cigarettes next to the glass ashtray and shook one out. I tore off a match, lit up, and dropped the pack onto the lacquered wood table as the waitress weaved through the room. She reminded me of Jean, something in the way she walked. The smile she offered was tired. I wanted a Manhattan, something strong, but I ordered a beer instead, a Beck's.

For all intents and purposes, I had the place to myself, so I sipped my beer and blew smoke rings through the dim shaft of light that speared my table from above.

"Nice," a voice said, and Hank Robins slid into the booth opposite me. He pointed at the ragged remains of the smoke ring. "Good form."

"You're late," I told him.

"Sue me," he said.

He took my hand and pumped it a couple of times, smiling through the smoke. "How are you, Work?" he asked, then went on without a pause. "I'm real sorry about all this. I know it's got to suck."

"You don't know the half of it."

"That bad?"

I shrugged.

"What's a guy got to do to get a drink around here?" he asked, then raised his voice. "Waitress. Two more."

Hank was an anachronism. He stood five eight, weighed about 140, yet was the most fearless man I'd ever met. I'd never seen it myself, but word was that he'd take on guys twice his size and come out on top. He had thick black hair, merry green eyes, and a chipped front tooth. Women loved him.

We'd worked a dozen cases together and I knew he was good. We got along, because neither one of us labored with illusion; we were realists, although he managed to do it without giving a damn. To him, the world would never make sense, so he just went with it. Nothing surprised him, yet he found humor everywhere he looked. I admired that about him. The world I saw was ragged.

Our waitress appeared with drinks and the same tired smile. She kept her eyes on Hank, so I studied her. Midforties, I guessed, with heavy features and bitten nails. "Thanks, doll face," he said, and gave her his dazzling chipped-tooth smile. She looked embarrassed, but she swept away with a livelier step.

"Do you ever piss them off?" I asked.

"Only the smart ones."

I shook my head.

"Hey," he said. "Everybody likes a compliment. It's a cheap way to make the world a better place." He sipped his beer. "So what's up with you? You look like shit."

"Where's my compliment?" I asked.

"That was your compliment."

"Thanks."

"Seriously, man. How are you?"

Suddenly, my eyes felt heavy. I couldn't pull them up from the bottle they stared at so intently. There was no answer for his question. Because no one wanted to hear the truth of how I was.

"Hanging in there," I finally said.

"I bet you're tired of giving that answer," he said, letting me know that I wasn't putting one over on him. Then he smiled to show that he was okay with that. "If you change your mind . . ."

"Thanks, Hank. I appreciate that."

"So," he said. "Let's talk business. I assume you want me to help figure out who killed your father."

My surprise must have shown on my face. But of course that was what he'd think; I should have seen it coming. I had to be careful. Hank and I were colleagues and occasional drinking buddies, but I had no idea how far his loyalty would extend. He was clearly puzzled.

"I never liked him much," I said. "The cops can handle that one."

"Okay," Hank said slowly, obviously at a loss but not wanting to push. He drummed his fingers twice on the table. "So . . ." He waited for me to fill in the blanks. So I did. Somewhat. It took a while. Then I told him what I wanted.

"Jesus," he said. "I didn't know you had such a high opinion of me."

"Can you do it?" I asked.

"I wish I could say yes, but I can't. You want to find out who tossed that chair down the stairs, and I don't blame you. But I'm not a fingerprint technician and I don't have access to AFIS or any other fingerprint database. What you need is a cop and a full crime-scene work-up. That's out of my league."

"The cops won't go there," I told him. "They don't believe me, and I'm not sure I want to push it."

"Then you're screwed, man. I'm sorry."

I shrugged. His answer didn't really surprise me. But I wanted to know who was responsible. It had happened, and it had happened for a reason. Maybe it had something to do with Ezra's death and maybe it didn't; either way, it was important. "What about the safe?" I asked.

"For that, you need a locksmith or a criminal. I'm neither."

"I thought that maybe . . ."

"What? That maybe I'd know someone?" I nodded. "As it turns out," he said. "I do. But he's in lockup. Ten to twelve. Why don't you just use a locksmith?"

"Because I don't know what's in there, and I don't want some stranger knowing, either. Not when the cops are so interested."

"You hoping to find the gun?"

I nodded. If the gun was in the safe, then maybe Jean hadn't killed him after all. And if she hadn't . . . then I'd get rid of the evidence. Besides, who knew what other secrets Ezra had tucked away in that safe?

"I'm sorry, Work. I feel like I'm letting you down. All I can tell you is this. People are predictable. When they set combination locks, they usually use numbers that are important to them. You should think about that."

"I already tried. Birthdays, Social Security numbers, phone numbers."

Hank shook his head sadly, but the twinkle in his eyes was not unkind. "I said predictable, Work, not stupid. Think about your father. Figure out what was important to him. Maybe you'll get lucky."

"Maybe," I echoed, unconvinced.

"Look, man. I'm sorry you wasted your time. I wish I could help."

"Well, there is one other thing," I told him. "It's personal."

"I can do personal." He pulled on the beer, waiting.

"It has to do with Jean."

"Your sister."

"Right." Then I told him what I wanted.

He took out a piece of paper and a pen. "Okay," he said. "Tell me everything you know about this Alex Shiften."

So I told him what I knew. It didn't take long.

He tucked the paper away in his shirt pocket just as two women seated themselves at the bar. They were both in their midtwenties, both beautiful.

They looked at us, and one of them waved minutely. Hank played it off, but I wasn't fooled. "Did you set this up?" I asked, gesturing at the women.

His grin gave him away even before he spoke. "I thought you could use the cheering up."

"Well thanks, but I've got enough women in my life right now. One more is the last thing I need." I started out of the booth. He stopped me with a hand on my arm.

"This one doesn't have to be in your life, Work. Just your pants. Trust me."

"Thanks anyway," I said. "Maybe next time."

Hank shrugged. "Have it your way. But listen, before you go." His voice was low and serious. "Take care, all right? This case is getting big press, even here in Charlotte. Whoever's working it won't care about stepping on toes. So watch your ass."

For a moment, I thought I'd been indiscreet, that I'd opened myself too much. That he'd guessed at the larger truth. But there was nothing in his eyes beyond simple goodwill.

"I'll do it," I told him, and put a twenty on the table.

"Hey, man. My treat."

"Buy your friends a round on me. We'll talk later."

Outside, the day died a slow, purple death, its breath a sigh of wind on the near-empty streets. A narrow blade of orange scarred the darkening clouds, then faded as I watched. I felt the heat of the day trapped in the concrete beneath my feet; it made me think of hell, yet cooled even as I walked.

If I was to save Jean, then I wanted to save her all the way, and that meant dealing with Alex. To do that, I needed information. That's where Hank came in. I wanted him to ferret out whatever truth made Alex tick. Jean loved Alex. Fine. But what did Alex want? Hard as I tried, I couldn't find the capacity for love in her. Yet she found something in my sister. I just wanted to make sure it was nothing bad.

CHAPTER

14

Back on the interstate, I drove as fast as the pickup could handle, and forty minutes later I turned onto her street. The streetlamps were burned out or broken, but I saw a glimmer of light behind her windows. I stepped out of the truck to the sound of a distant bark and the call of crickets in the brush along the track. Somewhere a television played. I climbed the shallow steps to her porch and glanced through the narrow crack of the curtains. The room beyond was dark, but I saw them in the kitchen, at the table. Jean had her back to me; Alex's face was a dim blur above her shoulder. There were candles on the table, a warm flicker, and I heard Jean laugh. Who was I to judge Alex? I'd not made my sister laugh since that long-ago night when her husband left with the baby-sitter and her world evaporated at a rest stop on I-85.

I almost left, but still there was a corpse, and the certainty that Mills would not rest. I knocked and heard the laughter die, the scrape of chairs. Then there was Jean, her eyes heavy as she said my name in surprise. Alex, behind her, frowned in annoyance and slipped an arm across Jean's throat, cupping her shoulder with long, tapered fingers.

"Hi, Jean," I said. "Sorry to bother you."

"What are you doing here?"

Her face was warmer than the last time I'd been here, and I flicked a glance to the flinty black points that Alex called eyes. "Didn't Alex tell you I came by earlier, looking for you?" Jean shifted and I saw Alex tighten her grip.

"No," Jean said uncertainly, her head turning a fraction before squaring back on me. "She didn't mention it."

I looked between the two, from Jean's pale face to the brittle lines of her lover's. Jean's eyes were moist, and I thought I smelled wine. "May I come in?" I asked.

"No," Alex said before Jean could reply. "It's late."

Jean put her hand on Alex's arm and gave it a squeeze. "No," she said. "It's all right. He can come in." She gave me a half smile, and I felt a wash of gratitude.

"Thanks." I entered her house, smelling the perfume Alex wore as I pushed past her. Jean turned on lights, and I saw that she was wearing a dress and pale pink lipstick. I noticed that Alex, too, was well dressed. The house still smelled of food. "Is this a bad time?" I asked. Jean hesitated, but Alex filled the void.

"We're celebrating an anniversary." She paused, as if she wanted me to ask. "Two years together." She moved her hand to the back of Jean's neck. Her point was plain, so I addressed myself to Jean.

"I need to talk to you. It's important." I saw Alex sneer, thought of her taunting words on my last visit. "I know this is a bad time, but it won't take long." Alex released my sister and flung herself onto the couch, her hands again behind her head, a look of wide-eyed expectancy on her face. "I'd like to speak to you alone," I said.

Jean's glance moved between us, confusion making her vulnerable, and I remembered how when we were kids, she would go anywhere with me.

"You should talk here," Alex said to Jean.

"We should talk here," Jean parroted, and I watched her sit next to Alex, the way she settled against her. "What do you want to talk about?"

"Yes, Work," Alex said. "What *do* you want to talk about?" Her eyes were laughing. *You have the right to remain silent.*

I tried to come up with the best approach, the best way to raise such a delicate subject, but all the rehearsed lines, all the clever ideas that had come to me during the drive to and from Charlotte dried up and blew away like dust.

"You don't have to talk to the police," I said. She tensed, alarmed, and turned to Alex. "In fact, it would be best if you didn't."

"I don't know what you mean," she said, her mouth working as if to find other words. "The police? What are you talking about?" She seemed frightened, nervous, suddenly alive on the couch. Alex laid a hand on her leg and she calmed visibly. Then, as if accepting the inevitable, she said, "Oh, you mean Detective Mills?"

"That's right." I nodded. "She's the lead detective on Father's murder investigation. We should have talked about this sooner. . . . I just want you to understand how this works. What your rights are—"

Jean cut me off, her eyes wild. "I don't want to talk about this. I can't talk about this." She struggled off the low couch.

"I don't—"

"Detective Mills said not to talk about this with anybody. She said I had to keep quiet."

Her behavior puzzled and concerned me. "Jean," I began.

"I didn't tell her anything about you, Work. Honestly. She asked a whole bunch of questions, but I didn't say anything about you."

Alex spoke into the silence of my dismay. "Just tell him, Jean. It's the only reason he's here."

"What are you talking about?" I demanded, and Jean stared at me as if I were a stranger. Her mouth opened; her lips silvered with saliva from her tongue.

"Mills thinks you did it," Alex said. "That's what she wanted to talk to us about. She thinks you killed Ezra."

"That's what she said?"

"Not in so many words."

"What did you tell her?" I asked, my eyes on Alex but the question meant for Jean. Alex didn't say a word, and Jean seemed to be slipping further away. She nodded several times.

"I can't talk about this," she said. "I can't. Just can't."

I saw that tears had gathered in her eyes. She looked panicked, pacing from side to side like a caged animal.

"It's okay, Jean," I told her. "Everything's okay."

"No!" she shouted. "No, it's not."

"Just take it easy."

"Daddy's dead, Work. He's dead. Killed. He killed Mom and somebody killed him. Somebody, somebody." Her voice trailed away with her eyes, which moved aimlessly across the floor. She stopped pacing and began to rock, her fingers twisted white against each other.

Looking at Jean, at her waxen face, I finally accepted the truth of my worst fear. She had killed Ezra. She'd pulled the trigger and the truth of that was unhinging her. Her mind was adrift, rudderless behind eyes that saw some unspeakable horror. How long had she been like this? And was she already too far gone?

I found myself on my feet, reaching to offer what comfort I could. I touched her shoulder and her eyes snapped up, wide and white. "Don't touch me!" she said. "Don't anybody touch me."

She backed away, hands outstretched. She found the bedroom door with her back and pushed it open. "You should just go home, Work. I can't talk to you."

"Jean," I implored her.

Her eyes were still wet, glazed under the dim bulbs. She backed farther into the bedroom, her hand on the door, ready to close it. "Daddy always said that done is done, and that's where we are. I said my piece, Work. I told that woman nothing about you. Now you go home. Done is done." A strange gurgling noise escaped her, half sob, half laugh. "Daddy's dead . . . and done is done." Her eyes moved from me to Alex. "Right, Alex?" she said. "That's right, huh?" Then, eyes still wild, she closed the door.

I felt light-headed. Jean's words filled my mind. Her words and her face, an expression I could never forget. I started when I felt Alex's hand on my shoulder. The front door was open and she pointed at it.

"Don't come back," she told me. "I mean it."

I gestured helplessly at the door that hid my sister. "What have you done to her?" I asked, knowing that, for once, Alex was not to blame. Knowing and not caring. My arm dropped to my side. "She needs help, Alex."

"Not from you."

"There's nothing you can say or do that will make me abandon her." I stepped closer. "Either you get her some help or I will. Do I make myself clear?"

Alex didn't back down, and I felt her finger, hard on my chest. "You stay away from Jean! From us and from this house!" She jabbed at me, her eyes fierce. "You," she said, jabbing again, "are the problem. You!"

We stood there. The line had been drawn, but in her eyes I saw a glimmer of terrible truth. I *was* the problem. Not entirely, but in part. I could taste the guilt.

"This isn't over," I told her.

"Get the fuck out," she said.

For once, I didn't argue; I just walked dumbly into the sweet night air. The door closed with a click and I heard the bolt drop.

I was outside the gates, and I was utterly alone.

I retreated into the womblike silence of the truck and, eyes on the darkened house, I relived the moments of Jean's deterioration. How long, I wondered, until she tried to kill herself yet once again? The signs were there, and some dark part of my mind spoke nightmare words.

The third time's the charm.

And I feared that it was only a matter of time.

I started the truck and the engine put a vibration inside of me. I felt the stutter in my heart as the truth of what I'd learned began to squeeze it. There could no longer be any question. Jean had killed him. My baby sister. She'd put two bullets in his head and left him to rot. Her words rang in my head—*done is done*—and I knew, more now than ever, that it would fall to me to save her. She could never do prison. It would kill her.

But what course to take? How to keep Mills from putting two and two together? It was not easy math, and I could only come up with one answer. Keep her eyes on me. I'd take the fall for Jean if I had to, but that was the last resort.

There had to be a way.

When I got to the park in front of my house, I realized that I couldn't remember the drive that had gotten me there. I'd been at Jean's and now I was at the park. Blink. Gone. Scary stuff.

I turned onto the side street that ran beside the lake, toward home, and saw a pickup truck parked at the curb, facing the lights of my house. As I drew closer, I recognized it. I slowed down, way down. It was Vanessa's.

I pulled up next to it and stopped. I turned off the engine. I saw her through the window, hands gripping the top of the steering wheel, her head on her hands, as if asleep or in prayer. If she knew I was there, she didn't show it, and for long seconds I watched her, aware of my breath in the silence. Slowly, reluctantly, she lifted her head and turned to face me. In the darkness, I could see little of her, just the outline of features I knew so well. I rolled down my window.

"What are you doing here?" I asked her.

"You scared me," she said stiffly.

"I didn't mean to." She sniffed and I realized that she'd been crying, watching my house and crying.

"I got your message," she said. "I thought I wanted to see you. But . . ." She gestured at the house, and I noticed for the first time that there were strange cars in the driveway and that all the lights were on. She wiped at her cheeks and I knew that I'd embarrassed her.

"You thought . . ." I began.

For a long minute, she said nothing. A car turned onto the road, and in its headlights she was drawn and beautiful. "You hurt me, Jackson." A pause. "I don't think I can let you hurt me like that again. But then you left that message. . . ." She broke then, and a tiny sob escaped before she clamped down again.

"I meant it. All of it."

"I've got to go," she suddenly declared. Her hand found the ignition.

"Wait," I said. "Let me go home with you. Back to the farm." I would tell her everything—about Jean, about Ezra, but mostly about my feelings for her, and about the shame I'd hidden from her all those years. "There's so much to say."

"No." Her voice was sharp and loud. Then softer: "I can't go there. Not again."

"Yes, you can."

"No, I can't. If I did, I fear you would destroy me, and I've decided that nothing is worth that." She put her truck into gear. "Not even you."

"Vanessa, wait."

"Don't follow me, Jackson."

Then she was gone, and I stared at her taillights; they grew smaller, turned, and disappeared. I closed my eyes but could still see red. Eventually, I went home, parked between a Mercedes and a BMW, and entered the kitchen through the garage. There was laughter in the dining room beyond; it rolled across me as I walked into the room.

"Oh, there you are," my wife said. "Just in time for the second course."

Then she was up and sweeping toward me, a smile creasing her face beneath eyes I could not read. There were two other couples there, the Wersters and a pair I couldn't name. They were smiling, amused, and suddenly Barbara was at my side, smelling of perfume and wine. She brushed at my shirt. Up close, I saw that she was worried. No, I thought. She looked terrified. She leaned into me, hugged me, and said very quietly, "Please don't make a scene." Then she leaned back. "We've been worried about you."

I looked beyond her; everybody was nodding and smiling, perfectly groomed above a linen cloth and polished silver. Red wine in cut crystal held the light of a dozen candles, and I thought of Jean and the melted wax on her wobbly kitchen table. I saw her in orange prison fatigues, in line for lunch as something brown and lukewarm was slapped from a spoon onto a molded metal tray. The image cut so deeply, I had to close my eyes. And when I opened them, Bert Werster still sat in my chair. "I'll go change," I said, then turned and walked out. I passed through the kitchen, picked up a bottle of bourbon, and walked straight out the back door.

As it closed behind me, I heard another burst of laughter. Outside, in the night air, I looked at the sky and tried to bleed away the tension. Then I heard more laughter, like the sound of passing traffic, and knew that it would not be that easy. How long, I wondered, until they realized I wasn't coming back? What excuse would Barbara offer for the imperfection of her marriage?

I walked around back, where I found Bone scrabbling to get under the fence. I put him in the truck, and I drove us away from that place without a backward glance. I couldn't save Jean, not tonight. But Vanessa was in pain, and I decided that it was time to deal with this shit once and for all. So as I watched the road, bright in the headlights, I thought of what I would say to Vanessa. I thought of the day we'd met. The day we'd jumped for Jimmy. I was twelve years old, and they said I was a hero. They said I was brave, but I wouldn't know about that. What I remember was being scared, and then being ashamed.

His name was Jimmy Waycaster. Everybody called him "Jimmy-One-T." There was a reason for that.

CHAPTER

15

Jimmy had only one testicle, a fact that followed him when he transferred in from some place out of county. His parents had no other children, which didn't stop Coach from putting him at shortstop the next spring. First game of the season, and Jimmy took one on the second pitch. When Jimmy dropped, there was stunned and absolute silence. Until he started screaming.

As it turned out, Jimmy's family was poor. And the surgery to save his last testicle was expensive. One of the other parents organized it, and two weeks later we jumped for Jimmy. It happened at the Towne Mall, back when it was open and fresh, before bodies were turning up in boarded-up stores. The plan was simple. Kids would collect pledges and jump rope in teams of four. So much for every hour the team jumped. It was supposed to last an entire day. There were twenty teams. Eighty kids.

Vanessa was one of them. So was I.

She was beautiful.

I guessed she was around fifteen, a freshman or a sophomore, which was pretty cool. Not many of the older kids turned out to jump for Jimmy's nut. I noticed her purple dress the minute I walked in. She was down the long corridor, across from *Sky City*. She caught me staring once or twice but didn't seem to mind. She even smiled, but it was a nice smile, not slutty or anything.

After that, I thought mostly about her smile, and what it would be like to kiss it. I thought about it a lot. It was that kind of smile.

There were a lot of parents, but none of them paid much attention. It was just a bunch of kids jumping rope. Every ten minutes, we'd switch, so you'd have thirty minutes before your next shift. Time to go to the arcade, hang with your friends, and watch the girl in the purple dress. Then it was your turn and you'd jump. It was an all-day thing. Parents appeared and disappeared, shopped and went for coffee.

Two hours into the day and I couldn't stop thinking about her. She had blond hair and wide blue eyes. Her legs were long beneath hips that flared just a little. She laughed a lot and was nice to the younger kids. I thought she was about the finest thing I'd ever seen, and with our eyes we seemed to find each other.

"Don't waste your time," a voice said. I recognized it without looking—Delia Walton, snotty bitch daughter of somebody or other. She and a couple of other girls pretty much ran the school. They were the popular ones, with flawless skin and gold beads that gleamed at their throats.

"What's her name?" I asked.

"Vanessa Stolen," Delia informed me. "She's old. In high school."

I just nodded, eyes still on Vanessa Stolen. Delia didn't like it. She knew what I was seeing.

"She's white trash," Delia insisted.

"Isn't it your turn to jump?" I asked.

"Yes," she said, and waved dismissively.

"Then go jump," I told her, and walked away.

Lunch came and went and the kids kept jumping. I heard an adult say that we'd probably raise over eight thousand dollars, which seemed like a lot for a nut.

It was about three o'clock when I saw the girl in the purple dress go outside. It didn't surprise me when I followed her, just scared me a little. But the day wouldn't last forever.

Outside, a hot wind blew; it carried the smell of exhaust into the parking lot. Cars flew by on the interstate. Birds watched from the power lines. Then I saw her, down by the creek, near where it flowed under the parking lot. She was watching her feet, kicking at tiny stones. She looked serious and I wondered what she was thinking and what I should say to her when I finally got the nerve.

She passed the last of the cars. We were far from the mall. No one else was around. No kids. No parents. Just us. She was almost at the creek, the tunnel dark along the steep overgrown bank. Clouds passed over the sun and it grew dark. The wind stilled itself and for a moment I looked up.

Then I saw Vanessa start, her hands flying up as if to catch something, but she didn't make a sound. She took a single step backward. Then a man, long-armed and bent, surged up and out of the creekbed. He had nasty clothes, red eyes, and a ragged beard. He snatched her up, hand over her mouth, and was gone, back into the creek and the tunnel that ran beneath the parking lot.

I looked for help but saw only empty cars and the mall, which seemed so far away. I stood paralyzed, but then I heard a muffled scream. Before I knew what I was doing, I was down the bank, so scared that I could barely breathe; then I heard her again, more a whimper than a scream, and the blackness swallowed me. I thought of the purple dress, and the smiles she'd given me. I took another step, into the black hole, and then it was just the three of us. But I thought of her face, her blue eyes wide above grimy fingers; I saw the flash of her pale legs as he dragged her down, how they kicked in terror—and I stumbled on, like in a dream. . . .

I rolled down the windows, wanting the wind. The images had not been this strong in years, and this time it was different, like someone wanted to hurt me. I thought of blue daisies that looked like open eyes, and then I was back in time, back in the dark, like it was happening now and not twenty-three years ago.

. . . Black water moved like tar in the darkness. I felt it in my sneakers and licking at my shins. I heard them ahead, a single high squeal and then only the creek—its murmur, a few faint splashes. I stopped and looked back at the square of light that was already so far away.

I wanted to go back, but that's what cowards did, sissies. So I moved on and it got darker. I put my hands out like a blind man; rocks tripped me and the dark tried to pull me down, but in my head I could still see the girl. Then there was pale light far ahead, and I thought I saw them.

I tripped, went down hard. My hands sunk into muck and I felt slimy water splash onto my face. Something moved against my arm and I almost screamed.

But I got up instead. Be strong, I told myself, then I put my hands out again and walked toward the distant light.

It was like being blind, but worse. So much worse . . .

A blind man would not have done what I did, and I said it under my breath as I pulled up at Vanessa's house and turned off the truck.

"A blind man would not have done it."

I ducked my head and peered through the windshield. Light burned in her house; it shone through the windows and cut into the dark like blades. Except for the windows that had been boarded up, I thought. They were dark and sightless.

Gouged out.

Blind.

. . . The girl screamed, a long, drawn out NO that was choked off; then I heard a man's voice, low and urgent.

"Shut up, you dirty little slut. Shut up or . . ."

The rest was lost. A rough mumble.

Then I saw them, definitely saw them, dark figures pinned against a spill of weak light. Her legs scrabbled, kicked up water, and he was shaking her as he dragged her. Her head looked twisted under his arm. Her arms beat against his, but they were small arms. She screamed again and he hit her. One, two, three times, and she didn't move again, just hung from his arms. She was helpless, and I knew then that there was no one else. Just me.

Suddenly, I tripped again, landed hard, facedown in water that tasted like gasoline and mud. When I looked up, half-blinded by the water in my eyes, I could tell that he had heard. He was still . . . looking back. I huddled down, blood loud in my ears. I didn't know how long he stood like that, but it felt like forever.

He would come back. He would find me and he would kill me.

But he didn't. Eventually, he turned and kept walking. I almost went back then, but I held on to her smile and prayed to God like I never had in church. I didn't know if he heard or not, but I went forward instead of back. I could still hear the sound of his fist against her face. One, two, three . . .

Don't let her be dead.

I heard his steps very clearly, dragging through the water as if he was running, and the light grew from pitch-black to dark gray, until I could see my hands. *The light was still far away, but I could see it. There was a storm drain, and I knew we must be far under the parking lot by now. I reached for the wall and found it, slimy concrete, like snot, under my fingers.*

They stopped beneath the drain, overlit by that half-dead light. A concrete shelf rose above the creek like an altar, and he threw her down. He looked in my direction, but I knew he couldn't see me. Yet he stared, as if he sensed me after all. Close to panic, I looked back the way I had come; the tunnel behind me stretched away, a throat.

Then his gaze was gone, torn away by his impatience. He was talking again, mumbling to himself, and it was in his voice, the eagerness.

"Yes, yes, yes. Oh yes . . ."

His fingers moved on her. I heard fabric tear and walked closer. His voice swelled up as her purple dress was ripped away. It spread beneath her, torn wings, and above it, in the light, her body shone like cold marble. His voice rose and fell, a chant, a crazy man's ditty.

"Thank you, Lord. Thank you. Yes. So long, so long, so long. Oh, my sweet, sweet Lord . . ."

He moved between us, his back to me, so that I saw her face and the bottoms of her legs. Again fabric tore and I heard his voice.

"Ohhh . . ."

It was a moan. Her panties floated past me on silent water. I looked down and watched them, blue daisies on a field of black—eyes staring in the dark. They drifted against my leg, spun away, and were gone, down the wet throat behind me.

I tore my eyes up, realizing how close I'd come, no more than twenty feet away, the light touching me. Her eyes were open and staring. Her mouth, too, gaped and I saw where he'd beaten her. Her lips twitched and a low gurgle escaped. Her fingers fluttered in my direction; then he struck her again, and her lips didn't move after that. Her eyes were still open but showed mostly white. I felt anger and I nursed it, needing it. It made me strong.

My foot touched something beneath the water and I knew what it was.

I reached down, my fingers closing on a rock the size of a baby's skull. . . .

I stared at the light that spilled from Vanessa's house, but it didn't drive the images away; so I closed my eyes, rubbed at them, fearing that I might start to tear at them instead.

. . . I raised the rock over my head and took another step, expecting him to turn and see me, to come for me, too. But he didn't. All he saw was the girl.

Another step, and the fear rose alongside the anger; and it was stronger. He would kill us both. I saw that. I should have gone for my father. This man was huge and he was crazy and he would kill us. He would kill us sure as shit. I was about to turn and run. Already I was beginning to accept it. Beginning to turn away.

Then he moved. And I saw her, a marble statue on a concrete pedestal. . . .

She was perfect.

I couldn't tear my eyes away. I'd never seen a naked girl before, not like that. Not a real one. I felt funny looking at her, ashamed and dirty, but I couldn't stop. And I noticed that my feet weren't moving. The rock felt loose in my hand, my head light on my shoulders. My breathing went funny, and she seemed to rush at me, until she filled my eyes. I looked at her breasts and then down to the soft blond hair that filled the space between her legs. I'd forgotten the man, my danger, everything but her, spread on that altar. It was only a few seconds but felt longer, and all I did was stare.

Then he moved, dirty fingers on her stomach, moving down, like snakes into a nest; then he was on her, grunting like an animal, baked-bean teeth dark on her pale and helpless breasts.

I couldn't move.

Then I saw her eyes, and I saw that there was nothing in them; and in that emptiness, I found myself again. My hand tightened; the rock came up.

I walked into the light. I took two steps before I saw his face, and his crazy eyes. They were on me. Right on me! And his lips were pulled back over those pudding teeth, and he was smiling, his body still pumping, like a separate animal. And his words, when he spoke, they penetrated me.

"You like what you see, don't you, boy?"

I froze.

"I seen you watchin'."

Red filled his eyes, making him less than human. But his body continued to move. Up and down. Up and down. Grunt. Grunt. Grunt. Eyes like grease on my face. And again that terrible smile. He knew.

"Well, get a good look boy . . . 'cause you're next."

And then he was off her, laughing, coming at me, his arm out, as if to put it around my shoulder.

"Lord, sweet Lord."

His mouth a dark, stinking hole. Fingers twitching. A wave of odor, like a dead dog I'd once found by the roadside.

"Adam and Eve!" he shouted. "Eve and now Adam." He leaned forward, bent low until he looked like a huge rat. "Let us pray."

He repeated the same words, over and over. "Let us pray. Let us pray. . . ." Until they bled into one high-pitched cackle that ended when he was mere feet away. Then with curled lips, he changed the words, and spoke them slowly. "Let us play. . . . Let us play."

Then his fingers were on me, and I began to scream.

But even as I screamed, I swung the rock, hit him somewhere, but he just laughed harder. I tried to hit him again, but he pulled the rock from my hand and tossed it down. I heard it splash, as if down a very deep well. Then my face hit the wall and I tasted blood. Again and again, until I could no longer scream. I felt his hands on me, all over me, but I couldn't move. I was barely there, just barely, but still . . . I felt his hands. The slickness of his tongue on my cheek.

. . . And I was sobbing.

But then there was flashing light, and distant shouting voices. I saw him squint, lips pulled back, tongue out like meat gone bad. Then he looked back down, caressed my face with one hand.

"You a lucky little boy," he said. "Yes, Lord." Then he dropped me in the water. My head cracked the wall again, and I saw stars. When they cleared, he was still there, crouched over me, eyes glowing but scared, his hand on my crotch, squeezing. "But I'll remember you. Adam on a cross . . . oh yes. You'll always be my little Adam."

Then he was gone, shambling down the tunnel, away from the light and the voices, which seemed so far away, but coming closer. I thought of the girl, naked and helpless, but this time it was different. I crawled through the mud and pulled myself up. I gathered the shreds of her dress and closed them about her. I placed her hands on her stomach, closed her bloodied legs.

That's when I saw that she was looking at me, the blue gleam of one eye just visible through the swollen flesh.

"Thank you," she said, and I could barely hear her.

"He's gone," I told her. "Everything's gonna be okay."
But I didn't believe it, and I didn't think she did, either.

I thought I was done, thought that it was safe, but another memory, like a predator, followed fast on the heels of the last.

It was something my father had said. I was in bed; it was late, but I couldn't sleep. I hadn't really slept in the two weeks since they'd pulled us out of that hole and into the wide-eyed crowd that pointed like we couldn't see them. The girl, broken, held together by the jacket they'd wrapped around her. Me, bloody teeth chattering, trying not to cry.

My parents were arguing in the hall, not far from my door. I didn't know what started the argument. I heard my mother first.

"Why do you have to be so hard on him, Ezra? He's just a boy, and a very brave one at that."

I crept to the door, cracked it, and peered out. My father had a drink in his hand. His tie was loose and he made my mother look very small in the dim light.

"He's no fucking hero," my father had said. "No matter what the papers say."

He knocked back the drink and put a hand on the wall above my mother's head. Somehow he knew my shame, the burning in my mind that kept me up at night. I didn't know how he knew, but he did, and I felt hot tears slide down my cheeks.

"He's having a tough time, Ezra. He needs to know that you're proud of him."

"Proud! Ha! He's just a dumb-ass kid who should have known better. It's sick the way you coddle him. . . ."

I didn't hear the rest. I closed the door and climbed back into bed.

He didn't know.

Nobody did. Just me. *And him.*

I seen you watchin'. . . .

I opened my eyes, done because I could do no more. Now I had to tell Vanessa how I'd failed her. She was raped at the age of fifteen and I'd watched it happen, allowed it to happen.

I should have done more.

I looked up at her house and felt a sudden twist of nausea. A man was standing on her porch, staring down at me. I'd not seen him come out. Had no idea how long he'd stood there. Who he was or why he was there. He came slowly down the steps. I climbed from the truck and met him at the front of it. He was younger than I, probably thirty, with thick brown hair and close-set eyes. He was tall, with big shoulders and large, heavy hands that hung like iron from the sleeves of a denim shirt.

"Ms. Stolen doesn't want to see you," he said without preamble, one hand out, fingers spread. "She wants you to leave."

"Who are you?" I asked.

"That's none of your business." He stepped closer, his hand mere inches from my chest. "Why don't you just get back in your truck and go home."

I looked past him and saw Vanessa's face, formless in the kitchen window. *I seen you watchin'. . . .*

"No," I said, angry. "*This* is none of your business." I gestured sharply, meaning the farm, myself, Vanessa. . . . I had things to say, and I meant them to be said. "I want to talk to Vanessa." I took a step forward and his hand settled like a weight onto my chest.

"I don't think so."

Suddenly, I was filled with rage, bursting with it. All the frustrations of my life seemed to boil up within a matter of seconds, and this nameless man represented all of it.

"Get out of my way." Low, cold, and dangerous, even to my ears.

"Not gonna happen," he said.

Anger. Rage. I was alive with it, like I might explode. His face was hard and heavy, and the pressure was building inside of me. The murder. The investigation. The searing need to talk to Vanessa. In a flash that smelled of prophecy, I saw Detective Mills cuffing Jean, and the way my baby sister sat in a darkened cell and sawed at her wrists with a piece of dull jagged metal. Everything was coming apart, and all I had was this moment and the fury that defined it with such perfect clarity. So that when he pushed me, I decked him, unloaded on him. And the shock of impact that traveled up my arm was a goddamn gift. He dropped to the ground, and I stood over him, hoping that he would get up and give me an excuse. But when he rolled off his back, sitting on the dirt, he looked surprised and hurt. "Jeez, mister. Why did you do that?" Suddenly, he looked much younger. More like twenty.

My anger bled away and left me old.

Then Vanessa was leaping off the porch, standing before me, hands on her hips. "What the fuck is wrong with you, Jackson? What is your fucking problem?"

I felt confused, drunk.

"How dare you come here and behave like that? I want you to leave. Right now. Go home. Get out of here."

She was helping him to his feet, her hand tiny in his. I saw them sleeping together, and felt new pain.

"I wanted to talk to you," I said, and it sounded lame even to me. I was lost, hands out.

"I told you not to follow me."

"This time is different."

But she walked away from me, until she was on the porch, holding the door for the man to move inside. Then she turned and looked down on me as if from a great height, and the porch light held her in its insubstantial grasp.

"Get off my property, Jackson. I mean it!"

I stood dumbly, awed by the pain that welled up to consume me; but it was not until she was gone, the door between us like a rip in the universe, that I realized she'd been wearing a purple dress.

Through the window I saw her at the kitchen table. She was crying, convulsing beneath the hand he'd placed on her shoulder.

I left, heavy with the words she refused to let me say. And it was only as I turned off the farm and onto the black pavement that I realized I had no bed to go to. So I went to the office, to Ezra's space, and with one lamp burning, tossing its warm light on the ceiling, I stretched out on the leather couch and pulled Bone onto my chest. He closed his eyes and was soon asleep. I stared at the ceiling until well after midnight, but my eyes kept wandering to the long, antique rug. I reached out my hand to touch it.

I thought of the safe and of the secrets my father had kept.

Eventually, sleep found me, but not before I realized that it was Monday and I had to be in court. That did not seem real.

CHAPTER

16

I woke in the dark; I didn't know where I was and I didn't care. I held on to the dream: two hands entwined, passing over green fields, the sounds of a dog and of laughter; a flash of blue skies that refused to end, and blond hair, like silk, against my face.

The dream had been of Vanessa, and of things that would never be.

There had been a child, too, with golden skin and her mother's cornflower eyes. She was four or five. She was radiant.

Tell me the story, Daddy. . . . Skipping through tall grass.

What story?

She laughed. *You know what story, Daddy. My favorite . . .*

But I didn't know. There was no story, no favorite; nor would there be. The dream was gone. I'd thought Vanessa would always be there. I'd thought that I had time. For some reason, I'd believed that things would simply work out.

What a fucking idiot.

Tell me the story, Daddy. . . .

I sat up and swung my legs off the couch, rubbed my hands across my face. It's never too late, I told myself; but in the dark the words felt lame, and I thought of the boy I'd once been. Then I said it again, out loud, stronger. "It's never too late."

I looked at my watch. Five-fifteen. Monday. Three days ago, I'd stood above my father's corpse. Now Ezra was gone, and so, too, the comfort of illusion; Vanessa had been so right about that. He'd been the structure and the definition, and I wondered where such power had come from? Was it a gift I'd made to him or something that he'd stolen? In the end, it didn't matter. My life was a house of cards, and the wind of Ezra's passing had knocked it flat.

I pulled on my shoes, thinking that the day already felt very much like Monday.

I found Bone on the overstuffed chair and guessed I'd been snoring. He was warm and loose as I carried him to the truck. At home, I put on a pot of coffee to perk while I showered and dressed. When I got out, Barbara was waiting. She sat on the counter, wrapped in the same fleece robe she'd worn the day before. She looked like hell.

"Good morning," I said noncommittally. She watched me as I toweled off, and I wondered what she saw.

"Hardly," she replied. "I didn't really sleep." I wrapped the towel around my waist, and she stated the obvious. "You didn't come home."

"No." I felt the need to say more but decided not to.

"Were you . . ." She hesitated. "Were you at her place?"

She did not need to elaborate. "No," I said.

"Then . . ."

"At the office."

She nodded and then watched silently as I rummaged in the closet. I'd forgotten that I had no clean suit, so I pulled on khakis and a rumpled cotton button-down that I usually wore around the house. I could feel her eyes on me but didn't know what to say, so I dressed in a silence made more awkward by our ten years of marriage.

"Work," she finally said. "I don't want to go on like this." I heard the forced calm in her voice, so I matched it with my own. I looked at her as I spoke; it was required.

"Do you want a divorce?" I asked.

She came off the counter, startled. Her voice rose. "Good God. No! Why on earth would you think a thing like that?"

I tried to hide my disappointment, realizing only then how desperately I wanted to be rid of this marriage.

"Then what . . . ?"

Barbara came to me and put her hands on my chest. She tried to smile, but it was pitiful to watch. Her breath explored my face, and I wanted to turn away. I'd been so sure. She took my hands and placed them around her waist, leaned into me.

"I want it to be like it was, Work. I want to fix things." She squeezed me, trying to appear playful, and failing. "I want to make you happy. I want *us* to be happy."

"Do you think that's possible?" I asked.

"Of course it is."

"We're not the same people we were, Barbara. We've changed." I removed my arms from around her waist and stepped back. Her voice, when she spoke, had an all too familiar edge. It was sharp and quick.

"People don't change, Work, only circumstances."

"Now, you see, that's where we're different." I pulled on my coat. "I have to go," I said. "I've got court this morning."

She followed me through the house. "Don't walk away from me, Work," she shouted, and I saw my father's face. I snatched my keys from the kitchen counter, ignoring the coffee, which suddenly smelled of bile. At the door, her hands found my arm and she pulled me to a stop. "Please. Wait just a minute." I relented and leaned against the wall. "There's still hope for this marriage, Work."

"Why do you say that, Barbara?"

"Because there has to be."

"That's no answer."

"Marriages have been made of less." She put her hand to my face. "We can make this work."

"Do you still love me, Barbara?"

"Yes," she said immediately. "I still love you." But I saw the lie in her eyes, and she knew it.

"We'll talk later," I said.

"I'll make dinner tonight," she said, suddenly smiling. "You'll see. Everything will be fine." Then she kissed my cheek and sent me off to work, like she had in the early days of our marriage. The smile was the same, as was the feel of her lips on my face, just like a thousand other times. I didn't know what that meant, but it couldn't be good.

I went out for breakfast and coffee. I had a bacon, egg, and cheese sandwich, which would have tasted great had I not found a copy of Sunday's paper. The story of Ezra's death and the ongoing investigation was still on page one, but there was not much else to say. For some reason, they showed a picture of his house. My house now. I scanned the article and was relieved to find my name absent. Another first.

I paid for the meal and walked outside. The day was crisp, with pewter skies and gusting winds. I shoved my hands into my pockets and watched the traffic pass. Somehow I was not surprised to see Detective Mills's car turn into the parking lot. It was one of those things that just felt right, like it had been preordained. I leaned into her window when she rolled it down.

"Are you following me?" I asked her. She didn't smile.

"Coincidence," she said.

"Is it?"

She gestured at the restaurant behind me. "I eat here twice a week," she said. "Wednesdays and Fridays."

I studied her: She had on a tight brown sweater and jeans. Her weapon was on the seat next to her. I couldn't smell her perfume. "Today is Monday," I told her.

"It's like I said. Coincidence."

"Really?"

"No," she said. "I stopped by your house. Your wife said she thought you might have come here."

I felt a foreboding chill, and I didn't know if it was because Detective Mills had been looking for me or because she and my wife had been breathing the same air.

"What do you want?"

"Douglas and I still want to get together with you about your father's files. Have you had a chance to go through them?"

"I'm working on it." A lie.

"Will you be in the office today?" Mills asked.

"I have court this morning. Then I'm going to the jail for an hour to see some clients. I'll be in the office by noon."

Mills nodded. "We'll be in touch." Then she drove away, and I stood watching after her. Eventually, I got into the truck and drove to the office. It was early still, and my secretary had not yet arrived, for which I was thankful. I could not bear her mournful eyes and the disappointment that seemed to shine from them whenever she looked at me. I ignored the stairs to the big office and settled into the chair in my own small office at the back corner of the building. The voice-mail light blinked at me until, with a small sigh, I pushed the button. It took ten minutes to get through all the messages, most of which were from various reporters. They all assured the utmost discretion . . . if I could just spare a moment to make a few comments about my deceased father. One, however, stood out. The call had come in that morning, about an hour before.

The reporter's name was Tara Reynolds; I knew her well. She worked for the *Charlotte Observer,* had the criminal beat for North Mecklenburg and the counties that bordered Charlotte to the north . . . Cabarrus, Iredell, and Rowan. Our paths crossed from time to time. She never misquoted me or abused the initial trust I'd given her. Murder cases were often tried in the press, and I was not above using her when circumstances called for it. She operated the same way; and yet there was an invisible line that neither of us ever crossed. Call it mutual respect. Maybe even liking.

Tara was in her midfifties, heavyset, with brilliant green eyes and a smoker's voice. She was beyond jaded, expected the worst of everyone, and believed that her job was the most important one in the world. She may have been right. She answered on the second ring.

"I want you to know that I never do this."

That was the first thing she said to me.

"What?" I asked.

"Just listen. I'm going to tell you some things and then we'll never mention this again."

She had my attention, yet she seemed suddenly hesitant. "What is it, Tara?"

"Just a sec. . . ." I could tell that her hand covered the mouthpiece. Muffled voices filtered through and then there was silence. "Sorry about that," she said. "I'm going to make this quick. You know that I've got sources?"

"I know that." Tara usually knew more about the murder cases in this county than everybody but the cops and the DA's office. I never learned how she did it, but she did.

"The word from inside Salisbury PD is that your name's coming up . . . a lot."

"What?"

"There's a lot of talk, Work. They're looking at you pretty hard for the murder." Her voice was low and urgent, as if she thought I'd not believe her.

"Somehow I'm not surprised."

"Just listen. There are a few things you might not know. First, they've identified the ammunition that killed your father. The bullets were Black Talons — fairly rare, illegal for awhile now. In and of itself, no big deal, but they checked the local gun-store records. Your father bought three boxes of Black Talons just before they were taken off the market."

"So . . ."

"So, it ups the odds that his gun was used. They think you had access to that gun." A pause. "Has it turned up yet?"

She was testing me, probing for information. "I don't know."

"Well, it hasn't, and until it does, that looks suspicious."

"What else?" I asked, knowing there had to be more. I could hear her breathing on the other end, the click of a lighter and the sharp inhale as she lit up.

"They're saying your alibi won't hold up." Another drag. "They're saying that you lied about your whereabouts."

There it was.

"Why do they believe that?" I asked, amazed that my voice sounded as calm as it did.

"I don't know, but it's firm. Add the money factor into it and it looks solid."

"You're talking about . . ."

"Yeah, yeah. The fifteen million."

"Word spreads fast," I said.

"You don't know the half of it."

"Are there other suspects?" I asked.

"You know, I'd have been worried if you'd not asked that question."

"Are there?" I pressed.

"Yeah. There are. There were several business deals where the other guy got the short end. Forgive me for saying this, but your father was a real ass. He was sharp but not exactly scrupulous. He screwed over a lot of people."

"Anybody in particular?"

"A few. But nobody else with such an obvious incentive. Some criminal defendants who got out around the time he was killed. They're being checked out. The DA was pulling out all the stops until some question came up about your alibi. Now Mills has forced his hand. He's not backing you anymore."

I was not surprised. Mills must have been all over Douglas about my going to the crime scene. She'd let me be there because he'd asked her to. Nobody would care about that if the case was shot because of it. In the end, it was her call. She'd swing if the wind blew the wrong way on this one. Normally, I'd have felt badly for Douglas, because our friendship had caused this problem, but not now. Now I couldn't have cared less.

Douglas would prosecute the case, whoever they arrested. Jean or me. That meant that Douglas was coming after the family, and the past was irrelevant. I remembered him from the parking lot, the way his face had hung so slackly around his ripe-plum nose. I was meat to him now; he'd swallow me or spit me out, just like anybody else.

"Who says my alibi is no good?" I asked, knowing she couldn't help me.

"Don't know. But it's somebody with a reason to know different. The cops believe it. Mills says she liked you from the get-go. She's all but accused you of hampering her investigation. But the pressure's on her. Everybody knows she let you onto the crime scene. Now she sees cracks in your story, and word is, she's like a kid in a candy store."

"Mills is a bitch."

"I try not to go there, but I can't disagree. I know she hates lawyers, but I can't blame her for that, either." She said it jokingly, but it fell flat. "Sorry," she said. "Just trying to cheer you up."

"My wife can swear that I was with her all night." I just wanted to try the alibi on, see what she would make of it.

"Biased testimony, Work. Any prosecutor worth a lick could shoot holes in it before breakfast."

She was right. Barbara's testimony was better than nothing, but not by much, especially in light of Ezra's will. A jury could well imagine a wife would lie for her husband. Throw in fifteen million dollars and it was a given.

"There's a bright side to all this," Tara told me. "Want to hear it?" She went on before I could answer. "Do you know this lawyer, Clarence Hambly?"

"Yes."

"He's saying that you knew nothing about the will. That your father gave explicit instructions that you not know of it under any circumstances. That's taken some of the wind out of Mills's sails. Hambly is very credible."

I pictured the old man staring down at me from his lofty height, a twist of distaste on his patrician mouth. But just because Hambly believed it didn't make it so. That's what Douglas would argue to the jury. I could hear him: I would never doubt the word of this upstanding gentleman. He would beam at the jury and place a hand on the old man's shoulder to show that they were on the same side. I am quite certain that he never discussed the will with this defendant. He'd stop and point his meaty finger, damning me. But there are other ways, ladies and gentlemen. And the defendant is a smart man, an educated man. Here he'd raise his voice. A lawyer! Who for ten years shared an office with the decedent. Who for thirty-five years had access to the poor man's home. . . . His own father!

That's how he'd play it. It's how I would. He'd need a motive.

Fifteen million dollars, ladies and gentlemen. A lot of money . . .

"And don't forget the obvious," the reporter said. "They still don't have a murder weapon. It's a big hole."

Not as big as the one in my father's head, I thought, amazed at my own callousness. If anything, my dislike for the man had grown since his death. "Is there anything else?" I asked.

"One more thing," she told me. "It's important."

"What?"

"I don't think you did it. That's why we're talking. Don't make me regret it."

I understood what she meant. If word escaped that she'd told me these things, her sources would dry up. She could face criminal charges.

"I understand," I told her.

"Listen, Work. I like you. You're like a little boy playing dress-up. Don't get caught with your pants down. It wouldn't be the same without you. I mean that."

Unsure what to say, I thanked her.

"And when the time is right," she said, "you talk to me and me only. If there's a story, I want an exclusive."

"Whatever you want, Tara."

I heard her light another cigarette. She muttered something under her breath. Then her voice firmed.

"This last bit's going to hurt, Work, and I apologize. But it's out of my hands."

A horrible pit opened in my stomach, and I felt my heart drop through it. I knew what she was going to say before she said it. "Don't, Tara," I said. "Don't do it."

"It's my editor's call, Work. The story's going to run. It won't be specific, if that helps. Sources close to the investigation say . . . that sort of thing. It won't say you're a suspect, just that you're being questioned in connection with the murder."

"But you'll use my name?"

"I can buy you a day, Work, maybe two, but don't count on it. It's going to run and it will be front page."

I couldn't keep the bitterness out of my voice. "Thanks for nothing."

After a long silence, Tara said, "I didn't have to tell you at all."

"I know. It doesn't make it any easier."

"I gotta go, Work. Take care." She hung up.

I sat in silence for a long time, thinking of what she'd said. I tried to picture it, the train wreck that was now bearing down on me, but I couldn't. The next day, or the day after that. It was too huge, too intense. I thought of the other things she'd said—because I had to. I absolutely had to.

Black Talons. They were hard to come by. That Ezra's own gun had been used against him now seemed a certainty. I thought of my last visit to his house, of the bed upstairs and the place where someone had curled up to rest or to weep. Jean had been there, looking for some kind of peace, I guessed. It was where it had started, on the night that now seemed so long ago. She would have gone there for the gun; we all knew that's where he kept it. How many times, I wondered, had she returned to that place, and what did she think while there? Would she undo the past if she could?

Then there was the fifteen million. No one would believe I had no use for it. It would appear to be an obvious and self-serving lie. And the cops knew that I'd not been home with Barbara. That presented a huge question. Where had that information come from? Suddenly, I thought of Jean, how her mouth had worked wetly beneath those kaleidoscope eyes. . . . *Done is done.* . . . *Daddy's dead and done is done.*

But I couldn't keep my mind off Tara. Why was she helping me? What was it she'd said? That I was like "a little boy playing dress-up." That's how she saw me, a little boy in his father's suit. She was right, I realized, but for the wrong reasons. It looked like dress-up because my father's suit would never fit. The problem, however, was not the size of the man, but the choice of suit, a truth I was gradually coming to accept. The vultures were circling, looking for a carcass, a body to feed the clanking machine that was justice. And I knew for fact that my father could never have put himself in the sights. He could never have made that sacrifice. I prayed that I would be strong enough to do what had to be done. I pictured my sister, and found that it helped. But the panic was still there, waiting, and I pushed the thoughts away, pounded them down with something like hatred.

Jean was right. The old man was dead, and done is done. Only one thing mattered now.

I leaned back in the chair I'd used for so many years and studied the walls, where diplomas and my law license hung; I saw the office as if for the first time.

There were no personal touches, no paintings or photographs, not even of my wife. It was as if a part of me had never accepted my life, and saw this all as merely temporary. Yet if that were true, it was a small part of me indeed. Until that moment, it had all seemed normal enough. Yet I knew I could move out of that office in five minutes, and it would be as if the past ten years had never been. The room would show little change. Like a prison cell, I thought. The building wouldn't miss me, and part of me wanted to torch the place. For what could it matter now? One cell was much the same as another.

There should be pictures on the walls, I thought, then placed a call to Stolen Farm. I told myself I was calling to apologize, to try one more time to set the past to rights, but that was not the whole truth. I needed to hear her voice. I wanted to hear her say that she loved me, just one more time.

No one answered.

By the time I left for court, the day had closed in on itself; the sky was shuttered with heavy clouds that threatened rain. I seemed to bow under the pressure of that sky, and I was bent by the time I walked into court. I'd expected to be treated differently, like everyone knew, but that didn't happen. I'd imagined the worst, a public shunning, but in the end it was just another day in court. So I sat through calendar call in near silence, addressing the court when my cases were called off the docket: one for plea, one for trial. Then I went to meet my clients in the crowded hallway.

They were petty cases, misdemeanors; I had to glance at the files to remember what my clients were charged with. It was typical Monday bullshit, except I had one guy who I thought might be innocent. I'd take his case to trial.

We stood in the burned tobacco smell by the outside door, a trash can for my desk. I dealt with the plea first. He was forty-three years old, overweight, and divorced. He nodded compulsively as I spoke, his lower lip loose over tobacco-stained teeth, his shirt already soaked through with sickly sweet perspiration. The "fear sweats" we called them. I saw it all the time. For most, criminal court was a foreign place, something that would never really happen. Then suddenly, it became real, and you heard your name called out in that room full of criminals, armed bailiffs, and the stiff-faced judge who sat above it all. By noon, the hall would be ripe, the courtroom even worse. There were 540 cases on the docket that day, a microcosm of greed, anger, jealousy, and lust. Just pick an emotion, and you'd find the crime to embody it. And they moved around us, an endless sea, each looking for his lawyer, his witness, or his lover. Some just looking for a smoke to kill the hours until their case was called. Many had been through the system so often, it was old hat. Others, like my guy, had the sweats.

He'd been charged with assault on a female, a class-A1 misdemeanor, just shy of a felony. He lived across the street from a very attractive young woman who'd been having marital problems with her pastor husband. How had my client known this? For several months, he'd used a scanner to intercept their cordless phone calls. During this time, he'd convinced himself that the cause of their problems was her infatuation with him, an assertion that anyone with working eyes could tell was absurd. And yet he believed it. He believed it now, just as he had six weeks ago, when he'd forced his way into her trailer, pinned her against the kitchen counter, and rubbed his crotch all over her. There'd been no rape, no penetration; the clothes had stayed on. He was reticent about why he finally left. I suspected premature ejaculation.

At our first meeting, he'd wanted to go to trial. Why? Because she'd wanted him to do what he did. He should not be punished for that. Should he? "It ain't right, I tell you. She loves me. She wanted it," he'd said.

I hated the sweaters. They'd listen to you, but they always wanted to get too close, as if you could truly save them. Three weeks before, we'd met in my office, and he'd told me his side of the story. The victim's side of it was unsurprising. She barely knew his name, found him physically repulsive, and had not slept through the night since the day it happened. I found her entirely credible. One look at her and the judge would drop the hammer on my guy. No question about it.

Eventually, I convinced my client that a plea of simple assault would be in his best interest. It was a lesser charge, and I'd worked a deal with the DA. He'd do community service. No time.

In the hallway, he licked his lips, and I saw dried spit at the corners of his mouth. I wanted to explain what was expected and how to address the court. All he wanted to talk about was her. What did she say about him? How did she look? What was she wearing?

He had all the makings of a client for life. The next time, it might be worse.

I warned him that the judge would order him to stay away from the victim, that going near her would be a violation of the terms of the plea. He didn't get it, or if he did, he didn't care; but I'd done my job, as disgusting as it was, and he could go back to his little hole and his dark fantasies of the preacher's wife.

The second client was a young black man, charged with resisting arrest. The cop said he'd hampered an arrest, that he'd incited a watching crowd by yelling at the cops to fuck off. My client had a different story. It had taken four white cops to catch the lone black man who had been arrested. When the charging officer had walked past my client, he'd been smoking a cigarette, at which point my client had said, "That's why you can't catch nobody, 'cause you smoking." The cop had stopped, said, "You want to go to jail?" My client had laughed. "You can't arrest me for that," he'd told him.

The cop had cuffed him and tossed him in the patrol car. And here we were.

This client, I believed, mainly because I knew the cop. He was fat, mean, and a chain-smoker. The judge knew it, too. I thought we had a good chance at acquittal.

The trial took less than an hour. My client walked. Sometimes reasonable doubt is easy to find. Sometimes it's not. As I was shaking his hand, moving away from the defense table, I looked over his shoulder and saw Douglas standing in the shadowed alcove at the back of the courtroom. He never came to district court, not without reason. I lifted my hand out of habit, but his arms remained crossed over his fat man's chest. I looked away from his hooded eyes to say good-bye to my beaming client, and when I looked back, Douglas was gone.

Like that, the last of my delusions fell away, leaving me naked before the truths I'd denied all morning. The room tilted and sudden dampness warmed my face and palms—the fear sweats, this time from the inside. I stumbled from court on weak legs, passed other lawyers without hearing or seeing them. I plowed through packed humanity in the hall, groping my way like a blind man. I almost fell through the bathroom door, and didn't take time to close the stall. Files slipped unheeded to the floor as my knees struck the damp, urine-stained tile. Then, in one unending clench, I vomited into the stinking toilet.

CHAPTER

17

Eventually, I got to my feet. I walked outside and found the wind; it gusted against my face as if to scrub it clean. Behind me, the courthouse rose up, pale against the monolithic sky. The light was silver and wan, a cold light, and people streamed past on the sidewalk below me. Normal people doing normal things, yet they seemed to bow beneath the pressure of the sky, leaning into the sidewalk as they forged uphill toward the restaurants and shops. None of them looked at the courthouse as they passed. They probably never gave it a thought, and in a way I hated them, but it was more like envy.

My eyes traveled up the street to the faded door of the local downtown bar. I needed lunch but wanted a drink. I wanted it so badly, I could actually taste it. Standing there, fantasizing about a cold beer, I realized just how much I'd been drinking the past few years. It didn't bother me. It was the least of my problems, a small revelation among the ugly multitude. But I decided against it. Instead, I turned for the office, moving down the broad courthouse steps.

I stepped onto the sidewalk and turned toward lawyers' row. I watched my feet, so it took several moments before I noticed the strange looks, but eventually I felt them. As I walked, people stopped and stared, people I knew: a couple of lawyers, a lady from the clerk's office, two patrolmen walking to court for trial. They all stopped to watch me pass, and it felt unreal, like they were frozen in time. I saw every expression with great clarity: disbelief, curiosity, disgust. There were whispers, too, as lawyers I'd known for ten years refused to meet my eyes and spoke behind raised hands. My steps faltered and slowed as I moved through this strange scene, and for a moment I thought that I'd been mumbling to myself or that my fly was open. Yet as I turned the corner onto lawyers' row, I saw the unbearable truth, and thus came to understand.

The police had come to my office, descended upon it. Patrol cars strobed at my front door. Unmarked vehicles leaned drunkenly, two wheels on the sidewalk, two on the street. Officers moved in and out of my office, carrying boxes. Bystanders stood in loose groups, and I recognized almost every one of them. They were the lawyers who worked all around me. Their secretaries. Their interns and paralegals. In one instance, a wife, her hand to her throat, as if I might steal her jewelry. I froze, yet somehow I clung to my dignity. Only one lawyer met my eyes, and it was as I'd imagined it would be. Douglas was distant, massive in a long gray coat that hung on him like a sack. He stood at the door and our eyes met in silent accord. Then he shook his head, and parted the crowd to walk toward me. It took an effort of will, but I moved forward to meet him on even terms.

He raised his hands, palms up, but I spoke first. People kept their distance and watched in silence.

"I assume you have a search warrant," I demanded.

Douglas took in my appearance and I knew that he saw what he expected to see. Red-eyed, haunted. I looked guilty. When he spoke, there was no sadness in his eyes. "I'm sorry it had to come to this, Work, but you left me no choice."

Police officers continued in and out of my office, and, looking over Douglas's shoulder, I saw my secretary for the first time; she looked small and beaten.

"There's always a choice," I said.

"Not this time."

"I'd like to see the warrant."

"Of course." Douglas produced the warrant and I looked at it without seeing it. Something was wrong with this picture and I needed time to figure out what it was. When it hit me, it hit me hard.

"Where's Mills?" I looked around. Her car was nowhere to be seen.

Douglas hesitated, and in that hesitation I saw the truth of it.

"She's at my house. Isn't she? She's searching my goddamn house!"

"Now, take it easy, Work. Just settle down. Let's do this by the book. We both know how it works."

I stepped closer, noticing for the first time that I was taller than Douglas. "Yeah. I know how it works. You get frustrated and I get screwed. Do you think people are going to forget this?" I gestured. "Look around. There's no going back."

Douglas was immovable and unmoved. He stared at my chin, so close that he could have stretched out his lips and kissed it. "Don't make this any harder than it has to be. Okay? None of us wants to be here."

I couldn't keep the sarcasm out of my voice. "You're forgetting about Mills."

Douglas sighed, the first sign of emotion. "I told you not to piss her off. I warned you." He hesitated, as if debating. "You shouldn't have lied to her."

"What lie?" I demanded, my voice rising higher than I'd planned. "Who says I lied?"

In shock, I saw his face shift. It seemed to soften. He took my arm and turned me away from the watching crowd. Together, we walked down the sidewalk until we were out of earshot. Seen from a distance, it would have looked like any normal day on lawyers' row, two attorneys consulting over a case or sharing a tasteless joke. But this was no normal day.

"I'm telling you this because it's on the affidavit supporting the warrant, and you'd have gotten around to it eventually. We couldn't get the warrant without probable cause. . . ."

"Don't lecture me on the law of search and seizure, Douglas. Just get to the point."

"It's Alex Shiften, Work. She contradicts your alibi. You told Mills that on the night your mother died, you, Jean, and Ezra left the hospital and returned to Ezra's house. You also told her that after you left Ezra's house, you went straight home and were there all night with Barbara. Alex says that's not true; she swears to it, in fact."

'True or not, how the hell would Alex know that?"

Douglas sighed again, and I realized that this was the part that pained him. "Jean told her. Jean went to your house later that night. She wanted to talk to you, she says. She got there in time to see you leave. This would have been late, sometime after midnight. She watched you drive off and then she went home and told Alex. Alex told Mills, and here we are." He paused and leaned in toward me. "You lied to us, Work. You left us no choice."

I lowered my eyes and closed them. The events of that night were becoming clear to me. Jean followed Ezra to the mall and killed him. Then she went to my house in time to see me leave for Stolen Farm. She knew that I'd left. She'd told Alex as much. But they did not know where I'd gone or what I'd done. What I wondered was why. Why had Jean gone to my house? And did she still have Ezra's gun when she got there?

When I looked up, I saw that Douglas had settled into a posture of patient complacency. I gave him a cold smile. "Your warrant's grounded on hearsay, Douglas."

"I don't need a lecture, either, Work. Alex came forward first; then we talked to Jean. She was reluctant—you should know that—but she corroborated Ms. Shiften's story."

I felt ill all over again as cold sweat explored my neck and rolled down my spine. I saw Jean's face, the wild abandon in her eyes as she'd sobbed. "Daddy's dead . . . and done is done. . . . Right, Alex? . . . That's right, huh?" What crushed me, however, was the knowledge that she'd told the police about it. Douglas knew that; it was in his eyes.

I felt Douglas's fingers around my arm. "You're not going to tell me that Jean lied, now are you, Work? Jean wouldn't lie. Not about something like that."

I looked past Douglas, watching the crowd of people who had been colleagues at worst, friends at best. Who now were what? Lost to me. Gone, as if I were already in prison. The fear snake uncurled in my belly, but I ignored it as I answered the district attorney as best I could.

"I can't imagine that she would make that up, Douglas. Not Jean."

It was true. I had left in the middle of the night, and apparently Jean had seen me. But what did she believe? Had she convinced herself that I'd killed our father? Was she that far gone? Or was she setting me up? If death was sufficient punishment for the man who killed her mother, what was appropriate justice for me? I'd made Ezra's truth my own. How badly did she hate me for that?

"Barbara supports my alibi, Douglas. I was with her all night and she'll testify to that fact. Just ask her."

"We have," Douglas said.

"When?" I asked, stunned.

"This morning."

Now I saw it. "Mills," I said. "She spoke to Barbara this morning." I pictured Mills at the restaurant. She'd known then that the warrants would be served. That's why she'd wanted to know my schedule. "Are you taking me into custody?" I asked.

Douglas pursed his lips and looked away, as if the question embarrassed him. "That would be premature," he finally said, which meant that he lacked sufficient evidence for an arrest. Then I understood. If Barbara had said anything different, Douglas would have served an arrest warrant, as well. That's why they'd waited so late to talk to her. They'd known what she'd say, and an alibi might have prejudiced their application for a search warrant. A judge might have hesitated. So get the warrant first, they'd figured. And if Barbara had told them anything other than what she had, then Douglas and I would have been having a different conversation altogether.

I nodded, studying the street scene one last time, as if to memorize all the little things I'd always taken for granted. "Fine. Then I'll get out of your way." I started to turn, when Douglas spoke.

"If you want to make a statement, Work, now would be a good time."

I turned back, leaned forward. "Fuck you, Douglas. There's your statement."

Douglas didn't bat an eye. "You're not helping yourself, Work."

"Do you want that statement in writing?" I asked.

Douglas frowned and glanced back at my office. "Don't talk to Jean about this," he said. "She's got enough on her plate without you adding to her troubles. I don't want you confusing the issues for her. She's given a sworn statement and that's all that matters."

"You don't have that authority, Douglas. You can't order me to stay away from my sister."

"Then call it another warning. Interfere with any phase of this investigation and I'll come down on you so hard, you won't believe it."

"Is there anything else?" I asked.

"Yeah. There is. Hambly probated your father's will today. Congratulations."

I watched him walk away. To my office. To my life. Such as it was.

He disappeared inside, and the crowd milled around my office door. In that instant, I was too furious to be scared, disturbed only by the ease with which the security blanket of my life had been ripped to shreds. Again the eyes were upon me, but they were not curious ones. And that, most of all, angered me to the point of disgust. These were people I knew, people who knew me. Yet there it was, plain in every glance. I was more than a suspect. I stood condemned, alone in a hostile country. So I left. I walked around the block and returned to the parking lot in back of the building. I got in my truck and I drove away, destination unknown.

Eventually, I arrived at the park, my house before me like a stranger's. It glowed in the eerie light, and loomed taller than normal against the gunmetal sky. The cops were there, too, at least a dozen of them; and my neighbors, like my colleagues, had gathered for the feast. Word would be all over town within the hour. In my head I saw the expressions of shocked disbelief, but the undercurrent of true emotion would be there as well, the dark thrill of another's utter collapse. Tongues would wag, and Ezra would emerge as the martyred hero, the hardworking, brilliant attorney who'd dragged his family from poverty, only to face this final reward. I saw it now. I'd killed him for the money.

I pictured the police in my house. Specifically, I pictured Mills, pawing through my things, my drawers, my desk. Looking in my closet, under my bed, and in my attic. Nothing would be sacred. Mills would see to that. My life would be stripped bare, tagged and bagged. I knew these people, damn it! And they now knew things about me that were nobody's business but my own. What I ate. What I drank. What kind of toothpaste I used. My wife's underwear. Our preferred method of birth control. The whole thing pissed me off, so instead of leaving, I drove to the house. Barbara was there, pacing the driveway in panic and despair.

"Thank God," she said. "Oh, thank God. I tried to call you. I tried . . ."

I put my arms around her out of long habit, feeling her bewilderment but nothing else. "I'm sorry. I've been in court. My cell phone was off."

She began to sob, her voice muffled by my chest. "They've been here for hours, Work. They're going through everything. And they're taking things! But they won't tell me what." She pulled back, her eyes wild. "Do something! You're a lawyer, for God's sake. Do something!"

"Did they show you a warrant?" I asked.

"Yes. They showed me something or other. I think that's what it was."

"Then there's nothing I can do. I'm sorry. I hate this as much as you." I tried to put my arms around her again, to offer what I could, but she pushed away, her hands hard on my chest.

"Goddamn it, Work! You are worthless! I swear to God. Ezra would never have let this happen. He'd have been so on top of this, the cops wouldn't have dared to cross him!" She turned away, hugging herself.

"I'm not my father," I said, meaning it in so many ways.

"You're damn right about that!" Barbara spat out. Then she gestured at the gathering crowd. "They're going to have a field day with this. That much I can tell you."

"Screw them," I said.

"No, screw you, Work. This is our life. My life. Do you have any idea what this means? Do you?"

"I think I know better than you what this means." But she didn't hear me. I tried again. "Listen, Barbara. They're going to do this with or without us. There's no reason to stay here. Let me take you somewhere. I'll go inside and try to get some of your things. Okay? You don't need to see this. Then we'll go to a hotel."

She was already shaking her head. "No. I'm going to Glena's house."

The momentary charity I'd felt toward my wife evaporated, leaving me chilled. "Glena's house," I said. "Of course."

When she turned to me, her face was bleak. "Tomorrow, Work. Tomorrow we'll talk, but right now I need to get away. I'm sorry." She turned away. As if on cue, a horn sounded, and I saw Glena Werster's black Mercedes at the curb below the house. When my wife turned back to me, I thought she'd changed her mind.

"You make this go away, Work." There was winter in her voice. "You make this go away. I can't take it." She began to turn.

"Barbara . . ." I stepped toward her.

"I'll find you tomorrow. Until then, please leave me alone."

I watched her all the way down the driveway, until she climbed into the sleek sedan. She embraced Glena and then they were gone, around the corner, toward the country club and the fortress of Glena's home. As I stared across the park, a horrible thought occurred to me. Barbara had never asked me if I'd done it. It'd never even come up.

Suddenly, I felt a presence behind me, and I knew it was Mills before I turned. She had on blue pants and a matching jacket; I didn't see her pistol. Her face was calm, which surprised me. I expected antagonism. I expected triumph. I should have known better. Mills was a professional; she wouldn't gloat until she had a conviction. After that, all bets were off. I'd probably get Christmas cards in prison.

"Where's your car?" she asked.

"What?" Her question took me off guard.

"Your BMW? Where is it?"

"I don't understand."

"Don't be an ass, Work. It's included in the warrant. I want it."

Of course she'd want the car. Who knew what a thorough forensic analysis might reveal? Ezra's hair in the carpet. Bloodstains in the trunk. Even as I spoke, I realized how my words would sound.

"I sold it."

She studied my face as if she could read something there.

"That's convenient," she said.

"Coincidence," I told her.

"When did you sell it?"

"Yesterday."

"Yesterday," she repeated. "You've had that car for years. You sold it days after Ezra's body was found, the day before I execute a search warrant, and you want me to believe that it's coincidence?" I shrugged. "Why did you sell the car? For the record." Her threat was more than implied.

I gave her reckless smile. "Because someone told me to stop being a pussy."

"You're playing a dangerous game, Work. I'm warning you."

"You're in my house! You're in my office! Warn me all you want. For the record, I sold the car because I felt like it, because it didn't fit anymore; something you'd never understand. But if you want to waste your time, you can find it on that car lot west of town, the one on Highway One-fifty. Help yourself."

She was pissed. With the car out of my control, its evidentiary value would plummet. I knew that it didn't matter—the car had nothing to do with Ezra's death—but she didn't know that, and for an instant I enjoyed her loss of composure. As victories went, it was cheap, but I'd take it.

"I want the truck, too," Mills said, gesturing at the old truck, which looked shrunken beneath the towering house. At the moment, it was all I had left.

"Is it in the warrant?"

Hesitation. "No," she finally said.

I gave an ugly laugh. "Are you asking for my consent?"

Mills eyed me. "You're burning up any goodwill that might be left. You know that."

"Oh. We've crossed that bridge. You want my truck, you get another warrant."

"I will."

"Fine. Until then, no way."

Our eyes locked, she swelled with bottled emotion, and I knew that this went way beyond professional. She hated me. She wanted me locked up, and I wondered if it was like this in every case. Or was there something about me or about this case? Something personal?

"Are you almost done in there?" I asked her, gesturing at the house.

She showed her teeth. They were small and white, except for one in the front, which was slightly yellow. "Not even close," she said, and I realized that she was enjoying herself. "You're welcome to come in and watch. It's your right."

My control slipped. "What is your problem with me, Detective Mills?"

"It's nothing personal," she said. "I've got a dead man, a missing gun, and a man with fifteen million reasons to lie to me about where he was the night in question. It's enough for me and it was enough for the warrant. If I had more, I'd arrest you. That's how sure I am. If that means I've got a problem with you, then yeah, I do. So come inside, stay out here, whatever. I'm just getting warmed up." She turned away and just as quickly turned back, her finger up like an erection. "But know this. I'm getting that car. And if it turns out that you lied to me about its location, then I'm going to have another problem with you."

I stepped closer, my voice rising to match hers. "Fine. Do your job. But I've made a career out of shredding search warrants. Not just how they're drawn but how they're executed. Be careful how you use it. Your case already has one big hole in it."

I was referring to my presence at the crime scene, and I saw my comment hit the mark. I knew what she was thinking. Any physical evidence linking me to the crime scene could have been carried in the day they found the body, not the day Ezra was killed. Any defense attorney worth his law license could use that to hang a jury. Mills had reason to worry. We'd squared off in court many times, and she knew that I could work the angles. If she screwed up with this warrant, the judge could throw the case out before it got to trial. Hell, she might not even get an indictment. Watching her mouth work, I felt some small satisfaction. Yes, I had to protect Jean, but nothing said I had to make this easy for Mills, Douglas, or anybody else. It was a thin line.

"I'm going in back to get my dog," I told her. "Unless you want to search him, too." She said nothing, just tightened her jaw. "And when this is said and done, I'll expect your apology." It was a bluff—no way would this end well for me.

"We'll see," she said, then turned and stalked away.

"Lock up when you're done," I called after her, but it was an empty gesture. I'd landed a couple of punches, but she'd won the fight, and she knew it. At the door, she turned and looked back. She gave me the same cold yellow-toothed smile, and then she went inside.

CHAPTER

18

I escaped into my truck and drove. I passed cars, stopped at signs, and turned from one street to another, but there was nowhere to go; all choices led back to the same life. It was a bad time, one of ugly questions and despicable truths. So I returned to the park, full of children, old men, and scattered windblown litter. Mills was still at my house. I parked at the curb and watched the police move in and out, tracking suspicion and indifference. It angered me, but it was a toothless rage. In this, I was helpless, and my fingers tightened on the wheel as if it were Mills's neck. When my cell phone rang, the noise jarred me; it took time to find the phone and bring myself to answer it.

"Hello."

"Hey, Work. How you doin'?"

It took a second to place the voice. "Hank?"

"Who else?" He sounded strained. Was it just the day before that I'd met him in Charlotte? It felt like a week. I tried to focus. "Sorry. What's up?"

"Are you okay?" he asked.

"Yeah." I paused, knowing that I was being short with him. Knowing also that I sounded far from okay. "Talk to me." I rubbed at my eyes.

"I called your office," he said. "A cop answered. He asked for my name." He hesitated, offering me the chance to say something, but I remained silent. What could I say? I almost laughed. "Then I called your house. Guess what?"

"I know. I'm in my car right now, watching the cops run in and out like it's on the parade of homes."

"I don't know what to say about this."

"Don't say anything, then."

"It's awkward, Work. It puts me in a bad position." He paused. "I take it they have a warrant?"

"I think they're hoping to find the murder weapon," I said. "Or anything else to incriminate me." I knew what he was thinking. They'd have needed probable cause to get the warrant. That meant they had something on me.

"Any real chance of an indictment?" he asked.

"Very likely," I said.

Hank went silent. Considering the news, I didn't blame him. We were acquaintances and drinking buddies, but not friends in any real sense. I could almost see the math. He relied on defense lawyers for most of his work, but no one in his position could afford to alienate the police. "That serious?" he finally asked. I knew the last thing he wanted was to get involved.

"Could be. The lead investigator's got it in for me. You'll probably read about it in tomorrow's paper."

"Mills?" he asked, not needing a response. I guessed he was playing for time, trying to decide how he felt about all this. "Is there anything I can do for you?"

His hesitation was clear. Getting involved in this could do him nothing but harm. It was to his credit that he'd even asked, but I knew what answer he wanted.

"Not now, Hank. But I appreciate it."

"Hey. Your dad was an ass, but I don't believe you murdered him."

"Well, thanks for that. It means something, Hank. Not many people are saying it right now."

His tone warmed. "Don't let them rattle you, Work. You've seen all this before. You know how it works."

You know how it works. Douglas had used the same words.

I decided to change the subject. "So what's up, man? Any chance of good news?"

Hank was no fool. He understood. I needed to move this conversation forward, onto neutral ground. "I went to Charter Hills this morning," he said. "I spent a couple hours poking around."

Charter Hills was a mental-health facility in Charlotte, one of the best in the state. It was where Ezra had finally committed Jean after her second suicide attempt. Even now, I saw it in stark clarity. Warm colors and fresh flowers did nothing to hide the pain of those condemned behind its tall brick walls; and condemned they were, whether their presence was voluntary or not. I'd visited Jean there many times; she'd never spoken to me, and her physician had told me that was normal. I hadn't believed him. How could I? She was my sister.

She'd been long months in that place. It was where she'd met Alex Shiften.

"Look, Hank . . ." I began.

"They have no record of a patient named Alex Shiften," he said, cutting me off.

"What?"

"No record at all."

"That's not possible," I said. "It's where they met."

"I don't think so, not unless she was there under a different name."

I tried to concentrate, but it was hard. "What are you saying?"

Hank sighed. "I don't know what I'm saying. That's the trouble. It doesn't add up and I don't have enough information to even speculate; but something stinks. I can smell it."

My mind was still so full of Mills that I had trouble focusing, but none of this would matter if Jean survived the investigation only to be left alone with Alex. She was trouble. Somehow I knew that, and I needed to handle this one detail. Before it was too late. Unfortunately, I was at a loss.

"What do you suggest?" I asked.

"I need a picture of Alex," he said without hesitation.

"What are you going to do?"

"I'm going back to Charter Hills. Then we'll see."

I felt a wave of gratitude. Hank would not cross the police, fine; but he'd go through with this, for me and for Jean. That made him a stand-up guy in a world that suffered from a lack of them. Somehow I'd make it up to him.

"Thank you, Hank." I paused because I had to.

"Forget about it. It's a little thing."

"Do you want me to mail you the picture?" I managed to ask.

"Too slow. Put it in your mailbox once the cops leave. I'll drive up to Salisbury sometime tonight. It could be late. If you're home, you'll see me. If not, I'll take it and go. Either way, I'll call you if I learn anything."

"That's awesome, Hank. I'll take care of it."

On the other end, Hank started to say something, then stopped. For a long second, I heard his breathing. "You understand? Don't you, Work?" He wasn't talking about Alex or Jean.

"Hey. Life's a bitch. I appreciate what you're doing."

"Okay. I'll call you."

Then he was gone, and I hung up the phone. I looked at Bone, but he was asleep on the seat next to me. How could so much happen at once? How could the world be normal one day and a smoking pit the next? I closed my eyes and pictured grass that bent in a wind from some faraway place. When I looked up, there was a man at my window, staring through the glass. I was too drained to be startled. It was Max Creason—same hunting cap, same sublime ugliness. He wore a bright red poncho, as if he, too, expected rain. I rolled down the window.

"Hey, Max," I said. "How are you?"

He studied me intently, his eyes bright behind his thick, filthy glasses. Then he gestured at my house. "There're cops at your house." His tone was more questioning than definitive, but I didn't take the bait. It seemed to anger him, for his lips pulled up over his stained teeth, and he made a strange sound deep in his throat. He leaned closer. "When I met you, I didn't know who you were. Didn't know you were the son of this murdered lawyer that's in the paper every day." It sounded like an accusation. He looked at the house and then back at me. "And now the police are in your house. They think you did it? You're a suspect?"

"I don't want to talk about it, Max. It's complicated."

"Talk is good."

"No. Talk is painful. It's good to see you again, but this is a bad time."

He ignored me. "Come on," he said, stepping back from the truck. "Let's walk."

"Thanks, but no."

It was as if he didn't hear me. He opened the truck door. "No, this'll be good. Just let the dog lie. You come on and walk with me." He gestured for me to get out of the truck, and I gave in. I had nowhere to go anyway.

So I left Bone to sleep in the truck and fell in beside Max. He led me down the hill to a narrow dirt footpath that ran beside the lake, away from my house. I didn't look back. He took long strides, and his poncho flapped around his legs. We walked for nine or ten minutes, past the lake, the public tennis courts, and across a gravel parking area. Neither of us spoke until the park was lost behind a small hill. We were on a narrow side street, lined with modest homes. Children's toys littered some of the yards. Others were immaculate. It was a transitional neighborhood. Newlyweds and nearly deads. But what did any of that matter?

"I'm gonna tell you a story," Max finally said. He rolled his eyes at me. "It's an important one, so listen up. I'm gonna tell you about my hands." He lifted them from his sides and then let them drop; they were dirty but pale against the red poncho, and his fingers were long.

"You remember. You asked me before. Now I'll tell you."

"Why?"

"I've got my reasons. Now shut up. No one in this town has heard this story and it's not easy for me to talk about."

"Okay."

"I got these in Vietnam," he said, and I knew he meant his hands. "I was just a guy, no different from anybody else, halfway through my second tour. We got caught, out on patrol, and we lost just about everybody. A few got away. Not me, though. I took a round through the leg and ended up in an NVA prison camp. There was a colonel running the place who thought I knew more than I did."

I saw his hands twitch.

"Either that or he was just plain mean. In the end, I guess it don't really matter. He worked on me for a few weeks, messed my hands up pretty good, then tossed me in a hole for five years. I almost died in that place." His voice seemed to trail off. "Five damn years," he said again, then fell silent. I could tell his mind was far away.

"Five years in jail," I said into the emptiness, trying to imagine it. His voice, when he replied, was bitter.

"Wasn't no jail, damn it. It was a dirt-floor cage eight feet wide. Five years, man. They let me out twice a month. Rest of the time, all I could do was sleep, shit, or pace. Mostly, I paced. Four steps and turn. Four and turn." He looked at me. "I can't handle closed spaces, Work. That's why I walk. When the walls close in, I just get out. You know, because I never could before." He gestured with his whittled-down hands—at the trees, the sky, everything. "You'll never know what this means." He closed his eyes. "This space."

I nodded, but I thought I might damn well find out one day.

"But why are you telling me this?" I asked him.

He opened his eyes and I saw that he was not crazy. Tortured and tormented, but not crazy.

"I have a problem with authority," he said. "You understand? I can't stand the sight of a uniform. And the cops round here have done nothing to make me feel any different. They don't exactly treat me with love and respect." A grin split his lumpen face. "I can't talk to the cops. I won't. You see?"

I understood, but I didn't get it. What did any of this have to do with me? I asked him. He didn't answer right away. Instead, he turned and walked. I hurried after him.

"You see how I walk," he said. "All the time. Anytime. Day or night. Don't matter. The walls close in and I walk 'cause I have to."

We turned right, onto a neat street, where the houses all had an individual charm. Max stopped in front of one, a small cottage with green grass and a hedgerow that separated it from its neighbors on both sides. The house was yellow, with blue shutters and a pair of rocking chairs on the front porch. Roses snaked up a trellis that bordered a stone chimney. I looked up at Max, suddenly realizing how tall he was.

"I'm talking to you because I won't go to the cops." My frustration must have shown, because he took off his hat and scratched at the matted hair beneath. "He was killed the night after Thanksgiving, right? It was raining."

I nodded, a strange sensation in my stomach.

"And they found his body in the Towne Mall, the empty one down by the interstate? Where the creek goes under the parking lot?"

"What . . ." I began, but he didn't respond to me. It was as if he were talking to himself, but with his eyes so hot on me, I could feel them.

"I'm tellin' you this story so you understand. It's important."

"What's important?" I asked.

"I'm tellin' you because I don't think you killed that man."

The sensation in my stomach expanded, heat rushing out into my limbs, my fingers tingling. "What are you saying?"

"I walk all the time," he said. "Sometimes by the tracks. Sometimes the park." A pause. "Sometimes by the interstate." I realized that I had seized his forearm. It was hard and scrawny beneath the slick plastic. He didn't even notice. "I remember that night because of the rain and because it was right after Thanksgiving. It was late, after midnight. And I saw the cars, near the mall. There are never cars there at night. It's a dark place with maybe a bum or two, maybe some junkies, but that's about it. Once I saw a fight there, a long time ago, but never cars. Not that late."

My heart was thudding, my lips dry. What was he saying? I peered through those thick, filthy lenses, looking for something. For some sense of what he was about to say. For some reason not to be afraid.

"You heard something?" I said. "Saw something? What?" I realized that I was squeezing his arm so hard that my hand hurt, but he showed no sign of discomfort. I forced my hand to relax.

"Maybe it's important. Maybe not. I don't know. But I think that maybe the cops should know. Someone should tell them."

"Tell them what?" It was almost a shout.

"I saw somebody come out from the mall that night—quick, but not running. This person moved past the cars and tossed something into the storm drain, then got in one of the cars and bailed."

The enormity of Max's revelation spilled over me. "Last year," I said. "Night after Thanksgiving. You saw a person exit the Towne Mall, throw something into the storm drain, and then leave in a car?"

Max shrugged. "Like I said."

"Did you see what this person looked like?" I asked.

"No."

Relief surged through me. He could not identify Jean.

"It was dark, raining, and this person was far away, wearing a coat and a hat. All dark. But I don't think it was you."

I released his arm, but he paid no attention. "Why not me?"

"This person was shorter, I think. Medium. You are too tall."

"Was it a man or a woman?"

"Who can say? Could have been either."

"But you are certain it wasn't me."

Max shrugged again. "For years I've seen you. You never do anything. You sit on your porch and drink beer. I've known a lot of killers, seen a lot of dead men; I don't reckon you could kill a man. But that's just me, my opinion."

I should have been offended, but I wasn't. He was right. In spite of going to law school, getting married, and running a practice, I never *did* anything. I coasted.

"What was this person wearing?" I asked.

"Dark clothes. A hat. That's all I can say."

"How about the cars? Can you tell me anything about them?"

"One big. One not so big. Not black, I think. But dark."

I thought for a minute. "Which car did this person leave in?"

"The smaller one. I'm sorry I can't tell you more. They were a ways off and I wasn't really paying attention."

"What happened to the bigger one?"

"It was still there when I left. I was just walking by. I didn't stay. Two days later, I walked by the same place, but the car was not there."

"What did this person throw into the sewer, Max? Did you see it?"

"Nope, but I have a theory, same as you."

"Tell me," I said. But I knew.

"When a person throws something into a hole in the ground, it's gonna be something they don't want to be found. The papers say the cops are looking for the gun that killed your father. I think maybe you look in the storm drain and you'll find it. But that's just me talking, and I'm just a guy."

I saw it through his eyes. Like I'd been there. Of course it was the gun. And if the cops found it? Game over. But the irony was like a fork in my guts. When they found Ezra in the Towne Mall, it was bad enough, but the memories of that awful day so long ago were just that, memories. But this was the tunnel, the throat, and I had to go there, to get the gun before the cops did. Before Max decided that he should tell someone else. Lord help me.

"You were right to tell me, Max. Thank you."

"You gonna tell the cops?"

I couldn't lie to his face, so I gave him the best truth I could. "I'll do what has to be done. Thanks."

"I had to tell you," Max said, and there was something in his voice, something unsaid. I turned back to him just as a car passed us. His eyes were on that car, and he watched it until it was gone; then he looked down upon me. "I've been in this town for nineteen years, Work, almost twenty. I probably walked ten thousand miles in that time. You're the only person who ever asked to walk with me . . . the only one who ever wanted to talk. That may not seem like much to you, but it means something to me." He put one of his shattered hands on my shoulder; his eyes were steady on mine. "Now that's not easy for me to say, but it had to be said, too."

I was moved by his sincerity, and realized that we'd traveled our own painful roads in this town. They were different, our roads, but maybe just as lonely.

"You're a good man, Max; I'm glad that we met." I held out my hand, and this time he shook it, best as he could. "So come on," I said. "Let's walk." I started to turn, but he didn't follow me.

"This is where I stop," he said.

I looked around at the empty street. "Why?"

He gestured at the yellow cottage. "This is my house."

"But I thought . . ." Fortunately, I stopped myself. "It's a lovely home, Max."

He studied the house as if looking for some imperfection, and then, finding none, he looked back at me. "My mother left it to me when she died. I've been here ever since. Come on inside. We'll grab a couple beers and sit on the porch."

I stood loose and still, embarrassed by all the years I'd seen him walk past my house, and by all the assumptions I'd made. In some ways, I was as bad as Barbara, and that fact humbled me.

"Max?"

"Yeah." His face twisted in a smile that no longer looked so gruesome to me.

"May I ask a favor? It's important."

"Ask away. I might even say yes." Another smile.

"If anything should happen to me, I'd like you to take my dog. Look after him. Take him walking with you."

It would be a good life, I thought.

Max studied me before he spoke. "If something happens to you," he said with great solemnity, "I'll take care of your dog. We're friends, right?"

"Yes," I said, meaning it.

"Then good. But nothing's gonna happen. You'll tell the cops about the gun, and take care of the dog yourself. Now come on. I bought beer just for you."

So we sat on his front porch, looked across his tidy lawn, and sipped beer from the bottle. We spoke, but not of important things; and for that brief time, I was not lonely, and neither, I thought, was he.

CHAPTER

19

I found Bone asleep in the truck, curled in the sun. One look up the hill and I could tell the house was empty, but I couldn't face it; that body was still warm. So I went to the office. It still felt like Ezra's building and I thought it would be easier to start there.

It was a little after four and the street was empty, sidewalks, too. I wanted to be angry, but walked like a victim. I went in through the back door and saw my office first. Drawers were pulled out, filing cabinets stripped bare. Case files, personal documents, all of it. My financial information, medical records, photographs. Even a journal I wrote in once in a blue moon. My whole life! I slammed the drawers shut, the sounds like breaking fingers in the quiet building. I glanced in the break room and saw that they'd helped themselves to drinks from my refrigerator. Cans and candy wrappers still littered the small scratched table, and the room stank of cigarettes. I scooped up trash and stuffed it violently into a plastic bag. I cleared half the mess, then flung the bag to the floor. There was no point.

I went upstairs to Ezra's office. It, too, was in shambles, but I ignored the mess and went straight to the corner of rug that hid the dead man's safe. I took a handful of fringe and pulled the rug back. Everything looked the same: two dented boards held fast by four nails—two of them cleanly driven, two bent and hammered into the wood.

The cops had not found it, which made me savagely content. If anyone had the right to tear down the old man's last secret, I did.

The hammer was where I'd left it, and I used the clawed end to pry at the nails. The bent ones came out, but the other two refused. The claw barely fit into the crack between the boards, but a hard yank brought them up with an animal squeal. I tossed them down and bent over the safe. Hank had said to think about what was important to Ezra if I wanted to open it without a locksmith. So I tried to think clearly of the dead man whom fate had made my father.

What was important to him? A simple question. Power. Standing. Prominence. Yet it all came down to money.

In the heart of my father's million-dollar house was his study, and on the desk there was a single framed photograph. It had been there forever, a reminder and a goad. How many times had I caught him staring at it? It was who and what he was: what he'd strived to bury yet couldn't bear to forget. In his heart, and in spite of his overwhelming accomplishments, my father had always been the same grubby boy with scabby knees. The dark eyes had never changed.

I'd been born into comfort, and both of us had known all along that I lacked his hunger. That hunger had made him strong, but it'd made him hard, as well. Ruthlessness was a virtue, and the lack of it in me was, to him, the surest proof that he had fathered a weakling. So where I searched for meaning, he'd sought power. His life had been a determined climb to the top, and it all came down to money; it was the foundation. Money had bought his house in the best neighborhood. Money had bought cars, paid for parties, and financed political campaigns. It was a tool, a lever, and he'd used it to shift the world around him, the people, too. I thought of my career, and knew I'd chosen the easy route. He'd bought me off. I could face that now. Maybe he'd bought us all, except for Jean. For her, the cost was too heavy, and, unable or unwilling to bend, she'd snapped under the weight of it. So in the end, Ezra had paid the price. The whole thing reeked of karma.

I studied the safe. I'd discovered it by accident and could have gone the rest of my life without knowledge of its existence, yet it weighed upon me.

Money and power.

I remembered my father's first million-dollar jury award. I was ten, and he took the family to Charlotte to celebrate. I could still see him, teeth clamped on a cigar, proudly ordering the best bottle of wine in the restaurant, and how he'd turned to Mother. "Nothing can stop me now," he'd said. And I remembered Mother's face, too, her uncertainty.

Not us. *Me.*

She'd put her arm around Jean, and at the time I didn't recognize it, but looking back, I knew she'd been scared.

That verdict was the beginning. It was the largest jury award in the history of Rowan County, and the press made my father famous. After that, people came looking for Ezra Pickens.

And he was right. Nothing could stop him. He was a celebrity, an icon, and his ego grew with his fame and with his fortune. Everything changed for him after that.

For us, too.

I still remembered the date of the verdict. It was the day Jean turned six.

I typed the date into the keypad. Nothing. I replaced the boards and hammered in four new nails. I took my time, and they sank into the wood, straight and clean. I spread the rug with a sigh and turned away.

It would have been too easy.

I moved around the office, closing drawers, turning off lights, and was about to leave, when the phone rang. I almost didn't answer it.

"Damn all generosity!" It was Tara Reynolds, calling from her office at the *Charlotte Observer.* "My editor is about to stroke out."

"What are you talking about, Tara?"

"Have you seen the *Salisbury Post?*" Unlike the *Observer,* it ran in the afternoons. It would have hit the stands less than an hour ago.

"No."

"Well, you should pick up a copy. You're page-one news, Work, and it's a freakin' injustice, that's what it is. I bust my ass on this story, I'm all set to break it, and some idiot from the *Post* gets a call that the cops are at your office and just walks on over and takes your damn picture."

My voice was cold. "I'm sorry to inconvenience you."

"'Police search home, office of slain lawyer's son.' That's the headline. There's a picture of you standing with the district attorney in front of your office."

"That was four hours ago," I said.

"Hey, good news travels fast. The article's short. Do you want me to read it to you?"

162

So, the story was now official. Fifty thousand people subscribed to the *Post*. In twenty-four hours, it would be in the *Observer*, which had close to a million readers. Strangely, I felt more calm than not. Once you lose your reputation, your worries become more concrete: life or death—freedom or prison. Everything else pales.

"No," I said. "I do not want you to read it to me. Other than making my day even worse, is there some reason you called?"

"Yeah. I want you to appreciate me. Because right now, I'm the only one doing any favors."

"Appreciate what?" I asked bitterly.

"News," she said. "With the same proviso as last time. You tell no one where you heard it, and I get the exclusive when this is said and done."

I didn't speak right away. I had a sudden splitting headache. None of this would go away. Not on its own.

"Do you have someplace else you need to be?" Tara demanded sarcastically. "If so, just tell me and I'm gone. I don't have to play games."

"No games, Tara. I just needed a second. It's been a long day."

She must have heard the despair in my voice. "Hey, I understand. I get caught up in things, the curse of the type A personality. I'm sorry."

She didn't sound particularly sorry, and my words, when they came, were short and bitten off. "It's okay," I said. "You use me. I use you. No reason to take it personally. Right?"

"That's exactly right," she said, oblivious. "So here's my news. The police have figured out why your father was in that old mall."

"What?"

"Actually, it would be more accurate to say that they've figured out how he was in that mall."

"What do you mean?"

"The property was going into foreclosure. Your father was retained to represent the bank. He would have had keys to the property."

This surprised me. While I didn't know everything about my father's practice, I should have been aware of the case, if only peripherally.

"Who owned the property?" I asked.

"I'm checking on that. All I know now is that it was a group of investors, some local, some not. They bought the mall several years ago, when it was about to fold. They pumped millions into renovations, but the tenants never materialized. They were hemorrhaging money when the bank finally dropped the ax."

"Is there any chance of a connection?" I asked. "Are the police looking into it?"

"I don't think so."

"Are you serious?" I demanded. "Ezra was foreclosing on a multimillion-dollar operation, was killed on the property, and the cops don't see a connection?"

I heard Tara light up a cigarette, pausing before she spoke. "Why would they, Work? They've got their man." She exhaled, and I pictured her wrinkled lips and the bright pink lipstick that bled into the cracks.

"No, they don't," I said. "Not yet."

"Well, that brings me to my second piece of news."

I knew trouble when I heard it. "What?"

"I don't have specifics, you understand? But word is that they found something in your house that incriminates you."

"That's not possible," I said.

"I'm just telling you what I heard."

"But . . . you must know more than that."

"Not really, Work. Only that Mills about had an orgasm. And that's a direct quote from my source."

I thought of all the people who had been in my house since Ezra disappeared, all the parties, dinners, and casual visits. Jean had been there once or twice, Alex, too. Even the district attorney. Christ, half the town had passed through those doors at some point in the past eighteen months. What in the hell was Tara talking about?

"You're not holding out on me, are you?" I asked. "This one is important."

"I've told you all I know. That's the deal." Another long exhale, and I knew she had something else to add. "Have you told me everything?" she finally asked.

"What do you want to know?"

"It all comes back to the gun, Work. They want the murder weapon. Have you had any more thoughts on that?"

I saw Max's face, and felt the dampness of that hole. I smelled mud mixed with gasoline, and suddenly couldn't breathe. For a moment, I'd forgotten.

"Still no sign," I finally told her.

"Would you like to make a statement? I'd be glad to put forth your side of the story."

I thought of Douglas. "That would be premature," I finally said.

"Call me if you change your mind."

"You'll be the first."

"You mean the only."

"Right."

She paused and I could almost smell the smoke; she liked menthols. "Listen," she said. "I'm not really such a cold bitch. It's just that thirty years of this has taught me a thing or two, like never get emotionally involved in the stories I cover. It's nothing personal. I just have to keep my distance. It's a matter of professionalism."

"Rest assured, you're very professional," I told her.

"That was uncalled for."

"Maybe. But I seem to be surrounded by professionals today."

"Things will work out," she said, but we both knew the truth. Innocent people went to jail all the time, and good guys bled as red as the rest.

"Take care," she said, and for an instant she sounded like she meant it.

"Yeah. You, too."

The line went dead and I settled the receiver back on its cradle. Suddenly, things weren't so clear. Why, on that night, did Ezra go to that nearly abandoned mall? His wife had just died. His family was coming apart at the seams. Who called him, and what was said in that hushed conversation? It was after midnight, for Christ's sake. Did he go first to the office, and if so, why? My father had driven a black Lincoln Town Car, so Max's big dark car had to have been Ezra's, but who owned the other one? Jean had a dark car, but so did a thousand other people in town. Was I wrong? Could there be some other reason for my father's death? I turned to an ugly reality, one that I'd shied away from because I simply could not face it. The old mall was less than a mile from where I sat. Its destruction was almost complete, but the parking lot was untouched, as was the low dank tunnel that ran beneath it. If Max was right and the killer had ditched the gun in the storm sewer, then it would be there still, lying in that grim place like the memories that had defiled my dreams, if not my very life. I would have to return, to claim the legacy of my father's last breath, and I didn't know if I could do it. But there was no choice. If the gun was Ezra's, I'd know it. Then I could dispose of it, so that Mills could never use it against Jean. And if it wasn't his gun? If by some miracle I was wrong, and it was not my sister that pulled the trigger?

I thought of Vanessa, pictured her face the last time I'd seen her. She'd kicked me out, spilled her tears on the hands of another man. Would she step forward if I asked? Would she utter the words to set me free?

I had to believe that she would. Whatever harm I'd done to her, she was a good woman.

My watch showed it was almost five. I glanced around the ruined office and, for a moment, considered cleaning it up, but this was not my life, so I locked up and left the place untouched. Outside, the clouds had pulled apart and a care-worn light filtered through. People were leaving the surrounding offices, packing up and going home to the same dreams that used to mean so much to me. No one spoke to me. No one raised a hand. I drove home and parked beneath high walls of peeling paint and windows as colorless as sanded lead. And when I finally went inside, it was like walking into an open wound. Our bed was pulled apart, my desk riffled, and clothing littered the floor. Every room was the same, yet each was worse than the last. I closed my eyes and saw Mills and her smug smile as she'd left me in the driveway to resume this slow and visceral penetration.

I wandered through the house, touched once personal and private things, then shuffled into the kitchen and took down a bottle of bourbon and a glass. It slopped as I poured it, but I didn't care. I sat at the breakfast table and downed half the glass before I realized what I was seeing, right there on the table before me. I slammed the glass down so hard that the remaining bourbon exploded out of its mouth and settled in a wide wet arc onto the face of the newspaper that Mills had so carefully placed there for me to find.

It was the *Salisbury Post,* and there I was on the front page. It was not the headline that enraged me, but the fact that Mills had put the paper there for me to find. And that act, so simple, had been calculated to inflict pain. She'd caught me at home, defenses down, and slit me open me with a fifty-cent newspaper.

My glass shattered on the wall. Then I was on my feet.

The writer didn't have many facts, but the implication was more than be-tween the lines. The son of a wealthy dead lawyer was being investigated. He was one of the last to see the victim alive and had somehow managed to compromise the crime scene. And there was a will, with fifteen million dollars at stake.

Not much, I thought, but more than enough for a public crucifixion. And soon there would be more, along with any unflattering information they could ferret out of my neighbors or colleagues.

I looked again at the paper and future headlines flashed through my mind.

LOCAL LAWYER GOES TO TRIAL . . . PROSECUTION RESTS . . . JURY SAYS GUILTY IN PICKENS MURDER TRIAL . . . SENTENCING TODAY . . .

The phone rang. I snatched it up.

"What!" Brutal and short.

At first there was silence, and I thought no one was there. But then I heard a wet snuffling noise and what was clearly a choked-off sob.

"Hello," I said.

Crying. Sobbing. A susurration of wet helplessness that dwindled to a keen so high, I could have been imagining it. I heard a dull and rhythmic thumping, and I knew it was Jean, striking her head on the wall or rocking so hard in her chair that it sounded in protest. My own problems dwindled into some distant place.

"Jean," I said. "It's okay. Calm down."

I heard a mighty intake of breath, as if her lungs were nearly starved yet had found the courage for one last, great effort. The air rushed in, and when it came out, it carried my name, but weakly, so that I almost missed it.

"Yes. It's me. Are you okay?" I tried to stay calm, but Jean had never sounded this bad, and I saw her blood on a sagging floor or spurting into hot pink water. "Talk to me, Jean. What is it? What's happening?"

More wet, stifled breathing.

"Where are you?" I asked. "Are you at home?"

She said my name again. A curse. A benediction. A plea. Maybe all three. Then I heard another voice, Alex's, but it was distant.

"What are you doing, Jean?" Footsteps boomed on wooden floors, accelerated, grew louder. "Who are you talking to?" Jean said nothing. Even her breathing stopped. "It's Work, isn't it?" Alex demanded, her voice louder, as hard as the receiver clenched like an ax in my hand. "Give me the phone. Give it."

Then it was Alex on the phone, and I wanted to reach through the line and beat her.

"Work?"

"Put Jean back on the phone! Right now, goddamn it!"

"I knew it was you," she said, and her voice was unruffled.

"Alex, I am so serious, you would not believe it. I want to talk to my sister and I want to talk to her now!"

"It's the last thing she needs right now."

"That is not for you to decide."

"Jean's too upset to know what she's doing."

"That still doesn't make it your decision."

"Whose, then? Yours?"

I said nothing, and for that instant I could hear Jean crying in the background. I felt a terrible helplessness.

"You know what she's been through, Alex. You know her history. For God's sake, she needs help."

"Yes, she does, but not from you." I tried to speak, but Alex cut me off. "Let me make one thing perfectly clear. Jean is upset because she saw your picture in the paper, you dumb shit. Black print implicating you in her father's murder. Is it any wonder she's upset?"

Then I got it. I understood. The article had compounded Jean's guilt. She'd killed her father, and her brother was taking the blame for it. No wonder she was falling to pieces. The possibility might have occurred to her—that day she spoke to Detective Mills—but the reality was different, and it was pulling her apart. The revelation staggered me. I was out of my depth, and knew I could do more harm than good. Poor Jean. What more must she endure?

"If anything happens to her, Alex, I'll hold you responsible."

"I'm hanging up now. Don't come over here."

"Tell her that I love her," I said, but Alex was already gone. I put the phone down and sat at the breakfast table, there in the back corner of my kitchen. I stared at the wall and then dropped my head into the cradle of my hands. Everything seemed to collapse—the room, my insides—and I wondered what further grief the day could possibly bring.

When I looked up, I saw the bottle of bourbon. I reached for it and pulled straight from the bottle. Hot liquor shot out and I drank too much, choking. I closed my eyes on the burn, wiped away something that felt like tears, and heard a gentle knock on the glass window of the garage door. I looked up, startled, and saw Dr. Stokes's face on the other side. I stared for a moment, and he cracked the door. He wore a seersucker jacket, a white shirt, and jeans. His white hair was neatly combed.

"I won't ask if this is a bad time," he said. "Mind if I come in?"

His was a welcome face, lined, warm, and sincere, and I nodded. He entered with economical movements, passing through a narrow space that closed quietly behind him. He put his back to the door and clasped his hands in front of his belt. His eyes moved over the kitchen, but it was a brief journey. He spent a little more time on me.

"Where do you keep the glasses?" he asked. He was stately and elegant, perfectly composed. I pointed at the cabinet, still uncertain of my own voice. He moved farther into the kitchen and stopped next to me. I thought he would offer his hand or pat me on the back. Instead, he reached for the newspaper and folded it closed; then he was past. He stepped over the shards of my broken glass and filled two fresh glasses with ice. "You don't have ginger ale, by any chance?" he asked.

"Under the wet bar," I replied, climbing to my feet.

"Sit down, Work. You look whipped." He returned to the table and poured bourbon over ice. "You like ginger ale with bourbon?" he asked.

"Sure. Yes." I remained standing. He was so matter-of-fact that nothing felt quite real. He studied me again as he finished making the drinks.

"Gonna burn your insides out, drinking it straight from the bottle like that." He handed me a glass. "Why don't we try the study?"

We walked through the long foyer and into the study, a small room with dark wood trim, green walls, and twin leather chairs flanking the cold fireplace. I turned on several lamps so that it would not appear so gloomy. Dr. Stokes sat opposite me and sipped his bourbon and ginger.

"I wouldn't have come over had Barbara been here," he said. He turned one palm up. "But . . ."

"She's gone," I said.

"So it would seem."

We drank in silence for a moment or two.

"How's your wife?" I asked, knowing how absurd it sounded under the circumstances.

"She's fine," he answered. "She's playing bridge down the street."

I looked down into the depths of the cold brown liquid that filled my glass. "Was she home when the police were here?"

"Oh yes. She saw the whole thing. Hard to miss, actually. There being so many of them and here for so long." He sipped. "I saw you in your truck, down by the lake. My heart went out to you, boy. I feel bad that I didn't come down, but at the time it seemed like the wrong thing to do."

I smiled at the old gentleman and at his understatement. "I would have been bad company, yes."

"I'm sorry that this is happening, Work. For what it's worth, I don't believe that you did it, not for a second. And I want you to know that if we can do anything to help, all you have to do is ask."

"Thank you, sir."

"We're your friends. We will always be your friends."

I nodded, thankful for the words, and we were silent for a moment.

"Have you ever met my son, William?" Dr. Stokes asked unexpectedly.

"He's a cardiologist in Charlotte. I've met him. But it's been four or five years since I saw him last."

Dr. Stokes looked at me and then down to his own glass. "I love that boy, Work, more than life itself. He is, quite literally, my pride and joy."

"Okay."

"Bear with me, now. I haven't gone senile just yet. There's a story coming, and there's a message in it."

"Okay," I said again, no less puzzled.

"When Marion and I first moved to Salisbury, I was right out of residency at Johns Hopkins, younger than you are now. In many ways, I was a damn idiot, not that I knew it at the time. But I loved medicine. I loved everything about it. And I was eager, you understand, ready to build a practice. All Marion wanted was to start a family. She'd been patient through my residency, but she was as eager for that as I was for my career, and eventually we had our son."

"William," I stated into a sudden silence.

"No," Dr. Stokes finally said. "Not William." He took another sip, draining the glass down to a pale liquid, more melted ice than anything else. "Michael was born on a Friday, at four in the morning." He looked at me. "You never knew Michael. He was way before you were born. We loved that boy. He was a beautiful child." He laughed a bitter laugh. "Of course, I only saw Michael in small increments of time. Dinner a few times a week. An occasional bedtime story. Saturday afternoons in the park down there." He gestured with his head, through the wall, down the hill, to the park we both knew so well. "I was work-ing hard, putting in the hours. I loved him, you know, but I was busy. I had a thriving surgery practice. Responsibilities."

"I understand that," I said, but he may not have heard me. He continued as if he'd not.

"Marion wanted other children, of course, but I said no. I was still paying off med-school debt and barely had time enough for one child as it was. I was just too busy. That's a hard thing for me to say, but there it is. She didn't like it, mind you. But she accepted it."

I watched shadows move on one side of the old man's face as he looked back down, and the way he tilted the glass in his seamed and heavy fingers. How he watched light move through the shifting ice.

"Michael was three and a half years old when he died. It took the cancer seven months to kill him." He looked up at me then, and I saw that his eyes were dry. That didn't prevent the pain from showing through. "You don't need the details of those months, Work. Suffice it to say, they were about as bad as a man could imagine. No one should live through times like that." He shook his head and paused. When he spoke again his voice had waned. "But if Michael had not died, we never would have had William. That's another hard thing to say, and most times I can't look at it straight on, not like it was a trade. Michael is a memory now, an unfulfilled promise; but William is real and he's been that way for almost fifty years. I can't picture what my life would have been. Maybe it would have been better. I'll never know. What I do know is the son I have, and I can't separate that out."

"I don't understand why you're telling me this, Dr. Stokes."

"Don't you?"

"I'm sorry. I'm not thinking very clearly right now."

He leaned forward and placed a hand on my shoulder. I felt the heat of it, and the pull of his weathered, knowing eyes.

"Hell is not eternal, Work. Nor is it devoid of all hope. That's what his death taught me, that you never know what's waiting on the other side. For me, it was William. There'll be something for you, too. All you need is faith."

I considered his words. "I haven't been to church in a long time," I said, and felt the firm grip of his practiced hand as he climbed to his feet and leaned on my shoulder. The light was full on his face when he spoke.

"It doesn't have to be that kind of faith, son."

I walked behind him as we moved back through the house, and I stopped him at the door. "What kind of faith, then?" I asked.

He turned and patted me on the chest, above the heart. "Whatever gets you through," he said.

CHAPTER

20

It was four in the morning, cold and damp. I stared at the hole, a rip in the earth, and a blacker black I'd never seen. Around it the world paled to gray, and I felt naked in that pallid light. I was squatting in weeds at the edge of the parking lot. A steep bracken-covered bank led down to the glint of water, and I heard it gurgle thickly around the storm-swept litter that had collected at the tunnel's mouth. What remained of the mall was a hundred yards away. Like everything, it felt alien in the skeletal light, a crumbled fortress surrounded by dozers and trucks, hard-edged and immovable. I heard distant noise, but here it was hushed. Only the water spoke, and it did so in the tongue of twelve-year-old boys. It said, Come, enter, be afraid.

I'd parked behind the tire store that bordered the mall property. It was closed, of course, but other vehicles were parked there and the truck would arouse no suspicion. I'd dressed for the job, in dark clothes and rubber boots. I carried a bat, and if I'd owned a gun, I'd have been carrying that, too. I also had a heavy flashlight, but the batteries weren't great. I hadn't checked them until I gotten there, and I knew that if I left now for new ones, I might not return. Ever.

From my position, the creek ran diagonally under the parking lot. It passed within a hundred feet of the mall before angling away to Innes Street. The first storm drain was the one I wanted. It was opposite the entrance where Ezra had been found. It was where the gun had been tossed. I knew what was beneath that drain: a concrete shelf that rose like an altar, and a red-eyed memory waiting to unman me.

"Fuck it," I said. "That was a long time ago."

I blundered through the brush, my feet loose and dangerous beneath me. I fell once but was quickly back on my feet, and then I hit the water with a splash that sounded too loud. My face was scratched from the brambles, but I still had the flashlight, still had the bat.

I was committed. I had to move soon. Slim chance or not, a cop could come by at any second. If I was found there, it would be over. Too many questions and not enough answers. So this time the blackness and the tunnel were my friends, a sanctuary, but my breath was loud in the windless space between the high banks.

I'd sworn I'd never go back.

I turned on the light and stooped into the low entrance. It was smaller than I remembered, lower, more narrow. The water came to midshin, and the bottom felt the same, a mixture of rock and deep muck. I shone the light down the length of the tunnel; it stretched away, square and wet, then faded to gloom. There was a lot of old trash and dead branches, and in places I saw narrow tracks of mud that rose from the water like alligator backs. I ran my fingers along the wall. The concrete was slick and wet. I remembered it vividly, and thought of blood, tears, and screams. I tapped the bat against the wall and walked on.

After two dozen steps, the tunnel mouth was a dull metal square, like a quarter I'd put on the tracks as a kid and pulled from the gravel after the train had passed. Twenty more and even that was gone. I was deep in the throat, but my breathing sounded steady and my heart rate was normal. I felt strong, and realized that I should have done this years ago. It was free therapy, and part of me wanted to find the bastard that had damn near ruined me. But he was gone. He had to be.

I pushed on, and each step took me further from those childhood terrors. But when I reached the shelf beneath the drain, it was bare. No gun. For a moment, I didn't care. In the cone of weak yellow light, the shelf was stained, as if by blood, and I stared, seeing a past that rose like an apparition, sudden, vicious, and so real, I could touch it. And I lived it again—the fear, the pain, all of it. But this time it wasn't about me. It was about her, and that's what I saw—the sticky blood that had looked black on her thighs, her battered eyes, and the brief blue glimmer as she'd thanked me.

Dear God. Thanked me.

I grew dizzy, and then my hands were on the concrete, my fingers clawing as if to gouge out the past. But it was just concrete, and my fingers merely flesh. I thought of a child on a playground, yelling for a do-over. But this wasn't childhood, and there were no do-overs. So I put it behind me, shoved it. Done is done.

I set the flashlight on the shelf and wiped at my mouth with the back of my sleeve. I plunged my hands into the water and felt along the bottom, my search becoming increasingly frantic. I found lots of mud and plenty of rocks, but no gun. The light flickered. I saw movement in the line where light met dark, a rat. Two of them, one crouched against the wall, one swimming against the current.

I dropped to my knees and widened the search. It had to be there! If it had entered the water, it shouldn't have gone far. There wasn't much current. But I thought about storms, and the heavy runoff that carried trash and dead branches so far into the tunnel. Could it carry a gun, too? Sweep it away?

I rocked back on my heels, shone the light down the tunnel; it ran for half a mile before exiting on the other side of the lot. A long way.

I looked for the rats. One was gone. The other seemed to watch me with something like contempt.

Maybe Max was wrong. Maybe this wasn't the right storm drain. Maybe the gun wasn't here at all. Someone might have found it. If I were looking for a place to smoke crack, this would be as good as any. People must find their way into this place from time to time.

I shone the light into the water, searched all around the concrete slab.

Nothing.

I sat on the slab, beaten, breathing hard, and the light flickered again. I didn't care. Let it go out. Leave me blind. The tunnel held no terror for me now. My demons were in the past and needed no substance to harm me. I leaned against the cold wet wall and splayed my fingers where Vanessa had lain. Did this place remember?

I shone the light on the walls around me, doubting it. It was just a place and had no need for memory. Then I looked up. It took a second for it to register, but when it did, I felt new hope. The storm drain did not empty straight into the tunnel; there was another ledge, three feet wide and half again as high, near the roof of the tunnel. It looked deep.

I clambered onto the slab, dirty, dripping, bent almost double. It was more than a ledge. It was another small tunnel. It ran back from the wall for three or four feet. I saw light from the storm drain at the end of it. The space was choked with debris: twigs, dried vegetation, litter. I reached in and began to pull it out; it rained around my legs, onto the slab and into the creek. I pulled out more and more. Faster. Frantically. I could not quite reach the very back. I strained harder, my face crushed into the concrete, tendons stretched. My mouth opened as I pushed. Then I felt something hard. My fingers scraped it, drew it closer. They seized it, knew it for what it was and ripped it out. It was a gun. Max was right.

I hunkered down onto the slab, a primitive man. I put the light onto the gun, knew right away that it was *the* gun, Ezra's gun. He'd never allowed me to handle it, not even to touch it, but I'd known it since childhood. Having seen it shoved into my mother's face, how could I ever forget it? It was a stainless-steel Smith & Wesson, with a custom pearl grip. Set into the pearl was a silver medallion, my father's initials carved into the metal. He'd been very proud of it, a rich man's gun, and it confirmed what I'd known for so long.

Jean had known where he kept the gun.

I cracked the cylinder: six shells, two of them spent. I saw the tiny divots made by the firing pin. Such small marks, I thought, touching them, to make such an enormous hole in my universe. I turned the pistol over. It was heavy, dull, and dirty. I didn't doubt that it would fire if I pulled the trigger. For a moment, I held the image in my mind, unable to deny the simple elegance of such an act, of my suicide, here of all places.

I snapped the cylinder closed, and for an instant the reality of my discovery overwhelmed me. This was the instrument of my father's death, the last thing he'd seen on earth. My fingers ached around the hard metal as I tried to picture my father's eyes. Had they begged? Held contempt? Or had they final!y shown some kind of love? What had he made of the fate that brought his daughter to use his own gun against him? Had he accepted responsibility, or had he been dismissive even at the very end? I ran my fingers over the cylinder. I knew the answer and it pained me. Jean lived with his contempt; it was all he'd ever had for her—her birthright and her dark inheritance.

What a shame. What a horrible, fucking shame.

Suddenly, I needed to get the hell out, away from the rats, the smells, and the memories. I had to get rid of the gun and figure out my next step. But first I used a bandanna to wipe the gun down. I opened it up again and wiped down the inner workings. I extracted every shell and wiped them down, too. I'd known people to fry for failing to do that. Then I reloaded it and wrapped it in the bandanna.

If the cops found me with the gun, Jean would be clear. In that, at least, I'd achieved something, but it wasn't enough, not yet.

I took one last look around that dismal place, then turned my back on it. I expected to feel something as I left, but there was nothing, just the echo of footsteps that carried me back to fresh air and to the moon, which made the world seem more than what it was. And in that silver place, between high banks that felt like walls, I wanted to kneel and give some kind of thanks, but did not. Instead, I climbed up, through the thorns, until I stood on top of the tunnel, above it, and the water's voice was a whisper I could barely hear.

CHAPTER
21

So it had come to this. I had the murder weapon in my hand, an accomplice after the fact. I was dirty, wet, and bloody, scared that the cops would find me before I did what I had to do. It was a bad place to be. I wasn't a wanted man yet, but I felt the noose and knew that it was only a matter of time. Five days had passed since they'd found my father's body, a lifetime in which I'd learned a few things about living, stuff the old man should have taught me. He used to say that everybody's got snakes to kill, and I thought I knew what he meant. But a man can't kill his snakes without opening his eyes to see them, a truth he forgot to mention.

I was alone on the bridge, five miles outside of town. The sun was almost up, and I could hear the river. It sounded resolute, and I leaned over the guardrail as if I could draw upon its strength. My fingers explored the pistol, and I thought of Jean, of what it must have been like for her to pull the trigger, to walk away, to try to go on. I finally understood her suicide attempts, and I wished I could tell her that. For in my own way, I'd traveled the same sad road. What before had seemed insane now made perfect sense. Oblivion. Release. I got it, the seduction and tender mercy embodied in those words. After all, what did I have to lose? A career I cared about? Family? The love of a woman I loved in return? Only the unbearable nearness of Vanessa, and the belief that it could have been something great.

If I had anything, it was Jean. She was the last of my family, and in this alone could I do something good for her. If I killed myself, here with this gun, they would blame me for Ezra's death. Case closed. Maybe then she could find some kind of peace; leave Salisbury and go to a place where the ghosts of loved ones lost haunted others but not her. Would that I could do the same with Vanessa.

But that would never happen. She had moved on, and rightly so. So to hell with it. One moment of courage.

I cocked the pistol, and there was finality in the sound of it.

Did I come to here to do this thing? No. I'd come to ditch the gun, make sure that it was never found and used against Jean. But it felt right, the thought of an ending. A single moment, a flash of pain perhaps, and Jean would be free of everything. Mills would have her pound of flesh, and my life, at the end, would serve some kind of purpose.

I stared over the river, watched new light touch the fog on the water and give it depth. A golden rim of sun appeared above the trees, my last, and I stared as it seemed to leap skyward. The world sprung into stark clarity, and I saw so very much of it: the green fields, the dark trees, and the muddy snake of river that steamed as if it, too, was being consumed.

I put the barrel under my chin, pressed it there, and sought the strength to pull the trigger, sought it in a wave of faces. Saw my mother as the floor fell away beneath her. Jean, crushed, and how she'd damned me for making Ezra's truth my own. I saw her face at the funeral, the disgust when I'd tried to take her hand. Then Vanessa — beaten senseless and fucked like an animal in the stinking mud. And shame so absolute that even now it poisoned me. It had driven Vanessa away, and I'd allowed it. That was the worst, and in a burst of resolute self-loathing, I found the strength I sought. The trigger moved under a finger that seemed to burn, and I pushed the gun so hard against my chin that it forced my head up. I opened my eyes to look again at the sky. It curved above me like the hand of God, and held therein a single hawk, wings spread and motionless. It seemed to hover, but it cared nothing for me. It circled, and I watched it. Then it cried once and flew off, and I knew that I could not pull the trigger.

The gun spun away; it hung from my finger, and in the silence the tears finally came. They burned down my cheeks, fell into the pool of my lap, and I did not look up as I dropped the gun into the river below. I knelt as my shoulders shook and I put my forehead on the cold metal rail. At first, I cried for the memories and for the failures, for all that should have been yet was not, but as the seconds slipped around me, they brought a great and terrible truth. I was alive, and I wept for that life. It was all that I had left, and so the tears came for it. Not for joy's sake, but for existence, for this breath that even now burned my lungs, and for the many times that I would look at the sky and remember.

And so I left the river. I felt new strength, a determination—something that felt like hope. I realized as I drove what had happened. I'd hit bottom again, and this time I'd bounced. I was not alive from a lack of courage, but from the sudden discovery of it. I could have pulled the trigger but did not. Why? Because life was not perfect and never would be. Max was right about that.

So I went home. I stopped at the bottom of the driveway and checked the mailbox. The picture of Alex that I'd left for Hank was gone, so he must have come at some point. In a way, I was glad to have missed him; I'd heard the mistrust in his voice and could not bear to see it in his eyes. Later, maybe, but now I was used up.

Exhaustion settled on me as I entered the kitchen. I could barely pull off my boots, and I could tell that the house was empty, not that I'd expected anything different. I wanted food and needed coffee, but the chair felt too good. So I sat at the small desk where Barbara spent so much of her day, writing small notes and talking to her friends on the telephone. I could almost feel her there, her smell and her practiced laugh of quiet amusement. I put my feet on the desk. My pants were damp and muddy, and they smeared her stationery. I sat like that for a long time, staring at the blinking red eye of the answering machine. Eventually, I pushed the button, and the machine's mechanical voice informed me that I had seventeen messages.

Thirteen were from reporters. I erased them. One was from Hank, confirming that he'd picked up the photo, and three were from Barbara. In the first, she was pleasant. In the second, she was polite. But in her last message, she was angry. She didn't shout, but I recognized the controlled, clipped tones. Where was I? That was the question, and I knew what she imagined. I was at Vanessa's.

I erased hers, too, and looked at my watch. It was 6:30, a new day. Sleep was impossible, so I went to put on some coffee. I had the pot in my hand, under the faucet, when the phone rang. I let the machine get it. By the time Barbara's outgoing message had played, I'd shut off the water and turned for the coffee machine. I froze when I heard Jean's voice. It was weak and strained, worse than before.

"Work, are you there?" A broken voice. "Work, please . . ." She coughed.

I dropped the pot in the sink and it shattered. I snatched up the phone. "I'm here, Jean. Don't hang up."

"Good," she said, and I could barely hear her. "Good. I wanted . . ." She began to cough. "I wanted to tell you . . ."

"Jean. What? I can't hear you. Where are you?"

". . . tell you that it's okay. That I forgive you. Will you remember that?"

"Jean," I shouted, suddenly frantic. "Where are you? Are you okay?"

For a time, there was only my voice and the sound of her breath, and when I spoke again, I begged her, "Please. Tell me what's going on."

"Tell me that you'll remember. I need to hear it."

I answered, not knowing why, knowing only that she needed to hear it and that I needed to say it.

"I'll remember."

"I love you, Work," she said, and I could barely hear her. "Don't let Alex tell you different." Her voice trailed away, then came back, seemingly stronger. "We were always family. Even when I hated you."

I knew then what she had done and I couldn't bear it.

Then her voice again, the barest whisper. "It should have meant more. I should have . . ."

"Jean!" I shouted. "For God's sake!"

I thought she'd hung up, for after my explosion there was only silence, but then I heard her, a thin wheeze that became a faint laugh, like wind through grass.

"That's funny," she said. "God." Then she inhaled. "I'll tell him."

I heard the phone drop from her hand and hit the floor, and then her voice, as if from a distance. "For God's sake," she said, but she was no longer laughing.

"Jean!" I screamed. "Jean!" But she did not respond, and those horrible words chased again through my head: *Third time is the charm.*

I put the phone down but kept the line open. I called 911 with my cell phone, told the dispatcher what had happened, and gave her Jean's address. She assured me that she would send EMT immediately, and I hung up. Then I dialed Jean's house, but the line was busy. That's where she was.

I pulled on the same muddy boots, grabbed my keys, and flew out the door. The truck was not built for the way I drove it, but there was no traffic yet and I beat the ambulance to her house. Loose boards vibrated beneath my feet as I crossed her porch at a run. I pounded on the door, shouting for Alex, but nothing happened. A dog barked at me from across the street. I aimed for the spot between the handle and the frame and I kicked the door. Wood splintered and I was inside, in the dark and the must, calling for Jean, shouting her name. Suddenly, Alex was there, framed in the bedroom door. She wore boxer shorts and a T-shirt, and her hair stood up in spikes. I could tell she'd just awakened.

"Where's Jean?" I demanded.

"What the fuck are you doing?" she yelled back. "Did you just break in my door?"

I crossed the room in three strides, grabbed Alex by the shoulders, and shook her so hard, I heard her teeth click.

"Where's Jean, Alex? Where is she?"

Alex tore away from me, stepped back to the bedroom door, and reappeared with a gun in her hand. She cocked the hammer, pointed it at me.

"Get the fuck out of my house, Work, before I put a hole in you."

I ignored it. For me the gun was inconsequential, like I'd never seen one before. "Damn it, Alex. Something's wrong with Jean. She called me. She's hurt. Where is she?"

My words found their way through her rage and the gun wavered. "What are you talking about?"

"I think she's trying to kill herself."

Uncertainty showed on her face. Her eyes darted around the house. "I don't know," she said. "She's not in bed."

"What do you mean? Come on, Alex."

"I don't know. I was asleep. You woke me up. She's not in bed."

"Your phone is off the hook. She has to be here."

"We take it off the hook every night."

I glared around the small house. There was only the bedroom, the kitchen, the bathroom, and the room we were standing in. I checked all the rooms, but Jean was not in any of them.

"Her car," I said, running to the kitchen window and throwing back the dusty curtain. But there was only Alex's car, the roots that rose from the bare dirt, and the oily stain where Jean's car should have been.

"Damn! It's not here." I went back to Alex, saw that her gun was on top of the television. "Where would she be? Think, Alex."

But she was at a loss, and stood uncertainly, shaking her head and muttering to herself. "She wouldn't do that. She wouldn't leave me." Alex reached out for my arm, and her eyes were fierce. Her voice steadied. "Not Jean. Not without me."

"Well here's a news flash. She did. Now where would she go?"

Alex started to shake her head, when suddenly it hit me, and I knew with absolute clarity where my sister had gone.

"Does Jean have a cell phone?" I asked.

"Yes."

"Oh my God. She's at Ezra's house."

"How do you know?"

"I just do." I turned for the door, my mind racing. "Do you know Ezra's address?"

"Yes."

"Call 911, give it to them."

"Then what?"

"Stay here, in case the ambulance shows up. If they do, then lead them to Ezra's."

"No," Alex said. "She needs me. I should be there."

"Not this time."

"You can't stop me, Work."

I turned at the door. "She called me, Alex. Not you."

Alex shrank under the words, but I took no satisfaction from the pain they caused her. Nevertheless, I had one more thing to say.

"I warned you, Alex. I told you she needed help, and I'm holding you responsible."

Then I was out the door and sprinting for the truck. My father's house was only a couple of miles away, but the roads were filling with cars. I passed three on a solid yellow line, going eighty in a thirty-five. I caught air over the tracks, then went the wrong way down a one-way street but shaved two blocks off the trip. I fishtailed into the driveway, clipped one of the box bushes, and stopped behind Jean's car. I hit the back door at a run and bounced off it. It was locked. Damn! I fumbled for my keys, realized I'd left them in the truck, and had to run back for them. But then I had the key in the door and it moved under my weight. I was inside, shouting, turning on lights. Her name echoed off marble floors, ran down paneled halls, and returned as if to haunt me; otherwise, the house wept with silence.

I moved as fast as I could: the kitchen, the study, the billiards room. It was a big house, and it had never seemed more so. She could be anywhere, I realized, and I thought of the bed upstairs; but then I knew, and I ran for the foyer. I rounded the corner and saw her at the foot of the stairs. She was unmoving, ashen, the rug beneath her sopping with blood.

I hit the floor beside her, my knees squelching in her blood. Her wrists had been opened with long vertical cuts, and I saw the razor blade, bright and red on the carpet.

Blood still pulsed weakly from the cuts, and I called her name. No response. I ripped off her shoes, pulled out the laces, and tied them around her arms, jerking them tight just above the cuts. The blood flow ceased, and I checked her pulse, feeling for the big vein beneath her jaw. I couldn't find it. I pushed harder, touched it. The pulse was hesitant, feeble, but it existed, and I thanked God under my breath. But I didn't know what else to do; I had no training. So I crossed her arms on her chest, tried to elevate them, then put her head in my lap and held her as best I could.

I studied her face, looking for a reason to hope, but it was bloodless and as pale as bone china. Blue veins showed through the skin of her closed eyelids, and they looked bruised. Her mouth hung loosely and I saw where she'd bitten down, bright red moons on her cracked lips. Her face was slack and her features sagged, but she was the same Jean, my sister. We used to laugh, damn it, and I swore then that I would make it better if she lived. Somehow I would do that, because it couldn't end like this. Not for her.

I stroked the hair from her face and talked to her. My words had no meaning beyond apology; they blurred, ran into the minutes that stretched away like hours, and later I could never recall them, although I might have begged her to please not leave me alone.

Then there was noise around me, the clatter of a gurney and calm, efficient voices. Hands were upon me and I did not know them, but they led me away and steadied me so that I could see. Jean was surrounded by men in white, and they moved over her, binding her wrists, slipping a needle into her arm, and covering her so that the last of her warmth should not escape. Someone asked me if the tourniquets were mine and I nodded. "Probably saved her life," the man told me. "A close thing."

I covered my face with my hands and dared to trust that she would live. When I looked up, Alex was there. She met my eyes over the stillness of her lover, and her old pride was back, her anger and her strength, but in that moment we shared the same thought: If Jean lived, it would be because of me, and Alex acknowledged that fact with her eyes and with fingers that fluttered before her mouth, as if to stop words that she could not take back. But I nodded nonetheless and she nodded back.

Then Jean was on the gurney and it took her from this place she'd chosen. For a moment, I was alone with Alex, and she came to where I sat slumped against the wall. Her jaw moved beneath sealed lips and her hands were fists, beating the tops of her thighs as she sought for words.

"Will you go to the hospital?" she finally asked.

"Yes. You?"

"Of course."

I nodded, looked down, and noticed that her feet were bare. She shifted her weight from one foot to the other.

"Do you think she'll be okay?" she asked.

I thought about the question. "I think she'll live," I said. "The paramedics think so." I paused, studied her face, saw that she'd been crying. "Do you think she'll be okay? I mean . . . well, you know what I mean."

"She's strong," Alex said. "Strong enough, I thought. But now I don't know. I feel like I don't know anything. I always thought . . . We always said . . ."

Her voice trailed away and she wiped at her nose. I thought of something she'd said back at Jean's house, and I understood, but the understanding left me chilled.

"You always said you'd go together? Is that it?"

Alex stepped back as if struck, and I saw that she'd left a bloody footprint on the hardwood floor, a perfect little foot. I could even see the lines.

I told her what was on my mind. " 'Not without me.' That's what you said."

"What?" Her voice was loud, and I knew that I was right.

" 'She wouldn't do that. . . . Not without me.' Those were your words. I want to know what they mean."

I climbed to my feet, growing angry. "Did you talk about this? Doing it together? Is that what you meant?"

"No." Another step back.

"Is that the kind of help you've been giving her? Is it?" A shout. "Then it's a miracle she's alive at all, and no damn wonder that she called me instead of you."

Alex stopped moving, and there was a sudden resoluteness in the way she stood and in the tone of her voice. She was no longer defensive, but upset herself, pissed-off—the Alex I knew so well.

"It wasn't like that," she said.

"It was a call for help, Alex, and she called me. Why did she do that? Why not you?"

"You couldn't possibly know how it was, and you could never understand. Don't flatter yourself. You're all the same."

"Who?" I demanded. "Men? Heterosexuals?"

"Pickens men," Alex replied. "All men. Take your pick. But mostly you and your damn father."

"Try me," I said. "Explain it to me."

"You have no right to judge us."

My voice rose and I let it. I was furious. I was scared. And I could not bear the comparison she'd made. I pointed at the empty door, toward the hall through which they'd rolled my sister to the ambulance.

"I do have the right," I shouted. "Goddamn you, Alex. I do. She just gave it to me, and you can't change that. If Jean lives—and you should pray that she does—then we'll see who has the right. Because if so, I'm going to have her committed, so that she can get the help she needs."

"If you're around," Alex said, and her eyes glittered with insect intensity.

"Are you threatening me?" I asked.

Alex shrugged, and her features dropped. "I'm just saying it seems like you've got other worries, other things to occupy your mind."

"What are you implying?"

"I'm not implying anything. I'm stating the obvious. Now, if you're finished with your tirade, I'm going to the hospital to be with Jean. But remember this." She stepped closer. "You have never had power over me, never, and as long as I'm around, you'll never have power over Jean, either."

I looked at Alex, at her bottled rage, and felt my own fall away. How had we come to this?

"She said that she loves me, Alex. In spite of everything, she still loves her big brother. So, you see, I don't need power over her. I don't want it. She called me and I saved her life. Just like I did before she met you. Think on that. Then let's figure out what we can do to help this person we both love so much."

If I'd expected Alex to back down, I should have known better.

"That's not what I meant, Work, and you know it. Stop being such a fucking lawyer."

She turned and left, her bare feet soundless as she fled the truth. I heard the door slam, the muffled sound of her car, and then I was truly alone in the great house I'd known for so long. I looked at the rug spread beneath the stairs, the lake of blood that filled the space with its own peculiar scent. Footprints led away from it, and tracks from the gurney, growing lighter, transparent, and then disappearing altogether. I saw Jean's cell phone and picked it up. I held it, studied the dried blood on it, and then placed it on the small table by the door.

I told myself I should go to the hospital, but I knew from bitter experience that Jean would live or die whether I was there or not; and I was so tired, so unable to deal with Alex again. I thought of the big bed upstairs, pictured myself on its snowy sheets; I wanted to roll into them, touch their cleanness, and pretend that I was a child again and had no worries. But I could not; I was not that person anymore, not a child and not a deceiver. So I lay down on the carpet, next to the drying wasteland of my sister's life.

CHAPTER

22

At the hospital, they told me that she would live. If I'd been a minute later, she would not have. That's how thin the margin was, around seventy heartbeats. They would allow only one visitor at a time, so I had the nurse ask Alex for five minutes. We passed each other in the hall outside Jean's room and both of us tried to be nice. It was awkward, and we looked like victims in the bright, clean light.

"How is she?" I asked.

"They say she'll make it."

"Brain damage?"

Alex shook her head, pushed her hands farther into the pockets of her grubby jeans. I saw where Jean's blood had dried between her toes. "They don't think so, but they won't swear to it."

"They sound like lawyers," I said, but Alex did not smile.

"Yeah."

"Has she regained consciousness?"

"No."

"Listen, Alex. When Jean wakes up, she'll need to see people who care about her, not people who hate each other. I'd like to give her that."

"You mean fake it."

"Yes."

"I'll do it for Jean, but the line's been drawn for us. Don't let my act fool you. You're bad for her, even if she doesn't see it that way."

"All I care about is getting her better, and I want her to know that people love her."

Alex looked down the hall, away from Jean and from me. "I'm going for coffee. I'll be ten minutes."

"Okay. Thanks."

She took two steps and turned. "I wouldn't have shot you," she said.

Her statement surprised me. Until then, I'd forgotten all about the gun in her hand and how steady it had seemed. "Thank you," I said.

"I just wanted you to know that."

Jean's hospital room was exactly like every other one in which she'd awakened after a failed suicide attempt. The bed was narrow and mean, with steel rails, stiff sheets, and a bright spread that somehow appeared colorless. Tubes snaked into her body, green in the light of her monitors, and the curtains were drawn. I walked around her bed and opened them. The morning light was warm, and in it Jean looked like a wax figure, pallid and incomplete. I wanted to mold her into something else, a survivor; but I lacked that qualification, and could still feel the barrel under my own chin. Only then did it occur to me how close we both had come, and standing above her, I tried to make sense of it all. I knew only that we lived, an immense but lonely truth. I sat and took her hand. When I looked at her face, I found her eyes open and watching me. Her lips moved, and I leaned closer.

"Am I alive?" she asked in a whisper.

"Yes," I answered in a cracked voice. "You are." I bit down on my lip. She was so weak. "It was a close thing."

She turned her head away from me, but not before I saw tears slip from beneath her tightly shut eyes. When Alex returned, she was asleep again, and I left without saying a word about it. Maybe I was selfish. I didn't care.

I leaned against the wall in the corridor for what felt like a long time. Before I left, I looked into the room, through the small window with wire in the glass. The curtains were pulled again, and Alex sat where I had, holding Jean's hand. Jean had not moved; she faced the wall, and I wondered if she was still asleep. Would she turn from Alex as she had from me? Or was Alex truly her life, whereas I was welcome only at the ending of it?

I almost left, but I saw Jean move; she turned, saw Alex, and covered her face with her hands. Alex said something and Jean began to tremble, the tubes dancing beneath her forearms. Then Alex was on her feet, leaning over her; she pressed her face to Jean's and they both grew still. So I left, an unwelcome member of our sad little family.

I had the elevator to myself, but when it opened into the lobby, I saw Detective Mills standing by the exit. She was looking out the window, but I knew she was waiting for me. I walked toward her and saw a marked patrol car idling at the curb. A uniformed officer leaned on the hood, his hand on the butt of his pistol. He was young and looked eager.

"Are you here for me?" I asked. Mills turned at the sound of my voice and studied me. I was bloodstained and filthy. Next to me, she looked every inch the instrument of justice; her shoes shone and I could still see the crease in her pants. When she spoke, I smelled her mouthwash.

"I am," she said.

"What about him?" I gestured at the young cop outside. Mills shrugged but did not respond.

"Cheap theatrics," I said. "There's no need."

Outside, the cop got into his cruiser and left. He did not look at Mills or at me. Mills watched him drive away before she turned back to me.

"A little jumpy, aren't you, Work?"

"Whatever."

She smiled. "I never said he was with me."

"How did you find me?" I asked.

"I heard about your sister," she said. "I figured you'd be here."

"Thanks for your consideration." I couldn't keep the bitterness from my voice.

"Your sarcasm isn't necessary."

"I'm not in the mood for you, Detective. Not this morning. Not in this hospital. So if you'll excuse me."

I stepped around her, walked through the exit and into the parking lot. The morning had warmed and the sky was clear and blue. Traffic was loud from the road beyond the manicured hedge, and people moved around me, but I felt Mills behind me. She wore heels, and her footsteps were loud and fast. I knew she wouldn't let me off the hook that easily, so I spun around to confront her.

"What do you want, Detective?"

She stopped a few feet away from me, a safe distance, and I saw the pistol butt hanging from beneath her jacket. She gave me the same cold smile.

"I hoped we might have a chance to talk. There are some things I need to discuss. Maybe there are some things you'd like to say. Either way, I've got nothing better to do right now."

"I do," I said, and turned.

"What happened to your face?" Mills asked.

"What?" I turned back.

"Your face. It's cut."

My fingers moved to my face as if guilty of some sin. "Scratches," I said. "Just scratches."

"How'd you get 'em?" Mills asked lightly.

"I went for a walk in the woods."

She looked away and nodded. "Is that where you got so muddy?" she asked.

"Is there some point to this?"

"Why were you in the woods?"

"I was burying bodies."

"More sarcasm," Mills noted disapprovingly.

This time, I shrugged.

"Maybe we should have this discussion at the station."

"The station," I repeated flatly.

Mills looked around the parking lot and up at the scrubbed blue sky as if she found it all slightly distasteful. When her eyes settled back on me, the expression remained.

"It might be more productive," she said.

"Do you have an arrest warrant?" I asked. Mills shook her head. "Then the answer is no."

"So you claim you've never seen your father's will?"

The sudden question threw me; it was unexpected, and a veil dropped over her face as she posed it. I sensed danger. "Why do you ask?"

Mills shrugged. "It's what you told me before. I just want to make sure that all my facts are straight. You said that you'd never seen the will, knew nothing of its contents. Is that about right?"

I knew what she wanted. Knowledge of the will meant motive, and alarm bells started ringing in the back of my head. Cops were like lawyers. The best questions were the ones to which they already knew the answer.

"I'm not prepared to discuss this. My sister just tried to kill herself. I'm still covered in her blood. Does this make sense to you?"

"I just want the truth, Work. Like everybody else."

190

"I know what you want, Detective."

She ignored my hostility. "Is that right?"

"If you want the truth, then why don't you look into the mall foreclosure? There were millions at stake there, too—angry investors, and my father in the middle of it. For Christ's sake, he was killed in the damn mall. Or is that not relevant to you?"

Mills frowned. "I didn't know that you were aware of that."

"There may be other things of which you're unaware. Are you looking into it or not? Do you even know who the investors are?"

"I'll run this investigation as I see fit."

"Obviously."

"Don't get smart with me, Work. It's not worth it."

"Then take your blinders off and do your job!"

Her voice dropped. "Your father was just the messenger. Killing him wouldn't stop the foreclosure. You're a lawyer. You know that."

"Murder is rarely cold-blooded; people kill in emotional states. Hate, anger, revenge, lust. If you don't know the players, how can you rule it out? There could be a thousand other reasons out there."

"You forgot one," Mills said.

"What?"

"Greed," Mills said.

"Are we done?" I demanded.

"Yeah. For now."

"Good," I said. "I need a bath." I turned away.

"Don't leave town," Mills called after me. I spun on my heels and stalked back to her.

"Don't play your little power games with me, Detective. I know the system, too. Arrest me or don't, but until you do, I'll come and go as I please."

Something glinted in her eyes, but she said nothing; so I walked to my truck and slammed the door against Mills and all she represented. The small space stank of mud, gasoline, and blood, yet the smell of her sickly sweet mouthwash overrode it all. I cranked the engine and drove out of the parking lot. I turned toward home, not realizing until I was almost there that Mills was behind me. I got her point: I could come and go as I pleased, but the last word was hers.

I parked at the top of my driveway and climbed out. Mills had stopped on the street, next to my mailbox. She honked twice and pulled away, but she didn't leave; she drove around the block and parked on the side street next to the lake. I saw her and she saw me, and that's how it was until I went inside.

In the kitchen, I gripped the counter until my arms shook, and anger made the room tremble. When I let go, the last of my strength had fled. In my body I was dead, yet my mind had resolved on a single purpose. Right or wrong, good or bad, I knew what I needed.

The phone was warm against my ear and for an instant I felt her beating heart, as if my head were on her chest. I sat on the floor and dialed her number. It rang, and I could hear it, as if I were there instead of in my own home—shrill in the kitchen, soft in the hall. I pictured her rushing to answer it, across the front porch, screen door banging, the smell of turned earth and the soap she used. I saw the curve of her lips as they crafted my name. But she never came, just her voice on the machine, and it was not the same. Not even close. I could not bring myself to leave a message.

So I replaced the phone on its cradle and climbed wearily up from the floor. I spent half an hour in the shower but could not get warm. When I ran out of hot water, I toweled off and climbed into bed. I thought I was too scared to sleep. I was wrong.

I dreamed in black and white, of shadows on the floor that stretched like bars across bare feet. My toes were dark with blood; I was running, in pain, and the shadows spun across me as if a giant fan stood between the sun and me. Light, then dark, faster and faster, and then there was only dark. I stopped running. I was blind. I was deaf. But still I felt it. Something approached.

"Hello, Barbara," I said without turning over.

"It's three o'clock," she said.

"I didn't sleep much last night," I told her.

"I know," Barbara said.

Reluctantly, I turned. She was wearing a pink Chanel suit with a pillbox hat. Her face was perfect, but the diagonal light cut tiny shadows at the corners of her mouth.

"How do you know?" I asked.

She put her purse on the dresser and began switching on lights. She moved as she spoke, as if she did not want me to see her face.

"When you didn't pick up the phone, I came over. At about four o'clock, I should say. I was worried. I felt bad that I was not here for you." She turned on the last light and stood uncertainly, smoothing her skirt as if it were wrinkled.

She still could not look at me. "You can't imagine how surprised I was to find an empty house."

"Barbara," I began, not knowing what to say.

"I don't want to hear your excuses, Work. I couldn't bear the insult. I can accept that you went to her because I was not here for you; in that regard, I share some of the blame. But I don't want to talk about it, and I don't want you to lie to me about it. You're not that good a liar."

I propped myself against the headboard. "Sit down, Barbara." I patted the bed beside me.

"Just because I'm talking to you doesn't mean that I've forgiven you. I'm here to tell you how things are going to be, so that we can get through this as an intact family unit. First, I don't think you killed your father."

I interrupted. "Well, thank you for that."

"I wasn't being sarcastic. Please let me finish."

"Okay, Barbara. Go ahead."

"You will not see this Vanessa person again, and I will stay here and help you get through this. Whatever has to be faced, we will face together. I will swear with my dying breath that you were with me when they say Ezra was killed." She finally looked at me. A strange light burned in her eyes, and her voice, when she continued, was as brittle and hard as shale. "We will smile at our neighbors. We will not hide as if in shame. When people ask how we are, we shall tell them. Splendid. We are splendid. I will cook for you and eventually I will sleep with you. All this will pass, and when it does, we will still have to live in this town."

Her voice had not changed, an unshakable monotone, and I watched her in disbelief as she continued to outline the way it was going to be.

"We'll stay in for the most part, but occasionally we'll go out, for appearances' sake. Everything will be as it always was. Glena has made some calls. Things are bad, but they'll get better. Once this blows over, we'll be okay."

"Barbara," I said.

"No," she shouted. "You do not interrupt me. Not now. Not after this." She pulled herself together, looked down on me, and painted a smile onto her face. "I am offering you a chance, Work. Once this is over, we can go back."

"Back to what?" I asked.

"To normalcy."

She chose that moment to sit and place a hand upon my leg. I started to laugh, a shabby noise, devoid of even rudimentary joy. I sounded crazy, even to myself, and I watched as if from behind plate glass as Barbara recoiled in confusion.

"'Normalcy,'" I parroted. "Our old life. That's no gift, Barbara. Or are you too wired into the program to even see that?"

She stood. "What are you saying?"

I climbed slowly from the bed, naked and not quite myself. I looked at this woman, this wife of mine. I thought of our past, felt the emptiness of our shallow joys and trivial dreams. I put my hands on her shoulders.

"There are few things that I know right now, and one of them is this. I'll never go back to the way things were." I thought of the shadow bars from my dream. "It's just another kind of prison." I stepped back and my hands fell to my side. Barbara's mouth hung open, then snapped shut. I looked down at myself. "I'm going to find some clothes," I said, and walked past her. She followed me into the bathroom.

"It's her, isn't it?"

"Who?"

"That bitch has already turned you against me."

I turned and said coldly, "To which bitch are you referring?"

"Don't play games with me. I won't be made a laughingstock and I won't lose you to some inbred country slut."

"I don't know anybody that matches that description, and if I did, this would have nothing to do with her. This is about me! This is about us! About choices and priorities. It's about opening your fucking eyes and seeing the truth we're drowning in! Our life is a joke. We are a joke. Can't you see that? Can't you admit it, even to yourself? We're together out of habit, because we can't admit the mistake we made and because the truth is too damn hard."

"Truth!" she said. "You want truth? Well, here it is. You think you don't need me anymore. All this money's coming your way, so now you can go and run off with your little country whore."

"What money?"

"That's funny, Work. We live in poverty for ten years and now that the end is around the corner, I'm not good enough for you. I read the papers. I know about the fifteen million that Ezra left you."

I laughed at the absurdity of it. "First of all, only you could think that we've been living in poverty, and never mind that I've given you every dime I've ever made. As for Ezra's will, I'll never see any of that money."

"That's right, because I'm your alibi and you're pissing me off."

"I don't want an alibi. I don't need it. Go keep up your own fucking appearances. Leave me out of it."

A crystalline silence fell between us, and I dressed behind her turned back. I was pulling on socks when Barbara spoke again. "I think maybe we both got a little carried away. I don't want to fight and I know that you're very upset. I think maybe you're projecting that onto me, I don't know. Let's just step back a minute."

"Fine," I said. "Whatever." I stuffed my feet into scuffed leather shoes and cinched up my belt.

"Let's just get through this trouble and then we can look at our situation a little more calmly. We've been together a long time. There's got to be a reason for that. I think we're still in love. I feel it. When this is behind us and our money worries are gone, everything will look different."

"There's not going to be any money, Barbara. I'd have to sell my soul for it, sacrifice what's left of my life, and I can't do that. I can't let him have the last laugh."

"What last laugh? Who are you talking about? For Christ's sake, Work. It's fifteen million dollars!"

"It could be a billion, for all I care." I pushed past her. "We can talk later, but I don't know what else there is to say."

"It's just the timing, Work. The situation." She followed me through the house. "Everything fades. You'll see. It'll get better."

I passed through the kitchen, grabbed my keys and my wallet. "I don't think so, Barbara. Not this time." Then I was in the driveway, and she filled the door behind me.

"You're my husband, Work. Don't walk away from me."

I started the engine.

"Goddamn it! You're my fucking husband!"

I drove away, knowing that in one thing my wife was right. Everything fades.

CHAPTER

23

I went to the office because I had to do something. If I didn't do something, I would drink, and if I drank, I would get drunk. The thought appalled me because it was so tempting. But booze was just more rank escapism, like denial and self-deception.

I sat at my desk, ignored the mess, and looked up the number for the medical examiner in Chapel Hill. He was an ex–football player, an ex-smoker, and an ex-husband. He was a good medical examiner and a decent witness on the stand. We'd consulted on several cases and we got along. He wasn't scared of a drink.

His secretary put me through.

"I don't know if I should be talking to you," he said without preamble. His tone surprised me.

"Why not?"

"We don't exist on some pedestal, you know. We do read the papers."

I knew where he was going. "So?" I asked.

"I can't discuss my findings with you."

"He's my father."

"For God's sake, Work. You're a suspect."

"Look, I know he was shot twice. I know the type of ammunition. I just want to know if there's anything else. Anything unusual."

"We go back a ways. I'll admit that. But you're putting me in a tough spot. There's nothing I can tell you, not until the lead detective or the district attorney clears it. Damn it, Work! You know better."

"You think I did it."

"What I think is irrelevant."

"You're the medical examiner. Nothing you think is irrelevant in a murder case."

"We're not having this discussion, Work. If this goes to trial, I'll not be sandbagged on the stand by allegations of impropriety. I'm hanging up now."

"Wait," I said.

A pause. "What?"

"I need to make funeral arrangements. When can you release the body?"

There was an even longer pause before he finally spoke. "I'll release the body when I get the paperwork from the DA's office. Same as always." He paused again, and I could tell that something bothered him.

"What is it?" I asked.

"I'd rather release it to your sister," he said slowly. "For the same reasons."

"She's in the hospital," I said. "She tried to kill herself this morning."

"I didn't know that."

"Well, now you do."

A silence stretched between us. He'd met Jean once or twice.

"I'll take it under advisement, Work. Until the paperwork comes. Then we'll see."

"Thanks for a whole lot of nothing," I said.

"I'll make a note of this conversation for the file, and someone from this office will contact you when the paperwork is finalized. Until this is cleared up, I don't want you calling here again."

"What is your problem?"

"Don't jerk me off, Work. Don't play me. I heard about your trip to the crime scene. You played Mills and now she's paying for it. It could cost her the case, maybe her job. I'll not be embarrassed like that and I'll not be manipulated. Not me and not this office. Now, good-bye."

He hung up, and I stared at the phone in my hand. Eventually, I put it down. What had he seen when he closed his eyes, held the phone to his ear, and heard my voice? Not a professional. Not a colleague and not a friend. He'd heard what he'd never heard, there in his rarified office, with the gleaming tables and the rows of silent dead. He'd heard the voice of the violator, the killer who filled his days with chemical smells and cold, unmoving blood. I'd known him for eight years and he thought I did it. I had been judged and found capable. Douglas, Mills, my wife. The whole damn town.

I closed my eyes and saw thin blue lips mouthing words I could not hear but recognized nonetheless. *White trash*, they said. They were a woman's lips, flanked by diamond earrings that sparkled like the sun itself. I saw the lips twist into a mirthless smile. *Poor Barbara. She really should have known better.*

Before I knew what I was doing, I was on my feet. I ripped the phone off the desk and threw it across the room. It struck the wall and cracked apart, leaving a hole the size of my forehead. I wanted to crawl into it and disappear. Instead I climbed to my feet and picked up the pieces of the shattered phone. I could not put them back together, so I dropped them on the floor. I touched the hole in the wall. Everything was coming apart.

I went to my secretary's desk because I couldn't bear the thought of my father's. I called the funeral home. If the mortician felt strange talking to me, it didn't show in his voice. It was liquid and measured, as if poured from one of the glass containers I always imagined filling the basement of his mortuary. Not to worry, he told me. All I needed to provide was a date for the service. Everything else was arranged.

"By whom?" I asked.

"Your father. He provided for everything."

"When?"

The mortician paused, as if speaking of the dead in anything but quiet respect required careful consideration.

"Some time ago," he said.

"What about the casket?"

"Chosen."

"The plot?"

"Chosen."

"The eulogy? The music? The headstone?"

"All provided for by your father," the mortician said. "He was, I assure you, quite thorough in his preparations." He paused. "In all respects, the perfect gentleman and the perfect client. He spared no expense."

"No. He wouldn't."

"Is there any other way in which I might be of assistance to you in this difficult time?"

He had asked that question so many times, I felt the insincerity of it even
through the phone.

"No," I said. "No, thank you."

His voice deepened. "Then may I suggest that you call again? Once things
have settled down. All I require is the date you wish for the service to be held."

"Fine," I said. "I'll do that." I almost hung up, but then I asked the question
that had lurked in my mind for the past minute. "Who did my father choose to
deliver the eulogy?"

The mortician seemed surprised. "Why, you, of course."

"Of course," I said. "He would."

"Will there be anything else?"

"No. Thank you."

I put the phone down and sat in silence. Could I deliver his eulogy? Perhaps. But could I say what he would want me to say? When Ezra made his
choice, I was a different man, his monkey boy and the repository of *his* truth.
Through my words, he would live one more time, and do it so that all present
would remember and be humbled. This is why he'd chosen me, because he
had made me, and because he was sure of his craft. Yet my words were merely
that, and memories dim with time. So he'd created the Ezra Pickens Foundation, through which his name would live in perpetuity. But still that was not
enough, thus the fifteen-million-dollar bribe, to ensure that I would continue
his grand tradition.

I wanted to throw my arms around him, tell him that in some small way I
would always love him, and then beat him half to death. For what is the price
of vanity, or the cost of immortality? A name is just a name, whether it's carved
in flesh or in marble; it can be remembered in many ways, and not all are
good. All we'd wanted was a father, someone who gave a damn.

I rested my head on the desk, on wood that was cool and hard. I turned my
cheek to it and spread out my hands. It made me think of high school. I closed
my eyes, smelled erasers, like singed rubber, and the room melted away. I was
in the past.

It was our first time; I was fifteen, Vanessa was a senior. Rain stuttered on
the tin roof, but the barn at Stolen Farm was dry, and her skin shone palely
in the premature twilight. When lightning flashed, it illuminated the world
outside and sealed us in our private place. We were explorers, and when the

thunder roared, it did so for us, louder each time, keeping pace with our bodies. Below us, in stalls that smelled of straw, horses stamped their hooves as if they knew and approved. I could still smell her. I could hear her voice.

Do you love me?

You know I do.

Say it.

I love you.

Say it again. Keep saying it.

So I did—three syllables, a rhythm, like our bodies had a rhythm. Then her voice was in my ear. It was soft. It said my name, Jackson, again and again, until it filled me, a spirit.

And then it was louder.

I opened my eyes and was back in my office. I looked up and she was there, flesh and blood, in the doorway. I was scared to blink for fear that she might simply vanish.

"Vanessa?"

She wrapped her arms around herself and stepped into the room. She seemed to solidify as she moved, as if she carried some new reality into the one I'd come to loathe. I wiped at my eyes, still fearing the emptiness of vision.

"I thought you might need a friendly face," she said, and her voice passed through me like the ghost of a loved one long dead. I thought of the things she needed to hear—of my wrongness, of my need, and of my sorrow.

But my voice betrayed me and rang harsh in the pregnant stillness. "Where's your new man?" I asked, and her face melted into that of a stranger.

"Don't lash out at me, Jackson. This is hard enough as it is. I almost didn't come."

I found my feet. "I don't know why I said that. I'm sorry. It's none of my business anyway." I paused, looked at her as if she might still disappear. "I'm an idiot, Vanessa. I barely know myself anymore." I reached out with empty hands and she stopped, safe on the other side of the room. I let my arms drop. "I feel transparent. I can't hold on to my thoughts." I pictured the shattered phone, the hole in the wall. "Everything's coming apart." I stopped speaking, but she finished my thought.

"It's been hard."

"Yes."

"It's been hard for me, too," she said, and I saw the truth of her words. The skin was stretched over the bones of her face, pulled tight by her own problems. Her eyes looked hollow and deep, and I saw new lines around her mouth.

"I tried to call you," I said. "No one answered."

She lifted her chin. "I didn't want to talk to you. But then this happened. I thought you might need somebody. I thought . . . maybe . . ."

"You thought right," I said.

"Let me finish. I'm not here to be your girlfriend or your mistress. I'm here to be your friend, because nobody should have to deal with this alone."

I dropped my eyes. "Everybody acts like I did it. People look away from me."

"What about Barbara?" Vanessa asked.

"She's using this against me. A weapon." I looked away. "It's over between us," I said. "I won't go back to her."

"Does she know?" Vanessa asked. She had reason for skepticism; I'd often spoken of leaving Barbara.

I lifted my head, found Vanessa's eyes, and tried to communicate directly through them. I wanted her to know the truth of what I said. "She hasn't accepted it. But she knows it."

"I suppose she blames me?"

"Yes, even though I told her different. She can't accept the truth."

"Ironic," Vanessa said.

"What?"

"Not long ago, I would have welcomed the blame. If it meant we could be together."

"But not now," I said.

"No. Not now."

I wanted to say something to make those words go away, but I was so close to losing her, and the thought of such utter aloneness paralyzed me.

Vanessa's face had paled and her lips made a thin line as she watched me search for words and fail.

"I'm thirty-eight years old," she said. "Almost forty." She walked across the room, confronted me over the desk. "I've only wanted three things in this life, Jackson, just three: the farm, children, and you."

She paled further, as if her blood had suddenly thinned. Her eyes looked enormous. I knew what this was costing her.

"I wanted you to be the father of my children. I wanted us to be a family." A tear escaped and she wiped it away before it could get very far. "I loved you more than I thought a woman could love a man. Since childhood, Jackson.

My entire life. We had what few people ever do; it would have been so right. And then you left me, just like that, after almost ten years. And you married Barbara. That damn near killed me, but I dealt with it. I got over you. But then you started coming around—once a month, twice a month, but I didn't care. You were there, with me again, and that was all that mattered. I knew that you loved me, even when you used me. Then Ezra disappeared, and you came to me that night, the night your mother died. I gave you everything I had. I held you. I poured myself into you, made your pain my own. Do you remember?"

I could barely meet her eyes. "I remember."

"I thought that with Ezra gone you would find yourself again, the boy I fell in love with. I so wanted that. I wanted you to be strong and I thought that you would be, so I waited. But you didn't come. For a year and a half, I didn't hear a word from you, not a sign, and I had to deal with losing you all over again. A year and a half, Jackson! I almost made it, too. But then, you bastard, you came back again, last week, and in spite of everything, I let myself believe. And why not? I asked myself. You felt it. Eighteen months and we still had the same passion, like no time had passed. But it had. I had finally pulled myself together, moved on. I had a life. I was as happy as I'd ever hoped to be. It wasn't bliss, but I could face the day. Then you showed up, out of nowhere, and you tore me apart."

She looked at me and her eyes were dry. "I don't think I can forgive you for that. But it taught me something, an ugly, brutal lesson that I've taken to heart."

"Please don't," I said, but she continued ruthlessly, impaling me with her words.

"There's something untouchable in you, Jackson, some part of you that is a wall between us; it's tall and it's thick, and it hurts when I hit it. I've left blood on that wall. I can't beat against it anymore. I won't."

"What if you didn't have to?"

Vanessa looked surprised. "You admit there is a wall?"

"I know what it's made of," I said.

"What?" Her voice rang with doubt.

"Once I tell you, there's no taking it back. It's ugly and I'm ashamed of it, but I've tried to tell you."

"Why didn't you?" Vanessa asked.

I hesitated. "Because you won't love me anymore."

"It couldn't be that bad."

"It's worse. It's the reason for everything bad between us. It's why I can't open up to you. It's why I let Ezra talk me into marrying Barbara, because I couldn't tell you this thing. Even now it scares me." I looked into her eyes and knew that I had never been so naked. "You'll hate me for it."

"How can you say that?"

"Because I hate myself."

"Don't say that."

"But I do."

"For God's sake, Jackson. Why?"

"Because I failed you when you needed me most, and because the reason that you love me is a lie." I reached across the desk and seized her hand. "I'm not what you think I am, Vanessa. I never have been."

"You're wrong. Whatever you think this is, you're wrong, because I know exactly who and what you are."

"You don't."

"I do." She retrieved her hand. "You're not as complicated as you think you are," she said.

"So, you want to hear this?"

"I need to," she said, and I understood. There's a difference between need and want. In spite of her brave words, she did not want to hear this.

I walked around the desk, and she stiffened. I feared that she would turn away, yet an animal stillness held her. She dwindled into herself and a mirrored glaze moved across her eyes. Then I filled the space before her, a clumsy giant, and in the shadow of her open, naked soul, I recognized the remarkable strength that was required to love me for so long and with such conviction.

I sat on the desk, but she would not allow our eyes to meet. I wanted to put my arms around her, knew better, and took her hands instead. Some emotion made them limp—fear, I guessed—and I knew that she had withdrawn to someplace inside herself. I presumed to tilt her chin and seek her in the depths of those mirrored eyes.

"Vanessa," I said.

Our faces were inches apart, her breath a feathered touch, and as she opened herself to me, her hands closed slowly around my own. I wanted to apologize, to explain, and to beg forgiveness, but none of that came out.

"I have always loved you," I said. "From the very first time I saw you. And I have never stopped loving you, not even for an instant."

She began to tremble and the façade that she'd carved onto her face crumbled as if made of sand. Tears filled her eyes, and I knew that I could hold nothing back; but emotion closed my throat, and in silence her tremors grew, until she tilted forward and leaned into me. She shook, and I armored her with my body; then the dam of her resolve burst and she began to cry, so that when she spoke, there was a distance between her words, as if they traveled from a deep place and required all the fuel of her breath to make themselves heard. I almost missed what she said.

"I told myself," she began, and then had to start over. "I told myself that I would not cry."

I held her tighter. I could not think clearly, so I murmured to her as I would to a child. "It's okay," I told her. "Everything will be okay."

I wanted to believe the words, so I repeated them. I did so time and again, like that long-ago day in the barn at Stolen Farm, when words and body heat seared our souls into something resplendent. It could be like that again, and so I told her: "Everything will be okay."

I did not hear the door open. I neither saw my wife nor heard her, not until she spoke.

"Well," she said, and her voice sundered the paper home I'd built with my words. "Isn't this cozy."

It was not a question.

Vanessa pulled away, turned to the door and the voice that could not have sounded crueler. Barbara stood ten feet away, flowers in one hand, a bottle of wine in the other.

"I must say, Work, I'm a little surprised." She tossed the flowers in a wastebasket and placed the wine on a side table.

"What are you doing here, Barbara?" There was no mistaking the anger in my voice. Vanessa backed away, but Barbara went on as if she had not heard me.

"The way you talk about this little slut at home, I thought you'd used her up." Barbara's eyes moved over Vanessa as if they could focus heat and char flesh at will. "I guess you wanted one more fling for the road." I saw Vanessa wilt, and felt my heart break. "For old time's sake." Barbara stepped closer, her eyes still hot on Vanessa. "I guess I was wrong."

"That's not true," I said. "None of it." But already Vanessa was heading for the door. Her name passed my lips, but my feet were slow. She passed Barbara before I could reach her, and my wife's words slipped through the thin armor of her exposed back.

"Did you really think you could compete with me?"

Vanessa turned, caught my eye one time, then slammed the door shut behind her. Barbara yelled at the silent door.

"Stay away from my husband, you white trash whore!"

Suddenly, I did not know myself. Rage carried me to Barbara's side and tightened my hand on her arm. Rage spun her around. Rage lifted my hand. But I brought it down. I slapped her so hard, I knocked her to the floor. Then rage filled me again, threatened to kick her, to crush her into utter and silent submission. Rage wanted blood. Rage wanted payback. And the rage was strong.

I had to fight it down, crush it through sheer will. Otherwise, I might have killed her.

Barbara must have seen it burn in my eyes, for she did not say a word until the killing light dimmed. In its absence, she saw what she expected to see, the man she'd been married to for ten years. The empty man. The shell.

If she'd seen the truth, she would have never opened her mouth to me again.

"Are you finished?" she asked. "Finished acting like what you think a man should be?"

"Is that supposed to hurt?"

"Truth sometimes does."

"Listen, Barbara. I told you before. We're finished."

She smoothed the back of her hand against her cheek. "We're through when I say we're through. I'll not be made a laughingstock. Not by that woman and not by you."

"You are so like my father," I said, and put my hand on the door. She smiled, and I stared, amazed that I'd not seen it sooner. She *was* like my father. Same values. Same detachment.

"I'll take that as a compliment," she said, climbing to her feet, straightening her clothing with a contemptuous air.

"It wasn't meant as one."

She breathed deeply through her nose. Her face was flushed, her eyes as shiny and hard as new dimes. "One of us has to be strong," she said. "And we both know who that is."

I paused halfway out of the office. "Don't kid yourself. You can call a lunatic a genius, but at the end of the day he's still crazy."

"What's that supposed to mean?"

"It means that an obsession for control is not the same thing as strength; it's just obsession." I thought of Vanessa. "I know what strength looks like," I said.

I don't know what she saw on my face: disgust, maybe pity. And the truth was this: My wife has never been strong, just angry, and there's a huge difference. Deep down she knew this.

"You need me, Work. Whether you know it or not, you will always need me."

As I passed down the empty hall in pursuit of Vanessa, I heard Barbara's final words. They rang with her confidence and I told myself that it was false. This time, she was wrong.

"You know where to find me," she screamed, and I walked faster. "You'll come back." I broke into a run. "You always do!"

I hit the exterior door with my shoulder. It flew open and the afternoon light blinded me. I squinted, shaded my eyes, and saw Vanessa behind the wheel of her truck. She reversed out of her parking spot and sped toward the exit. She slowed at the street but didn't stop, then turned right and accelerated, blue smoke spewing from the exhaust. I ran behind her, called her name. I smelled burned oil, heard my breath and my beating heart. People stared, but I didn't care. I sprinted down the yellow line and I called Vanessa's name.

She didn't stop.

But I wasn't going to let her go, not this time, so I ran back for my truck. I'd catch her on the road or at home. Somewhere. And we'd finish what we'd begun.

I was out of shape and breathing hard when I hit the grass strip that separated the parking lot from the road. I stumbled, caught myself before I went down, then fumbled for my keys. I found the right one, shoved it into the lock, and turned it. She couldn't be too far away, no more than a mile.

I looked up as I opened the door and saw Barbara standing by the rear entrance of the building. Her face was expressionless as she watched me. I, for one, had nothing to say. My eyes probably said it all.

Then I was inside the truck, the engine hot, my foot on the gas. I backed out of the spot, pointed the truck toward the exit. And just like that, my universe changed. Suddenly, there were cars everywhere, pouring into the parking lot. Flashing lights. Uniforms. I was blocked in, surrounded by vehicles.

Nobody drew weapons, but I saw the guns and my heart stuttered. I found it hard to breathe; I knew what was happening. Then Mills was at my door, and she knocked on my window, her face surprisingly empty.

I'd created this scene in my mind on countless occasions: lying awake at night, feeling the wheels turn, so grinding and relentless. Somehow I'd thought that it would never happen, but I'd pictured Mills, and always, without fail, I'd imagined a fierce glee. Somehow, this nothingness was worse.

I rolled down the window, not really feeling my arms.

"Would you turn off the engine and step out of the car, please." A stranger's voice.

I did what she asked, and the ground felt rubbery beneath my feet.

Mills closed the truck door behind me, and I was very conscious of the sound it made, a metal door slamming shut. Uniformed officers flanked me; I didn't recognize them, and I realized that Mills must have chosen them personally.

Mills continued, and as she spoke, I felt hands turn me, bend me over the hood of my own vehicle.

"Jackson Pickens, you are under arrest for the murder of Ezra Pickens. You have the right to remain silent. . . ."

The metal was hard, unforgiving. I saw rust I'd never seen before. I smelled my own breath. I heard a grunt and realized it was mine.

"Anything you say can and will be used against you in a court of law. . . ."

I looked up and saw Barbara. She was still against the building and I sought her face. It was almost as empty as Mills's had been, but something bent her features and it looked like anger.

I felt the cuffs cinched tight around my wrists. Somebody pulled me upright by the back of my shirt. People had collected on the sidewalk and they stared. I stared back as Mills finished reading me my Miranda rights from a card.

"You are entitled to an attorney." Here she looked up and met my eyes. "If you cannot afford one, one will be appointed to represent you."

I didn't want to look at her face, so I tilted my face to the sky, suddenly thinking of the hawk I'd seen from the bridge. But this sky was empty, and if redemption moved in it, it did so in a place that I could not see.

"Do you understand these rights as I have explained them to you?"

Finally, I looked at her. "Yes. I understand them." Another stranger's voice, this one from my own mouth.

"Search him," Mills said, and again the hands were upon me. They patted me down, ran up my legs, groped my crotch and my armpits. They took my wallet and my pocketknife. Under the public eye, they took my belt. I was not a person anymore. I was part of the system.

I knew how it worked.

I was escorted to one of the patrol cars and placed in the backseat. Again, my ears resonated with the metallic clang of a slammed door. The sound lasted a long time; when it was gone, I saw that the crowd had grown, and saw also that Barbara was gone. She would not want to be seen, but I imagined her in one of the windows, one eye on me and one on the crowd. She would need to know who had personally witnessed my public disgrace.

Outside, Mills spoke to several of the uniformed officers. My truck would be impounded and searched. I would be taken to the Rowan County Jail and processed. I knew the drill.

I would be stripped, subjected to a cavity search, and dressed in a loose orange jumpsuit. I would be given a blanket, a toothbrush, a roll of toilet paper, and a pair of used flip-flops. I would be given a number. Then I would be given a cell.

Sooner rather than later, I would be questioned, and I knew that I had to prepare for that.

But right now, it didn't matter. I couldn't see it. Instead, I saw Vanessa, and how she would hurt when I failed to come after her.

How long would she wait before she closed the door on me forever?

The answer was unavoidable.

Not long, I thought.

If at all.

I thought of Jean and tried to remain calm. Reasons, I told myself. There are reasons for this. Good ones. If not me, then Jean. I focused on that, and it kept me grounded. This was just the first step. They were taking me to jail, not prison. No one had convicted me yet.

But I couldn't fool myself for long, and as we drove away, I waited for the fear sweats to find me.

CHAPTER

24

The room was square and had wire cages over the lightbulbs; it smelled of feet. Time-bent black linoleum tiles rippled across the floor and gave the room a warped feel, like giant hands had twisted it, and I wondered if it was bad construction or my state of mind. The room was at the back of the police station, and like similar rooms at the jail, this one had green walls, a metal table, and two chairs. It also had a mirror, and I knew that Mills was behind it. She knew that I knew she was behind it, and that just made it silly.

In spite of everything, I felt a strange smile cross my face. Maybe it was because I knew that I had an alibi. If I broke, I had an out, and that made everything surreal. Maybe I was closer to the edge than I realized. Whatever the case, the feeling persisted.

They'd brought me in the back, through the parking garage, then down a concrete hall to this place that smelled like feet. They'd removed my cuffs and left. I'd been sitting there for an hour but had not touched the water pitcher on the table. I'd heard cops joke about the technique. Suspects with full bladders often spoke too freely, just to get it over with and get to the john. The wait was also common. They liked for the reality to settle in; they liked the fear sweats.

So I sat still and tried to prepare myself, but what I really wanted was a cigarette. I thought of all the clients who had been in this room before me.

When Mills came in, she brought the ripe-peach smell with her. Another detective followed her in, and I knew his face but not his name. Mills sat opposite me and he leaned against the wall, next to the mirror. He had big hands and a small head; he hooked his thumbs in his pockets and watched me without blinking.

Mills put the usual things on the table—pad, pen, tape recorder, manila file folder. Then she put a piece of paper in front of me and I recognized the Miranda waiver form. She turned on the tape recorder and announced the date and the time. She identified everyone present, and then she met my eyes.

"Mr. Pickens, you have previously been advised of your Miranda rights. Is that correct?"

"May I have a cigarette?" I asked.

Mills glanced at Detective Small Head and he produced a pack of Marlboro Lights. I took one from his hand, slipped it between my lips. He leaned across the table, lit it with a cheap pink lighter, and retreated to his place against the wall.

Mills repeated the question. "Have you previously been advised of your Miranda rights?"

"Yes."

"Do you understand those rights?"

"I do."

"Before you is the standard North Carolina Miranda waiver form. It explains your rights. Will you please read the form out loud?"

I picked up the paper and read it for the benefit of the tape recorder and any judge who might be asked to scrutinize the legality of this interrogation.

"Do you understand these rights?" Mills was taking no chances.

"I do."

"If you are willing to speak to us at this point, I'd ask you to indicate your willingness on the waiver form, then date and sign it."

All such waiver forms have a box you can check if you're willing to proceed with the interrogation. Under the law, once a suspect is in custody and requests the presence of counsel, the police are required to suspend the interrogation immediately. Anything said after that time is inadmissible in court; in theory, so is any evidence the cops find based on such statement.

I told all my clients the same thing: "Don't ever sign that damn waiver. Ask for a lawyer and keep your mouth shut. Nothing you say will help you."

I ignored my own advice, signed the waiver, and passed it over. If Mills was surprised, she hid it well. She slipped the signed form into her manila folder, as if afraid I might change my mind and tear it up. For a moment, she appeared uncertain, and it occurred to me that she'd never anticipated that I'd cooperate. But I needed information, and I wouldn't get it without playing along. They'd found something. I wanted to know what it was. It was a dangerous game.

I took the initiative. "Have I been indicted?"

"This is my interrogation." Her demeanor remained calm; she was still the detached professional, but it wouldn't last long.

"I can always retract my waiver," I said.

Few people realize this. You can sign a waiver in blood, answer questions all day, and then still change your mind. They then have to stop the interrogation, a thing that no cop wants to do until he's ready. I saw a muscle twitch in Mills's jaw. The deck is stacked in the cops' favor, and they often benefit from people's ignorance of the system.

"No. There's no indictment."

"But you have an arrest warrant?"

She hesitated again, but then answered. "Yes."

"What time did you get it?"

Her mouth constricted into a narrow pucker, and I saw Detective Small Head straighten against the wall.

"That's not important."

I could see the struggle on her face. Her answer would piss me off, but so would her silence. And I knew Mills; she wanted me to talk, wanted it so badly, she could taste it. If I talked, she could trip me up, score an early victory. If I exercised my right to remain silent, she would be denied that pleasure. But she wanted the early hit. She wanted blood, and had faith in her ability to get it.

"One o'clock," she finally said.

"Yet you waited until after five to arrest me."

Mills looked down at her pad, embarrassed to have this conversation as part of the official interrogation tape. Cops have rules, too. Don't let suspects take control of an interrogation.

"I just want to make sure we understand each other," I continued. "I know why you waited." And I did. By arresting me after five, I had no chance to go before a judge on a bail motion, not that day. That meant at least one night in jail, and that was personal, like the newspaper she'd left on my kitchen table. She wanted me to feel the noose, plain and simple.

"Are you finished?" she asked.

"Just so we understand each other."

"Then let's get on with this." She began systematically, and I had to admit that she was good. She established my identity, my relationship to the deceased, and my occupation with minimum dialogue. She wanted a clean, crisp transcript. She questioned me about the night my father died, and she was thorough. She wanted every moment accounted for, and I gave her the same story I'd given before. Mother's accident. The hospital. Ezra's house. The phone call. His sudden departure. I played down the severity of his argument with Jean, and I confirmed once again that after I'd left Ezra's house, I was at home for the rest of night. "No," I told her. "I never saw my father again."

"What about his gun?" she asked.

"What about it?"

"Did you know where he kept it?"

"Lots of people did."

"That doesn't answer my question."

"I knew where he kept it."

"Do you know how to fire a gun?"

"You point and you pull the trigger. It's not rocket science."

"Do you know where it is now?"

"No," I told her. "I have no idea."

So she went back to the beginning. She went over every detail again and yet again. She approached my story from different angles, searching for inconsistencies, the tiny lies that every guilty person tells. "What time did you go to bed? How about your wife? What did you talk about? Tell me about the argument. Tell me what happened at the hospital. What else did your father say before he left? How about the phone call? Let's go over that again."

On and on, for hours. "How did you get along with your father? What was your financial arrangement in regards to the practice? Were you partners or were you an employee? Did you have a key to his house? Did he lock his office at night? How about his desk?"

I asked for water and Mills poured a glass from the pitcher. I took a small sip.

"When did you first learn about the will?"

"I knew he was leaving me the house, but I knew nothing else about it until I met with Hambly."

"Your father never discussed it?"

"He was a secretive man, especially about money."

"Hambly tells me you were angry about the terms of the will. He says you cursed your father's name."

"Jean was not included."

"And that bothered you."

"I think it's cruel."

"Let's talk about your mother," Mills said. I stiffened.

"What about her?"

"Did you love her?"

"What kind of question is that?"

"Answer the question, please."

"Of course I loved her."

"What about your father?"

"He loved her, too."

"That's not what I meant."

"He was my father."

"That doesn't answer the question," she said.

"I think it does."

She leaned back in her chair, enjoying this power she had over me. "Were you friends?"

I thought about it, and almost lied. I wasn't sure why the truth came out, but it did. "He was my father and my business partner. We were not friends."

"Why not?"

"He was a hard man. I don't think he had many friends."

Mills flipped the pages of her pad, looking back over some previous notes. "The night your mother died."

"That was an accident," I said, a little too loudly.

Mills looked up, the pages still held between her fingers. "So you've said. But questions were asked. There was an inquest."

"Haven't you read the report?" I asked.

"I've read it. It raised some questions."

I shrugged as if this wasn't killing me. "People die. Questions are asked. That's how it's done."

"Where was Alex Shiften?" she asked.

The question took me off guard. "Alex?"

"Yes. During the argument. After the argument. Where was she?"

"I don't know," I told her truthfully.

Mills made a note on her pad and then changed tack seamlessly. "You've never seen your father's will. Is that right?"

She'd asked this before. "I've never seen his will," I told her. "I never knew any details. Until I spoke with Clarence Hambly, I had no idea that his estate was so large." I sensed movement and looked at Detective Small Head. He hadn't actually moved, but the razor's edge of his mouth had turned up at one corner, and suddenly I felt the true danger of the game I was playing. I couldn't see Mills's trap, but I sensed it. My next words were spoken slowly. "I certainly didn't know that he'd left me fifteen million dollars."

I put my eyes back on Detective Mills and saw the first gleam of triumph. Whatever she had up her sleeve, I was about to find out. She opened the manila folder and removed what looked like a document sealed in a clear plastic evidence bag. She read the evidence number into the record, took the document out, and then laid it before me. I knew what it was before it hit the table. A glance confirmed my suspicions. "The Last Will and Testament of Ezra Pickens," it read.

"You've never seen this document?" she asked.

"No," I said, a hollow place opening in my stomach. "I've never seen it."

"But according to the title of this document, it is your father's will. Is that a fair statement?"

"It purports to be the last will and testament of my father, yes. You'd need Clarence Hambly to confirm it."

"He has," Mills said, making her less-than-subtle point. Everything would be confirmed. Every word I said. "And you've never seen it before?"

"No."

"No, you've not seen it?"

"That's correct."

Mills picked up the document.

"I am turning to page five," Mills said. "There is a sentence here that has been marked with a yellow Hi-Liter. The last three words of that sentence have been underlined three times in red ink. I'm going to show this to you and ask you if you have ever seen this."

She presented the document, placing it faceup on the table. The feeling of surreal calm that had enveloped me started to crumble.

"I have never seen this before," I said.

"Will you please read the highlighted portion."

I felt Detective Small Head detach himself from the wall. He crossed the room and stood behind Mills. In a shallow voice I read my father's words; it was a voice from the grave, and it damned me.

"To my son, Jackson Workman Pickens, I leave, in trust, the sum of fifteen million dollars." Red ink underscored the dollar figure. Whoever did it had pressed down hard, as if in anger or expectation. I could not bring myself to look up. I knew what the next question would be. It came from Mills.

"Will you explain for us how this document, which you have never seen, came to be in your house?"

I could not answer them. I could barely breathe. My father's will had been found in my house.

They had their motive.

Suddenly, a hand crashed down on the table before my eyes. I jumped in my chair, looked up at Mills. "Damn it, Pickens! Answer the question. What was this doing in your house?"

Mills continued, pounding me with words as she'd pounded the table with her open palm.

"You knew about the will," she said. "You needed the money, and you killed him!"

"No," I finally said. "None of that is true."

"Hambly told us that your father planned to change the will. He was cutting you out, Pickens. Fifteen million dollars was about to fly out the window, and you freaked. So you put two in his head and you waited for the body to be found. That's how it happened, isn't it? Admit it!"

I was stunned. He was going to cut me out? Hambly had never mentioned that. I filed the issue away, concentrated on the present. This was a hard blow, a strategic nightmare, but I'd faced worse. I had to think. I had to be calm. I took a slow, deep breath, told myself to think about the transcript of this interview, think about a future jury. This was a deposition, I told myself. Nothing more.

I almost believed it.

"Are you through?" I asked, leaning against the back of my seat. My voice was quiet, and I knew that the sound of it made Mills's histrionics seem extreme. She was on her feet, leaning over the table. She studied my face and straightened. "May I pick this up?" I asked, indicating my father's will.

Mills nodded, took a step back, and sat down. Much of the color had faded from her face. "As long as you're still planning to talk to me," she said.

I declined to answer. I lifted the document from the table and slowly flipped through the pages. I needed something. Anything.

I found what I was looking for on the signature page.

"This is a copy," I said, laying the document back down and squaring the edges.

"So?" I saw brief concern tighten her eyes. It showed in her voice, too.

"So there are only a few originals of any will. Usually the client keeps one, as does the drafting attorney. Two originals, then. Maybe three. But copies, by their very nature, can be limitless in their number."

"That's irrelevant. All that matters is that you knew the terms of the will."

Arguing with me was her first real mistake. She'd opened the door, given me license to speculate, and it was my turn to lean forward. I wanted my next words on the transcript; I spoke clearly.

"You acquired a copy of the will from Clarence Hambly. You did so prior to the search of my home. That's one person that we know of who had a copy — you. I can also assume that you gave a copy to the district attorney. That's two. Clarence Hambly, of course, had one of the originals, so he could also have made a copy. That makes three people with copies of the will who have also been inside my home within the past few days." I counted on my fingers, bending each one back as I spoke. "Hambly was at Ezra's wake the night after his body was discovered. That's one. The district attorney stopped by the other day to speak with my wife. He made a special trip to visit her at the house. Nowhere else. The house. That's two. And you were there during the search. That makes three. Any one of you could have planted that copy."

"Are you challenging my integrity?" Mills demanded. "Or that of the district attorney?" I saw that the color was back in her cheeks. My words had hit the mark. She was getting angry.

"You're challenging mine. So why not? Three people, all of whom had a copy of the will, all of whom have been in my house within the past several days. That's a compelling problem for you, Detective Mills. People love a good conspiracy theory. And let's not forget Hambly's office staff. He has fifteen support people working there, plus another five lawyers. Any one of them could have copied that document. Have you checked them out? I bet a hundred bucks could buy a copy of a dead man's will, if you found the right person. What's the harm in that, right? Barbara and I have had countless people in our house over the past year and a half. One of them buys a copy of the will and plants it in our house. That's a simple picture. You should check them out as well."

Mills was furious, which was how I wanted her. Her voice rose as she spoke. "You can twist this all you want, but no jury will buy it. Juries trust cops, trust the district attorney. The will was in your house. You knew about the fifteen million."

"I wouldn't be so quick to insult the juries of this county. They're smarter than you think. They may surprise you."

Mills saw the danger of letting me take control just as I smiled. I was calm. She was not. She had called the jury stupid. I had paid them a sincere compliment. It was on the record.

"This line of questioning is over," Mills said. Her eyes burned with conviction, and I saw real hatred there.

I wasn't ready to let it go. Not yet. I wanted one more theory on the record. "Then there's the person that broke into Ezra's office," I said. "The one who tried to kill me with the chair. I wonder what he was after. Maybe he stole a copy of the will."

"That is enough." Mills was back on her feet, her hands clamped on the table's edge. I would get nothing further from her; that was plain.

So I said the only thing left to say.

"Very well. I withdraw my Miranda waiver and assert my right to remain silent. This interview is over."

Mills swelled as blood suffused her face. She had tasted the kill and liked it; but then I'd shut her down, blown massive holes in her theory. It would not be enough by itself—I knew that—but it made her look bad, cast some small shadow of doubt. She'd not fully considered the significance of the will being a copy. An original would have been much more damning. But it was all smoke and mirrors in the end. She had what she wanted. I was on record. I'd never seen the will, yet it was found in my house.

And fifteen million dollars—that would sway most juries.

Yet as Mills stormed out and left me alone with these thoughts, I had to deal with two more questions that, in their own way, were even more troubling: Why did my father want to cut me out of the will, and why hadn't Hambly told me about it?

I rubbed my hands across a face that felt as if it belonged to another man. Razor stubble, deep lines—I ground my palms into raw eyes, opened them when I heard Detective Small Head approach the table. He dropped a telephone onto the surface.

"One phone call, counselor. Better make it a good one."

"How about some privacy?" I asked.

"No chance," he replied, and moved back to lean against the wall.

Already the interview was moving behind me. I looked at the telephone and remembered Vanessa's face as she'd fled the sound of Barbara's voice. I had one phone call, so I thought of all the lawyers I knew, then dialed the only number that made any sense whatsoever. I heard the phone ring at Stolen Farm and squeezed the receiver so tightly that my hand ached. Was I looking for my alibi? Maybe, for a moment, but most of all I wanted her to know that I'd not abandoned her. Please, I begged silently. Please pick up. But she didn't, just her voice, indifferent, asking that the caller leave a message. But I couldn't. What could I say? So I lowered the phone back to its cradle, dimly aware of the detective's curious stare, and the fact that, far from here, an unfeeling machine carried the sound of my anguished breath.

CHAPTER

25

In my imagination, the cells were always cold, but the cell they took me to was hot. That's the first thing I noticed; after that, it was the size. Narrow and mean, eight by six, with a small window where I'd always pictured bars. But the glass had wires in it. I noticed this as I pressed my face against the window, trying to see more of this place to which Mills had sent me. I'd not seen her after she stormed off, but she didn't leave me alone for long. Detective Small Head and two uniformed officers had cuffed me again and led me through a warren of hallways to the heavy steel door that guarded the entrance to the police station's parking garage. Then into a cruiser for the short ride to the county jail, where I was processed.

That part was worse than I'd ever imagined. They took my name, took my clothes, and with a flashlight and a rubber glove, they took the last pitiful rag of my dignity. Detective Small Head watched, and lit a cigarette when they spread my cheeks.

Eventually, someone tossed me an orange jumpsuit and I put it on, ashamed of my eagerness. The legs were too short, and the crotch drooped almost to my knees. My heels hung off the back of the flip-flops, but I stood as straight as I could. Detective Small Head smiled as he said, "Sleep well, counselor." Then he was gone, and I was alone with the guards, who contrived to act as if they'd never seen me before, instead of two or three times a week for the past ten years.

I stood there for another ten minutes while the senior guard finished his paperwork and the younger one ignored me. No one else entered and no one else left. Ten minutes, the three of us, and not a word spoken. The pen rasped across paper in triplicate, and his meaty forearm left a damp spot on the desk as he moved down the form. Even the top of his head looked bored. I wanted to sit, but the only other chairs had leather straps and I couldn't go there. They were thick, stained with sweat and blood, and one had teeth marks in it. I stepped away from it.

"Going somewhere?" the older guard asked wryly. I shook my head. "Just relax, counselor. Time is the one thing you've got plenty of." Then he went back to work, and the younger one sat on the edge of the desk, picking at his fingernails.

I studied the walls, the floor, and tried not to look at the door that led to the interview rooms. I'd walked through it a thousand times, but that was not my destination. This time, they would take me through another door, into the general population; and as I stood there, I felt the truth of the guard's words. Time was the one thing I had, and in that time I felt it—the reality. Not the concept or the possibility, but the bones of it, the flesh and hair of it. I was in jail, accused, and in that blink of time the fear sweats descended upon me. They warped the room, soured my stomach, and I fought a sudden surge of nausea.

I was in jail. I would go to trial.

Finally, the older guard finished his paperwork and looked up. His eyes flicked over me and I saw the recognition in them, but he ignored my obvious distress. He'd seen it all before. More times than he could probably count. "Pod four," he said, indicating to the younger man where he was to take me.

I followed the guard out of central processing and into a world where nothing felt real. They'd taken my watch, but I felt the lateness. We passed blank doors, and I saw the flickering reflection of my face in the tiny black windows with the guillotine wire.

I lost track of the turns, aware, in any real sense, of only the sounds and the smells: the guard's polished shoes cracking on the concrete floor, the whisper of flip-flops worn as thin as skin. Sounds of a distant argument abruptly ended. Metal on metal. The smell of antiseptic, packed humanity, and the faintest whiff of vomit that was not my own.

We moved deeper into the institution, down an elevator, down another hall, away from the last hint of fresh air. I followed his back, and it led me deeper. Once he looked at me and mouthed a question, but I had nothing to say; my thoughts bled together, shattered, and were lost. I felt hunted, and I shied away from blind corners and dark recesses. I smelled my fear, and envied the guard his casual arrogance. In that long walk, he became a god, and I came to dread the moment he would cast me loose in this place.

And so I followed him as far as he would lead me, into the hard-cornered space that was pod four, an octagonal area with doors on its perimeter. There were eight of them, and I saw more than one face pressed against the small glass panes. One door stood open, and the guard gestured toward it. At the door, he turned, and I saw that he was not a god after all. He looked uncertain. He seemed to shuffle his feet without actually doing so. Finally, he met my eyes.

"I'm sorry about this, Mr. Pickens," he said. "You were always very polite to me."

Then he gestured me inside, closed the door, and left me alone. I heard the door to the pod slam shut, and thought about the guard. I could not recall ever having seen him before, but I must have; and his kind words, in this unkind place—they almost broke me.

So, like those other nameless charges of the great state of North Carolina, I now pressed my face against the glass as if by sight alone I could expand the black hole that had become my world. Looking across the pod, I found another face, a pair of dark eyes that seemed to hang above a glass-flattened nose and the black slash of a mouth. For a long moment, our eyes locked; then he pulled back from the glass and kissed it with thin whiskered lips. I recoiled from the sight but couldn't look away, not until his eyes were back, and I saw that he was taunting me. So I flipped him off and dropped onto the narrow, rigid mattress of my bunk. My heart hammered, my hurried breath a fog around me. I lay for a minute, then a harsh buzzer resounded through the tight metal confines of my new world. The sound had barely faded when the lights went out, leaving me in a darkness so profound, it could only originate from the soul itself. The world constricted around me, and in that horrible second I was again a boy, crippled beneath the earth. Those hands were upon me, that voice in my ear, and the smell of breath like rotting meat.

But this was different. The guard had called me by name, Mr. Pickens, and that childhood was lost behind me. So I forced myself to my feet, gripped the steel sink until my breathing slowed, and then I paced in the blackness, feeling my way like a blind man. And suddenly I thought of Max Creason. Four paces and turn, for five years—four and turn. He gave me strength, and I made the cell my own, and the darkness with it. I walked it, and while I knew that I could survive this interlude, I knew as well that I could never do life behind bars. Better I'd pulled the trigger on the bridge. So I paced and I thought, and as the night wore on, one thing became very clear. If I managed to get out of this, I would never take freedom of choice for granted. I'd spent most of my life in a prison of my own making, trapped behind bars of fear, expectations and the opinions of others; and none of that mattered, not a whit. That it took the murder of my father and my own arrest to see this almost made me laugh, but this was not a laughing place and never would be. So I searched for a way out. The next day I would be taken to court for my first appearance. With any luck, I would be arraigned and given an expedited bail hearing. Somehow I would make that bail. Then there would be some time before I went to trial. I would figure something out or I would go back to the bridge.

One way or another.

The night wore away, until it too was as thin as skin, and as it did, I paced and I thought; I thought about a great many things.

CHAPTER

26

The courtroom was crowded with lawyers, reporters, and other defendants. There were families, friends, and witnesses, the usual mix, but mostly I saw the other lawyers; they filled the space before the bar, motionless, as if in my absence they'd claimed the right of judgment. I searched their faces as I entered the room, flanked by guards, steel on my wrists. What did I search for? A friendly smile. A nod. Anything from the life I used to have. But I got nothing. The eyes turned away, or they glazed, as if looking at a stranger. So I was led past them, beyond them, to the defense table where I'd sat a thousand times as one of their number; and there was Douglas, who used to be my friend, and with him was Detective Mills. They watched me from the prosecution table, and like the others, they'd found veils for their eyes.

I'd prepared myself for this moment, in the small predawn hours, and so was able to keep my back straight as I assumed a position behind the chair reserved for the accused. The manacles clanked as I placed my hands on the back of that chair, and the bailiffs stepped back. A quiet descended on the room, remarkable only in its completeness. Normally, there was a background hum, as lawyers muttered behind raised hands, bailiffs maintained order, and defendants practiced lines they hoped would sway the judge. I'd heard people pray and I'd heard people weep. Some screamed obscenities and were manhandled from the court. I'd heard it all, a daily cacophony that every lawyer learned to tune out, but I'd never encountered a silence as expectant as this.

The judge was the same older woman who'd given such heartfelt condolences to me on the day after my father's body had been discovered. Even now her eyes were not unkind. I looked from her to Douglas, who seemed uncertain for a moment. But then he turned my way, and he straightened to a more predatory stance when he saw me watching. There would be no help there; he was committed, and would fight me every step of the way.

The judge spoke, and even though she spoke softly, her words were an avalanche in the silence. "Bailiff," she commanded. "Remove Mr. Pickens's handcuffs, please."

A murmur ran through the double row of attorneys seated before the bar. Douglas leaned into the prosecution table.

"I object, Your Honor. The defendant is accused of murder."

The judge cut him off. "Are you suggesting that attorney Pickens presents some physical threat to this court?" Her mockery was thinly masked, and I saw a faint blush creep into the district attorney's neck.

"The defendant is in custody. The defendant is accused of murdering his own father."

"The defendant is a member of this bar! He will be treated as such until such time as he is proven guilty. Do I make myself clear?"

I felt a lump in my throat and an overwhelming gratitude for her words.

"Yes, Your Honor," the DA said. "Perfectly clear."

"Good. Bailiff, remove the cuffs." The bailiff stepped forward and I held out my hands. The cuffs fell away. I wanted to thank her but could only nod.

The judge looked at me more closely. "Will counsel approach the bench," she said. I hesitated, unsure if I was included in her summons. "That means you, too, Mr. Pickens," she said. I rounded the table, nearly brushing shoulders with the DA, and together we approached the bench. We had barely arrived when Douglas addressed the judge in a harsh whisper.

"I protest again, Your Honor. This man is here as a defendant, not as a lawyer. This display is undermining my position in this courtroom and in this case."

The judge leaned forward. "And I have made my position very clear on this, as well. Unlike you, Mr. DA, I will await the evidence before I convict this man, in my mind or in any other manner. He has served as an officer of this court for ten years, and I am not willing to pretend otherwise."

"I want my objection on the record."

"Fine. On the record. But this is my courtroom, and I will run it as I see fit. Mr. Pickens will not be treated like a common street thug."

"Justice is supposed to be blind, Your Honor."

"Blind but not stupid," the judge responded. Then she looked directly at me. "And not without some feeling."

"Thank you, Your Honor," I managed to say.

She studied my face for long seconds before speaking. "How did you come by that black eye, Mr. Pickens?"

My fingers moved of their own accord, touching the swollen purple flesh beneath my left eye. "Nothing serious, Your Honor. A disagreement with another inmate. Earlier this morning."

"Bailiff?" She turned her eyes on the bailiff.

He cleared his throat. "One of the prisoners was trying to intimidate him, Your Honor. But just verbally. Mr. Pickens started it."

"That's not the entire story, Your Honor."

She looked back down at me. "Would you like to elaborate?"

"It's not important." I thought of the inmate across the pod. Although I'd never represented him, I'd seen him in and around court for years. He was a drug addict and a wife beater. He'd come straight for me as soon as the cell doors opened and we lined up for breakfast.

The judge, however, continued to hold my eyes, and it was clear that she wanted an answer, so I shrugged. "He wanted my orange juice, Your Honor."

She turned her hawkish eyes on the district attorney. "You assured me this man would be kept out of the general population," she said, and looking at her intent features, I realized something. She had signed the arrest warrant. She felt responsible.

"I did, Your Honor. I cannot control events inside the jail."

Again her eyes found mine; they moved over my face, and in them I saw a profound sadness.

"Very well," she said. "That will do."

We returned to our respective places and the proceeding continued. The judge advised me of the charges against me, first-degree murder, and informed me of my right to an attorney.

"Do you wish to have an attorney to represent you, Mr. Pickens?"

"No, Your Honor." At my words, a ripple moved through the lawyers assembled behind me, and I had another revelation. They wanted the case, each one of them; it would be a high-profile one, with lots of press. Television interviews, newspaper, radio—even a loss would make a reputation for the attorney who represented me. A victory and the attorney might succeed Ezra himself. "I intend to represent myself," I said. The last thing I wanted was another person prying for a truth better left uncovered.

"Sign the waiver," I was told. A bailiff handed me the form wherein I waived my right to court-appointed counsel. This was a mere formality. Only the indigent qualified for state-sponsored lawyers. I signed the form and the bailiff passed it up.

Now we came to the crux of the matter. Normally, this would have concluded a defendant's first appearance. Later, he would face a probable-cause hearing, wherein the state carried the burden of convincing a judge that sufficient probable cause existed to bind the defendant over to superior court, there to stand trial for whatever felony charge he faced. Once past probable cause, a person could request bail, but all of this took time. And there was one significant problem, and I knew of only one way around it.

"Your Honor," I said. "I move for an expedited bail hearing."

Douglas surged to his feet. "I object, Your Honor. I most strenuously object."

"Sit down," the judge said, exasperation clear on her withered features. "Of course you object." She turned her attention to me, laced her fingers, and leaned into her words. "This *is* very unusual, Mr. Pickens. You know that as well as I. There are procedures to be followed. Steps. We'll need to have the probable-cause hearing. Your case will have to be bound over to superior court." She paused, as if embarrassed by her lecture. Clearly she was puzzled.

"I waive probable cause," I said, and my words generated a windstorm of conversation among the lawyers seated behind me. The judge leaned back, as surprised as the rest. No defense attorney going to trial waives probable cause. The state has to show its case at the probable-cause hearing. Not all of it, necessarily, but the broad strokes. It's a perfect opportunity to probe for strengths and weaknesses. Beyond that, there is also the possibility that the judge will find insufficient probable cause and dismiss the charges. I knew this, of course, but I knew something else, as well. Douglas would object to any local judge hearing the matter. Too much bias, he'd claim. The judge would have to recuse. Another judge would be brought in, someone from out of county. And that would take time, time in jail, time behind bars. It could be days.

Gradually, the buzz of conversation faded and the courtroom settled again into near-perfect silence.

"Are you aware of the ramifications of your request?" the judge asked, rustling beneath her robes. "The probable-cause hearing is one of the cornerstones of procedural due process. I am loath to proceed at this point, Mr. Pickens. I fear that your judgment maybe clouded."

I focused on a point beyond the judge and looked neither right nor left as I spoke. "Shall I renew my motion, Your Honor?"

She sighed, and her words descended into the courtroom as if weighted down with regret. "Very well, Mr. Pickens. Let the record show that the defendant has waived his right to a hearing on probable cause and moves this Court for an expedited bail hearing." She raised her voice as Douglas came to his feet. "A motion that this Court is inclined to grant."

"I object," Douglas almost shouted.

The judge settled back into her chair and waved a narrow hand. "Approach," she commanded. "Both of you." At the bench, she looked down on us with the stern disapproval of a schoolmistress and used the same parchment hand to cover the microphone. Douglas opened his mouth to speak, but she rode him down with iron-shod words. "What is the problem here, Douglas? You've arrested him, charged him, and brought him before this Court. Do you honestly think that he's a flight risk? . . . No? Neither do I. Now, I've seen your evidence, and between us, it's got holes in it. But that's your bailiwick, not mine. What's mine is this decision." She looked pointedly at my face, and I felt her eyes linger on the injuries. "You intend to rebut these charges, do you not, Mr. Pickens?"

"I do."

"And you intend to do so in court. Is that not also true?"

"Yes."

"So you'll be here."

"I wouldn't miss it," I said.

"There, Douglas," the judge said. "He wouldn't miss it." I thought I heard teeth grind. "Now, we are off the record and speaking in private, and since I will not preside over the trial, I am going to say what I must." She directed her next words at me. "I signed the warrant because I had no choice. On paper, probable cause to arrest did exist, and if I'd not signed it, some other judge would have." She turned to the district attorney. "I don't think he did it, Mr. DA, and if you quote me on that, I'll deny it. But I've known this man for ten years, and I cannot believe he killed his father. I won't. So you can stand up in this court and argue against bail. You can rant and rave. Your choice. But I'll not have this man put back into the general population. That's *my* discretion. *My* prerogative."

I looked at Douglas, whose calcified features barely moved as he spoke. "It will stink of favoritism, Your Honor."

"I'm sixty-nine years old, and have no plans to run for reelection. Do you think I give a damn? Now, step back. Both of you."

My feet carried me back to the defense table, where I sat down. I risked a glance at Douglas, who was red-faced and studiously ignoring Detective Mills.

"Mr. Pickens," the judge said. I came to my feet. "Do you have anything further you wish to offer the Court in support of your motion?"

"No, Your Honor." I sat down, grateful to the judge for many things. Standing before this crowd to argue the reasons why I should be trusted outside of lockup would have been unpleasant at best. She had spared me that humiliation.

"Anything from the state?" she asked. If Douglas wanted to raise hell, he could. He could argue a great many points, many of which would make sense. He could make the judge look bad, and I hoped he would not do that. Slowly, he stood, his eyes on the tabletop, stretching the moment until it almost burst.

"The state requests only that bail be reasonable, Your Honor."

Again, an excited stir ran through the packed courtroom, an energy wave that broke against my back before receding into yet another hushed expectancy.

"Bail is set at two hundred and fifty thousand dollars," the judge said. "The defendant is bound over to superior court and remanded into custody until such time that bail is satisfied. This court will stand in recess for fifteen minutes." Then she banged her gavel once and rose to her feet, looking small and withered inside the black robe of her office.

"All rise," the bailiff thundered, and so I did, then watched in stillness as she slipped through the door behind her bench and the courtroom erupted into unabashed speculation.

I looked at Douglas, who had not moved. Muscles worked in his jaw as he stared at the door through which the judge had exited. Then his head swiveled, as if he felt me. He gestured to the bailiffs, and within seconds the cuffs were back on. Our eyes locked. Mills mouthed near-silent words into his ear, but he continued to ignore her. There was something in his eyes, and it was something unexpected. I knew this even though I could not recognize what it was. I knew only that it was not the normal look I'd seen him give other defendants. Then he surprised me by smiling. He stepped to my side, and his voice was like warm oil.

"I'd say that went rather well for you, Work." Mills remained at the table, her face inscrutable. Behind us, several lawyers turned to watch, but none approached. We existed in a pocket of silence that seemed to belong to us alone. Even the bailiffs felt momentarily insubstantial. "You should be back on the street within a couple hours."

I tried to pin him with my eyes, but in the orange coveralls and steel bracelets, I'd lost that power. His smile blossomed, as if he, too, had arrived at the same conclusion. "Why are you talking to me?" I asked.

"Because I can," he replied.

"You're a real ass, Douglas. I wonder how I've missed it all these years."

His smile vanished. "You missed it because you wanted to miss it, like all defense lawyers. You want the deal. You want to be my buddy, so I'll make your job easier. It's a game and always has been. You know it as well as I do." His eyes flicked left and right and he raised his voice ever so slightly. "But the game's over, and I don't have to play it anymore. So enjoy your little victory. The next judge won't be so easy on you, and you can rest assured that I won't be."

Again, something felt odd, something in his eyes, maybe, something in what he said or how he said it. I tried to figure it out, when suddenly it became clear. Douglas was playing to the audience. Lawyers were watching, and Douglas was playing to them. I'd never seen him grandstand before. Looking at his face, sorting this out, a question occurred to me. I'd thought about it the night before, yet I had almost forgotten it. Before I'd considered my words, they were out, and their effect was immediate.

"Why did you let me go to the crime scene?" I asked.

Douglas looked uncomfortable. His eyes darted at the surrounding lawyers, then settled back on me. His voice dropped.

"What are you talking about?" he asked.

"The day they found his body, when I asked for permission to go to the crime scene. I didn't think you'd agree; no reasonable district attorney would have. But you did. You almost ordered Mills to show me the body. Why did you do that?"

"You know why I let you go," he said.

"For Jean."

"For Jean. That's right."

A silence stretched in the wake of his words. For both of us, Jean had that power, which was probably the only thing that remained common to us both.

"It won't help you as much as you think," he said, referring to my presence at the crime scene. "I won't allow it to."

"Maybe it already has."

"What's that supposed to mean?"

"It means that a man has a lot of time to think in jail, Douglas. A whole lot of time."

I was taunting him, and he finally realized it. But I'd scored a point; I'd made him doubt, if just for an instant. His face closed down like a carnival ride. The power just drained away, leaving everything still. For an instant, we had an eye thing going, the kind of unspoken communication I'd only had once or twice in my life. It was not so much a message as a feeling, one of cold, the kind I'd expected to find in jail yet, strangely, had not. But like that cell, his eyes were empty, dark, and timeless. Then some unfathomable emotion twisted his mouth into a cruel smile, and with a nod to the bailiffs, he sent me away.

The next hours dragged, as I waited, perhaps in vain, for someone to bail me out. They'd given me a phone again, and I'd called the only person I could. But Barbara was not there, or she chose not to answer. So I left a message for my wife and waited to see if she would leave me to rot.

They put me in a padded detox cell down the hall from central processing. The judge's doing, I guessed. At some time, the walls may have been white. Now they were a mixture of browns, like burled wood. At times, I wanted to throw myself at them, scream as if I were indeed strung out. I'd never lived a longer day. The room seemed to shrink with each passing hour, and I came to wonder just how much my wife had come to loathe me. Would she leave me in jail out of spite? I honestly couldn't say.

Eventually, they came for me, processed me in reverse. I tipped the stained manila envelope onto the counter. My watch spilled out, followed by my wallet, which contained money, credit cards, identification. All present and accounted for; I signed the little piece of paper that said so. They gave me back my clothes—wrinkled, my belt, my shoes. And as I put them on, I felt the change come upon me. I became a human being again, and again I passed through the jailhouse doors, this time walking into the musty lobby, where normal people waited for people like me. What did I expect? Barbara? A faceless bail bondsman? Truthfully, I had not thought about it, not since I'd first felt underwear against my skin. In the mounting excitement of my rebirth into the human race, I expected to walk beneath blue skies, breathe fresh air, and eat a decent meal. My future was so uncertain, that was all I could expect. I did not expect Hank Robins. I did not expect what he would eventually tell me.

"What are you doing here?" I asked him.

He gave me a crooked smile, one that showed his chipped front tooth. "I should ask you."

"Yeah. I guess so."

There were two other people in the room. One was a washed-out woman who could have been thirty or could have been fifty. She sat on the hard plastic chair, head tilted against the wall, mouth open; she reeked of tobacco and hard living, all wrinkle and no laugh line. Her sunburned thighs hung loosely under cutoffs too short for a teenager. She clutched her purse like a talisman, and I wondered how long she'd been waiting, and for whom. The other person was a uniformed cop. I watched him sign in at the bulletproof window, then check his weapon into one of the steel lockboxes mounted on the wall. He never turned his back on us, not completely, and Hank watched him with ill-concealed distress. I knew that Hank did not wish to be associated with me under my current circumstances, and I wondered what could have brought him to see me.

"Come on," I said. "Let's talk outside. I've had enough of this place."

Hank nodded around another smile. "You don't have to tell me twice. Place gives me the screamin' willies."

Outside, the air was a tonic, and we leaned against the chest-high concrete wall and watched the traffic crawl along Main Street. It was late afternoon, the sun low and golden in the sky. Two of the district criminal courts were still in session and there were a few defendants lingering about, waiting for their cases to be disposed of. I'd seen two attorneys in the hall as we left, but there were none outside, a fact for which I was grateful.

"You don't have a cigarette, do you?" I asked.

"No, sorry. But hang on a sec." Before I could tell him not to worry about it, Hank had approached one of the few people scattered along the wall. When he returned, he had a crumpled pack of Marlboros and a book of matches. He handed them to me.

"Guy over there," he said and gestured with his thumb, "he was in court today, same as you. He said, 'Give 'em hell.'"

I lit a cigarette and wondered briefly what the guy's crime had been. I tucked the pack in my shirt pocket.

"Don't take this the wrong way, Hank. But you're not the person I expected to see."

He leaned against the wall, back to the passing traffic, and crossed his arms. He didn't look at me right away.

"I was in court this morning, too," he finally said. "Came up to talk to you and caught your performance. I figured somebody ought to call your wife, seeing as how she wasn't there. Thought somebody should tell her to arrange for bail."

"I tried to call her."

Hank nodded, looked at me with something like pity. "Me, too. No answer. But I wasn't in stir, so I went to see her." Hank looked up at the roofline of the jail, where it connected to the courthouse. "She didn't answer when I rang the doorbell, so I went around back. I found her on the patio, sipping iced tea and reading *Cosmo*."

A silence fell between us, and I knew that telling me this made Hank uncomfortable. "Maybe she didn't know," I said, meaning my court appearance.

"She knew," Hank said. "She looked guilty as hell when she saw me."

"She knew, and she wasn't going to bail me out?"

"Not as bad as all that. She'd made some calls, she said, and was waiting for the money to be put together."

"What calls?" I asked. Hank shrugged.

"Didn't ask. Don't know. But she asked me if I would meet you."

"That's it?" I asked.

Hank twitched and then patted his pocket. "I almost forgot. She asked me to give you this." He handed me a note, folded twice. I recognized her stationery. She used to spray perfume on it. Because she loved me, she said. I opened the note and read it. It was brief and unscented.

"She wants me to know that she still loves me, very much, and that some dirty bum stole my dog."

"I know," Hank said. "I read it."

I refolded the note and put it in my pocket.

"I'm sorry, man," Hank said. "Life's a bitch."

I nodded.

"So is your wife."

"Why are you here, Hank?" I asked again.

"Maybe to save your ass," he said, and I looked up from my shoes, searching his face for the punch line. "I'm serious," he said. "Look. I had my doubts, okay. I mean, who wouldn't? Fifteen million dollars is a lot of jack. So, sure, I thought you might have popped him. But I told you I'd check up on Alex, and I did."

Had I been walking, I would have stumbled. Driving, I would have wrecked. "What does Alex have to do with any of this?"

"Maybe nothing. Maybe something. That's what we're going to find out."

"Let's back this up, Hank. What the hell are you talking about?"

Hank took my arm, turned me toward the wide, shallow stairs that led off the concrete platform. "Not here, okay. In the car."

"Are we going somewhere?"

"Raleigh," he said.

"Raleigh," I repeated.

"To ask a few questions."

"Of whom?" I asked. We reached the top of the stairs. Beneath us, the sidewalk beckoned. I hesitated, wanting answers. Hank's hand settled on my shoulder, seeming to urge me down the stairs.

"Just keep walking," he said, and something in his voice made me turn. He was looking back over his shoulder, and I followed his gaze to the courthouse door. Sunlight gilded the glass, and I did not understand. I almost missed it. Then a thin tissue of cloud blotted the sun's face, and I saw him there, behind the glass: Douglas, watching us, a frown of concentration on his heavy features.

"Forget about him," Hank told me. "He's tomorrow's problem."

I turned away, let the private investigator lead me down the stairs. "I'm parked over here," Hank told me. We walked down the hill, past three parked sheriff's cars, the secure judge's entrance, and a street crew that worked with loud, foul-smelling equipment that ripped at a small section of asphalt. Hank gestured down the narrow side street that ran along the unmarked cemetery where free blacks had been buried almost two hundred years earlier. We turned left, and the noise dwindled behind us. I started to feel like myself again, less like a punch-drunk fighter. We separated at his car, a dark green Buick sedan, and I stepped off the curb and walked to the passenger door. He unlocked the doors, but I caught his eye over the roof before I got in.

"Alex?" I asked, but he ignored me, and I felt his door slam shut. The car rocked, as if agitated; so I got in, and took my question with me.

"It's not her real name," Hank told me five seconds later. "That's why I couldn't find a record of her at the hospital in Charlotte. Jean was in the system, plain as day, but no Alex Shiften. To me, that stank of something, but I couldn't tell what. Not until I went back with that picture you gave me."

"So you got the picture?" I asked numbly, dealing with the little detail because I could not focus on the great big one that sat like an elephant on my lap.

"Early," Hank responded. "A little after five, and then I drove back to Charlotte in time for the shift change at the hospital. I flashed the photo, asked my questions, and eventually found the right guy, an orderly with a deep appreciation for Benjamin Franklin."

"What did he tell you?"

"He knew Alex all right, but not by that name. According to him, her name is Virginia Temple. She'd been at Charter Hills for three months before Jean showed up. Apparently, they hit it off pretty quick. For a couple months there, your sister spoke to no one but her."

"Virginia," I repeated. The name felt made up. Alex Shiften was too hard to be a Virginia, too sharp, like calling a razor blade a butter knife.

"It gets worse," Hank said. "She transferred in from Dorothea Dix."

"The hospital in Raleigh?"

"The state hospital in Raleigh. The place where they keep the criminally insane."

"Not everybody there is a criminal," I said. "Just some."

"That's right. Just some. But some of those eventually get out, and usually they're transferred to a place like Charter Hills. A stepping-stone to normal living, like a halfway house."

"And you think that may be the case with Alex?"

Hank shrugged.

"Well shit," I said.

"Exactly," Hank replied, and started the car. "That's exactly what I thought."

He dropped the transmission into drive.

"I'm not supposed to leave the county," I said. "It's part of the standard bail arrangement."

He put the car back into park and turned to face me. "Your call, Work. I can drive you home if you want and check it out myself. No sweat at all."

I didn't want the judge to regret her kindness, but this was too important to play by the rules; and rules, I had recently decided, weren't necessarily good.

I'd played my whole life by the book, and that life wasn't looking very pretty right now. "Screw it. Let's go."

"That's my boy."

"But we have to make a couple stops on the way out of town."

"It's your life," Hank said, accelerating away from the curb. "I'm just driving."

CHAPTER

27

I t was a short drive to Clarence Hambly's office. Like most lawyers in town, he worked close to the courthouse. Hank pulled into his parking lot, a crowded space, its brick accents designed to make the cracked concrete look less austere. The building itself was over two hundred years old, a four-over-four antebellum structure with a large addition in back, hidden from the street.

"So, what are we doing?" Hank asked.

"I have to ask some questions. It won't take long."

The lobby was crowded with criminal defendants whom Hambly would shuck off on some junior associate for a buck twenty-five an hour or a flat fee, based on the charge and the likelihood of their taking a plea. He had a rear entrance and private stairwell for his more august clients. They'd go straight up, to the personal assistant who guarded his office. I knew that I'd never get past her unannounced, so I didn't even bother. Instead, I cut through the crowd in the main lobby and put my hands on the gleaming cherry-wood counter. One of Hambly's assistants, an older woman, asked if she could be of some assistance, then stepped back once she looked up and recognized me.

"I'd like to see Clarence," I said.

"That's not possible," she replied.

"I'd like to see him now. And I'm very willing to raise my voice. So please just let him know that I am here."

She looked me up and down, thinking about it. I knew for a fact that she'd handled hundreds of frustrated, angry clients, so she had to size me up. After a few seconds, she picked up the phone and told Hambly's assistant that I was there to see him. It took a good minute.

"You can go up," she said.

Hambly met me at his office door and stepped aside to let me in. The office was long and elegant, with views of the courthouse on the other side of Main Street. He did not ask me to sit, just studied me from above his paisley bow tie.

"Most people make an appointment," he said.

"This won't take long," I replied, closing the door. I took a step closer to him and planted my feet widely. "I want to know how a copy of my father's will came to be in my house."

"I didn't realize that one had."

"Who had a copy?"

"This conversation is highly inappropriate," Hambly said.

"It's a simple question."

"Very well. I gave two originals to your father and kept one here. If he made copies, that was his own business. I have no idea how one ended up in your house."

"You've seen the one that the police have in their custody?"

"I have, but I cannot say for certain that it is the one found in your house. They asked me to identify it and I did."

I pushed. "Yet, it is an accurate copy. You verified that for them."

"Yes," he conceded.

"Why didn't you tell me that Ezra was going to cut me out of his will?"

"Whatever gave you that idea?"

"Mills," I said.

Hambly smiled tightly, a gleam in his eyes. "If Mills told you that, she did so for her own reasons. Yes, your father contemplated some minor changes, but he never intended to remove you as a beneficiary. He was quite firm on that. I suspect that Mills was trying to trick you into some indiscretion."

"What changes?"

"Nothing significant and nothing that was ever put into place. Ergo, nothing that concerns you as the beneficiary of his estate."

"Is your copy of the original accounted for?" I asked.

"Filed with the probate court. I'm certain that they would show it to you, if you asked."

"Yet you made copies."

"Of course, I made copies. This is a law office. I represent the estate."

"Who else did you give copies to? Mills? Douglas? Who else?"

"Don't raise your voice to me, young man. I won't tolerate it."

"Try this on then, Clarence. If I am convicted of Ezra's murder, can I inherit under the laws of North Carolina?"

"You know that the state will not allow a killer to profit from his crime in that way."

"Then who retains control of Ezra's assets?"

"What are you implying?" Hambly demanded.

"Who?"

"All of your father's assets pass to the foundation."

"And who controls that foundation?"

"I do not appreciate your insinuation."

"You would have control of the entire forty million dollars. Isn't that correct?"

Hambly stared at me, his face tight with barely contained fury. "I find you and your petty machinations insufferable, Work. Get out of my office."

"You were in my house. For the first time ever since I bought it, you were in my house. Why?"

"I was there because Barbara invited me to be there. And because it was the respectful thing to do. I should not have to explain that to you. Now, get out," he said, and took me by the arm. Outside of his office, before the pretty young assistant who had come suddenly to her feet, I jerked my arm free.

"Somebody planted that document in my house, Clarence. It had to come from somewhere."

Hambly straightened to his full height and looked down the length of his nose. I saw color in his face, and the pulse of blood in the big veins that ran down his neck. "Earlier today, I held some pity for you, Work. But that's gone. I will look forward to your trial date." He pointed a thin arm toward the stairwell, and I saw that it trembled. "Now, please leave."

"Very well, Clarence. Thank you for your time." I walked down Hambly's private stairs and did not look back. I heard his office door slam.

I found Hank in the car, his arm out the open window.

"How'd it go?" he asked.

"I don't know," I said.

"Really?"

I looked at Hank. "Really."

"So where to now?"

"Highway Six-oh-one, toward Mocksville. I'll show you where to turn."

We rolled out of town, and as we drew closer to Stolen Farm, I felt the spring inside of me grow tighter. My head was heavy with densely packed emotions. It grew more so as we approached Vanessa's house and stopped in front of it.

"Wait here," I told Hank, getting out of the car, leaning in through the open window.

"Jesus, Work."

I held up my hands, palms out. "Last time," I told him.

Stolen Farm lay in the shadow of the neighboring woods. Thin fingers of light reached for the farmhouse but fell short, satisfied with the faded red wall of the old barn. We'd parked in the rutted drive, house to the left, barn to the right. I didn't see Vanessa's car, but her nameless man was there; he watched me from the gaping mote-filled cavern that bisected the barn. If I'd looked up, I would have seen the door to the loft, where Vanessa and I found what we'd thought would last forever. I didn't look up. I looked at her man. He'd been working on the tractor. Grease covered his hands and the heavy wrench he held. He leaned against the tall molded tire with a proprietary air and studied me as I crossed the dry dirt toward him. He looked bigger than I remembered; he was heavily muscled, and depressingly young, but definitely the same guy.

"That's far enough," he said. I stopped, still ten feet away, and held up my hands.

"I'm not looking for any trouble," I told him. "I just want to talk to Vanessa."

His mouth opened to an unasked question, and he put the wrench down on the engine cowling of the tractor. He moved toward me, wiping his hands on his pants. Worry creased his face.

"I thought she was with you," he said.

I dropped my hands, feeling foolish. I might have decked him the other night, but it was clear to me now that he was not intimidated.

"What are you talking about?"

He stopped, towering over me. He searched my face as if for something specific, then flicked his eyes at the house. I followed his glance, hoping to see Vanessa, but the old place was still and dark.

"She didn't come home last night."

"What?"

"And I haven't seen her all day."

A familiar pit opened in my stomach. Something moved in the young man's eyes, and I knew it for what it was. I stepped closer.

"Start at the beginning," I told him. "Tell me everything."

He nodded and swallowed hard. He wanted to tell me. The thing in his eyes made him need to tell me. It was fear; the young man was afraid, and suddenly I was, too.

CHAPTER

28

"So what was that all about?" We were on the interstate, ten minutes north of town. Hank had started to speak at least five times, but something in my face had stopped him. I didn't want to answer him. I didn't want to say the words, yet for some reason I did. Maybe I hoped they wouldn't sound so bad if spoken out loud.

"Someone important to me has gone missing."

"Someone important? Who do you—Oh, I get it. A girlfriend?"

"More than that," I said softly.

"Plenty of fish in the sea, Work. Trust me on that."

I rolled down the window because I needed the smell of something clean. Wind buffeted my face, and for a moment I could not breathe.

"You're wrong about that, Hank," I finally said.

"Then we're swimming in different bodies of water."

Not swimming, I thought, *drowning,* and for a moment I was.

"So who was the guy?" I didn't answer, and Hank looked his question at me a second time. "The guy?"

I settled back into my seat, the headrest soft and sweet-smelling on the heels of jail-issue bedding. "Just drive, Hank. Do you mind? I need to think."

His words came from far away. "Sure, man. Whatever. It's a long trip."

He was right. It was.

But we made it to the crowded parking lot of Dorothea Dix Hospital by late twilight. We didn't speak until he killed the engine. I peered up through the windshield. Of all the miserable places in this world, I thought, this one must hold the darkest secrets. I thought of Bedlam, and screams choked with vomit. "Talk about the screaming willies," I said.

"It's not as bad as you might think," Hank said.

"You've been here before?"

"Once or twice." He did not elaborate.

"And?"

"And I've never been on the secure floors. But the rest of it is just like any other hospital."

I studied the grounds again. "Except for the razor wire," I said.

"There is that."

"What now?" I asked.

"How much money do you have?"

I checked my wallet instinctively, forgetting that I'd already counted the money when it was returned to me. "Three hundred and seventy dollars."

"Give it to me." He separated out the three hundred-dollar bills and gave me back the rest. "This should do it." I watched him fold the bills together and tuck them into the front pocket of his jeans. "Ready?" he asked.

"As I'll ever be," I said, meaning it. He punched me lightly on the shoulder.

"Relax," he told me. "This will be fun."

When we got out of the car, he donned a windbreaker and checked something in the inside pocket. I couldn't tell what it was, but he grunted lightly, as if satisfied. I looked up at the hospital, black and sharp-edged against the dark purple sky. Light seemed to jump from the windows and die on the way down.

"Come on," Hank said. "Try to relax."

We started toward the main entrance to the hospital. "Hang on," Hank said. I watched him trot back to the car, unlock it, and reach inside. He came back with the picture of Alex that I'd left in the mailbox. "Might need this," he said. The picture flashed in the weak light, but I saw Alex's face perfectly. Like the building, it had sharp edges, and I wondered, not for the first time, what had brought her to this place. What had brought her here and what had she carried away? What had she taken home to my sister, and was it as evil as my troubled mind made it out to be?

I needed an answer, and looking at Hank, I thought we had a good shot at finding one.

We walked into the lobby. Halls shot off in multiple directions. An elevator bank faced us. The hospital smell was overwhelming.

Hank approached a row of newspaper machines and dug some change from his pockets. "Have you read the Charlotte paper today?"

I shook my head. "No."

He dropped his change into the machine that vended the *Charlotte Observer*. He retrieved a paper and handed it to me. "You'll need this," he said.

I didn't understand. "What for?" I asked, holding the paper as if I'd never seen one before.

"Are you serious?" he asked, and turned away.

"Oh." I tucked the paper under my arm. Hank looked up at the bewildering proliferation of signs and seemed to find what he wanted. I didn't have a clue what that was, but when he told me to follow him, I did. Soon we were lost in the maze, and the ever-present signs beckoned us deeper into the hospital. Hank kept his eyes down, like he knew exactly where he was going. He looked at no one and no one looked at him. I tried to follow suit. Eventually, we turned onto a hall that ended at a small waiting room. In the corner, on the wall, a television showed us its blank screen. A sticky note informed passersby that it was out of order.

A row of vinyl seats lined one wall. Two more halls ran away in opposite directions, their polished floors agleam with the reflection of fluorescent lighting from above. Voices echoed around us: passing nurses, medical students, a box on the wall paging doctors. Across from us was a blue swinging door beneath a sign that said EMPLOYEES ONLY.

"This is the place," Hank said. I looked around again, sure I must have missed something. Hank fished a plastic identification badge from his jacket pocket and clipped it onto his shirt. It had his picture on it, a name I'd never heard before, and the name of the hospital. It looked just like every other employee identification badge I'd seen since we entered.

"Where did you get that?" I whispered.

"It's forged," he replied curtly.

"But . . ."

He flashed his crooked grin. "I told you I'd been here before."

I nodded. "Okay. What do you want me to do?"

"Wait here," he said. I followed his gaze to the row of uncomfortable red vinyl seats. "Read the paper. This might take a while."

"I want to come," I said.

"I know you do, and I don't blame you, but people will talk to one person when they might not talk to two. One is a friendly chat. Two is an interrogation."

He read the emotion on my face, knew how important this was to me.

"Relax, Work. Read the paper. If there is an answer to be found here, I'll find it. Okay? This is what I do. Trust me."

"I don't like this."

"Don't think about it." Hank turned away, then just as quickly turned back. "Give me the sports section," he said. I fumbled it out of the paper and handed it to him. He rolled it up and saluted me with it. "Icebreaker," he said. "All-important in this business."

I sat stiffly on the hard chair and watched as Hank walked boldly through the door designated for employees only. He didn't look back, and when the door swung shut, it swallowed him whole.

I settled back. I opened the paper and stared blankly at words that swam. When people passed, I tried to look normal, as if I belonged, but it was hard, for in my racing mind I was a criminal.

I sat there for what my watch said was only fifty-five minutes. The watch lied. It was a lifetime.

Time and again, that blue door swung open. A black man came out the first time, then a white woman and a fat man who could never be mistaken for Hank Robins. Another woman. Two men. An endless stream, and they all wore the same badge of identification. Again and again the door swung wide, and each time it did, the spring of my body wound a little tighter. Hank had been found out. He wasn't coming.

Then I saw him, in the brief flash as the door swung shut behind an old man pushing a bucket. He was coming out, and the next time the door opened, it was for him. He did not smile, but in his eyes I saw a fierce satisfaction. He took me by the arm before I could say a word; then we were walking, our footsteps loud in the hard-tiled and resonant halls that were the arteries of this place.

"That wasn't so bad, was it?" he asked in a voice so normal, it surprised me. I'd expected a whisper.

"Did you get it?" I asked, meaning the answer to our question.

The fierceness moved from his eyes to his mouth, and he smiled. "Oh yes. I got it."

I wanted to shake it out of him. "And?"

"And it's something."

We walked in a silence that just about killed me, but eventually we made it to the car. Hank slipped behind the wheel, started the engine, and hit the door-lock button. He still had not said a word. He backed out of the parking spot and navigated us through the inland sea of parked vehicles. Finally, he looked at me. "Buckle up," he said.

"Are you fucking with me?" I asked. "Because this is not a good time." He did not respond, and his eyes remained steady on the road.

"I'm just getting my thoughts together, Work. There's a lot to say and I'm trying to figure out the best way to do it. I don't want to freak you out."

"You're freaking me out right now."

But he would not be rushed, and he kept his mouth shut until we were on Interstate 40, driving west at exactly nine miles over the speed limit.

"Have you ever heard of East Bend?" he finally asked.

"Maybe. I think so."

"It's a little place. Pretty, with horses. It's on the Yadkin River, not far from Winston-Salem."

Headlights flashed on Hank's face from across the grassy divide, unidentified cars driven by nameless people. In the dark intervals, Hank's face was a blurred profile. Then he turned to look at me.

"You should go there sometime. There's this little vineyard there, right on the river. . . ."

"Is there some reason you're stalling?"

He looked at me again, and headlights filled the space around us. "Alex is from there. It's where she grew up. For the first fourteen years anyway."

"And?"

"Look, Work . . . the details are sketchy. All I've got is what the nursing assistant told me, and bought information isn't always reliable. I haven't verified any of this."

"Fine. You're absolved of the consequences of any misinformation. Just tell me what you heard."

"She killed her father, Work. She cuffed him to the bed and set it on fire."

"What?"

"She was fourteen. Her mother was in the bed, too, but she survived. It was Daddy she was after." He paused. "And she got him, too. Cooked him right to the bed."

I felt Hank's eyes on me, gauging my reaction, but there was none; then Hank continued, his voice a flat line.

"She waited for him to stop screaming, and then she called 911 and walked out of the house; she watched it burn. When the fire truck arrived, she met them at the curb, said her mother might still be alive. They found her under the bedroom window, burned over seventy percent of her body. She was cut up pretty bad, too, from diving through the glass. When the police showed up, the girl told them what she'd done. She didn't lie about it, but she didn't gloat, either. Rumor is, she didn't shed a single tear. The nursing assistant didn't know if she went to trial or not, but the state sent her to psychiatric lockup. She spent four years at Dorothea Dix, but she was a minor when she did the job. So when she turned eighteen, they released her to Charter Hills, where she met Jean."

"That was only three years ago," I said.

"She's young."

"She doesn't look it."

"She's led a hard life, no mistake there. It'll age a person."

"Are you sympathizing with her?" I asked.

"Not at all," Hank said. "But they couldn't tell me what went down before she killed him. She must have had a reason, and it's not too hard to guess what it was." I sensed him shrug. "I have a soft spot for hard-luck cases." He left the rest unspoken. I didn't have the details, but I knew that Hank's childhood had been no picnic.

The silence drew out. Cars passed us.

"That's it?" asked. "That's all we know?"

"I tried to buy a copy of her file, but the guy wouldn't go there. He said gossip was one thing, stealing documents was another; but he was pretty sure of what he told me. Said it was common knowledge among the staff."

Hank checked his mirror and passed a pickup truck. One of its headlights was out, so it seemed to wink at us as we passed. I saw the sign for Interstate 85, and we remained silent until we'd left I-40 and pointed south, toward Jean and the woman who guarded so well the secrets of her violent past.

Hank reached into his pocket and handed me back two of the hundred-dollar bills. "It only took one," he said.

"So that's it?"

"Basically."

I sensed Hank's hesitation. "What does 'basically' mean?" I asked.

Hank shrugged again. "The guy was scared of her."

"Of Alex?"

"Alex. Virginia. He said everybody was pretty much scared of her."

"Except Jean," I said.

I felt his eyes again, measuring me in the dark. "Except Jean," he finally said. "Jean loved her."

I nodded silently, then looked again at Hank. There had been something in his voice.

"Is there something you're not telling me?"

He shook his head. "Not really. Just something I heard at Charter Hills."

"What?"

A shrug. "Something a guy said. Another floor worker, one of the guys I talked to the other day. I asked him about Jean and Alex, and something he said stuck with me. He said that Jean loved her like a preacher loves his God." Hank took his eyes off the road. "His words, not mine."

I pictured them together.

A *preacher and his God.* Obedience. Subservience.

"Could she really love her that much?"

"Who the hell knows? I've never had anything like it." He sounded wistful. I said nothing for a long time, and Hank, too, seemed content with his own thoughts.

"Do you think Alex could have killed my father?"

"Assuming you didn't do it?"

"Very funny." I wasn't laughing.

"Do you know where she was the night Ezra went and got himself shot?"

"No."

"Did she have a reason to want him dead?"

I thought of Ezra, and of his persistent disdain for Alex. I saw the fight between him and Jean, the night that everything went to shit. The fight had been about Alex. Ezra had tried to force them apart.

"She had a reason," I said.

"And seven years ago, she cooked her father to his bed."

I nodded to myself. "I guess it's possible."

"There you go."

CHAPTER

29

We rolled into Salisbury after midnight. The town was quiet, with few cars moving and fewer lights burning. I felt like a ghost as we whispered through the stillness. Even Hank was subdued, and I guessed that, like me, he could not shake the image of what Alex had done.

When Hank pulled into my driveway, I got out and walked around to his window. He rolled it down.

"Listen, Hank. I really appreciate what you've done; it means a lot."

"You'll get my bill," he replied.

"Better send it soon," I said.

"You're not going back to jail, Work. We both know how this is going to end. Alex is your man. Take what we learned to Mills and get her to check it out."

"Maybe. We'll see." I still had to talk to Jean. "Listen, about the bill . . ."

"It's going to be a big one."

"Bigger than you think," I said.

He eyed me. "What do you mean?"

I put my hands on the frame of his window, leaned against the car. "I need you to find somebody for me. It's important."

"Your girlfriend?"

"Her name is Vanessa Stolen. You know where she lives. I need to find her. I need to talk to her. I need . . ." My voice trailed away, then came back. "I just need her."

An overwhelming conviction came over me that she was dead. "She never leaves like this." That's the last thing the big farmhand told me, there by the tractor at Stolen Farm. "Not without making provision for her animals. She'd never leave them unattended."

"What about you?" I'd asked.

"I just work here, mister. If she needs me to take care of things while she's gone, she always calls. I've got my own place to look after, too. She knows that."

In my mind I'd seen them together, her body alive under his heavy calloused hands. I'd thought she'd given herself to him, and that her gift had killed the last, best part of me.

"Just find her for me, Hank. There are things that need to be said."

"What else can you tell me about her? Anything that might help me find her. Family. Friends. Places she might go. That sort of thing."

"She has no family. She's the last. I don't know if she has any friends, and as far as I can tell, she rarely leaves the farm. The place is her life."

"When did you see her last?"

"Right before I was arrested."

"I hate to ask this," Hank said. "But is it possible that she doesn't want to be found? People get to that point, Work. Sometimes we just need to disappear for awhile." He looked away, as if he had to in order to finish his thought. "You're married. You were arrested for murder. Maybe the fling wasn't worth it anymore. Maybe the cost was too high."

"It wasn't like that," I said. "Don't try to make it like that."

"Take it easy, man. I see it all the time. I had to ask."

"It wasn't like that."

Hank just nodded, still not looking at me, and an awkward silence formed around us. He looked at his watch. "It's late. I'm going home. But I'll look for your missing friend tomorrow. Okay? I'll find her."

"You're a good man, Hank. I appreciate it."

"I'll call you later."

He rolled up the window and drove away; and it was only then that I noticed that Barbara's car was gone. I walked into an empty house and found another one of her notes on the kitchen counter. She was staying at Glena's house for the night.

I was too keyed up to sleep. For it seemed increasingly possible that Alex was responsible for Ezra's death. She'd killed her own father. Why not mine? But there was more to the story, and I wanted to know it all. I had to. It felt like a piece was missing. Once I had it, and once Hank found Vanessa, then I would go to Mills. But not before.

I turned on my computer and did a White Pages search for East Bend, North Carolina. I found two Temples listed, a husband and wife and a Rhonda Temple. I wrote down her address. Then I realized that I had no vehicle. Mills had impounded the truck when she'd arrested me. I considered waiting until morning, but I could not face six hours awake in that depleted house. In the end, I called Dr. Stokes. He met me at his back door. He had on striped pajamas. His hair was in disarray.

"I'm sorry to wake you up, Dr. Stokes, but it's kind of important."

He waved away my words. "I said I'd help and I meant it. Plus, it's been a long time since someone called me with an emergency in the middle of the night. I kind of miss it." He stepped out of the house and we stood on the concrete driveway. He looked small under the porch light. "Which car do you want?" He gestured at the two cars parked there, a dark blue Lincoln and a wood-paneled minivan.

"Whichever. I don't care."

"Then you'd better take mine," he said. He walked back inside and came out with a set of keys. He handed them to me.

I looked at the Lincoln. It was large and polished. I knew that it would be fast. I gestured toward it as I spoke. "I'll take good care of it," I said.

Dr. Stokes chuckled. "That's Marion's car, Work." He continued to shake his head. "I drive that one." He pointed at the minivan. It had to be nine years old.

"Oh. Okay. I'll be back by midmorning."

"Take your time. I have no plans tomorrow."

I found the town of East Bend at 2:30 in the morning. It was a bump on Highway 67, thirty miles outside of Winston-Salem. There was not much there: a restaurant, a real estate office, a few convenience stores. I walked into the only store that was open, bought a cup of questionable coffee, and asked the clerk if they sold maps of East Bend. He was probably twenty, with long hair under a camouflage hunting cap. He laughed at my question.

"That's a good one," he said. "I'll have to remember that one."

"I'm looking for Trinity Lane," I said as I paid.

"You'll never find it."

"That's why I'm asking for directions."

"It's not a real road. That's why you won't find it. It's just a dirt road, the kind where they let you make up a name for it, but the sign is blue instead of green. That's how you can always tell if it's a real road or not. Green means real. There's an *e* in both of them—*green* and *real*. That's the best way to remember."

"There's an *e* in blue also."

"Shit. You're right."

"I'm looking for a woman named Rhonda Temple." He didn't answer me. He stood behind the counter, patted his belly, and stared back. "I don't mean her any harm, if that's what you're worried about."

He laughed again and showed his stained teeth. "You can kill her, for all I care. That woman is without doubt the meanest bitch I ever did meet. What do you want to talk to her for?"

"Was she in a fire seven or eight years ago?"

"That's her."

"That's what I want to talk to her about."

"Hell, everybody around here can tell you about that. That crazy kid of hers set the place on fire. Cuffed her old man to the bed and left him to burn."

"Alex."

"Naw. Not Alex."

"Virginia, I mean. The daughter's name is Virginia."

"That's her."

"Did you know her?"

"Not really. She was only a year or two older, but she was damaged goods. She was like fourteen when they sent her away."

I leaned on the counter. "Any idea why she did it?" I asked.

He lifted his cap and scratched his head. "Just mean, I guess. And crazy as a shithouse rat."

"So how do I find this woman's house?"

"Oh. Go on down that way and take a left at the blinking yellow. Look for the blue sign on the left, a dirt road. She's at the end of it."

I looked at him. "I thought you said I'd never find it."

"Well you wouldn't have if I hadn't told you. You going down there tonight?"

"Maybe," I said. "I haven't decided."

"Well, I wouldn't if I were you. Going down blue sign roads at three in the morning is liable to get you shot."

I thanked him and turned to leave. "Hey, mister."

"Yeah."

"Don't let her scare you." I waited for something more. "She's ugly as shit."

As much as I wanted to speak with Rhonda Temple, mother of Virginia Temple, aka Alex Shiften, I knew that the store clerk had a point. I sipped coffee in the parked car and thought about how I would handle it. I thought about Dr. Stokes and his feelings on faith, hell, and the chance of salvation. Eventually, I dozed.

I found Trinity Lane at a few minutes before seven, right where it was supposed to be, although I almost missed it. At some point, a car had hit the blue sign and now it leaned at an angle, twisted and almost hidden in the scrub growth that bordered the two-lane blacktop. Trinity Lane itself was a rutted dirt track, a gash in the wooded verge. It curved away before me, a dim alley in the weak morning light. I passed derelict single-wides as I moved deeper into the woods. Some were burned out, others simply worn down and abandoned. Fiberglass insulation hung from places where siding had been stripped away, and rusted appliances bled slowly into the weed-choked red clay. It was a dismal place.

The road ended five hundred yards in, at the rear bumper of a twenty-year-old Dodge Omni. It was parked in the bare dirt yard of the last trailer, a single-wide with a satellite dish beside it. I climbed warily from the car. There was a refuse pile behind the trailer, at the point where the land fell away to the river. A few lifeless items hung from a clothesline. A light burned behind one of the windows.

I knocked on the aluminum door.

The woman who opened the door was clearly the woman I sought. Her face and hands were severely scarred, not only from the fire but from the glass of the window she'd leapt through to escape the flames. The right side of her face, from the nose to the ear, was a textured nightmare, and long scars, puckered and white, crisscrossed her face. She had wild gray hair, thick glasses in pink frames, and a cigarette with a plastic filter on the end.

"Who the hell are you?" she asked. "And what the fuck are you doing at my house this early in the fucking morning?"

"Ma'am, my name is Work Pickens. I drove up from Salisbury. I'm sorry to bother you so early, but it's very important that I speak to you about your daughter."

"Why the hell should I talk to you?"

"I honestly don't have an answer for that. You don't know me and you don't owe me. I'm just asking."

"You want to talk about my daughter? Are you a cop or a reporter or something?" She looked me up and down.

"No. I'm none of those things."

"What are you, then?"

I ignored her question. "Virginia Temple. She's your daughter, right?"

She took a drag on the plastic filter, studied me with reptile eyes. "She came out of me, if that's what you mean. But she's no daughter of mine."

"I don't understand," I said.

"That girl was ruined by the time she was ten. She wasn't my baby no more, even then. But when she did this to me, when she set the fire and killed my Alex, well, I decided then and there that she weren't no child of mine. Not then and not ever again."

I couldn't help but look at the scars, and I thought of what it must have been like to wake up engulfed in flame. "I'm sorry about your husband."

"Are you stupid?" she asked. "I don't care about that worthless shit. He got what he deserved and I'm better off with him dead. I'm talking about my Alex." Her eyes misted and she swiped at one of them.

"Alex? I don't understand."

"Alex was the only thing good in my life."

I stood there, confused. "Ma'am . . ."

"Goddamn it. Alex was my other daughter, my baby. She was seven when it happened. That bitch Virginia killed her, too. Or didn't you know that?"

CHAPTER

30

Rhonda Temple pretty much shut down after her outburst. She wouldn't talk much at all, not about Virginia and not about why she'd done what she did. But she did tell me how Alex, her youngest daughter, had come to die. The story stayed with me on the drive back to Salisbury, and I knew that the time had come to confront Jean. I had to ask the question. I had to know.

I parked Dr. Stokes's car and walked to the entrance of the emergency room. I nodded at a doctor who stood smoking outside, then entered the brightly lit hospital. It was quiet, and for a moment it felt more like a mausoleum than a hospital. The triage nurse's desk was empty. No one sat on the long benches or chairs in the waiting room. I could hear the hum of fluorescent lighting and the pneumatic hiss of the door as it slid shut behind me. I saw movement behind a glass partition, a flash of white coat, but that was it. The place was dead. So, feeling more like a ghost than ever, I passed through the reception area and into the long hall. It led me past vending machines, telephones, and the closed doors of the small hutchlike offices where low-grade administrators worked from nine to five. I found the bank of elevators and stepped inside. I pushed the button for the third floor.

The nurse's station on Jean's wing was empty and I walked quickly past it. As I reached my sister's room, a nurse turned the corner, moving toward me, but her head was down. She didn't see me, so I went inside and closed the door. The room was dark after the hallway, but not entirely without light. Some filtered in from outside, and the monitors cast their eerie glow. I half-expected to find Alex there, and honestly didn't know what I'd do if I did. Fortunately, she wasn't there. I needed Jean's attention, not another pissing contest.

When I took Jean's hand, it felt desiccated, as if she had bled out after all; but it was warm, and I looked down at her as I held it. Her eyes moved beneath her lids, and I wondered what she was dreaming about. Something bad. Her life was a nightmare. There would be no reprieve behind closed eyes. I wanted to wake her but did not. I sat in the chair by her side and held her fevered hand. Eventually, I put my head on the narrow margin of bed, and leaning forward, perched on that unyielding chair, I finally fell asleep.

At some point, I, too, must have dreamed. I felt her hand on my head and heard her voice. *How could you, Work? How could you do it?* Her hand fell away, along with her words, but in the clairvoyance of dreams, I knew that she was weeping.

When I woke, it was with a start. Jean's skin was washed charcoal, her eyes twin slits of darkness, but then she blinked, and I knew that she was awake and had been watching me.

"When did you get here?" Her voice was as arid as her hands. I rubbed my eyes.

"Do you want some water?" I asked her.

"Yes, please."

I poured some into the plastic cup on her bedside table. "There's no ice."

"It doesn't matter." She drank the water and I refilled her cup.

I looked at the saline bag suspended above her, followed the tube to where its needle entered her arm beneath a white X of tape. It was easy to recall the red sea of her blood on the floor of our parents' house. She'd probably be dehydrated for a week.

I looked at her face, saw the slackness around her mouth, and wondered what she was on. Antidepressants, maybe? Sedatives? She saw me looking and turned away.

I did not want to ask her the things that had to be asked. She was transparent, and I knew that I had never seen a more fragile person.

"How are you, Jean? Are you holding up okay?"

She blinked at me, and for an instant I thought she wouldn't answer. She drew up her knees, puddled into herself, and I thought she was going to turn away from me, as she'd done the last time.

"They say you saved my life." The statement was utterly devoid of emotional context.

They say your car is blue. Like that.

I almost lied. I didn't want her to hate me for doing what I'd done. "I might have," I said.

"Even Alex says it. She says you found me and put tourniquets on my arms. She says one minute later and I would have died."

I looked at my fingers, remembering the slipperiness of her blood; how hard I'd jammed those fingers into her neck, looking for a pulse. "You called me," I said. "I came."

"That's the third time," she continued. I felt her movement and looked up in time to see her turn her face away. "You must hate me," she said.

"No." I put my hand on her arm, turned her back so that I could see her face. "Never, Jean. Don't you ever think that. I could never hate you." I squeezed her shoulder and said the words that should have come easily but never had. "You're my sister. And I love you."

It was her turn to nod. She did so in fitful jerks as folds closed over her eyes like curtains and tears pooled on the shelf of her wasted cheeks before spilling down her face in two long, hot arcs. She swiped at the tears with one arm, scrubbing them away with the heavy bandage that covered her wrist. She opened her mouth to speak but then closed it, the words unsaid. Instead, she continued to nod. But I understood. The words were hard. That's how we were raised.

Do you need anything? I wanted to ask. More water? Another pillow? I meant to ask these things, but that's not what I said. There was a larger question, a dangerous one. But it couldn't wait any longer. I needed to know. I couldn't go to Mills until I heard it from Jean herself.

"Did you do it?" I asked.

Jean looked horrified.

"What?" Almost a moan, and the tears came faster, but I couldn't stop. Every action of the past week had been based around my assumptions that Jean had pulled the trigger. I'd gone to jail for those assumptions. I now faced life in prison for them.

"Did you kill him?" I asked again. "Did you kill Ezra?"

Jean's mouth gaped and then collapsed. "I thought *you* did it," she said. It was her child's voice, so vulnerable that I saw the truth of her words. She really believed that I'd done it.

"Is that what Alex told you, Jean? Is that why you think I did it? Because she told you I did it?"

Jean shook her head, hair moving over her eyes, coming to rest on her forehead. I saw that she'd pulled the sheet to her throat. Her eyes spilled confusion.

"You did it, Work. You had to have done it."

"I thought you did it," I said, and Jean rocked as if my words were bullets. Her eyes widened and she pushed deeper into the pillows that mounded behind her.

"No." She shook her head again. "It had to be you. It had to be."

"Why?" I asked, leaning closer. "Why me?"

"Because . . ." Her voice trailed off. She tried again. "Because . . ."

I finished her thought. "Because if you didn't do it, and I didn't do it, then Alex did. Is that what you were going to say?"

This time, she did roll away; she curled into a fetal ball, as if I might kick her, and for that moment I was at a loss. Jean hadn't done it. Had I not known the truth about Alex, I would not have accepted that fact.

I'd been so damned sure.

"There are some things about Alex, Jean. Some things you might not know." I had to jolt her out of her complacency, force her to accept the truth.

She spoke from across the chasm I'd opened between us. "I know everything there is to know about Alex, Work. There's nothing you can tell me."

"Do you know that's not her real name?"

"Don't do this, Work. Don't try to come between me and Alex."

"Did you know it?" I asked again.

Jean sighed. "Virginia Temple. That's her real name. She changed it when she was released."

"Do you know she killed her father?" I asked.

"I know," she said.

"You know about that?" I couldn't believe it. "Do you know how she killed him?" Jean was nodding, but I couldn't stop. The horror of it was still too fresh in my mind. Cooked meat. Charred lungs. Alex watching and her mother sliced to ribbons. "She handcuffed him to the bed and set it on fire. She burned him alive, Jean. For Christ's sake, she burned him alive!"

Suddenly, I was on my feet. Beneath me, Jean contracted even further. She was hugging her knees to her chest, cringing, and I saw that the line from her saline bag had a kink in it. The sight calmed me down, forced me to get a grip on my raging emotions. I knew that I was losing it. It was all too much. I took a deep breath, then leaned over to straighten the kink, but when my hand brushed against her arm, she flinched.

"I'm sorry, Jean. I'm really sorry." She declined to respond, and her body rose up as she sucked in a mighty breath. I found the chair again and fell into it. I buried my face in my palms, pressed against my eyes until I saw sparks. But for her wet breath, the room was silent. I took my hands away and looked at her. She was still clenched in a ball.

"It scares me, Jean. It scares me that she killed her father, and it scares me that she has this power over you." I paused, looking for better words. "It just scares me."

Jean did not respond, and for a long time I watched her in silence. After a few minutes of this, I felt the need to move, to do something. I got up and went to the window. I pulled back the curtain and stared across at the parking deck. A car pulled in and turned on its headlights.

When Jean spoke, I could barely hear her.

"She had a pool. Growing up, she had a pool."

I walked back to the bed. When she rolled her face off the pillow, I could see the wet spot of her tears. "A pool," I said, letting her know I was there and that I was ready to listen. I sat down. Her eyes were huge and raw; she showed them to me briefly, then turned back to the wall. I looked at her back and waited for her to go on. Finally, she did.

"It was one of those aboveground pools, like we used to make fun of when we were kids. A poor kid's pool. She didn't care that it was cheap or flimsy. She didn't care that it sat behind a single-wide or that it was visible from the road. She was a kid, you know. And it was a pool." Jean paused. "The best thing that ever happened to her."

I could see it as if I were there; yet I already sensed the truth of it. It was the way she said it. The pool was not the best thing that ever happened to her. Not by a long shot.

Jean continued. "When she turned seven, her father implemented the new policy. That's exactly how he said it. 'We're implementing a new pool policy.' He tried to make a joke out of it. She didn't care one way or another. But if she wanted to hang out around the pool, she had to be wearing high heels and makeup. That was the policy." She paused, and I heard her sharp intake of breath. "That's how it started."

I knew where this was going, and I felt my insides clench in disgust. Hank had been right.

"The policy didn't include her mother. Just her. She told me once that her mother stopped hanging out at the pool after that. She didn't do anything about it. She just didn't want to see it. Her father was out of work that year, so that's what they did. They hung out at the pool. In the summer, I guess, that was enough. Watching, I mean. But two weeks after they closed up the pool for the winter, it started."

I did not want to hear this. I wanted her to stop. But I had to hear it and she had to say it. We were trying to find the road.

"He didn't just fondle her, Work. He raped her. He sodomized her. When she fought back, he beat her. After that summer, she wasn't allowed to have pajamas. For God's sake, she had to sleep naked. Another policy. It didn't start slow and build up. It exploded into her life. One day she was seven. The next day she was getting it regular. His term. But in spite of that, it somehow got worse over time, like he got bored with her and had to find new ways to make it fun. She can't talk about some of the things he did, not even now. And she's the strongest person I know.

"It went on for years. He never did go back to work. He drank more and he gambled more. On three occasions, he loaned her out to cover his gambling debts. A hundred dollars here, two hundred there. She was eleven the first time. The guy was a shift foreman at the rubber plant in Winston-Salem. He weighed three hundred pounds. Alex weighed a little over seventy."

"Her mother . . ." I began.

"She tried to tell her mother once, but she didn't want to hear it. She accused her of lying and slapped her. But she knew."

Jean fell silent.

"She could have gone to the authorities," I said.

"She was a child! She didn't know any different. By the time she turned thirteen, it started to get a little better. He molested her less and beat her more." Jean rolled her eyes to me. "She was getting too old for him. She hit puberty and he started to lose interest."

"She was fourteen when she killed him," I said. "Well past puberty."

A sound escaped Jean's throat, part laugh and part strangled cry. She turned her entire body over, raised herself up on one elbow as if to meet me eye-to-eye. "You don't get it, Work."

"If he'd stopped abusing her—"

"She had a sister!" This time, she yelled. "That's why she did what she did. A seven-year-old sister named Alexandria."

Suddenly, I understood. I understood everything.

"On the day that Alex killed her father, her sister had just turned seven years old. Her party was the day before. Guess what her daddy gave her."

I knew the answer.

"High heels, Work. Her own high heels and a tube of lipstick. For daddy's little girl. And she loved it. She didn't know what it meant; she just wanted to dress up like her big sister. That's why Alex killed him."

I didn't want to speak. I didn't want to hurt my sister further, but knew that I probably would. Hank had told me that Jean loved Alex like a preacher loves his God. So be it. But this was no divine being, no benevolent soul. She was damaged, a killer, and Jean had to understand the truth of this. For her own good.

"What happened to her sister?" I asked. "Did Alex ever tell you that?"

Jean sniffed loudly, but her voice was calmer. "She doesn't talk about her sister. I guess they lost touch after Alex was locked up. Her sister probably didn't understand, not at that age."

I had to do it fast, before I froze. She had to know.

"Her sister died, Jean. She ran back into the house and she burned to death along with her father."

Jean's mouth formed into another silent, seemingly toothless black circle.

"Accident or not, she killed her sister. And for some reason, she took her name. Alexandria, Alex. It can't be a coincidence. She killed her father, she killed her sister, and, as far as I'm concerned, she killed Ezra, too."

Jean's body trembled. "She would have told me," she said, then looked suddenly suspicious. "Why are you doing this?" she demanded.

"I'm sorry, Jean. I know it hurts, but I had to tell you. You deserve the truth."

"I don't believe you."

"I swear it, Jean. On our mother's name, I swear it's the truth."

"Get out of here, Work. Get out and leave me alone."

"Jean . . ."

"You always took Dad's side. You've always hated her."

"She killed our father, and she wants me to fry for it."

Jean rose from the mattress, a gray and quaking shadow of herself; her sheets fell away and she swayed on the narrow bed. I feared she would tumble off and crack her skull on the hard floor. Her finger stabbed at me, and I saw the denial in her. I'd pushed it too hard, too fast.

I'd lost her.

"Get out!" she screamed, and burst into tears. "Get out! Get out of here, you fucking liar!"

CHAPTER

31

I fled the room because I had no choice. Jean was distraught; I'd pushed her to a dangerous place. She had two things in this world, Alex and me. But right now, Alex was all that mattered to her, and I'd tried to take that away.

But at least I had the truth, finally. Jean had not killed Ezra. She was not a murderer, and without that weight on her conscience, she might eventually pull out of the nosedive that had brought her to this hospital in the first place. Yet the alternatives could be equally devastating. Someone was going down for Ezra's murder, and the way it looked now, it would either be Alex or me. Could Jean recover from either of those eventualities? She would have to. It was just that simple.

For me, things had changed dramatically. I might have been willing to take the rap for Jean, but not for Alex. No way in hell.

I leaned against the wall. It was hard and cold under my back, and I closed my eyes. I thought I heard her weeping, but then the sound was gone. Imagination, I told myself. Guilty conscience.

When I opened my eyes, a nurse was standing in front of me. She looked worried.

"Are you okay?" she asked. The question took me by surprise.

"Yes."

She studied me. "You're as pale as a sheet and look dead on your feet."

"I'm okay. Just tired."

"I'm not going to argue about it," she told me. "But if you're not a patient, you'll have to leave. Visiting hours aren't for another hour."

"Thanks," I said, and walked off. When I looked back, she was watching me, a puzzled look on her face. I could almost read her mind. Don't I know you from somewhere? She was thinking. Then she turned away.

As I followed the hall toward the elevators, I thought about Alex. I was no shrink, so I could only guess at the state of her mind, but it had to be a wreck. Why the name change? I could understand wanting to escape her childhood, but why take her dead sister's name? Because she'd died untouched and un-spoiled, purified by her innocence and by the fire that killed her? Or was it guilt, and the desire that she live on in some small way? I would probably never know. But one thing was crystal clear, and that is what scared me. Alex Shiften was fiercely loyal, and she would take drastic measures to eradicate any per-ceived threat to herself, to Jean, or to their relationship. She killed her father to protect her sister. She killed Ezra to protect her relationship with Jean. Now I was the threat, and she was setting me up for the murder. She'd turned Jean against me. She'd undermined my alibi, somehow acquired a copy of the will, and planted it in my house.

Suddenly, I froze, paralyzed by a thought that came unbidden yet with hor-rifying clarity. Alex had undermined my alibi. She knew that I was not home with Barbara when Ezra was shot. Did she know where I was that night? Did she know about Vanessa? Dear God! Did she know that Vanessa could give me an alibi? Now Vanessa was missing.

She didn't come home last night.

I couldn't finish the thought. But I had to. There was no time left for fear or denial. So I asked the question. If Alex knew that Vanessa could ruin her plans, would she kill her?

The answer was unequivocal.

Absolutely.

The elevator opened. I pushed through the waiting crowd of green shirts and white coats and nearly sprinted for the exit. Outside, I realized that I had no plan. Nowhere to go. I looked at my watch. It was 10:30. I called Stolen Farm, knowing better than to hope, yet doing so with every fiber of my being. Just pick up. Please, pick up. The phone rang four times, and each unan-swered ring was a nail in my heart. Alex had killed her. She was dead.

The grief almost overwhelmed me, yet through the pain, like a whispering traitor, came a single selfish thought. I had no alibi. I could go to jail for the rest of my life. The presence of that thought made me think that maybe I should. I squashed it and it did not resurrect itself, for which I was grateful.

Next, I called Hank. I had to talk to him, now more than ever. He didn't answer at home, so I tried his cell phone.

"I was about to call you," he said.

"Hank, thank God."

"Shut up for a minute. We've got big fucking problems." I heard his hand go over the mouthpiece, heard muffled voices. Almost a minute passed before he came back on the line. "Okay. I'm outside."

"Listen, Hank. I think I'm onto something about Vanessa."

"Work, I mean this in the most polite way, but we don't have time to deal with your missing girlfriend. I'm at the police station now."

"In Salisbury?"

"Yeah. I came here to check accident reports before I started looking for your friend. But it's a damn hornet's nest down here. We need to talk, but not on the phone. Where are you right now?"

"I'm at the hospital. I'm standing outside the emergency-room exit."

"Stay there. Try to stay out of sight. I'll be there in a couple of minutes."

"Hank, wait." I caught him before he hung up. "What the hell is going on?"

"They found the gun, Work. The one you threw in the river."

"What?"

"Just sit tight. Two minutes." He hung up, and I stared at the dead cell phone in my hand for what may have been the longest two minutes of my life.

They'd found the gun. Could Alex have been responsible for that, too?

When Hank turned into the parking lot, I met him at the curb. I climbed into his sedan. He neither looked at me nor spoke. He turned left out of the parking lot, made several seemingly random turns, and then stopped at the curb. We were in a residential neighborhood. It was quiet, nobody in sight. Hank stared wordlessly through the windshield.

"I'm waiting for you to speak," he finally said, looking at me.

"What do you mean?"

His face was hard; so were his eyes. When he spoke, I found that his voice had chilled, as well. "What river? What gun? Those are the questions you should have asked. It concerns me that you did not ask those questions."

I didn't know what to say. He was right. An innocent man would have asked the questions.

"I didn't kill him, Hank."

"Tell me about the gun."

"There's nothing to tell." The lie came instinctively.

"You don't have many people in your corner, Work, and you're about to be all alone. I don't help people who lie to me; it's that simple. So you take a minute, and think about the next words that come out of your mouth."

I'd never seen Hank so tense, like he could punch me in the face or rip his own hair out. But it was more than anger. He felt betrayed, and I couldn't blame him.

If Jean hadn't pulled the trigger, then I had no reason to lie about the gun. In fact, I should want the police to have it, if that would help convict Alex. But I'd wiped it down and ditched it, a crime in and of itself. Yet all that mattered right now was finding Vanessa, and if Hank could help me do that, then I would tell him anything he wanted to know. I had one question first.

"How'd they find the gun?"

Hank looked like he was about to drive off and leave me, so I spoke again.

"Swear to god, Hank. Just tell me that and I'll answer your questions."

He seemed to mull it over. "Someone called in an anonymous tip, said that they'd seen someone toss a gun into the river. A diver from the sheriff's department went down this morning and found it right where the caller said it'd be. That was about an hour ago. They know it's Ezra's gun because it has his initials right there on it."

"Do they know who made the call?" I was thinking about Alex. She would have had to know that the gun was clean before she'd do something like that. She would not want it traced back to her.

"The guy didn't identify himself, but he described someone who looks a hell of a lot like you. Same build, same age, same hair, same car. They're trying to track him down to do a lineup. If they find him, you'll be the first to know. Mills will have you downtown so fast, your head will spin. And if he identifies you, that's it; you're as good as convicted."

"It was a guy?" I asked. "The caller?"

"Didn't you hear me? They're trying to link you to the gun."

"But the caller. It was a man?"

Not a woman?

"Look. That's what I heard, okay? It's not like I was on the phone. I heard it was a guy. Now tell me about the fucking gun. I don't want to ask again."

I scrutinized his features. He wanted me to be innocent; not because he liked me, although I thought that maybe he did, but because he did not want to be wrong, not about something like this. Hank Robins would never help a killer, and, like everybody, he hated to be played.

"You want to know why I ditched the gun if I didn't kill him." It was a statement, not a question.

"Now we're getting somewhere."

So I opened my mouth. I started talking and didn't stop until I'd explained it to him. He didn't say a word until I was through.

"So, you were going to take the heat for Jean."

I nodded.

"That's why you ditched the gun."

"Yes."

"Tell me again why you thought that Jean had pulled the trigger."

I'd been vague about this. No way could I discuss the night Mom died, not with Hank or anybody else. I didn't know if he'd accept my theory without understanding what could have driven my sister to murder, but that was the chance I'd have to take. That body was buried, and I meant for it to stay that way.

"Jean has not been well, mentally, for a long time now. She and Ezra had problems."

"Hmmm," Hank said, and I knew that I was losing him. "Problems."

"It's a family matter, Hank. I can't talk about it. You can believe me or not. Help me or not. But that's all I can say about it."

He was silent for a full minute. He didn't look away from my face, and I could almost see the wheels turning.

"There's a lot you're not telling me."

"Yes. But like I said, it's family stuff." I hesitated. I didn't want to beg but knew that I was close. "I didn't kill him, Hank. He was deceitful, arrogant, and a first-class bastard. All right. I admit that. But he was my old man. I could have beaten him bloody on any number of occasions, but I could never have killed him. You've got to believe me."

"And the fifteen million dollars?" Hank asked, doubt again clouding his features.

"I've never cared about making money," I said.

Hank raised an eyebrow at me. "Making money's not the same as having it. Your father was born poor. I bet he understood that."

"I don't want it," I reiterated. "Nobody gets that, but I don't. He left me the house and the building outright. That's probably one point two million. So I'll sell them, give half to Jean, and still be richer than I'd ever planned on being."

"Six hundred grand ain't fifteen million."

"It's enough," I said.

"For about one guy in a million." Hank paused. "You that guy, Work?"

"I guess I am."

Hank settled back in his seat. "I'd take the fifteen million," he said, and I knew then that he would help me.

He put the car in drive and eased away from the curb. We drove in silence for a few minutes.

"So what do you want me to do?" Hank asked. "The way I see it, we have a couple choices. We dig deeper on Alex or we go talk to Mills, let her check Alex out. Now I understand if you don't want to talk to Mills, so I'll be glad to handle that. That would probably be the best idea, the more I think about it. You'll have to come clean about the gun, but nobody says that has to be done quickly. Once Mills is convinced, once she's built a case against Alex, maybe then we'll tell her. Of course, if they find the anonymous caller, that point will be moot. It's not going to be pretty, no matter how we do it. Mills would chew your face off if she could get away with it. She won't be easy to convince. She wants you to be guilty. It's almost personal."

I was barely listening; my mind was elsewhere. "I think Alex will come looking for me," I said.

"What do you mean?"

"I told Jean about my suspicions. Alex won't sit still for that. She'll come looking for me."

Hank was already shaking his head. "If she's the killer, that's the last thing she'll do. She'll play dumb. She'll wait for the world to land on you. All the hard work's done. She can relax and watch her tax dollars at work."

"Maybe," I said, but was not dissuaded.

"So, do you want me to talk to Mills?"

"I want you to find Vanessa," I said. "That hasn't changed."

"Damn it! This is not the time to waste energy looking for some missing person. I don't care how you feel about her. As soon as Mills finds that caller, you'll be arrested, and as far as we know, they've already back-traced it. They could do a photo lineup easily enough. They could be coming for you already, and this time there won't be any bail. Not after attempting to destroy evidence. No judge alive would let you out. You'll rot in jail, Work. So get your priorities straight! Playtime is over."

"I want you to find her, Hank."

"For fuck's sake, Work. Why?"

I didn't want to say this, because it was not the most important reason, and I already felt bad enough. But Hank had to hear it.

"She's more than my girlfriend, okay? She's my alibi."

"What?" Hank's disbelief was plain on his face.

"I was with her when Ezra was shot. I was at Stolen Farm."

"Well, Jesus, Work. Why didn't you just tell me that?"

"For Jean's sake, Hank. But there's one other thing. And I hope I'm wrong about this."

"What?" Hank asked.

"I think Alex knew that Vanessa was my alibi. It's possible that she went after her; she may have already killed her."

Hank settled into my revelation; his features solidified into resigned determination. "I'll find her, Work." He did not smile. "Alive or dead. I'll find her."

"Find her alive, Hank," I said, but he didn't respond. He looked at me once, then put his eyes back on the road.

"Is your car at the hospital?" he asked.

"I have a car there."

When we arrived at the hospital, I directed him to Dr. Stokes's minivan. "I want you to go home," Hank told me.

"Why? There's nothing for me there."

"Actually," he said. "There is. Toothbrush, razor, clothes. I want you to pack all that crap up and find a motel room somewhere off the beaten track. Not too far away, just someplace you can lay low for a day or so. Get cleaned up. Get some sleep. Once I find Vanessa, we'll go to Mills. But I don't want to do that until we can walk in her front door with a sworn alibi."

I got out of the car, leaned in the open door. "What are you going to do?"

"My job, Work. If she can be found, I'll find her. Once you're set up, let me know where you are. Call me on my cell."

"I don't think I can just sit around." I tried to find the words to express what I felt. It was difficult. "I don't want to hide anymore."

"Twenty-four hours, Work. Thirty-six at the most."

"I don't like it." I started to close the door.

"Hey," Hank said. I turned back, and he said, "Don't waste any time at the house, okay? Get in and get out. Mills could be looking for you already."

"I understand," I said, and watched him drive away.

I got in the minivan and went home. I looked at the high walls where once-white paint had grayed and then peeled. Barbara had always said the house had good bones, and she was right about that; but it had no heart, not with us living inside it. In place of laughter, trust, and joy, there was a hollow empti-ness, a kind of rot, and I marveled at my blindness. Was it the alcohol, I won-dered, that had made it bearable? Or was it something else, some inner failing? Maybe it was neither. They say that if you drop a frog into boiling water, he'll hop right out. But put the same frog into cold water and slowly turn up the heat, and he'll sit quietly until his blood begins to boil. He'll let himself be cooked alive. Maybe that's how it was for me. Maybe I was like that frog.

I thought about that, and then I thought about what Hank had said. His heart was in the right place. His head, too, for that matter. But I couldn't go to a hotel. I couldn't hide and I couldn't pretend that this would just go away. If Mills came for me, she came. Alex, too, for that matter.

Done is done, I thought, and went inside.

I found Barbara in the kitchen, poised ten feet from the door, as if frozen or about to turn away. For a split second, her face seemed fluid, but then her mouth opened in a half smile and she ran to meet me. I stood there, straight-armed and stiff, as she threw her arms around me and squeezed.

"Oh, Work. Oh, honey. I'm so sorry I didn't meet you at the jail. I just couldn't." The words came fast from her overeager mouth, and the feel of them against my jail-grimed neck unsettled me. She pulled back, framed my face with her hands. Her words accelerated onto a slippery track. They ran over one another, tripped, and fell. They were soft and too sweet, like chocolate left in the sun. "People have been looking at me, you know," she said. "The way people look sometimes, and I know what they're thinking. And I know it's no excuse, not compared to what you've been through, of course, but still it hurts. And I couldn't go there, not to the jail, not to see you like that. I just knew that wouldn't be a good thing for us. Unhealthy, you know. So when your Mr. Robins showed up, I asked him if he would meet you. I hope that was okay. I thought it would be. But then you didn't come home, and you didn't call, and I didn't know what to think." She sucked in a breath. "There're just so many things I wanted to say to you, and not being able to, why, that was just about the worst."

She fell silent, and in the absence of my response, awkwardness blossomed between us. She took her hands from my face, slid them to my shoulders, and squeezed me twice before allowing them to fall away. Eventually, they clutched the front of her shirt and settled there, white-knuckled.

"What was it?" I asked. She looked startled, as if she did not expect me to speak after all. "What was it that you wanted to say to me?"

She laughed, but it was born small and died a second later. She unclenched a hand and rubbed my right shoulder. She did not look at my face.

"You know, honey. Mainly just that I love you. That I believe in you. Those sorts of things." She finally risked a glance at my face. "The kinds of things I hoped you'd want to hear, especially at a time like this."

"That was very considerate of you," I managed to say, for the sake of civility.

She actually blushed and smiled. She cast her eyes at the floor as if her carefully groomed eyelashes could still entice me. When she looked up, her uncertainties had vanished. Her voice firmed, as did her eyes and the renewed grip on my shoulders.

"Listen, Work. I know this is difficult. But we'll get through it, okay? You're innocent. I know that. There's no way you'll go back to jail. This will pass, and when it does, we'll be fine. We can be the perfect couple again, like we were in the old days. People will look at us, and that's what they'll say: What a perfect couple. We just have to hang on and get through this. Get through it together."

" 'Together,' "I parroted, thinking of the frog.

"It's just a glitch. Huge and unfortunate, but just a glitch. That's all. We can handle it."

I blinked, and this time I actually saw the frog. The water bubbled and his blood began to boil. I wanted to scream, to warn him, but did not; and as I watched, his eyes boiled away. Poof. Right out of their sockets.

"I need a shower," I said.

"Good idea," Barbara agreed. "You take a nice hot shower, and when you get out, we'll have a drink. We'll have a drink and everything will be okay." I started to turn away, but she spoke again, so softly that I almost missed it. "Just like old times," she whispered. I looked at her eyes, but they were impenetrable, and her lips curved into the same half smile. "I love you, honey," she said. I turned out of the kitchen, and she called after me, her voice already fading. "Welcome home."

I went to the bedroom, where I found the bed perfectly made and flowers in a vase. The shades had been opened and light flooded in. In the mirror above the dresser I looked old and stepped upon, but there was resolution there, too; and I watched my eyes as I emptied my pockets and shed my days-old clothing. They did not look so old or so stepped upon as the rest of me.

In the shower, I turned the water as hot as I could bear. I lifted my face to the nozzle, let the water beat upon me. I didn't hear the shower door open. I felt the draft, and then I felt her hands. They settled on my back like autumn leaves. I might have flinched.

"Shhh," Barbara said gently. "Be still." I started to turn. "Don't turn around," she said.

She reached around me and wet her hands in the shower. She ran the soap between them and replaced it on the soap dish. Then she put her hands on my chest, which grew slick beneath them. She must have felt my resistance, in my tense muscles, in my unyielding posture—perhaps in the rigidity of my silence. Yet she chose to ignore it, and her hands lathered a path from my chest to my stomach. She molded herself against my back and I felt the firm press of her flesh against my own. Water cascaded across my shoulders, forced its path down the joining of our bodies, and she opened herself to it, let it wet her. She slithered against me, insinuated her slender leg between my own. And her hands worked down to a place where in the past they had always been welcome.

"Barbara." My voice was an intruder. Her fingers worked harder, as if persistence alone could make me want the absolution she thought was in her power to offer.

"Just let me do this," she said.

I did not want to hurt her. I wanted nothing to do with her at all. "Barbara," I said again, more insistently this time. I reached for her fingers. She pulled me around to face her.

"I can do this, Work."

The front of her hair was wet, the back still dry, and her face was so serious that I almost laughed; yet there was desperation in her eyes, as if this was all she had left to offer and she knew it. For a moment, I did not know what to say, and in that moment she lowered herself to her knees.

"For God's sake, Barbara." I could not keep the disgust out of my voice, and I pushed roughly past her; I opened the door and grabbed my towel. Steam followed me out, along with a dread silence. The water stopped. I did not look back. When Barbara stepped out next to me, she didn't bother to cover herself. She ignored the water that ran into her eyes and pooled on the floor; and I ignored her until I knew she would not simply walk away. So I turned and faced her, my towel heavy with cooling damp, my heart just heavy.

"My life's falling apart, too," she said. But it wasn't sadness I saw in her eyes. It was anger.

CHAPTER

32

In my closet I found a row of empty hangers, which was fine. I would never wear a suit again; I was pretty sure of that. I pulled on a pair of jeans, an old button-down shirt, and running shoes that I'd worn out years ago. On the top shelf was a battered, disreputable baseball cap, and I put that on, too.

I found Barbara in the kitchen. She was making a pot of coffee; her robe was cinched tight.

"What can I do to make it right?" she asked. "I want it to be right with us, Work. So just tell me."

A week before, I would have wavered and broken. I'd have told her that I loved her and that everything would be all right. Part of me would have believed it, but the rest of me would have screamed its thin scream.

"I don't love you, Barbara. I don't think I ever did." She opened her mouth, but I continued before she could speak. "You don't love me, either. Maybe you think you do, but you don't. Let's not pretend anymore. It's over."

"Just like that," she said. "You say so and it's over." Her anger was obvious, but it may have been ego.

"We've been on a downward spiral for years."

"I'm not giving you a divorce. We've been through too much. You owe me."

"'Owe you'?"

"That's right."

"I don't need your agreement, Barbara; I don't even need cause. All it takes is a year's separation."

"You need me. You won't make it in this town without me."

I shook my head. "You might be surprised at how little I need." But she ignored me and moved across the kitchen floor on feet that were invisible beneath the hem of her robe.

"We have our problems, Work, but we're a team. We can deal with anything." She reached for me.

"Don't touch me," I said.

She allowed her hands to drop, but they did so slowly. She looked up at me, and already she seemed to be retreating.

"Okay, Work. If that's what you want. I won't fight you. I'll even act civilized. That's what you want, isn't it, a dry, emotionless parting? A clean break. So that you can get on with your new life and I can try to figure what mine will be. Right?"

"My new life might well be prison, Barbara. This may be the biggest favor I've ever done for you."

"You won't go to prison," she said, but I merely shrugged.

"I'll do the best I can for you, moneywise; you won't have to fight me."

Barbara laughed, and I saw some of the old bitterness steal into her eyes. "You don't make enough money now, Work. You never have, not even when Ezra was alive, and nobody made money the way he did."

Her words rang in my head, and something clicked. "What did you just say?"

"You heard me." She turned away, picked up a pack of cigarettes, and lit one. I didn't know when she had started smoking again. She was in college the last time I saw a cigarette between her lips, but this one danced in her mouth as she spoke. "You could barely make it with Ezra looking out for you. As it is, I don't know a single lawyer in town who makes less money than you do." She blew smoke at the ceiling. "So keep your empty promises. I know what they're worth."

But that wasn't what struck me.

Making money's not the same as having it. Hank's words.

"Would you say that Ezra liked making money?" I asked. "Or did he like having it?"

"What are you talking about, Work? What does any of that matter? He's dead. Our marriage is dead."

But I was onto something. The pieces weren't in place, but something was there and I couldn't let go of it. "Money, Barbara. The achievement of it or the possession of it? Which was more important?"

She blew out more smoke and shrugged, as if nothing mattered anymore. "Having it," she said. "He didn't care about working for it. It was a tool."

She was right. He depended on it. He could use it, and suddenly I knew. Not the exact combination to his safe, but I knew where to find it. And just like that, opening the old man's safe became the most important thing in my world. It was something I had to do, and I knew how to do it.

I've got to go," I said. I put my hand on her arm and she did not flinch away. "I'm sorry, Barbara."

She nodded and looked at the floor, more smoke writhing from her lips.

"We'll talk more later," I said, and picked up the keys. I stopped at the garage door and looked back. I expected her to appear different somehow, but she didn't. She looked as she always had. My hand was on the door when her voice stopped me a final time.

"One question," she said.

"What?"

"What about your alibi?" she asked. "Aren't you worried about losing your alibi?"

For an instant, our eyes locked. She let her shutters drop, and I saw into the depths of her. That's when I knew that she knew. She'd known all along; so I said the words, and with their passing, a weight seemed to fall away, and in that instant even Barbara was untainted.

"You were never my alibi, Barbara. We both know that."

She nodded slightly, and this time the tears came.

"There was a time I would have killed for you," she said, and looked back up. "What was one little lie?"

The tears came faster, and her shoulders trembled as if finally exhausted by some invisible load. "Are you going to be okay?" I asked.

"We do what we need to do, right? That's what survival is all about."

"It's just a question of getting to the point where it has to be done. That's why we'll both be okay. Maybe we can part as friends."

She sniffed loudly, and laughed. She wiped at her eyes. "Wouldn't that be something?"

"It would," I agreed. "Listen, I'll be at the office. I won't be long. When I get back, we'll talk some more."

"What are you going to the office for?" she asked.

"Nothing, really. I just figured something out."

She gestured at the pain-filled space around us: the room, the house, maybe the entirety of our lives together. "More important than this?" she asked.

"No," I replied, lying. "Of course not."

"Then don't leave," she said.

"It's just life, Barbara, and it gets messy. Not everything works out the way you want."

"It does if you want it badly enough."

"Only sometimes," I said. Then I left, closing the door on the life behind me. I started the car and turned around. The children were still in the park, tiny flashes of color as they ran and screamed. I turned off the radio, put the car in drive, and then I saw Barbara in the garage. She watched me in utter stillness, and for an instant she did look different. But then she waved at me to wait and ran light-footed to the window.

"Don't go," she said. "I don't want it to end like this."

"I've got to."

"Damn it, Work. What's so important?"

"Nothing," I said. "Nothing that concerns you."

She wrapped her arms around herself and leaned over as if her stomach hurt. "It's going to end badly. I know it will." Her eyes grew distant. She looked down at the park, as if the sight of the children affected her, too. "Ten years of our lives, and it'll all be wasted. Just gone."

"People move on every day, Barbara. We're no different."

"That's why it never could have worked," she said, and I heard blame in her voice. She looked down at me. "You never wanted to be special, and there was nothing I could do to make you want that. You were so ready to be satisfied. You took the scraps from Ezra's table and thought you had a banquet."

"Ezra was chained to that table. He was no happier than I was."

"Yes, he was. He took what he wanted and took pleasure in taking it. He was a man that way."

"Are you trying to hurt me?" I asked. "Because this is unpleasant enough as it is."

Barbara smacked her hand on the top of the car. "And you think it's pleasant for me? It's not."

I looked away from her then, turned my eyes down the hill to the flashes of color that stained the dark green grass. Suddenly, I wanted to be away from this place, but something remained to be said. So I said it.

"Do you know what our problem is, Barbara? You never knew me. You saw what you wanted to see. A young lawyer from a rich family, with a near-famous father, and you assumed you knew me. Who I was. What I wanted. What I cared about. You married a stranger, and you tried to turn him into someone that you recognized. For ten years, you beat me down, and I let you do it; but I could never be what you wanted. So you grew frustrated and bitter, and I grew despondent. I hid from myself, as if it would all just go away, and that makes me as bad as you. We married for the wrong reasons, a common-enough mistake, and if I'd been man enough, I would have ended it years ago."

Barbara's lips twisted, "Your self-righteousness makes me ill," she said. "You're no better than me."

"I don't pretend to be."

"Just go," she said. "You're right. It's over. So just go."

"I'm sorry, Barbara."

"Save your fucking sympathy," she said, and walked back to the house.

I let her go, and for that moment I seemed to float; but the absence of pain can pass as pleasure for only so long, and I still had things to do. I pointed her car toward the office.

A psychiatrist could probably explain my obsession with opening Ezra's safe. In tearing down his last secret, I was replacing him, assuming his power. Or struggling to understand him. To outdo him. Truthfully, it was nothing that complicated. I'd worked in that building for ten years, thirteen if you counted the summer jobs during law school. During that time, my father had made no reference to the safe. We were family. We were partners. He shouldn't have kept secrets from me. Yes, I was curious, but more than that I was disturbed; and some part of me believed that tearing down this secret would make my father known to me once and for all. Our truest self is often the person we allow no one else to see—who we are when we are alone. In the real world, we edit. We compromise and prevaricate.

I wanted to see the man behind the curtain.

For what I'd realized was this, and I should have seen it sooner. Ezra cared about having money; it was the curse of growing up dirt-poor. Money bought food. Money fixed the roof. Having it meant survival. So the million-dollar jury award that made him famous and ultimately rich was not the most important thing after all. I'd been wrong about that. Because big-dollar jury verdicts are appealed, and even if they're not, nobody cuts a check the day of the verdict. Making money versus having money. In that equation, only one date matters: the day you deposit the check.

I didn't know what date that was, but there would be records. Somewhere in the office was a deposit record showing a cash infusion of $333,333.33, exactly one-third of one million dollars. By the time he died, a few hundred grand amounted to chump change, but that was the money that had made him. I should have seen it.

I parked in back and looked up at the tall, narrow building. Already I felt like a stranger there, and Barbara's words echoed in my mind: *ten years . . . wasted. Just gone.*

I got out of the car. No one was around, but in the distance I heard sirens, and I thought of Mills. She was looking at Ezra's gun, slapping her open palms against the hard muscles of her thighs. She would find the anonymous caller and I would be identified. I would be arrested, tried, and convicted. All I had was Hank, and the faded hope that Vanessa Stolen could save both body and soul.

Inside, the office was musty, as if weeks or months had passed since last I'd been there. Shadows stretched through slatted blinds, and dust hung in the alternating bars of light. The place was silent and unwelcoming, as if my thoughts had betrayed me. I did not belong. That was the message. The building knew.

I locked the door behind me, moved down the short hall and into the main reception area. Sound was muffled; I pushed through air that felt like water, and accepted that much of what I felt was formless dread. I tried to shake it off.

The cops had seized my computers, so I went down the narrow, creaking staircase to the basement, where boxes rose in jagged mounds and a single bare bulb dangled as if from a gibbet. The place was packed with old case files, tax records, and bank statements. I saw broken furniture, an exercise machine that dated to the seventies, and eight different golf bags. It was a mess, and the oldest stuff was in the very back. I waded through it, trying to figure out the system. The boxes were stacked haphazardly but were grouped together by dates. So the files from any given year would be found together, buried in a mass grave.

I located what I thought would be the right year and started tearing open boxes. There was no order to it at all, which surprised me. Ezra had always been meticulous in his affairs. Files numbered in the thousands, crushed into misshapen cardboard cartons. And inside the larger boxes I found smaller containers holding monthly calendars, receipts, message slips, dried-out pens, and paper clips. There were half-used legal pads and discarded Rolodex cards. It was as if Ezra had emptied his desk every year and then started fresh with new supplies. I opened his day planner for December, saw the small exclamation point he'd placed on December 31, and realized then why this was so different. It was a finished year, and like so much of his past, Ezra had boxed it away to be forgotten. Ezra had always cared about the future. Everything else was one step above refuse.

I found what I was looking for in the bottom of the seventh box, buried beneath a foot and a half of divorce pleadings. I recognized the well-creased spine of the thick black ledger book that Ezra had always preferred. It made a cracking sound when I opened it, and I fingered the green paper, now browned at the edges, and saw the rows of Ezra's precise figures. My first impression was of smallness. Small writing and small numbers—nothing like his stature or the billings he would soon come to achieve. I found the deposit entry on the thirty-third page. The deposit above it was for fifty-seven dollars, the one below for an even hundred. His handwriting was unvaried, so that one-third of a million dollars might well have been a daily deposit. Looking at it, I could only imagine the satisfaction that entry must have given him. Yet, it was as if he'd bottled up any symptoms of joy or pleasure. Maybe he'd been selfish with it; maybe he'd just been disciplined. But I could still remember the night he took us out to celebrate. "Nothing can stop me now," he'd said. And he'd been right, until Alex shot him in the head.

I left the basement and turned off the light. The smell of moldering cardboard followed me as I headed for Ezra's office. I paused at the foot of the stairs, remembering the sound of a heavy chair crashing down; but now there was only silence, and so I broke it, my feet heavy on the timeworn stairs. The rug looked different; maybe it was the light, but it seemed to ripple at the far corner. I pulled it back, wondered again if my mind was playing tricks on me. The wood was chipped at the edge, gouged around the nail heads. The marks were unfamiliar, small, as if made by a flathead screwdriver. I ran my fingertips over them, wondering if someone else had been here.

I dismissed the thought. Time was not on my side, and I had a number burning holes in my brain. I grabbed the hammer and went to work on the nails. I tried to slip the claw beneath the heads. I gouged more wood, scratched the nail heads shiny, but could not get them out. I rammed the claw into the crack at the boards' ends and leaned back on the handle. No give. I pulled harder, felt the tension in my back as I heaved. But the four big nails were too much.

I ran back to the basement, back into the weak light of that one dangling bulb, then around the cardboard junkyard to the tool corner, where I'd seen a snow shovel, a ladder, a busted rake, and an old car jack. I found the lug wrench that went with the jack; it was two feet long with a sharp, tapered end. Back upstairs, breathing hard, I pushed the narrow end between the boards, pounded the other end with the hammer. Steel slipped into the crack where that yellow-white wood seemed to smile at me. I jammed the hammer against the base of the wrench for leverage, held it there with my foot, and then I put one hundred and ninety pounds on that long wrench. I leaned into it, heard wood crack and then splinter. I shifted down the board. Pried up one ragged piece and then another, until the whole thing came loose. I ripped the boards out, felt splinters in my palm and ignored them. I threw the ruined boards aside.

The safe challenged me, and for a moment I was afraid; but I pictured my old man's ledger entry, knew it was the right number. I was ready to tear him down, ready to know, so I dropped again to my knees. I knelt above this last piece of him, said a silent prayer, and typed in the date that he'd made the largest deposit of his life.

The door swung up on silent hinges, opened to darkness; and then I blinked.

The first thing I saw was cash, lots of it, banded together in stacks of ten thousand. I removed all of it. The money was solid in my hand, a brick of currency that I could smell over the mustiness. At a glance, it looked like almost $200,000. I put it on the floor beside me, but it was difficult to look away. I'd never seen so much hard currency. But I wasn't here for money, so I returned to the gaping hole.

There were pictures of his family. Not his wife and children. Not that family. But the one that raised him, the impoverished one. There was a faded picture of Ezra and his father. Another of his father and his mother. One of several dirty, blank-eyed children who may have been siblings. I'd never seen these before, and I doubted that Jean had, either. The people looked used up, even the children, and in one group shot I saw what had made Ezra different. It was something in his eyes, like in the photo on his desk at home. There was strength in them, as if, even as a child, he could move worlds. His brothers and sisters may have sensed this, for in the photographs they seemed to hover around him.

But they were all strangers to me. I'd never met a single one of them. Not once.

I put the photos next to the money and returned to the safe. In a large velvet box I found some of my mother's jewelry—not what she was wearing when she died, but the really expensive stuff, which Ezra once referred to as "fuck-you baubles," and only brought out when he wanted to impress a man or make the guy's wife look cheap. Mother hated to wear them, and she once told me that they made her feel like the devil's concubine. Not that they weren't beautiful; they were. But they, too, were tools, and never intended as anything else. I put the box aside, planning to give it to Jean. Maybe she could sell them.

The videotapes were on the bottom, three of them, unmarked. I held them as I would a snake, and wondered briefly if I'd been wrong—that maybe there were things about a father that a son should never know.

Why would he keep videotapes in a safe?

A VCR and a television sat in the corner. I picked a tape at random and put it in the player. I turned on the television and pushed the play button.

At first, there was static, then a sofa. Soft lights. Voices. I looked at the long leather couch behind me, then back at the screen. They were the same.

"I don't know, Ezra." A woman's voice, somehow familiar.

"Humor me." That was Ezra.

I heard the sound of a gentle smack, a burst of girlish laughter.

A woman's legs, long and tan. She ran past the camera, flung herself onto the couch. She was naked, laughing, and for an instant I saw a flash of white teeth, and equally pale breasts. Then Ezra heaved into view, filling the screen. He shrank as he moved to the couch, but I heard him mumble something. Then her voice: "Well, come on, then." Her arms above her head, face obscured. Her legs opened, the left finding the back of the curved leather couch, the right circling his waist, guiding him down.

He collapsed onto her, buried her under his massive body; but I saw her legs, and she had the strength to rise up beneath him. "Oh yeah," she said. "Like that. Fuck me like that." And he did, slamming her, driving her down and into the yielding leather. Narrow arms escaped from beneath him, found his back, and dragged claw marks into his skin.

Watching, I felt sick, but I could not look away. Because some part of me knew. It was the voice. The way her legs joined. That brief, horrible flash of teeth.

I knew, and in bleak disbelief I watched my father nail my wife to the couch.

CHAPTER

33

The images were hammer blows. He used her, manhandled her, and her eyes, when I saw them, glowed like an animal's. There was no office, no world; it was gone, obliterated, and I could not feel the floor that rushed up to meet my knees. My stomach clenched, and my mouth may have filled with bile, but if it did, I never tasted it. Every sense was overwhelmed by the one that I could forever do without. Sights no man should see swelled and burst like rotten fruit. My wife, on her back, then on her hands and knees. My father, hairy as any farm animal, grunting over her as if she, too, were mindless flesh, and not the wife of his only son.

How long? The thought found me. *How long had this gone on?* And then, quick on its heels: *How could I have missed it?*

And just when I could take no more, the screen went dead. I sagged into myself and waited for a collapse that never came. I was numb, staggered by what I'd seen and by what the sight implied. Her voice, when she spoke—it shocked the hell out of me.

"You nailed the boards down."

I turned and saw her. She stood by Ezra's desk. I hadn't heard her come up the stairs and so had no idea how long she'd been there. She lowered the remote control to the desk. I climbed to my feet. She looked calm, but her eyes were glazed and her lips were damp.

"Do you know how many times I've tried to open that damn safe?" She sat on the edge of the desk and looked at me; her face remained pale, and her voice was equally colorless. "Late at night, usually, while you slept. It was the best thing about being married to a drunk. You were always a heavy sleeper. I knew about the tapes, of course. I shouldn't have let him do that, but he insisted. I didn't know he kept them in the safe until it was too late."

Her eyes were lightless, and when she blinked, her body seemed to tilt. She looked drugged, and may well have been. I didn't know her. I never had.

"Too late for what?" I asked, but she ignored me. She pulled at her ear with one hand and kept the other hand behind her back. I knew then that I'd been wrong about a great many things.

"It was you that night," I said. "You pushed the chair down the stairs."

I looked around the office. There was only one way out.

"Yes," Barbara said. "I'm sorry about that. But I guess it was bound to happen, sooner or later. I've been up here so many times." She shrugged, and the gun appeared. It was in her left hand, and she acted as if it weren't there. I froze at the sight of it. It was small and silver, an automatic of some kind. She used the barrel to scratch at her cheek.

"What's the gun for, Barbara?" I tried to make my voice as nonthreatening as possible. She shrugged again and looked at the gun. She tilted it this way and that, as if fascinated by the play of light along its glittering edge. Her face was slack. She was clearly not herself, and I thought she had to be stoned or mentally adrift.

"Something I've had for awhile," she said. "This town is getting so dangerous these days, especially for a woman alone at night."

I knew that I was in danger, but I didn't care.

"Why did you kill him, Barbara?"

Suddenly, she was on her feet, jabbing the gun in my direction, and the vacuous calm of her eyes disappeared, replaced by something entirely different. I flinched, expecting the bullet.

"I did that for you!" she screamed. "For you! How dare you question me? I did it all for you, you ungrateful bastard."

I held up my hands. "I'm sorry. Try to calm down."

"You calm down!" She took three uneven steps toward me, holding the gun as if she meant to use it. When she stopped, she didn't lower the gun. "That son of a bitch was going to change the will. I fucked him for six months before he agreed to do it right in the first place." She laughed, the sound like fingers on a chalkboard. "That's what it took, but I did it, and I did it for us. I made that happen. But he was going to undo all of that, put it back the way it was. I couldn't allow that. So don't you pretend that I never did anything for you."

"That's why you slept with my father? For money?"

"Not for money. Money is a thousand dollars or ten thousand. He'd never trust you with fifteen million dollars. He was going to leave you three." She laughed bitterly. "Just three. Can you believe it? Rich as he was. But I convinced him. He changed it to fifteen. I did that for you."

"You didn't do it for me, Barbara."

The gun began to shake in her hand, and I saw her fingers whiten where she gripped it. "You don't know me. Don't pretend that you know me. Or what I've been through. Knowing that the tapes were here. Knowing what it would mean if somebody else found them."

"Can you put the gun down, Barbara? It's not necessary."

She didn't respond, but the barrel drifted lower, until it pointed at the floor. Barbara's eyes followed it and she seemed to slump. For an instant, I dared to breathe, but when her face came up, her eyes sparkled.

"But then you started seeing that country whore again."

"Vanessa didn't have anything to do with us," I said.

The gun came up, and Barbara screamed, "That bitch was trying to steal my money!"

I had a horrible revelation. "What did you do to her?"

"You were going to leave me. You said so yourself."

"But that had nothing to do with her, Barbara. That was about us."

"She was the problem with us."

"Where is she, Barbara?"

"She's gone. That's all that matters."

Inside, I felt something tear. Vanessa was the only reason I had left for living. So I said what was on my mind.

"I've slept with you enough times to know when you're faking." This time, I stepped toward her. My life was over. I had nothing. This woman had taken everything and I let my anger build. I gestured at the blank screen, but in my mind I still saw her, and the way she screamed. "You loved it.

You loved fucking him. Was he that good? Or did you just like the idea of hurting me?"

Barbara laughed, and the gun came up. "Oh. Now you're a man. Now you're a tough guy. Well, let me tell you. Yes, I loved it. Ezra knew what he wanted and knew how to get it. He had power. I don't mean strength. I mean power. Fucking him was the biggest rush I ever had." Her top lip curled. "Coming home to you was a joke."

I saw something in her face, and had another revelation. "He dumped you," I said. "He liked having sex with you because of the power he held. He controlled you, manipulated you; but then he realized that you liked it, and once that happened, he got bored. So he dumped you. That's why you shot him."

I was right. I knew that I was. I saw it in her eyes, and in the way her lips twitched. For a moment, I felt a fierce joy, but it didn't last.

I saw her pull the trigger.

CHAPTER

34

I dreamed again of contentment, of green fields, the laughter of a small girl, and Vanessa's cheek pressed softly against my own; but dreams are fickle deceivers, and they never last. I caught a final fleeting glimpse of cornflower eyes and heard a voice so faint, it must have crossed oceans; and then the pain hit with such ferocity that I knew I was in hell. Fingers peeled back my eyelids, and red light was everywhere, beating at the world. Hands ripped at my clothes, and I felt metal against my skin. I struggled, but bone-white fingers forced me down and bound me. Blank faces flickered in and out; they floated, spoke a language I couldn't understand, and then were gone, only to return again. And the pain was ever constant; it pulsed like blood, it channeled through me, and then there were more hands upon me and I tried to scream.

Then there was motion and a white metal sky that rocked as if I were at sea. I saw a face I'd come to loathe, but Mills did not torment me further. Her lips moved, but I couldn't answer; I didn't understand. Then she left, just as I understood, and so I called out. I had the answer. But bloody hands forced her back, until she pushed them away, found the place above me, and leaned into my words. I had to shout, because I was in a deep well and falling fast. So I did. I screamed, but her face fell forever into the white sky and I crashed into the powdered ink that filled the bottom of the well. And my last thought as darkness settled around me was to wonder at a white sky in hell.

But even in that blackness, time seemed to pass, and on occasion there was light. The pain rose and fell like the tides, and when it was weak, I imagined faces and voices. I heard Hank Robins arguing with Detective Mills, who, I sensed, wanted to ask more questions; but that didn't make sense. Then Dr. Stokes, looking old with worry. He held a clipboard and was talking to a strange man in a white coat. And once Jean was there, and she wept with such force that it killed me to see it. She told me she understood, that Hank had told her everything—about the jail and my willing sacrifice. She said that she loved me but knew that she could never spend life in prison for me. She said that made me better than her, but that didn't make sense, either. I was in hell, but it was hell of my own making. I tried to explain that to her, but my throat wouldn't open. So I watched in silence and waited for the well to pull me back in.

Once, I thought I saw Vanessa, but that was hell's cruelest joke, and I did not rise to it. I closed my eyes and wept for the loss of her, and when I looked up, she was gone. I was alone, cold in the dark. The cold seemed to last forever, but eventually the heat found me, so that I remembered. I was in hell. Hell was hot, not cold. And hell was pain, so that when I woke and found it all but gone, I thought the dream had returned. I opened my eyes, but there was no child, no field, and no Vanessa. Perhaps the torments of this place were more than purely physical.

When finally I woke, I blinked in the cool air and heard the rustle of movement; so that when a face appeared above me, I was prepared for it. It was blurry at first, but I blinked it into focus. It was Jean's.

"Relax," she said. "Everything's fine. You're going to be okay."

A stranger appeared beside her, the man in the white coat. He had dark features and a beard that glistened as if oiled. "My name is Dr. Yuseph," he said. "How do you feel?"

"Thirsty." A dry croak. "Weak." I could not lift my head.

The doctor turned to Jean. "He can have an ice chip, but only one. Then another in ten minutes or so."

I heard the clink of a spoon, and Jean leaned over me. She slipped an ice chip into my mouth. "Thanks," I whispered. She smiled, but there was pain in it.

"How long?" I asked.

"Four days," the doctor replied. "In and out. You're lucky to be alive."

Four days.

He patted me on the arm. "You'll recover; it'll hurt, but you'll get there. We'll put you on solid foods as soon as you feel up for it. Once your strength returns, you'll start physical therapy. It won't be long before you're out of here."

"Where am I?"

"Baptist Hospital. Winston-Salem."

"What about Barbara?" I asked.

"Your sister can tell you anything you want to know. Just take it easy. I'll be back in an hour." He turned to Jean. "Don't tire him. He'll be weak for some time yet."

Jean reappeared at the bedside. Her face was swollen, the flesh around her eyes as dark as wine. "You look tired," I said.

She smiled wanly. "So do you."

"It's been a tough year," I said, and she laughed, then turned away. When she looked back, she was crying.

"I'm so sorry, Work." Her words broke, and the edges seemed to cut her. Her face reddened and her eyes collapsed. The tears devolved into sobs.

"For what?"

"For everything," she said, and the words, I knew, were a plea for forgiveness. "For hating you." Her head bowed, and with terrible effort I reached for her. I found her hand and tried to squeeze it.

"I'm sorry, too," I whispered. I wanted to say more, but my throat closed again, and for a long time we shared a bittersweet silence. She held my hand with both of hers and I stared at the top of her head. We couldn't go back to the way it had been for us; that place was a garden overgrown. But looking at her, I felt as close to our childhood as I ever had. And she felt it, too, as if we'd reached back to a time when apologies mattered and do-overs were a simple word away. I saw it in her eyes when she looked up.

"Did you see all your flowers?" she asked with a timid, brittle smile.

I looked past Jean and saw the room for the first time. Flowers were everywhere, dozens of vases with cards.

"Here's a card from the local bar—every lawyer in the county signed it." She handed me an oversized card, but I didn't want it. I still saw the way they'd looked at me in court, the ready condemnation in their eyes.

"What about Barbara?" I asked, and Jean put the card, unopened and unread, back on the table. Her eyes moved over the room, and I was about to re-peat the question.

"Are you sure you're ready to talk about this?" she asked.

"I have to," I said.

"She's been arrested."

I exhaled a mixture of relief and despair; part of me hoped that her betrayal had been the dream. "How?" I asked.

"Mills found you. You'd been shot twice, once in the chest and once in the head." Her eyes drifted upward, and I touched my head. It was bandaged. "The one in your chest went through a lung. The head shot just grazed you. At first, she thought you were dead. You almost were. She called the paramedics and they transported you to Rowan Regional. Eventually, you were brought here."

"But what about Barbara?"

"You were conscious in the ambulance. You managed to tell Mills who'd shot you. She arrested Barbara two hours later."

Jean's voice trailed off and she looked away.

"What?" I asked. I knew there was more.

"She was having a late lunch at the country club, as if nothing had hap-pened." Her hand settled onto mine. "I'm sorry, Work."

"What else?" I had to move on. I could see her so clearly, sipping white wine, a fake smile plastered to her face. Lunch with the girls.

"They found the gun at your house, hidden in the basement, along with a lot of money and Mother's jewelry."

"I'm surprised Mills doesn't think I put them there and shot myself." I could not keep the bitterness from my voice.

"She feels terrible, Work. She's been here a lot, and she's not afraid to admit her mistake. She wanted me to tell you she was sorry."

"Mills said that?"

"And she left something for you." Jean got up and walked across the room. When she came back, she held a stack of newspapers. "Most are local. Some are from Charlotte. You look good in print. Mills even made a public apol-ogy." She picked the top copy off the stack. I saw a picture of Barbara being led from a police cruiser. She was cuffed, trying to hide her face from the cameras.

"Put it down," I said.

"Okay." She dropped the papers onto the floor by the bed and I closed my eyes. The picture of Barbara brought it all back, the pain and betrayal. For a moment, I could not speak. When I finally looked at Jean, her eyes were veiled, and I wondered what she was seeing.

"Do you know?" I asked.

"About Barbara and Daddy?"

I nodded.

"Yes, I know. And don't you dare apologize."

I closed my mouth; nothing I could say would make it go away. It was a part of us now, as much his legacy as the color of my hair.

"He was a horrible man, Jean."

"But now he's gone, so let that be an end to it."

I agreed, even though I knew there would never be an end to it. His presence among us lingered, like the smell of something dead but unburied.

"Would you like some more ice?" Jean asked.

"That would be nice."

She fed me the ice, and as she hovered there, I saw the fresh scars on her wrists. They were tight and pink, as if the skin had stretched too tightly over the veins. To better protect them, perhaps. I didn't know. With Jean, I never did; but I hoped, and I thought that maybe it was not too late to pray.

"I'm fine," she said, and I realized that I'd been staring.

"Are you really?"

She smiled and sat back down. "You keep saving my life," she said. "There must be some value in it."

"Don't joke, Jean. Not about this."

She sighed, leaned back, and for a moment I feared I had pushed too hard. The line between us had grown vague, and I didn't want to step over it. But when she spoke, there was no resentment, and I realized that she was taking her time and wanted me to understand.

"I feel like I've come through a long, dark tunnel," she said. "It doesn't hurt to stand straight anymore, like something's let go inside of me." She clenched her hands in front of her stomach and then opened them, a ten-petaled rose. "It's hard to explain," she said, but I thought I understood. Ezra was gone; maybe that brought closure. Maybe not. But it was not my place to fix Jean. That was a truth I'd come to understand. She had to do that herself, and looking at her smile, I thought she had it in her.

"And Alex?" I asked.

"We're leaving Salisbury," she said. "We need to find a place of our own."

"You didn't answer my question."

Jean's eyes were expressive and very real. "We have issues, like everybody, but we're dealing with them."

"I don't want to lose you," I said.

"I feel like we just found each other, Work. Alex understands that. It's one of the things we've been dealing with; and while she'll always have issues with men, she swears that she'll make an exception for you."

"Can she forgive me for dredging up her past?"

"She knows why you did it. She respects your reasons, but don't ever mention it to her."

"So we're okay?" I asked.

"Wherever we go, you'll always be welcome there."

"Thank you, Jean."

"Have some more ice."

"Okay."

She fed me the ice and I felt my eyes grow heavy. Suddenly, I was exhausted, and I closed my eyes as Jean moved around the room. I was almost gone when she spoke.

"There's one card you might like to read. It's more of a letter, actually." I cracked my eyes. Jean was holding an envelope. "It's from Vanessa," she said.

"*What?*"

"She was here for awhile, but said she couldn't stay. She wanted you to have this, though." She handed me the envelope, which was thin and light. "She thought you would understand."

"But, I thought . . ." I couldn't finish the sentence.

"Hank found her at the hospital in Davidson County. She'd gone to the feed store in Lexington and was crossing the street, when somebody hit her."

"Who?" I asked.

"Nobody knows. All she remembers is a black Mercedes that came out of nowhere."

"Is she okay?"

"Broken ribs and bruises all over, but she'll survive. They kept her at the hospital overnight. She was pretty doped up on painkillers."

"I thought she was dead."

"Well, she's not, and she was pretty broken up to see you like this."

Suddenly, I couldn't see. The letter in my hand was hope for the future, something I thought I'd lost. I wanted to read her words, to see the letters made by her hands. But my fingers were clumsy.

Jean took the envelope from my hands. "Let me," she said.

She tore it open, removed the folded page, and put it back in my hand. "I'll be outside if you need me," she said, and I heard the door close behind her. I blinked, and when my vision cleared, I looked at the note Vanessa had left for me. It was short.

Life is a torturous journey, Jackson, and I don't know if I can handle any more pain. But I'll never regret the day we met, and when you're ready to talk, I'm ready to listen. Maybe some good can come of all this. I hope so, but I know too well the cruelness of fate. No matter what happens, re-member this—every day I thank God that you're alive.

I read it three times, and fell asleep with it on my chest.

When I opened my eyes again, I felt ten times better. It was late, dark out-side, but someone had turned on the lamp in the corner. I saw Mills in the chair, and I managed to sit up in bed before she looked up from the book she was reading.

"Hey," she said, getting up. "I hope you don't mind, but Jean has been here around the clock and was exhausted. I told her I'd stick around." She stood, looking uncertain. "I thought you might have some questions."

"I guess I should say thanks," I said. "For saving my life."

If possible, Mills looked even more uncomfortable. "And I owe you an apology."

"Forget about it," I said, surprising myself. "The past is dead. I don't intend to think about it too much." I gestured at the chair next to the bed. "Sit down."

"Thanks." She sat and put her book on the table. I saw that it was a mystery, and for some reason that struck me as funny, her being a detective and all.

"I really don't know what I want to hear," I told her. "I haven't had much time to think about any of this."

"I have a couple questions," Mills said. "Then I'll start at the beginning and tell you anything you want to know."

"Okay."

"Where did you find your father's gun?" she asked, and I told her about the creek, about my nighttime search down the throat.

"I sent a team through that tunnel," she said, visibly upset. "They should have found it."

I explained how I'd found it wedged deep in the debris-choked crevice, but

I refused to tell her how I knew to look there. She pushed, of course, but I wasn't going to give Max to her.

"Somebody tipped me off, Detective. That's all I can tell you."

When finally she let it go, she did so as a favor, her way of making up for the harm that she'd done to me. But moving the conversation forward was awkward; letting go was not easy for Mills.

"So you did what you did to protect Jean? Because you thought she might have been involved?"

"That's right."

"But why? Why would you think Jean killed him?"

I thought about her question. How much could I give her? How much did she really want? Most importantly, was I still the guardian of Ezra's truth? I had come to terms with what had happened, with how my mother passed from this place. But would the truth serve any good purpose? I had to ask myself: Would Jean sleep any better? Would my mother's soul?

"Jean was not at home after she left Ezra's. I went there looking for her."

Mills interrupted. "She went for a drive. She was upset and went for a drive. Then she went to your house to talk things over. She got there in time to see you leave."

I nodded. It was the simplest explanation, but it had never occurred to me. "Jean has not been right for awhile, Detective. She was angry, unstable. I couldn't take the chance."

I would keep Ezra's truth, but not for him. Some truths are best left alone; it was really that simple.

Mills was clearly frustrated. "There's a lot you're not telling me, Work."

I shrugged. "Not as much as you think, and nothing that will affect your case."

"Was Jean the real reason you wanted to visit the crime scene?" she finally asked, and in her eyes I saw that she already knew the answer. I'd gone to the crime scene for one reason only; and, in spite of what I'd told Douglas, giving Jean details was not it. And now, safe on the other side of everything, I allowed myself a very small smile.

"No."

Mills did not return the smile. She knew that I'd worked it out in advance and she knew why. My manipulations had caused her great embarrassment and could have cost her much more—the case, her reputation, her job. But I saw that she understood. I'd gone to the crime scene for one very specific reason—to hamper my eventual prosecution. I'd been willing to take the fall for Jean, but I hadn't wanted to go to prison unless I was forced to. I'd figured that if it went to trial, I could use my presence at the crime scene to confuse the issue—maybe hang the jury, maybe get an acquittal. While no guarantee, it had been something.

"I had to do it," I said to her. "When Ezra never came back, I eventually figured out that he had to be dead. I thought that Jean had done it. I couldn't let her go to jail." I paused, thinking about Ezra's long absence and the dark thoughts that haunted me during that time. "I had eighteen months to think about things."

"You had it planned out—from that first day when Douglas called you into his office. The day we found his body. That's why you pushed Douglas to let you onto the crime scene."

"*Plan* is too big a word. I just figured that it couldn't hurt."

"You know what I think?" she asked. "I think you're a better lawyer than Ezra ever gave you credit for."

"I'm no lawyer," I said, but Mills didn't seem to hear me.

"You're a good brother, too. I hope Jean knows what you were willing to do for her."

I looked away, embarrassed.

"Let's talk about how you saved my life," I said.

"All right. I'll start there, and if something occurs to you, then stop me."

"Okay."

She leaned forward and put her elbows on her knees. "I was coming to arrest you," she said.

"Because of the gun?" I asked. "Because you identified me?"

For a moment, she looked startled, and then angry. "Hank Robins told you. That little bastard. I knew he was sniffing around, but I thought I'd kept that information bottled up pretty tight."

"Don't hold it against him, Detective. Not everyone thought I was guilty."

Mills looked pained by the tone of my voice. "Point taken," she said. "But it's funny how things work out."

"How so?"

"If we hadn't identified you, I wouldn't have gone there to arrest you. You'd have bled to death on your office floor."

"A close thing," I said.

"They often are."

"Who identified me?"

"Just some guy out fishing. He was about a hundred feet upriver, sitting on an old bucket and waiting for something to bite. He didn't want to identify himself because he'd been drinking all night and didn't want his wife to know."

"A bad witness," I said, wondering if he had also witnessed my despair, seen the barrel pressed so hard under my chin. I tried to read Mills, to see if she knew, but she was inscrutable.

"A bad witness," she agreed, her eyes shifting away from my face. And I knew that she knew.

"And Barbara?" I tried to keep my face straight and my voice level, but it was hard. For good or bad, I'd spent ten years of my life with her; I couldn't pretend this wasn't killing me.

"We arrested her at the country club. She was poolside, having lunch with some of her friends."

"Glena Werster?" I asked.

"Yeah, she was there."

"Glena Werster has a black Mercedes."

"So?"

"Vanessa Stolen was run down by a black Mercedes."

Suddenly, Mills was a cop again. "Do you think Ms. Werster was responsible?"

"Do I think she would put herself at risk to help one of her friends? No. Their friendship was a parasitic thing; Barbara used Glena for her prestige and Glena used Barbara like a dishrag. What I do believe is that Barbara wanted Vanessa out of the way, and she was too smart to use her own car."

"Do you think Ms. Werster could have been aware of this?"

"I think it can't hurt to ask."

"I intend to," Mills said.

The thought of Glena Werster trying to deal with Detective Mills made me smile. "I wish I could be there," I said.

"You don't care for Ms. Werster?"

"No, I don't."

"Then I won't go easy on her," Mills said in total seriousness.

"Will you let me know?"

"I will."

"Then let's get back to Barbara," I said.

"At first, she acted tough, you know, angry. But by the time the cuffs went on, she was crying." Mills showed me her teeth, and I recognized her animal grin. "I enjoyed that part."

"You always do."

"Do you want me to apologize again?"

"No," I said. "Go on."

"I've spent a lot of time with your wife."

"Interrogating her?"

"Discussing things," Mills said.

"And?"

"And she refused to confess. She said I'd made a grave mistake. She threatened to sue. The same innocent act I've seen a hundred times. But then she learned that you were alive, and something in her seemed to break."

"She confessed?" I asked.

Mills shifted in her seat. "That's not exactly what I meant."

"What then?"

"I mean she broke. She's incoherent."

I tried to absorb this. "Is it an act?"

Mills shrugged. "We'll see, but I doubt it."

"Why?"

"She babbles. She lets things out, little pieces of information no sane person would tell the cops. We've pieced it together from what she's said. The will, her affair with Ezra. And we found the tapes, along with the money and the jewelry."

I hesitated, but had to ask. "Is that common knowledge?"

"Her and Ezra? I'm afraid so."

A silence stretched between us as I thought about what Mills had said. Eventually, she broke it. "Frankly, I'm surprised she didn't destroy the tapes. They were pretty damning."

"She loved him," I said. "In some sick, twisted way I'll never understand. But she did." In my mind I saw her face, and the way her eyes seemed to glow.

"It takes all kinds, I guess."

I thought back to the night this all started, the night my mother died. "So it was Barbara who called Ezra that night, after we left the hospital."

"Actually, it was Alex."

My jaw may have dropped, but Mills continued evenly.

"She knew about the fight between Jean and your father; she knew what it was about. She called Ezra. She offered to leave town for fifty thousand dollars. She said she would disappear, leave Jean alone. The mall is next to the interstate. She told him to meet her in the parking lot with the cash. She'd get on the road and leave Salisbury forever. I believe he went to the office for the cash, his gun, too, probably. Then he paid her off and she left. That was the last time anybody saw him alive, except for Barbara, of course."

"I can't believe Alex would do that." *Take his money. Leave Jean.* "None of that makes sense to me."

"She didn't spend the money. She didn't want it, not like any other person would. She just wanted to show Jean the kind of person her father was. She wanted to drive them apart. And it would have worked, too, I bet, but it wasn't necessary."

"Ezra disappeared and that was that. Alex had what she wanted. Namely, my sister."

"Free and clear," Mills said.

Except for me, I thought.

"So after Alex left, did he call Barbara or did she call him?"

"A lot of what I believe is just theory right now, but it seems to fit, based on things that Barbara has said and the information that I've collected throughout the investigation. Here's how I see it. The night your mother died, the three of you were at Ezra's house after you left the hospital. Ezra got the phone call, which we now know was from Alex; he left to get money from his office and to meet her near the interstate. Jean left right after he did, which is, in part, why you thought she might have been responsible. If he went to the mall, Jean could have followed him. You checked her house and found that her car was gone. It makes sense, assuming she had a motive." Mills looked hard at me. "It still troubles me that you won't explain what you think that motive might have been. . . ." I returned her measured gaze and said nothing. "But I guess I'll have to let that one go, as well.

"So, Ezra went to his office and collected fifty thousand in cash from his safe. Maybe he got the gun there. Maybe it was in his house or in his car. We'll never know. But he meets Alex at the mall and pays her off. Alex leaves, satisfied that her plan has worked. Now we have Ezra at the mall. This is about the time that you left home and went to Stolen Farm—let's say one in the morning, maybe a little later. I don't think Ezra would have called your house, knowing that you were probably there. That means that Barbara called him, shortly after you left, I would imagine. She wanted to talk to him about his wife's death or about the will. Maybe she just wanted a tumble. I don't know that part yet. But let's assume Ezra gets the call while he's at the mall. . . ."

"She loved him," I said.

"You said that before."

I rolled my shoulders. "Maybe she thought that he would take her if she left me. Maybe she saw a window of opportunity with my mother gone. Maybe she wanted to talk to him about that."

Mills studied me for long seconds as my words dwindled. "Are you okay to talk about this?" she asked.

"I'm okay," I said, but I wasn't.

"All right. For whatever reason, they meet at the mall. Ezra has just finished manipulating Alex out of his life. His wife is dead. My guess is that he wanted a clean slate and told your wife as much. I think that he called it off, told her that it was over and that he was going to change the will back to the way he wanted it. He's done with her, right? So your wife gets her hands on the gun somehow. He couldn't have seen that coming. She orders him into the closet and shoots him dead; puts a second one in his head to make sure. She closes the closet door, walks out of the empty building, and tosses the gun into the storm drain. Then she gets into her car and goes home, arriving there well before you do. By this time, Jean is at home with Alex, knowing that you left your house on some mysterious errand. There's no one there to see Barbara leave and then return; so that when Ezra goes missing and then turns up dead, Jean assumes you were involved. Or maybe she didn't assume that, at least not until his body turned up. But then you gave me a false alibi, one that Jean knew to be factually inaccurate. She thinks back to the night in question and draws a reasonable conclusion."

I was already nodding to myself. "It makes sense."

"It would have looked something like that. Exactly like that? Who knows? Only Barbara can tell us for certain. But she won't. I don't know if she even can. In time, maybe . . ."

"What about Ezra's car?"

"Stolen, probably. Barbara would have wanted the body discovered in due course so that the will could be put into probate. The car would have eventually drawn some kind of attention, so she left it there. She kept Ezra's office keys in order to enter your office at night to try to retrieve the tapes. The car keys were probably in the car, an invitation to whoever stole it." Mills showed her teeth in a brief smile. "It must have killed her—these past eighteen months—knowing that all that money was in reach if only someone would find the body."

"There's still one thing I don't understand."

"What's that?" Mills asked.

"If Barbara was in this for the money, why did she try to kill me? She can't inherit if I'm dead. So why didn't she take the money and jewelry from the safe and just leave? Why put herself at risk by sticking around if she had nothing to gain?"

For the first time, Mills looked genuinely pained, and she stared at her folded hands for a very long time.

"Detective?" I'd never seen her this hesitant. Finally, she looked up, and there were shadows in her eyes.

"It's true what you told me, isn't it? You never read your father's will."

"The only time I saw it was when you showed it to me."

She nodded and looked back down at her hands.

"What?" I asked.

"Barbara did convince Ezra to increase the amount of money left to you in trust. She was telling the truth when she told you that. Here's what she didn't tell you. There was an unusual clause in the will. It must have been Barbara's idea. According to Clarence Hambly, your father had it inserted into the will about six months before he died. This would have been after they started sleeping together, Ezra and Barbara. But Ezra changed his mind. Hambly says that he intended to have the clause removed. Maybe he understood what an incentive it could be."

"I don't understand."

"I think your father came to sense just how dangerous your wife could be. I don't know this, Work, but I feel it. I think at the end he understood. He saw that it put you at risk. Your father asked Hambly to draw up new documents; they had scheduled a meeting so that he could sign them. Barbara killed him before he could make the change official."

"What did it say, this clause?"

I heard Mills's breath, and when she looked up, she was the most human I'd ever seen her. Her voice was flat, but I saw that this hurt her. "In the event of your death, the fifteen million would go into trust for any offspring you had. Barbara would be the executor of that trust and would have almost unlimited discretion in how to use the money."

"I don't understand," I said, but then I did. "Barbara's pregnant," I said.

Mills could barely look at me. "She *was* pregnant, Work. She miscarried yesterday."

CHAPTER

35

Douglas stopped by once; he hung in the door until I saw him, then offered a smile that played more like a grimace. The skin was loose beneath his eyes and under his chin. He looked like hell. He tried to apologize, and explained that it was just his job, nothing personal; but he shied from my eyes, and, unlike Mills, he didn't mean a word he said. He'd sunk his teeth into me and liked the taste of it. I'd seen it in court, and in the way he smiled when the bailiffs put the cuffs back on me. Any regret was born of embarrassment, and the knowledge that another election was just around the corner. For even in Rowan County, no voter liked a fool, and the papers had crucified him. He told me that he wouldn't prosecute me for attempting to destroy evidence, then looked away and said that, nonetheless, it was his duty to report my behavior to the state bar. We both knew that such a report would result in my eventual disbarment. But the thought of that didn't bother me in the least, and he looked surprised when I told him not to worry about it. When he attempted another smile, I suggested he have a nice day, then told him to get the fuck out of my hospital room.

I had other visitors, too: lawyers, neighbors, even some old friends from school, all of whom were probably just curious. They all said the same things, and they all rang false with me. I knew who had believed in me, and a few flowery words would never make me forget those who had not. But I did what I had to do. I thanked them for the visit and wished them a happy life. Dr. Stokes was a different story. He stopped by several times, and we talked about small things. He told me stories of my mother, and of things I'd done as a child. He was good for me, and I felt a little stronger after each conversation. On his last visit, I held out my hand and told him that he had a friend for life. He gave me a smile, told me that he'd never doubted it, and insisted that the next drink was on him; then he shook my hand gently but solemnly, and there seemed to be a light upon him as he walked from the room.

Jean and Alex came by on the day before they released me. They were packed and ready to leave.

"Where?" I asked.

"Up north. Vermont, maybe."

I looked at Alex, who returned my gaze with the same unswerving strength as always. Yet this time there was no animosity, and I knew that Jean had not lied to me. When the time was right, I would be welcome.

"Take care of her," I said.

She put out her hand and I shook it. "I always will," she said.

I looked back to Jean. "Send me your address," I told her. "I'll have some money for you once I sell the house and building."

"I wish you would reconsider. We don't want anything of his."

"It won't be from him. It will be from me."

"Are you sure?"

"I want you to have it," I said. "Use it well. Build a life."

"It's a lot of money."

I shrugged. "I owe you more than money, Jean. This is the least I can do."

Jean looked at me then, looked so deeply that I could not hide the emptiness I felt, the reverberation of utter aloneness. Nor could I hide the guilt that rose within me every time I looked at her. Eventually, I had to turn away.

I heard her voice, and there was something new in it. Strength, maybe? A clarity of her own? "Will you give us a minute, Alex?"

"Sure," Alex said. "Take care, Work." And then we were alone behind the closed hospital door. Jean pulled up a chair and sat beside me.

"You don't owe me anything," she said.

"I do."

"For what?"

I marveled that she could even ask the question. "For everything, Jean. For not protecting you better. For not being a better brother." My words fell into the narrow place between us. My hands twitched beneath the thin sheet, and I tried again because I wanted her to understand. "For not having faith in you. For letting Ezra treat you the way he did."

Then she laughed, and the sound of it hurt me; those words had not come without cost. "Are you serious?" she asked.

"I'm serious."

The smile fell from her face. She settled back into her chair and studied me with overly moist eyes. But she wasn't on the verge of tears, far from it. "Let me ask you a question," she said.

"Okay."

"And I want you to think about it before you answer."

"All right."

"Why do you think he brought you into the practice?"

"What?"

"Why did he encourage you to go to law school? Why did he give you a job?"

I did like she'd asked. I thought about it before I answered. "I don't know," I finally said. "I've never thought about it before."

"Okay, another question. Was there a time when your relationship with him changed? And I'm talking about a long time ago."

"Do you mean like childhood?"

"I mean exactly like childhood."

"We used to be close."

"And that stopped when?"

"Look, Jean, what's the point of all this?"

"When did it change?"

"I don't know, all right? I don't know."

"Jesus, Work. You can be really dense sometimes. It changed overnight. It changed on the day we jumped for Jimmy. Before that, you were a chip off the old block, but then you went into that creek. After that, everything changed between you. I never understood why, not then. But I've thought about it, and I think I do now."

I didn't want to hear any more. The truth was too ugly; it never shut up, and this is what it said. It said that my father sensed something different about me after that day. He felt the change, and knew to be ashamed of me, even if he didn't know exactly why. It said that he could never respect me after that. He smelled my degradation like old garbage, and so he turned away. Even now I know that he died despising me.

I finally looked at my sister, expecting to see some small shadow of the same emotion.

"You know?" I asked.

"You started that day a boy, Work, Ezra's little boy—a reflection of him, perhaps, but no more than that. Something he could look down on with vague pride, point to, and say, That's my son; that's my boy. But you came out of that hole a man, a hero, a person everyone looked up to, and he couldn't handle that. You were the center of attention, not him, and he hated that, hated it enough to grind you down and keep you down, so that you would never surpass him like that again. That's when it changed for you and that's why it changed."

"I don't know, Jean."

"How many grown men do you think would have gone down that hole all alone? Not many, I can tell you that, and certainly not our father. I saw his face when they pulled you out and the crowd started cheering."

"They cheered?" I asked.

"Of course they did."

"I don't remember that," I said, and didn't. I remembered scornful eyes, ridicule, and pointing fingers. I remembered Ezra, drunk and telling my mother that I was just a dumb-ass kid. "He's no fucking hero." That's what he'd said.

"Vanessa Stolen would probably have died that day, raped and killed at fifteen. How many twelve-year-old boys have saved a life? How many grown men? It's a rare thing, and it took courage. Only our father could make you blind to that, but that's what he did, and he did it intentionally."

Her words were destroying me. I was no hero. He'd been right about that. But what she said next penetrated some of the fog that filled my mind.

"Ezra brought you into the practice to keep you beneath him."

"What?"

"You're not cut out to be a lawyer, Work. You're smart as hell, no question, but you're a dreamer. You have a big heart. Nobody knew that better than Ezra. He knew that you could never be cutthroat like he could, and you would never care about money like he did; that meant that you could never succeed like he had. Having you in the law kept Ezra safe. As long as you were there, you would never be the man that he was. Never as strong, never as confident." She paused and leaned toward me. "Never a threat."

"Do you really believe that?" I asked.

"Trust me."

"None of that lets me off the hook, though. I still owe you."

"You just don't get it, do you? He treated you worse than he ever treated me. For me, it was simple misogyny. I was female and therefore of little value. But for you, it was personal. He waged a campaign against you, Work. He went to war, and no one can do that like our father could. Good or bad, he was a force." She laughed again, a bitter and dismayed sound. "You talk about protecting me from him. Jesus, Work. You never had a chance."

"Maybe," I said. "I'll have to think about it."

"You do that," she said. "He's dead. Don't let him drag you down any further."

Suddenly, I was too tired to talk about Ezra anymore. It would probably take years to sort out the mess he'd made of my head, but the carnage seemed less absolute. And maybe Jean was right. Maybe I needed to give myself a break. I was only twelve when it happened, and that seemed terribly young to me now.

"I'm going to miss you, Jean."

She stood and put her hand on my shoulder. "You were going to go to prison for me, Work. That makes you a very good man. Better than anyone I've ever known. You remember that when things get you down."

"I love you, Jean."

"I love you, too," she replied. "And that's what family is supposed to be about." She crossed the room and stopped at the door. She opened it and looked back. "I'll call you when we get where we're going."

Then she stepped out of the room, and as the door swung shut, I saw Alex materialize beside her. She slipped her arm around my sister and turned her down the hall. I watched until the door closed between us, and saw, in that last second, that Jean was crying; but it was a good cry, a healthy cry, and I knew that when they found their place, she would call. I took great comfort in that.

I was packing my few belongings the next day when Max appeared in the door of my room. He looked exactly the same.

"You want your dog back?" he asked without preamble.

"Yes," I said.

"Damn!" he said, and walked off. I heard his raised voice from down the hall. "You come to me when you want him. Maybe I'll let him go, maybe not, but we'll have beer regardless."

I laughed for the first time.

An hour later, I went home to a house that rattled when I walked inside. I wouldn't miss it, I knew, but I took a beer onto the front porch and sat where I liked to sit. I watched the sun descend on the park across the street. It touched the treetops and I thought about another beer. But I didn't get up, and the sun went down as I watched. I sat there long into the night and listened to the sounds around me. They were comfortable sounds, city sounds, and I wondered if I would miss them.

The next day, they'd put Ezra in the ground, and once he was there, I planned to seek out Vanessa. I would say what I had to say, make whatever promises were necessary. I wanted her back, if she would have me, but only after the truth was told. If I had to beg, I would. That was the curse of clarity, and the price I would happily pay. For I saw things now like I never had before. I was ready to make my own path, but I wanted her to walk it with me; I wanted to make the life I should have had all along.

So when the sun came up the next day, I took my time in shaving. I brushed my teeth and I combed my hair. I put on my favorite jeans and a pair of sturdy boots. The funeral was at ten, but I had no plans to go. Jean said it best, really, when I asked her if she would attend.

"He died for me that night, Work. Like I've always said. They can't bury him any deeper."

I did drive past the church, however, and I saw the long black car that would carry him to the hole they'd dug. And when they came out, I was still there. Maybe I wasn't like Jean; maybe I needed to see. But whatever the reason, I followed the line of cars to the cemetery outside of town. When they turned in the main gate, I continued past. I found the feeder road that ran along the ridge and drove until I found a place where I could watch. There was a tall tree there, and I leaned against its dimpled trunk and looked down on the gray mourners as they departed their expensive cars. They puddled around the rectangular pit, which looked so small from where I stood, and I saw a man, probably the preacher. He held out his arms as if for silence, but his words were lost in a sudden wind, which was just as well. For what could he say to make it right for me?

I stayed until they shoveled in the dirt, and when all were gone, I walked down to look upon the settling mound. There was no headstone yet, but I knew what it would say. They'd come to me for the words, and I'd done the best I could.

Ezra Pickens, it would read. *His Truth Travels with Him.*

I stood there for a long time, but mostly I looked at the place where my mother lay. Would she thank me for putting him there? Or would she rather have been left alone? Again, I'd done the best I could. What I thought she would want. By his side, she had lived, uncomplaining; so be it in death. But in my heart I was angry, and knew that I would always question the wisdom of this choice. But what I'd told Barbara was true. Life gets messy, and death, it seemed, was no exception.

When I heard a distant engine, I paid it no attention. I probably should have known better, so that when Vanessa appeared beside me, I would have had a smile to greet her; but all I saw was fresh-turned earth and the hard edges of my mother's graven name, until she spoke and touched me on the shoulder. I faced her then, and she took my hand. I said her name and she took all of me. Her arms were slim and strong, and she smelled like the river. I leaned into her, and her hand moved on the back of my neck. When I pulled away, I did so for a reason. I wanted to see her eyes, to see if there was cause to hope. And there was, for there was clarity there, too; and I knew, before I even spoke, that we would be okay.

Yet the words had to be said, although not in the shadow of Ezra's mounded earth. So I took her farm-worn hand and led her slowly up the hill to the shady place I'd found. I told her first that I loved her, and she looked away, down to the rows of chiseled stone. When she looked back, she tried to speak, but I stopped her with a finger. I thought back to the day we met, the day we jumped for Jimmy. It's where it started, where everything changed, and where our future almost ended. If we were to have a chance together, she needed to hear about that day, as I needed to tell her; so I said what I had to say, and truer words have never been spoken.

EPILOGUE

Many months have passed, and the pain has lessened to an occasional throb. I still have trouble sleeping at night, but I don't mind; my thoughts are not unpleasant. I keep Vanessa's letter in the drawer of my bedside table, and I read it from time to time, usually at night. It reminds me of how close I came, and that life is not a given. It keeps me honest, and maintains what I've come to call "this precious clarity."

The clock reads just after five, and although my days start early now, there is no hurry; and the dream is still fresh upon me. So I swing my feet onto the cool floor and walk from the room. In the hallway, there is light from the moon, and I follow it to the window. I look down on still fields, then to my right and to the river. It winds into the distance, a silver thread, and I think of currents and of time, of things that have been swept away.

The courts ruled that the cash and jewels from my father's safe were part of his estate. They would go to the foundation. But the buildings sold quickly, and for a better price than I'd hoped. In the end, I sent over $800,000 to Jean, and she used it to purchase a cabin on the wooded shores of Lake Champlain. I've not visited yet. Still too soon, Jean told me, the world still too entirely theirs. But we are talking about Christmas.

Maybe.

As for my share of the money, I used it as best I could. I restored the aging farmhouse, bought a decent tractor, and acquired the adjacent two-hundred-acre parcel. It is good land, with rich soil and a bold stream. I also have my eye on eighty acres that borders to the south, but the sellers know my ambitions and their price is still too high. But I can be patient.

I hear the door swing open behind me and smile in spite of myself. She only wakes when I find my way to this window. It's as if she knows I'm here and rises to join me in looking down on this garden we've made. Her arms slip warm across my chest, and I see her face in the window—Vanessa, my wife.

"What are you thinking about?" she asks.

"I had the dream again."

"The same one?"

"Yes."

"Come back to bed," she says.

"In a minute."

She kisses me and returns to bed.

My hands find the windowsill and I feel the cold draft coming through. I think of what I've learned and of those things I have yet to discover. Farming is a tough life, replete with uncertainty, and much of it is new to me. Yet I've grown lean and welcome the long hours that have made my hands so hard. It suits me, this life. There is no rush, neither to judgment nor to action; and that, perhaps, has led to the greatest change of all, for I have yet to face a single regret.

Yet I remain my father's son, and it is not possible to escape fully the reprehensible choices he made. I know that I can never forgive him. But fate, which can be so wayward, is not without a sense of justice. Ezra played his games with Barbara, manipulated her for his own twisted ends. At her insistence, he changed his will, inserted a clause providing that any child of mine would inherit the fifteen million dollars in the event of my death. It was Barbara's idea, her safety valve, and I am quite certain that my father planned to change it once he was through with her. But she killed him before he could sign the new documents. Maybe that's why she shot him. I'll never know. But I realized, when I finally read through his will, that there was no time limit involved. So I did the research, and what I learned was this: When I die, whenever that might occur, my child will inherit a large part of Ezra's millions. I filed a caveat on the matter, seeking declaratory judgment. Hambly fought it, of course, and the loss still embitters him. But the will was specific, and the law favored my interpretation.

After awhile, I retrace my steps and slip under the covers. She's warm, on her side, and I flatten myself against her. The dream seems more real each time, and each time takes longer to leave me. We walk over green grass, the three of us.

Tell me the story, Daddy.

Which one?

My favorite.

I reach for Vanessa, my hand finding her belly. She sinks deeper under the covers and nestles back against me.

"I hope it's a girl," I whisper.

"It is," she says, and settles her hand upon my own.

I can't say if she knows this or simply feels it. For me, it is enough. I hear her voice from the dream—my little girl—and I contemplate the vast fortune that will one day be hers. I think for the last time of my father, and of his feelings about women and money. There is poetry in this, an irony that completes the circle, and I wonder if he is restless in that dark and forever grave.

I stay in bed for a few more minutes, but the day beckons and I am restless. I pull on jeans and a sweater, and Bone follows me downstairs. It is cold outside, and I stand on the porch in the predawn light. I take a breath that fills me up and look out across the silent fields. There is a low mist in the hollow places, and the hilltops rise to meet the coming sun.